THE TALE OF
CUCKOO BROW WOOD

The Tale of
Cuckoo Brow Wood

The Cottage Tales of
Beatrix Potter

Susan Wittig Albert

BERKLEY PRIME CRIME, NEW YORK

THE BERKLEY PUBLISHING GROUP
Published by the Penguin Group
Penguin Group (USA) Inc.
375 Hudson Street, New York, New York 10014, USA
Penguin Group (Canada), 90 Eglinton Avenue East, Suite 700, Toronto, Ontario M4P 2Y3, Canada
(a division of Pearson Penguin Canada Inc.)
Penguin Books Ltd., 80 Strand, London WC2R 0RL, England
Penguin Group Ireland, 25 St. Stephen's Green, Dublin 2, Ireland (a division of Penguin Books Ltd.)
Penguin Group (Australia), 250 Camberwell Road, Camberwell, Victoria 3124, Australia
(a division of Pearson Australia Group Pty. Ltd.)
Penguin Books India Pvt. Ltd., 11 Community Centre, Panchsheel Park, New Delhi—110 017, India
Penguin Group (NZ), Cnr. Airborne and Rosedale Roads, Albany, Auckland 1310, New Zealand
(a division of Pearson New Zealand Ltd.)
Penguin Books (South Africa) (Pty.) Ltd., 24 Sturdee Avenue, Rosebank, Johannesburg 2196,
South Africa

Penguin Books Ltd., Registered Offices: 80 Strand, London WC2R 0RL, England

This is an original publication of The Berkley Publishing Group.

This is a work of fiction. Names, characters, places, and incidents either are the product of the author's imagination or are used fictitiously, and any resemblance to actual persons, living or dead, business establishments, events, or locales is entirely coincidental. The publisher does not have any control over and does not assume any responsibility for author or third-party websites or their content.

Frederick Warne & Co Ltd. is the sole and exclusive owner of the entire rights titles and interest in and to the copyrights and trademarks of the works of Beatrix Potter, including all names and characters featured therein. No reproduction of these copyrights and trademarks may be made without the prior written consent of Frederick Warne & Co Ltd.

First edition: July 2006

Library of Congress Cataloging-in-Publication Data

Albert, Susan Wittig.
  The tale of Cuckoo Brow Wood / by Susan Wittig Albert.—1st ed.
    p. cm.
  ISBN 0-425-21004-9
1. Potter, Beatrix, 1866–1943—Fiction.   2. Women authors—Fiction.   3. Women artists—Fiction.
4. Human-animal relationships—Fiction.   5. Animals—Fiction.   6. Villages—Fiction.
7. England—Fiction.   I. Title.
  PS3551. L2637T347   2006
  813'. 54—dc22   2006002224

PRINTED IN THE UNITED STATES OF AMERICA

10 9 8 7 6 5 4 3 2 1

Publisher's Note: The recipes contained in this book are to be followed exactly as written. The publisher is not responsible for your specific health or allergy needs that may require medical supervision. The publisher is not responsible for any adverse reactions to the recipes contained in this book.

Dedicated to
the Gentle Readers who will always hold
Beatrix Potter's "Little Books"
close to their hearts

Can it be—it must be—that you are that embodiment of the incorporeal, that elusive yet ineluctable being to whom through the generations novelists have so unavailingly made invocation; in short, the *Gentle Reader?*—

HENRY JAMES

Acknowledgments

My grateful thanks go to Dr. Linda Lear, Senior Research Scholar in History at the University of Maryland, Baltimore County, and Research Professor of Environmental History at George Washington University, who has helped me resolve several problems of fact and emphasis and has been a generous and gracious friend since I began this project. Those who admire the work of Beatrix Potter are eagerly awaiting Dr. Lear's forthcoming biography, to appear in 2007: *Beatrix Potter: A Life in Nature.*

Special appreciation also goes to my editor, Natalee Rosenstein, who has supported my work for over a decade, and to my husband, Bill Albert, who has cheerfully driven all over the Lake District—on the wrong side of very narrow English roads, in an English car with the steering and gearshift on the wrong side, in the pouring English rain. Many thanks, Natalee and Bill. If it weren't for you, these Potter books would never have been written.

Susan Wittig Albert

When you are young so many things are difficult to believe, and yet the dullest people will tell you that they are true— such things, for instance, as that the earth goes round the sun, and that it is not flat but round. But the things that seem really likely, like fairy-tales and magic, are, so say the grown-ups, not true at all. Yet they are so easy to believe, especially when you see them happening.

EDITH NESBIT
The Enchanted Castle, 1907

Lake Windermere

CLAIFE HEIGHTS

Fern Vale Tarn

10

Path to Tarn

Cuckoo Brow Wood

FAR SAWREY

To the Ferry

Ferry Landing

Sawrey Hotel

Sawrey School

13

12

11

14

NEAR SAWREY

½ mile

N

9

7

8

6

4

5

2

3

1

1. Hill Top Farm
2. Tower Bank Arms
3. Courier Cottage
4. Croft End
5. Meadow Croft Cottage
6. Post Office
7. Belle Greene
8. Anvil Cottage
9. Tower Bank House
10. Raven Hall
11. Tidmarsh Manor
12. St. Peter's Church
13. The Vicarage
14. Holly How Cottage

* Near and Far Sawrey are about a half mile apart.

Cast of Characters

(* indicates an actual person or creature)

People

Beatrix Potter,* renowned children's author and illustrator, divides her time between her farm at Hill Top, in the Lake District village of Near Sawrey, and her parents' home in London.

Sarah Barwick lives in Anvil Cottage, where she operates the Anvil Cottage Bakery. Also known as Sarah Scones, she is the best baker in the Land between the Lakes.

Dimity Woodcock lives with her brother, Captain Miles Woodcock, in Tower Bank House. *Elsa Grape* keeps house and cooks for the Woodcocks.

Captain Miles Woodcock is Justice of the Peace for Sawrey District, and Dimity's brother.

William (Will) Heelis* is a solicitor who lives and has an office in Hawkshead. He is a good friend of both Captain Woodcock and Major Christopher Kittredge.

Major Christopher Kittredge, master of Raven Hall, has recently returned to the Land between the Lakes with his new wife, *Diana Kittredge,* about whom there is much mystery.

Mr. Augustus Richardson is a London property developer who plans to build villas along the western shore of Lake Windermere.

Vicar Samuel Sackett is the vicar of St. Peter's Church in Far Sawrey. He lives at the vicarage, which is tended by his housekeeper, Mrs. Thompson.

Harold Thexton, an antiquarian and folklorist, is staying at the vicarage while he collects information about the Lake District. His wife, *Gloria Thexton,* is also a guest at the vicarage.

John and *Becky Jennings* operate Hill Top Farm for Miss Potter and live in the new addition to the old farmhouse. They have three children.

Lucy Skead, the village postmistress, lives at Low Green Gate Cottage, also the site of the village post office. *Dolly Dorking,* Lucy's aged mother (known to the villagers as *Auld Dolly*), lives there as well.

Mathilda and *George Crook* live at Belle Green. Mathilda boards guests; George owns and operates the village forge.

Hannah Braithwaite is the wife of the village constable, *John Braithwaite.* They live at Croft End Cottage and have three children, *Jack, Sally,* and the baby.

Grace Lythecoe is the widow of the former vicar. She lives in Rose Cottage and plays an influential role in village affairs.

Margaret Nash is Head Teacher at Sawrey School. She lives in one of the Sunnyside Cottages with her sister, *Annie*, a piano teacher.

Daphne Hammond, a widow, is the Assistant Teacher at Sawrey School, in charge of the infants class (children up to age 7).

Dr. Butters, the much-loved village doctor, lives in Hawkshead.

Deirdre Malone, eleven, lived in an orphanage before she came to help take care of the Suttons' children at Courier Cottage.

Caroline Longford, twelve, lives with her grandmother, *Lady Longford,* at Tidmarsh Manor, a large estate at the edge of Cuckoo Brow Wood. In *The Tale of Holly How,* both grandmother and granddaughter were rescued by Miss Potter from the skulduggery of Lady Longford's personal companion.

Jeremy Crosfield lives with his aunt Jane at Holly How Farm. Jeremy, thirteen, is an artist and naturalist and spends as much time as possible in the woods and fields. In *The Tale of Hill Top Farm,* Miss Potter defended him against a serious charge of theft and encouraged him to draw.

Animals of the Village, Hill Top Farm, and Cuckoo Brow Wood

Tabitha Twitchet is the senior village cat, respected for the quality of her ideas and advice. She lives with the Crooks at Belle Green.

Crumpet, a sleek gray tabby cat, lives with the Stubbses in Lakefield Cottage, but is welcome in every kitchen in the village.

Felicia Frummety belongs to the Jennings family at Hill Top Farm; she is a lazy mouser who has allowed a ragtag rabble of rats to overrun the farmhouse. To manage the rats, several other cats are hired: *Max the Manx, Fang, Claw, Lion, Tiger,* and *The Cat Who Walks by Himself.*

Rascal is a Jack Russell terrier. He lives with the Crooks at Belle Green, but spends most of his time managing affairs in the village.

Ridley and *Rosabelle* are the resident rats in the Hill Top attic.

Tibbie, Queenie, and their lambs are Miss Potter's Herdwick sheep.

Professor Galileo Newton Owl, D.Phil., is a tawny owl who lives in Cuckoo Brow Wood. He studies celestial mechanics and the habits of small furry creatures, and keeps a watchful eye on things from the skies above the village.

Bosworth Badger XVII lives in The Brockery, at the edge of Cuckoo Brow Wood. Bosworth is responsible for *The Brockery Badger History and Genealogy.* A wide assortment of residents and guests live in The Brockery.

THE TALE OF
CUCKOO BROW WOOD

1

"Something Really Must Be Done!"

The tale I am about to tell you begins on a bright, clear, April-sweet morning in the Lake District village of Sawrey. The sun had just begun to work its magical morning alchemy, burnishing the blue surface of Esthwaite Water to a sparkling silver, turning the leaves of larch and willow to an iridescent opal, and transforming every apple blossom in the village to pure gold. The sky was scattered with white clouds, as if a playful breeze had tugged yesterday's laundry from the drying-lines in the village gardens and flung them into the brilliant blue heaven, where they stuck, tattered and wind-torn.

It was a magical morning, and the little village seemed more than ever to occupy a magical place in the world. To the east lay Lake Windermere, the longest, deepest, bluest lake in all of England, a barrier of sorts against any modern encroachments that might creep into the village, which proudly described itself as "old-fashioned." To the west lay Esthwaite Water, a small but perfect jewel among the other sparkling lakes in the District. And beyond Esthwaite Water rose Coniston Old Man, its bald head in the clouds, its steep, stern shoulders covered with winter-brown bracken and heather. And beyond Coniston, right the way to the Irish Sea, there was nothing but desolate moorland and silent fell, and all still in winter's unrelenting grip.

But in the Land between the Lakes (as people like to call it), winter was magically turning to spring. If you have ever visited this part of England, of perhaps seen pictures of it, you can envision the hawthorn coming into bloom, and primroses, violets, and cowslips splashing the roadsides with pastel pink and purple and white and gold. The meadow grass is dappled with daisies and clover blossom, and the trees along the beck flaunt that joyful, optimistic green that belongs only to spring. On such mornings, even the breeze is in a celebratory mood, playing gently with the flowers, tossing their sweet scents into the air and whispering delightedly of even sweeter pleasures to come, as April becomes May and all the green land wakes from its winter sleep and comes joyfully alive.

The rising sun always enjoyed its first glimpse of the twin hamlets of Near and Far Sawrey, for the setting was uniquely beautiful and the villagers led such quaint and engaging lives. But this morning, it looked with an even greater interest at the two cats sitting on the stone fence along the garden at Hill Top Farm, the country residence of Miss Beatrix Potter (who was at that very moment asleep in her second-story bedroom, the covers pulled over her head). Of course, you have often observed cats sitting on fences, and if you know anything about cats, you know that they like to do this because it gives them a vantage point: above the fray, as it were, keeping a close eye on everything that is going on.

Tabitha Twitchit, the senior village cat, was a calico with a handsome orange and white bib and mahogany markings. Crumpet was younger, slimmer, and sleeker, with gray fur, a red collar, and a gold bell. The pair might look as if they were simply enjoying the sun's first caressing glance, but in reality, they had come on an urgent errand of great importance to the entire village of Sawrey. And it wasn't long before the object of their concern—a ginger-colored cat with a white-tipped tail and delicate features—came prancing prettily down the flagstone path.

"Good morning, ladies," she said. *"I'm sure you won't mind if I join you. It's a lovely morning for a nap in the sun."* And with that, she jumped up beside Crumpet and began to wash a pretty white paw.

Tabitha Twitchit leaned forward and gave her a disapproving glare. *"Felicia Frummety,"* she said sternly, *"you should be working, not napping. Hill Top Farm is simply swarming with rats. You have not been doing your job."*

Tabitha, who lived with Mr. and Mrs. Crook at Belle Green, was in her third term as the president of the Village Cat Council. Her most important duty (at least *she* thought it was important, and perhaps you will agree) was supervising the other cats in the crucial business of keeping Near Sawrey free of rats, mice, voles, and other objectionable creatures. And Tabitha was the sort of cat who took her responsibilities seriously.

Crumpet gave a sarcastic mew. *"What? Miss Felicia Frummety, condescend to catch a rat? I doubt it, Tabitha. She's afraid to get those pretty white paws dirty."*

Tabitha sighed. *"I fear you're right, Crumpet."* She fixed Felicia Frummety with a long look of rebuke. *"We seem to have a shirker in our midst."*

"*I am NOT a shirker!*" Felicia exclaimed, annoyed. "*I just don't see the point of bothering with rats, that's all.*" She turned down her mouth in an expression of disgust. "*A mouse is a sweet, delicate morsel, and nutritious, too. But rats—*"

She shuddered all the way down to the tip of her tail, which was exceedingly clean and white. "*They're tougher than old boot-leather, and covered with indigestible hair. They smell like a rubbish-bin, and they bite!*"

"*Biting,*" Crumpet said darkly, "*is in the nature of rats.*" She was quite out of patience with Felicia, a conceited young puss who gave herself airs. The other members of the Cat Council each took a turn at patrolling the gardens for voles— all but Felicia, who felt she was too good for what she disdainfully called "common alley work."

"*Rats are formidable foes,*" Tabitha said, in the tone of one who knows whereof she speaks, "*and every cat worth her salt has been bitten more than once. We wear our scars proudly, as a badge of honor.*" Now retired from active duty, Tabitha herself had one torn ear, a slash across her nose, and a missing claw, testimony to her reputation as a respected ratter. "*But you have no scars, Felicia, for you are afraid of being bitten. Fear is not in the nature of cats. Cats,*" she added emphatically, "*have courage.*"

"*You may call me Miss Frummety, if you please,*" Felicia retorted loftily. "*And I am not afraid! Not two days ago, I chased a rat right down his rat-hole. I frightened him so thoroughly that he hasn't shown a whisker since.*"

"*Ha,*" grunted Crumpet skeptically. "*Probably skipped straight out the back way. You're lucky he didn't come round and bite that pretty tail of yours, MISS Frummety.*"

"*Be that as it may, Felicia,*" Tabitha said, "*I have been instructed by the Council to inform you that you have been officially censured for your inability to keep Hill Top Farm free of rats. We have countenanced your refusal to participate in the nightly vole patrol, but dereliction of duty is intolerable."*

Felicia arched her back, hissed, and jumped off the wall. *"Dereliction of duty!"* she spat furiously. *"Rubbish!"*

Tabitha went on as if Felicia had not spoken. *"Understanding that the situation at Hill Top is out of control, the council has authorized me to offer you a special assistant—a volunteer cat who will come in and help you get rid of the rats."*

"Help ME!" Felicia exclaimed indignantly. *"Stuff and nonsense. Hill Top Farm is my affair, and mine alone. You know the Rule, Tabitha Twitchit. No poaching on private property. So you and your council can keep your collective noses out of MY house, MY barn, and all MY outbuildings."* Having delivered this tart riposte, she twitched her gingery tail disdainfully and stalked off in the direction of the barn, her nose high in the air.

"How . . . how insulting!" Tabitha sputtered heatedly. *"The nerve of that young hussy, taking that tone to me!"*

"Don't take it to heart, Tabitha," Crumpet said soothingly. *"Felicia will come to regret her impudence. But something really must be done, you know. The Hill Top rats are completely ungovernable. Why, at nine o'clock last night, while the Stubbses were sitting beside the fire, a pair of Hill Top rats attempted to raid the bread cupboard."* Crumpet lived with the Stubbses and prided herself in keeping their cottage free of both mice and rats. She grinned ruthlessly. *"I showed them my teeth."*

"Yes, something most certainly must be done," Tabitha muttered. *"But Felicia is quite within her rights to invoke the Rule."*

The Rule (properly known as the *No Poaching Rule*) was the foundation of each cat's amicable relationship with every other cat in the village. Any cat might kill a rat, mouse, vole, or other vermin in another cat's front or back garden, but

NOT in the house or in any outbuilding unless expressly invited to do so by the human owner. No one knew who had made this Rule or how long it had been in existence, but it had been passed down from one generation of cats to another as long as anyone could remember and was held to be absolutely inviolate. To break it would be to risk the disintegration of the social order.

Crumpet knew this rule, of course, and never hesitated to invoke it when one of the younger cats strayed into her territory. She did not like to think, however, that an equitable solution to the problem of the rats at Hill Top Farm might be constrained by the Rule. Surely, there was a way to deal with the matter.

"The problem is that Miss Potter is a city lady," Crumpet muttered. *"She's owned Hill Top for nearly two years now, and she likes to think of herself as a farmer. But she still has a great many lessons to learn when it comes to animal management. She seems to find it difficult to take a firm position on the matter of rats."*

"Yes," said Tabitha. *"In fact, I've heard her say that she once kept a rat as a pet. His name was Sammy, and she was very fond of him."* She closed her eyes and shuddered. *"A pet rat—when she might have had a nice, companionable cat!"*

"Even the best of humans are often illogical," Crumpet said sadly. *"And if Miss Potter allows the rats at Hill Top to carry on as they are, the entire village will soon be overtaken. You know rats, Tabitha. They have no restraints and not an ounce of pity, and they multiply faster than rabbits."* She laid back her ears. Thinking about the menace, she felt cold and frightened. *"First Hill Top, then the Tower Bank Arms and Anvil Cottage, and after that, the entire village. No cottage will be safe from the ravaging horde. We will be completely overrun!"*

"*We will indeed,*" agreed Tabitha in a somber tone. *"But I have an idea, Crumpet. What do you think of this?"*

When Crumpet had heard Tabitha's plan, she cheered up immediately—and I think you will, too, when you have heard what it is.

2

Miss Potter Flings Down the Gauntlet

Beatrix Potter awoke a little later than her usual hour, jumped out of bed, and opened her window wide to take an eager breath of the fresh spring air. She had arrived at Hill Top Farm late the previous night, having spent a tiresome Tuesday on the railroad train from London. But a night's sleep between lavender-scented sheets had entirely refreshed her. If any traces of the winter's London fogs lingered in her lungs, they were whisked away by that first breath of clean, clear air. And if any London worries clouded her mind, they were gone as well, banished by the cheerful sight of green hills, wooly white sheep, and bright blue sky. It was as if she had awakened on the first day of spring and found the world a newly marvelous, magical place.

All around her, Hill Top Farm, too, was wakening from its long winter sleep, stretching in the morning sunlight, taking a deep, full, happy breath of spring, and contemplating the beginning of another lovely day. In the barnyard beyond the garden, Blossom, the new black-and-white Galway calf, bawled for her breakfast. Beatrix's favorite Berkshire pigs, Aunt Susan and Dorcas, chuckled merrily in the mud of their pig sty, as a trio of busy red hens—Mrs. Bonnet, Mrs. Shawl, and Mrs. Boots—scurried past on their way to the garden to see if the early worms might be out and about. A parade of gleaming white Puddleducks headed in the opposite direction, on the way to Wilfin Beck for their morning swim. Mustard, the big yellow dog who had recently come to work at Hill Top, kept a watchful eye on things from the barn doorway, at the same time warming his creaky old bones in the morning sun. And on the fence, in companionable contemplation, sat two of the village cats, Tabitha Twitchit and Crumpet, while Felicia Frummety, the Hill Top cat, was making her way to the barn, to search (it was to be hoped) for rats.

Beatrix smiled down at the scene before her. If she could only open her arms wide enough, she would embrace every single wonderful thing, from the cats on the fence to the clucking chickens in the garden and the tiniest of the Puddleducks dabbling heads-down, tails-up in the beck. Not to mention the lambs on the hillside and the larks in the sky and—

"Good morning, Bea!" a woman's cheery voice called. "I've brought you a fresh-baked loaf of bread for your breakfast."

Beatrix looked down. Sarah Barwick was standing on the flagstone path below, her sleeves rolled to the elbows, a basket in her hand.

"Good morning, Sarah," Beatrix said. "My goodness, you're out and about early."

"You're late getting up," Sarah replied in her downright way. "I've been baking for hours already. But I s'pose you can be forgiven, poor thing, since you must've been very tired from your journey. I'll just go inside and put your kettle on, shall I?" And without waiting for an answer, Sarah disappeared through Beatrix's door. The two cats leapt down from the fence to follow her.

Beatrix hurried to comb her hair and dress in what she had come to think of as her farm costume—a simple blue blouse, gray tweed skirt, and a gray knitted cardigan—and hurried downstairs. Sarah had poked up the fire until it blazed brightly and was busily slicing bread and setting out butter and marmalade. A pot of sausages was warming on the range while tea brewed in the green china pot.

Sarah looked up from her task. "Thought you deserved a bit of a welcome home," she said with a wide smile. "What's it been since you were last here? Two months?"

Beatrix made a face. "Eight weeks and five days."

She had been trying to get away from her parents for the past fortnight, while her mother—always a hard woman to satisfy and rarely pleased with anything Beatrix proposed to do—came up with first one thing and then another that must be done before she might leave. But Beatrix was determined. While she might have to live in the gloomy house at Number Two Bolton Gardens, Hill Top Farm and Sawrey Village were her true home. Now that she was finally here, she didn't intend to waste a single instant. There was so much she wanted to do! Meet the new lambs and piglets, work on drawings for her new book, take a long walk in the woods to sketch the spring flowers—

"We've missed you, dear," Sarah said, picking up the teapot, "and that's God's truth. The village isn't the same without you."

Beatrix sat down at the table and let Sarah pour her a cup of steaming tea. "How kind of you, Sarah," she said gratefully. "Thank you." She smiled down at the two cats peeping out from under the tablecloth. "Hello, Tabitha. Hello, Crumpet. Nice to see both of you."

"Hello to you, Miss Potter," Crumpet returned politely. *"Tabitha Twitchit and I should like to be among the first to welcome you home."*

The cats had another reason, of course, for coming into Miss Potter's house—for trespassing, that is, on Felicia Frummety's territory. Tabitha had proposed to Crumpet that they persuade Miss Potter to invite another cat to deal with the rats at Hill Top. If Miss Potter herself extended the invitation—well, then, Felicia should simply have to accept it.

"Kind? Oh, I shouldn't say so," Sarah rejoined, sitting down and helping herself to a sausage. "I have to eat, don't I? And since I'd put my buns to rise, I thought I'd just pop on over and we'd both have a bite of breakfast while I caught you up on the news."

Sarah—also known as "Sarah Scones"—owned Anvil Cottage Bakery. Although she had been in business for only a little over a year, she was already considered the best baker between Kendal and Hawkshead. No one would ever call her pretty: her nose was too prominent, her mouth too wide, and her face too emphatically freckled. But her dark eyes sparkled with an unquenchable good humor, and she was unusually courageous and bold. She dared to smoke cigarettes in public, for instance; and she had a great deal of down-to-earth practicality, evidenced in her brown corduroy trousers and red jumper. The villagers had been scandalized when this trousered New Woman inherited Anvil Cottage from Miss Tolliver and set up a bakery there. But even Mathilda Crook had to admit that there was not an unkind bone in Sarah Barwick's body, and Elsa Grape (who prided herself on her baking) conceded that Sarah's muffins were really quite tasty, although her scones could do with some improvement.

"Oh, yes, the news!" Beatrix said happily, with her mouth full. "I'm as hungry for news as I am for your fresh bread, Sarah. I hope I'm not a gossip, but I want you to tell me *everything.* Has Grace Lythecoe's arm mended? What's been heard from the Crabbe sisters? And how is Caroline Longford getting along?"

Beatrix missed the villagers while she was in London, and when she returned, she was always anxious to find out how they had got on in her absence. Learning who had been born and who had died, who had acquired a new pig or a new piece of land or a new spouse—this sort of thing connected her once again to the little village, which was so full of life and energy and delightfully vivid people. And Sarah Barwick was always a reliable source of news, since she was out and about so often on her bakery route.

"Oh, well, *gossip,*" said Sarah, with a dismissive wave of the butter-knife. "There's plenty of that, if you like. But to answer your questions, Dr. Butters has pronounced Grace's arm on the way to mending, although she's still wearing it in a sling. The Crabbe sisters remain in Bournemouth, but the elder Miss Crabbe died just before Christmas."

Beatrix made a regretful noise, although she doubted that many mourned the passing of Miss Crabbe, the former head of the village school. She had been responsible for a great many misunderstandings in the last few months of her tenure.

"And Caroline is not doing well in school, I'm sorry to say," Sarah went on. "Mrs. Beever tells me that her grandmother won't allow her to keep company with the village children. Lady Longford blames them for Caroline's difficulties."

Beatrix frowned. Mrs. Beever was the cook at Tidmarsh Manor, and would certainly know what was going on there. The report made Beatrix sad. She was especially fond of

Caroline, and did not like to think that the girl might be lonely and was not doing well in school. She should have to see whether something could be done about the situation.

Sarah took a bite of bread-and-butter. "But it's the doings at Raven Hall that have got the village tongues wagging at both ends. Christopher Kittredge—he lost an eye and an arm to the Boers in South Africa—has come back and brought a new wife with him. She's quite a mystery. Everybody's keen to find out more about her."

Beatrix was about to ask what was meant by "quite a mystery," but Sarah was going on. "And Rose Sutton is expecting again, which will make eight, won't it?"

"Seven," Tabitha amended. *"I was over there just this morning. The Irish lass who's come to live there—Deirdre, her name is—gave me a plate of fresh milk, which I call very kind."*

"Seven, I think," Beatrix said. The Suttons were her neighbors, just down the hill in Courier Cottage. Desmond Sutton was a veterinarian; his wife Rose helped him out in the surgery, when she wasn't tending to their rapidly growing family.

"Yes, seven," Sarah said, counting on her fingers. "Anyway, the Suttons have taken a girl from the orphanage—Deirdre, her name is—to live with them and help out, which does make eight, of course. And the vicar has had company ever since Christmas. Some sort of distant cousins, and not a happy pair, either, from their sour looks. They—"

Whatever Sarah was about to say about the vicar's unhappy guests was interrupted by a knock at the door. "Come in!" she shouted with enthusiasm, and then, covering her mouth apologetically, added, "Oh, sorry, Bea. It's your house."

The door opened. "Good morning!" chirped Dimity Woodcock. "Mrs. Jennings told me you'd got back last night,

Beatrix. How lovely to see you!" She set down a basket and took out some covered dishes. "Elsa thought you might not have enough in the house for a good breakfast, so she sent some potted tongue, a bowl of stewed rhubarb, and a plate of kippers. Hello, Sarah."

"Kippers!" Tabitha cried enthusiastically. *"I do love a bit of kipper for breakfast."*

"Jolly good," said Sarah heartily. "Sit down, Dim, and join us. We'll have ourselves a feast." She looked under the table. "I'll just put a taste of kipper on a saucer for the kitties, shall I?"

"Do," Beatrix said, feeling very comfortable and happy. It was so good to have friends, and to be away from London and her parents. She picked up the teapot. "May I pour you a cup of tea, Dimity?"

"Yes, please," Dimity said, taking off her jacket and smoothing her brown hair. She and her brother Miles lived in Tower Bank House, on the hill above and behind Anvil Cottage. Captain Woodcock served as the District's Justice of the Peace, and Dimity was a regular parish volunteer. Sawrey couldn't get along without either them. "Shall I leave the door just ajar?" she asked. "The outside air is so fresh."

"Yes, please," Beatrix said. "Mrs. Jennings airs the house every week while I'm gone, but it's still fusty."

Mr. and Mrs. Jennings had been living at Hill Top when Beatrix bought the farm nearly two years before. Mr. Jennings took care of the sheep, cows, and pigs, while Mrs. Jennings tended the garden and managed the poultry and dairy. They had recently moved, with their three children, into the two-story addition Beatrix had built for them at one end of the old farmhouse. Mrs. Jennings, who had at first been very unhappy about Beatrix's purchase of the farm, seemed much more content now that her family were comfortably accommodated.

Beatrix was delighted, as well. With the Jenningses settled, she had the old part of the house all to herself and could get on with her plans for turning it into the home she had always wanted. Not the home of her dreams, perhaps—that, she would have shared with Norman Warne, had he lived. She glanced down at Norman's ring, then pushed the bleak thought away. The day was too pretty to dwell on sadness.

Crumpet, seeing the expression on her face, whispered to Tabitha, *"She's thinking of her fiancé. The one who died the month after they were engaged."*

"Such a sad story," Tabitha whispered back. *"Pulls the heart right out of you just to think of it."*

Crumpet and Tabitha had once overheard Miss Potter telling Miss Woodcock what had happened. Miss Potter's parents had been dead set against the match. Mr. Potter refused to let his daughter marry a man who was in trade, and Mrs. Potter insisted that her only daughter's place was at home, looking after her parents as they grew older. Miss Potter had defied them and accepted the proposal, only to have her world come crashing down when Mr. Warne died just a month later, of leukemia. Tabitha had been much affected by the tale, for she had lost her only true love when he was kicked in the head by Mrs. Crook's cow, and had never ceased to grieve.

Sarah put down a plate of kippers for the cats as Dimity looked around, admiring. "I don't think I've been here since you've finished this room, Beatrix. It's delightful, just delightful!"

"Thank you," Beatrix said with pleasure.

She herself was happy with the way it had turned out. She'd had a new, separate kitchen built beside the garden, and turned this room, formerly the Jenningses' kitchen, into the main living area—the "hall," to use the old North

Country term. She'd made a great many changes, pulling down a partition, replacing the modern shelves with an old oak cupboard she had bought at an auction, papering the walls and ceiling in a green-and-white flowery print that freshened the room and made it light and airy. She'd spread a sea-grass rug on the blue slate floor and a shaggy blue rug in front of the fireplace recess, which held a black cast-iron range with a large oven at one side. The red curtains and pots of red geraniums at the deep-set window added the final cheerful touch that made the room warm and bright and as comfortable as an old friend.

"Have a sausage, Dim," Sarah said, forking one onto Dimity's plate. "I was just telling Bea all she's missed in the last two months. I'd got through Raven Hall and the Suttons' new baby and the Irish girl who's living with them, and as far as the vicar's cousin and his wife."

"Oh, yes, the Thextons," Dimity said, and pulled down her mouth. "I pity the poor vicar."

"Why?" Beatrix asked with concern. "He's not ill, is he?" Samuel Sackett was a sweet man, studious and a bit distracted, perhaps, but always attentive to the cares of his flock. He was one of her favorite people.

"Not ill, exactly," Dimity replied, adding marmalade to a slice of Sarah's bread. "Just weary."

"And well he might be," said Crumpet, wiping a trace of kipper from her whiskers with one paw. *"Those Thextons are really dreadful people, you know. I met Mrs. Thexton in the shop, where she was charging ribbons to the vicar's account. Fancy!"*

"We're not here to gossip, Crumpet," Tabitha said severely. She finished licking the saucer clean. *"We must think of a way to persuade Miss Potter to invite a new cat to Hill Top."*

"Weary is right," said Sarah spiritedly. "I should be weary, if I had to put up with that pair. They're out to take advantage, if you ask me. Bea, have some of Elsa's potted tongue, do. It's delicious. What does she season it with, Dim?"

"She'll never tell us," Dimity replied. She tasted. "But I'd say nutmeg and cloves. And sage?" She tasted again, and considered. "Yes, sage, I believe."

"Think I'll try making some myself," Sarah said appreciatively.

"I don't suppose," Beatrix remarked, "that the vicar's quite up to booting them out, even if they are taking advantage." The vicar was a mild man with a simple nature, hospitable and generous to a fault.

"Well put!" applauded Sarah. "That's the point, exactly. He'd like to be rid of them, but it's the getting rid that's troubling." She cocked an ear. "Bea, what in the world is that rustling noise?"

This was exactly what Crumpet and Tabitha had been waiting for.

"It's rats in the wall," Crumpet said urgently, coming out from under the table. *"Rats—that's what you're hearing."*

Tabitha rubbed against Miss Potter's ankle. *"What's needed here is a cat, Miss Potter. A ratter who isn't afraid of getting bitten, not that silly, harum-scarum Felicia Frummety."*

Beatrix gave a resigned sigh. "I'm afraid you're hearing our Hill Top rats, Sarah. There's a very old spiral stair in the wall, which used to give access to the upper floor. It was blocked up when the other stair was built, but it seems that the rats delight in using it. Mrs. Jennings wrote me that they were becoming a problem, and last night, I heard them for myself, scurrying up and down the stair."

"Oh, rats," Dimity said with a shiver. "You really have to get after them, Beatrix. If you don't, they'll take over the rest of the village, and everyone will be annoyed at you for letting them get a foothold. Doesn't Mrs. Jennings have a cat?"

Sarah chuckled. "The current Hill Top cat is a bit like our vicar. Not quite up to giving the rats the boot."

"*Precisely,*" said Crumpet, twitching her tail. "*What's wanted is a cat with a mouthful of sharp teeth and the will to use them.*"

"*Exactly, Miss Potter,*" Tabitha said. "*I know of several cats who are currently looking for assignments—creatures of substance, with plenty of claw and sinew. I should be glad to send them around, and you can give them a trial.*"

"Bless me," Sarah said admiringly. "Just listen to all that mewing. You'd think the creatures were talking to us, wouldn't you?"

"Perhaps they are," Beatrix said with a little laugh. "I imagine that they are remarking that what Hill Top needs is a new cat."

"*Yes, yes, yes!*" shrieked the cats, in unison. "A new cat!"

"That should be easy enough," said Dimity.

"I suppose," Beatrix sighed. "Unfortunately, I'm rather partial to rats. I had a white one once, you see, as a pet. Sammy—a very sweet and affectionate fellow. And some cats can create as many problems as they solve. But in the present circumstance, I'm afraid I have to agree. One simply cannot have rats running riot."

"*You see, Tabitha?*" Crumpet said with satisfaction. "*Miss Potter isn't like the other humans. She really DOES understand what we say.*"

Crumpet and Tabitha (in fact, all of the animals in the Land between the Lakes) were sadly aware that the Big Folk rarely understood them when they tried to communicate what they knew or how they felt. Some were different, though. Miss Potter often seemed to understand, as did Jeremy Crosfield and several of the other children—the quiet ones, who preferred to sit still and listen rather than run around screaming and waving their arms all the time.

"I can't think what she means, though," Tabitha said with a frown, *"about cats becoming part of the problem. How could that be true?"*

Sarah handed Dimity a dish of rhubarb. "I told Bea about the Kittredges coming to Raven Hall, but I didn't go into detail. You know more than I do about it, I'm sure."

"I know Major Kittredge, of course," Dimity said slowly. "The Kittredge family has lived at Raven Hall for generations, so everyone in the village is acquainted with him." She took a spoon and busied herself with her rhubarb. "The major was quite a handsome man before he got shot up in that appalling war."

"All wars are appalling," Beatrix said soberly. Her parents had brought her up as a Unitarian, but she occasionally attended Quaker meetings, and leaned toward the Quakers' pacifist ideals.

Dimity nodded distractedly. "I haven't seen the major since he returned, but I understand that he lost an eye and an arm. He spent quite a lot of time in hospital after he got back." Her eyes filled with sadness. "Such terrible luck for such a good man."

"Raven Hall," Beatrix said, pouring herself another cup of tea and pretending not to notice that Dimity seemed unusually affected by the major's plight. "That's the Gothic mansion at the top of Cuckoo Brow Wood?" She walked in that direction occasionally, following a path that took her to Fern Vale Tarn, and had glimpsed the house through the trees, a forbidding pile of stone, with turrets and towers and a darkly unpleasant look, although someone had told her that it had been designed by David Bryce, the architect who built Balfour Castle.

"Raven Hall is where the servant girl drowned last year," Sarah put in. "And where the housekeeper went mad and shut herself in the pantry." She shuddered. "The villagers say it's haunted by a woman in a gray silk dress, who drifts about, jangling a great lot of old-fashioned keys."

"The villagers say all sorts of silly things," Dimity said sharply. Softening her tone, she added, "There's been no one living there—except for the staff, of course—since Major Kittredge's parents and his older brother were killed in a carriage accident five years or so ago. The major had just gone off to South Africa at the time, to fight the Boers." She sighed. "There's been a great deal of misfortune in the family, I'm afraid, in spite of the Raven Hall Luck."

"In spite of—" Beatrix frowned in confusion, thinking that something didn't make sense. "I don't understand."

"That's Luck with a capital L," Sarah told her. "The Luck is a fancy glass goblet, said to have been handed over to one of the Kittredge ancestors by the Fairy Folk who live in Cuckoo Brow Wood. As long as it stays in one piece, the place is supposed to have good fortune." She snorted contemptuously. "A lot of good that magic Luck has done 'em. If the Folk offer me a goblet, I'll tell 'em they can jolly well keep it for themselves."

Dimity sighed. "One can hope that having the master at home will change the luck of the place, even if his new wife—" She broke off.

"Even if she what?" Beatrix prompted. This was the second time the new Mrs. Kittredge had been mentioned with hesitations and odd looks, and she was getting curious.

"Nobody quite knows who she is, you see," Dimity said lamely.

"And if there's anything that this village can't abide," said Sarah, "it's not knowing who somebody is, when they think they ought. And in the case of the mysterious Mrs. Kittredge, they smell a rat."

"I am confident," said Dimity loyally, "that Major Kittredge would not have married someone who is not perfectly nice, in every imaginable way."

"Oh, no doubt," Sarah said. "But the real difficulty is that she has red hair, you know. Well, we *don't* know, actually," she amended, "because none of us have seen her. But that's what the head housemaid at Raven Hall told her sister, and her sister told Lydia Dowling. Although of course, it's not just the red hair. It's her manner. Mrs. Kittredge's manner, that is."

"What's wrong with red hair?" Beatrix asked with interest, reflecting that her own, while mostly brown, had rather a reddish hue.

Sarah lowered her voice dramatically. "The ghost of Raven Hall is supposed to have red hair. Some are saying that the new Mrs. Kittredge is the Raven Hall ghost, come back to life. And Lydia Dowling says she must be a witch. Witches always have red hair."

"*A witch?*" Tabitha inquired with immediate interest, not surprisingly, since it is widely known that cats are quite familiar with witches. "*We haven't had a witch in the District since my grandmother's days, when old Mrs. Diggle practiced the Craft. I wonder what kind of witch Mrs. Kittredge is, and whether she—*"

She stopped suddenly and grew very still, her eyes narrowing, her whiskers twitching. "*Look, Crumpet,*" she said, very low. "*There, in the corner, just by the cupboard door!*"

Crumpet crouched, every muscle tensing. "*Not to worry, Tabitha. I'll take care of him.*"

"*No!*" Tabitha put out a warning paw. "*Remember the Rule!*"

"That witch business is nothing but old-fashioned superstitious rubbish," Dimity said heatedly. "I do wish Lydia

Dowling would keep her opinions to herself. It's appalling to call the major's wife a—" She broke off. "A rat!" she shrieked, and jumped up onto her chair.

"Get that rat, Crumpet!" Beatrix cried.

And then, Miss Potter having given a direct order (so that the Rule was no longer in question), Crumpet bounded across the floor and pounced fiercely on the bold, whiskery fellow who had ventured out of the cupboard. She gave him two savage shakes. The rat uttered a single terrified squeal and went limp as a rag doll.

"There, there, Dim," Sarah said in a comforting tone. "You can come down from your chair. Crumpet's taken care of the foul beast." She chuckled. "You see, Bea? What you need is a really first-rate ratter."

"I'm afraid you're right," Beatrix said, as Dimity climbed off the chair. "It is time to fling down the gauntlet. I shall look into getting another cat straightaway—although he will have to live in the barn."

"How about Crumpet?" Sarah asked. "That was an impressive catch."

"Mrs. Stubbs wouldn't part with her." Beatrix went to the door and opened it wider. "You were very quick in dispatching that fellow, Crumpet. Now, take him outside, will you? That's a good cat."

"Glad to oblige, I'm sure," Crumpet said, around her mouthful of warm rat. She strutted out the door with an envious Tabitha at her heels, feeling quite proud of herself—as I daresay you would, if you had just rid the world of an exceedingly ugly rat.

"Let's see," mused Sarah, as Beatrix came back to the table. "We were talking about the mysterious Mrs. Kittredge, who may or may not be the Raven Hall ghost come to life. And

Dimity was feeling cross with Lydia Dowling for saying that she's a witch."

Dimity took a sip of tea to steady herself. "I'm sure Lydia was only trying to be funny," she said. "But this is a very old-fashioned village. There are some who still believe in witches and ghosts and fairies. One has to be careful about what one says," she added sternly.

"Is Mrs. Kittredge from around here?" Beatrix asked. She knew from her own experience that the villagers were clannish and apt to feel antagonist toward off-comers.

"From London," Sarah replied. "Of course, that's part of it. That, and her clothes. The housemaid said she's never seen so many grand dresses and so much fine jewelry. Must have set the major back thousands of pounds."

"Sawrey is a bit out of the way of things," Beatrix remarked. "And as Dimity says, it's very old-fashioned. No electric lights, no telephone, no entertainments. It suits me exactly, but I wonder whether Mrs. Kittredge might find life dull here."

"I doubt it," Dimity said stoutly. "Mrs. Kittredge could not possibly find it dull. Christopher—Major Kittredge—is a very interesting person. Marriage to him would be—"

She stopped abruptly, coloring, and looked away, but not before Beatrix—who often noticed what others might like to hide—understood that Dimity Woodcock had once cared a very great deal for Christopher Kittredge and was forcing herself to set her feelings aside and accept the fact that he now had a beautiful new wife. Realizing this, Beatrix felt a great sympathy for Dimity, for she herself knew what it was like to lose the one person you loved. Married, Major Kittredge was as irretrievably lost to poor Dimity as Norman was to herself.

"That's as may be, Dim," Sarah said, tossing her head carelessly. "But p'rhaps you'll forgive me if I am just a tiny bit glad that the villagers have happened on something new to keep their tongues wagging—besides my trousers and my bicycle, that is." She smiled at Beatrix. "You won't want to miss the reception, Bea. Saturday afternoon, at Raven Hall. The whole village plans to turn out to ogle the mysterious Mrs. Kittredge and stuff themselves with sandwiches and sweets. *My* sweets," she added proudly. "The Raven Hall cook isn't up to such a large crowd, it seems. I've been asked to provide cakes and tarts and other sweets."

"Oh, yes, you must come, Beatrix," Dimity said in a rush, obviously relieved to leave the subject of the Kittredge marriage. "Raven Hall may look forbidding on the outside, but the interior is really quite spectacular, with a minstrel gallery and a view over Lake Windermere, and some fine old pieces of art. Including the Luck, of course, which is quite famous." She fell silent again, and Beatrix guessed that she was thinking of a time when she had seen herself as the mistress of Raven Hall.

"I'm not sure I'll go," Beatrix said apologetically. She was shy and self-conscious in crowds, and avoided large social gatherings when she could. "There's so much to be done here, and I promised my mother that I would only stay away a fortnight. If the weather is fine, I should very much like to get into the garden."

"Nonsense," Sarah said decidedly. "You have to go, and that's all there is to it." She glanced at the clock and stood up. "My buns have risen, so I'm off to put them into the oven. Lovely to have you back, Bea. Do get another cat, will you, before I have rats in my bread bin? Ta, Dim. See you at Raven Hall."

"I'm off, too," Dimity said, as Sarah bustled out the door. "I must go down to the school this morning and look for the May box."

"The May box?" Beatrix asked curiously.

"The crowns and May Pole ribbons," Dimity said. She sighed. "Mrs. Peachy always manages the May Pageant, which is just a week away. But she's gone to Edinburgh to help her sister, who's ill. So I agreed to take her place."

"That's no surprise," Beatrix said with a smile. Dimity was always agreeing to do this, that, or the other thing, usually on very short notice. But perhaps the May Pageant was good for her. It might keep her mind off Major Kittredge and his mysterious new wife.

"I know." Dimity made a face. "But the children always look forward to the May Pole. I couldn't find it in my heart to say no." She picked up her basket. "So you're staying just a fortnight?"

"Yes," Beatrix said, going with her to the door. She glanced out at the stone wall, where Crumpet was perched, victorious, with her prize. "And it looks as if I shall have to spend a good part of it dealing with *rats*."

3

Ridley Rattail Arrives at
a Conclusion

At the same moment that Miss Potter was asserting her determination to do something about the rats, Ridley Rattail was pacing around his parlor in the northwest corner of the Hill Top attic, his hands clasped beneath his coattails. He and Miss Potter were puzzling over the very same problem.

Ridley, a stout, mild-tempered gentleman rat from the Midlands, had come to live at Hill Top at the invitation of his friend Rosabelle, just about the time Miss Potter had purchased the place. His introduction to the Lake District had been most unpleasant, as you will remember if you read a book called *The Tale of Hill Top Farm*. If you've not read it or have forgotten the story, perhaps I ought to tell you that Ridley had been cheated out of some money (never mind how he acquired it) by a pair of very disagreeable rats, and that he had just missed being snatched up by an enormous

owl, and had lost most of his clothes when he was forced to
swim across Wilfin Beck in the middle of the night. He had
arrived in Rosabelle's attic wet, miserable, and thoroughly
frightened.

But Rosabelle was a most gracious and hospitable friend.
Various guests who had stayed with her over the years had left
one thing or another behind, and Ridley was able to outfit
himself quite handsomely in the way of trousers, shirtfronts,
waistcoats, slippers, and a fine briar pipe, to which he added
his own possessions, forwarded from his previous residence.
The Jennings family, who occupied the rooms downstairs,
were also generous (or careless—it amounted to the same
thing in the end), and there was a regular supply of beans,
bacon, and cheese, with the occasional savory bubble and
squeak, and no end of delicious cake and pie. In fact, Ridley
had never before enjoyed such substantial provender, and as a
result, his already stout figure had grown several sizes stouter,
and he could no longer button his waistcoat and jacket.

It wasn't just the fine dining that Ridley enjoyed, either.
For when the renovations to the farmhouse were completed
and Miss Potter took up residence in the older part of the
house, she brought with her a great number of handsome
leather-bound books, gilt-framed paintings, pieces of antique china and porcelain and silver, and so many other
fascinating treasures that Ridley felt he was living in what
might fairly be called an art museum—exactly the right
sort of residence for a gentleman of fine taste.

What's more, Miss Potter was an artist and children's
author of wide reputation, and she liked to do her artwork
on the table in front of the window in what had once been
Mrs. Jennings's kitchen. So Ridley had the rare opportunity
to enjoy her little books before they were seen by the public.
He often lurked in the chimney corner until she went up to

bed, so he could have an admiring look at her current project. He very much liked the one she was working on now, which involved a pair of rats, something like himself and Rosabelle, who captured an impertinent young kitten and tied him up with string, preparatory to wrapping the saucy fellow in pastry and steaming him like a roly-poly pudding.

Miss Potter had not yet got to the end of her book, so Ridley could not be sure how the story came out. But if it went as it seemed to be going, he knew he should like it very well. It included a stunning passage that made him shiver with fright and grin with delight at the very same time, for in it he recognized Hill Top itself, with its staircase hidden in the wall:

> *It was an old, old house, full of cupboards and passages. Some of the walls were four feet thick, and there used to be queer noises inside them, as if there might be a little secret staircase. Certainly there were odd little jagged doorways in the wainscot, and things disappeared at night—especially cheese and bacon.*

Miss Potter's fictional Hill Top seemed dark, somehow, and sinister, as though its walls and passages might hide macabre secrets beneath the serene ordinariness of everyday life. This description made Ridley shiver because it gave him the sense that disruptive powers might lurk behind any respectable façade, and since he was so comfortably contented, this little *frisson* of horror was pleasurable indeed.

And all taken together, Ridley Rattail enjoyed every domestic pleasure that any rat might wish. He and Rosabelle lived a sedate, self-satisfied, and entirely pleasant life, rich in civil discourse and the pleasures of gentility, always careful not to call attention to themselves in any way. Of course, had there been a mouser downstairs who paid the proper attention to larder or dairy, it might not have been so easy to escape notice, and get away with the cheese and bacon. But the only cat was a young, inexperienced feline named Miss Felicia Frummety, who belonged to Mrs. Jennings but liked to boast that she was Miss Potter's cat. Felicia, a vain creature who spent a great deal of time grooming herself, could not be bothered to notice, so the rats' forays into the kitchen and dairy went unchallenged.

But Ridley's contentment was short-lived. It happened that Rosabelle's sister Bluebell and Bluebell's husband and four children had been left without a home when a storm blew the roof off their barn on the other side of Esthwaite Water. Rosabelle, generous to a fault, hospitably offered them refuge.

And that was when things had turned sour, Ridley thought darkly, taking another turn around his comfortable, nicely furnished parlor. He could not in good conscience object to a brief visit from Rosabelle's homeless relatives. But then Bluebell's husband Rollo, a brash, brutish fellow with menacing whiskers and bad breath, had invited three or four of his bachelor friends—ne'er-do-well rogues from Hawkshead—for a fortnight's holiday. They had set up a dartboard and a billiard table at the east end of the attic, rolled a keg of ginger beer and a round of ripe yellow cheese up the spiral stairs in the kitchen wall, and commenced to enjoy themselves long and loudly.

Ridley deeply resented this intrusion into his tranquil life, the life of a self-satisfied gentleman rat settled in comfortable lodgings, which heretofore had been altogether civilized and enjoyable. Finally, one midnight, when the gaiety had reached an unendurable pitch, he went to the east end of the attic (he had taken to calling it the Hill Top Saloon) to remonstrate. But Rollo took immediate offense.

"Wot's all this, eh?" he growled, raising himself up on his back legs and glaring down his whiskery nose at Ridley, who found himself feeling suddenly rather short and out of trim. *"Interferin' wi' me gennulmen friends, are ye?"*

"Well, no," replied Ridley nervously. *"I only—"*

"Stow it," Rollo growled. His tail twitched threateningly. *"Give me any more o' yer lip, Rattail, and I'll punch ye in the nose."*

In the circumstance, Ridley thought it just as well to allow the party to continue. He took himself off to his room and comforted himself with the reminder that this was only a temporary situation. Rollo's riotous friends would be gone soon, the Saloon would be closed, and attic life would return to its normal, decorous state.

But the fortnight came and went and Rollo's friends showed no signs of departing. Instead, they invited *their* friends to join them. More cheeses were pilfered from the Hill Top dairy and supplemented by mutton, bacon, bread, and scones from the Jenningses' kitchen, as well as apples from the apple barrel and corn from the barn. When the ginger beer ran out, it was replaced by bottles of stout pinched from the nearby Tower Bank Arms. And all the while Felicia Frummety slept on the warm hearth below, allowing the renegade rats to run rampant wherever they liked.

So, just when Ridley had hoped that these unwanted guests would be gone and the attic restored to its former broad expanse of dusty peace, the party in the Saloon only grew louder and larger. One of the rats had engaged a concertina player, who sat on a stool and entertained the crowd—the *growing* crowd—with bawdy songs he had learned from veterans of the war in South Africa. After a few days, the concertina player invited a trio of can-can dancers, who kicked up their heels on a wooden crackerbox stage that their admirers had cobbled together, with curtains made of scraps stolen from Mrs. Jennings's workbasket.

Poor Ridley. He who had preferred the quiet life and liked to retire early to his chambers found himself kept awake almost until dawn by the sound of rats enjoying themselves in his attic. *His* attic, he thought resentfully, as he lay sleepless through the night, with bits of cotton wool stuffed in his ears and the covers pulled over his head.

Bad as the situation was, it was about to get worse—oh, much, much worse. Quite a few of the fellows noticed with approval that the Hill Top attic was clean and dry and undisturbed (Miss Potter had better things to do than bother about the attic), and decided to bring their wives and children and all their family furnishings to take up lodgings there. And of course, rats—as Tabitha Twitchit has already pointed out—multiply faster than rabbits. In no time at all, there were some six dozen rat families in permanent residence. (This was according to the January census, which could not be relied upon as accurate, for several large litters had been produced since the count was made and more were on the way.) The roomy attic no longer seemed roomy at all, and Ridley—who valued his privacy more than anything else in the world—could scarcely manage a ten-minute nap in his favorite chair without having his slippered feet tread upon or his tail pulled by rowdy, ill-behaved rat children.

"We would not have this problem," Ridley grumbled to Rosabelle when they had a private moment in the kitchen, *"if you were not so obliging."*

"You are making too much of it, Ridley," Rosabelle said mildly, rolling up her sleeves in preparation for the washing up. *"You should be a little forgiving, and allow the children to have their play."*

"I could tolerate the children during the daytime," Ridley retorted, *"if I could get my sleep at night. It's the music and dancing and laughing and the crack of billiard balls*—crack! crack! crack!*—on and on until the wee hours. That's what's got me down, Rosabelle."*

"You might speak to Rollo," Rosabelle suggested, stacking the dirty dishes. *"I'm sure he'd be willing to*—"

"I spoke to Rollo," Ridley said glumly. *"He offered to punch my nose."*

Rosabelle gave him a sympathetic look. *"I urge you to try again,"* she said, ever the peacemaker. *"I'm sure he*—"

"I invite you to allow Rollo to punch your nose." And with that pained retort, Ridley stalked off to his private apartment, where he closed and locked the door and began to pace back and forth, feeling deeply injured.

But the sense of injury was soon overtaken by a growing sense of . . . well, shame, that's what it was. Rosabelle had been too kind to call him a coward, but she didn't need to, for he knew himself all too well. He was a rat of no courage, a rat who was too meek and mousy to do what had to be done. He was a coward, and the knowledge cut like a sword to the heart.

Ridley stopped pacing and stood very still, trembling, until finally the dark shame of his cowardice began to transform itself into something like resolve. What was needed in this situation was not brawn, but brains; not muscle, but mental acuity. Surely, if he put his mind to it, he could think of a way to rid the Hill Top attics of this infestation of uninvited, unwelcome, and unruly rats. He could think of a solution.

Now, if you have ever been acquainted with rats (and most of us have, in one way or another), you know that they are astonishingly intelligent along practical lines: where to find the best cheese and bacon, how to be stealthy when stealth is required, and which is the quickest means of escape when danger threatens. But you may also know that rats are not among the most intellectual of animals. Disciplined thought is a challenge for the entire species. Their minds are apt to wander off into pleasant topics, having to do with crumbs in kitchen cupboards and corn in feed bins and bright trinkets lying in a dish on the bureau top—crumbs and corn and trinkets that might be put to better use by an enterprising rat. In fact, their rat brains are full of a great many things all tumbled about with no particular order or method, so finding anything specific in them is even more difficult than finding a needle in a pile of hay.

Nevertheless, within the hour, and by dint of applying himself with rigorous and exhausting mental effort, Ridley Rattail had come upon the solution to his problem. He felt at once proud of having thought of it and foolish that he had not thought of it before.

What was needed to rid the Hill Top attic of the plague of unwanted rats was, quite obviously and simply, a *cat*.

A cat unlike Miss Felicia Frummety, who disdained to chase rats and spent her time either asleep on the hearth or admiring herself in the mirror.

A fierce and stalwart cat who had an insatiable appetite for rats.

A cat who had enough fortitude to face an army of rats if necessary.

A cat who—

And then, just as Ridley was getting well started on the list of important feline qualifications required to deal with this unfortunate situation, he heard a commotion in the hallway outside his rooms, and a loud shrieking and wailing.

Startled, he opened his door and put out his head. *"What's happened?"* he inquired anxiously. *"What's wrong?"*

"There's been a murder!" a rat shouted, tearing at his ears and running in frenzied circles. *"A foul, filthy, fiendish murder! Oh, it's too horrible, too hideous for words!"*

A shiver started between Ridley's ears and quivered all the way down to the tip of his tail. *"A murder, you say?"* he whispered. *"Who was murdered?"*

"Rollo," the rat cried. *"Our wonderful, hospitable host! He was killed by a vicious cat when he went to fetch a bun from the kitchen, not five minutes ago. Oh, horrors, oh, woe! Oh, dear, departed Rollo!"*

"Oh, really," murmured Ridley.

Now, we all know that we are supposed to forgive our enemies, even those who have kept us awake until all hours and offered to punch us in the nose when we complained, and to be sorry when something bad has happened to them.

But I am afraid that Ridley was not so sorry as he ought to have been. Instead, hiding a rattish sort of smile, he went back into his apartment, shut the door, and danced a jig of pure delight.

4

At Sawrey School

The village of Sawrey is made up of twin hamlets, the two separated (or joined, if you will) by a lush green meadow with Wilfin Beck threaded like a long silver ribbon through the middle. The hamlet nearest the market town of Hawkshead (some three miles to the northwest) is called Near Sawrey, logically enough, whilst the hamlet a half-mile farther along the road to the east, closer to the ferry crossing over Lake Windermere, is called Far Sawrey. Near Sawrey, its inhabitants have always judged, is the more important because that's where the Tower Bank Arms is located, and the smithy and joiner and bakery. It is also where the Justice of the Peace lives, and John Braithwaite, the village constable. Those who live in Far Sawrey, on the other hand, consider that hamlet to be the more important, because they possess St. Peter's Church, and the vicarage, and the Sawrey Hotel, and Sawrey School. (Both hamlets boast a post office and a shop, so these are generally left out of the calculation.)

Miss Margaret Nash, the new headmistress at Sawrey School, was one of the fortunate people who lived in Near Sawrey and worked in Far Sawrey, and thought this arrangement gave her the best of all possible worlds. At half past three on Wednesday afternoon, as she stood at the school door and watched as her jubilant charges skipped out of the school yard, the girls in companionable pairs and trios, the boys leaping and shouting from sheer joy, she thought again how singularly fortunate she was to live in such a beautiful place and to have work that gave her such an enormous sense of satisfaction. She had been appointed head teacher upon the retirement of Miss Myrtle Crabbe, although Margaret herself had at one point given up hope of having the position. If it had not been for Miss Potter's discovery that Margaret's chief competitor for the post was a sham and a fraud, she was sure she would not have had it.

But all's well that ends well, Margaret reminded herself cheerfully. She picked up Jane Jackson's blue hair ribbon, Tommy Tyson's grimy sweater (recognizable by the hole in the elbow), and an arithmetic exercise paper with Willie Adams's name printed crookedly at the top. She placed all three articles prominently on the Lost and Found shelf, where their careless owners might see and claim them. Then she picked up the broom and applied it industriously to the patch of dried mud in front of the boot-box.

Things could not have turned out better, she thought happily, as she finished her sweeping and replaced the broom in the teachers' pantry. The members of the school board (which included the vicar and Captain Woodcock) were entirely supportive. Margaret's junior pupils were all that she might have wished in the way of interesting academic challenges. And Mrs. Daphne Holland, who had assumed Margaret's place as teacher of the infants class, was an energetic and highly qualified young lady who had been widowed the year before and was glad of a job and a little money coming in. Mrs. Holland always presented a bright, cheerful countenance to her small charges and (perhaps because of her youth) seemed to like nothing better than to romp with them at the recess interval.

Just now, Mrs. Holland joined Margaret in the pantry, for the cup of tea and the bit of talk they always shared after the children had gone home for the day.

"Oh, Miss Nash," she said, "I wonder if you and your sister will be going to tea at Raven Hall on Saturday. I've been invited and thought perhaps the three of us might go together." She smiled. "Not that I'm shy, of course. But I did think there might be strength in numbers."

Margaret filled the kettle, put it on the gas ring, and reached for the biscuit tin. "Annie and I should like that." She smiled. "I suppose I'm as curious as the next person to see the inside of Raven Hall, which has always struck me as a gloomy, forbidding old place."

"It's the new Mrs. Kittredge I'm dying to see," Mrs. Holland confided gaily. "You know what they're saying in the village." She leaned closer, her eyes sparkling in her round, girlish face. "They're saying the lady's a *witch*. Or maybe she's the ghost of Raven Hall, come to life."

"Mrs. Holland!" Margaret exclaimed in a scandalized tone. "You shouldn't repeat such wicked things."

"Oh, pooh," Mrs. Holland said breezily. "It's all balderdash, and of course one doesn't believe it. But it's what the villagers are saying."

Margaret gave her a severe look. "You and I, as teachers, are supposed to be above common superstition. And if we are heard to repeat such idle nonsense, the children and their parents might think we're giving them leave to do the same.

We have to set an example, you know." And then, because she sounded like a scold, and since she hadn't heard the gossip herself, she added, in a softer tone, "Who's saying this?"

"Bertha Stubbs," Mrs. Holland replied, getting down the cups and saucers from the shelf.

"Oh, Bertha," Margaret said dismissively. "She's liable to say anything that comes into her mind." Bertha Stubbs was the school's daily woman, and an inveterate gossip. Even worse, she was a cantankerous complainer. No part of her work suited her, from scrubbing the floors to stoking the stoves and cleaning the blackboards. Margaret often found herself wishing that Bertha would give in her notice (as she regularly threatened to do) so they could find someone more compatible.

"And then I heard it again on my way home from school yesterday," Mrs. Holland added, "when I stopped at Lydia Dowling's shop to get some apples. I suppose it's because she—Mrs. Kittredge, that is—has red hair. She's said to be frightfully smashing."

Margaret frowned at Mrs. Holland's schoolgirl slang. "I suppose it's because she's a mystery. People don't know her, so they make up all sorts of things about her."

"Of course," Mrs. Holland said. She turned a serious face to Margaret. "It's all rubbish, I grant you, and people ought to know better. But there is quite a lot of talk, silly or otherwise. And Deirdre Malone, poor child, has flaming red hair. She's being tarred with the same brush."

"Oh, dear," Margaret sighed. "So that's what it's all about. I saw Harold teasing the girl. She seemed to be holding her own, though."

Deirdre Malone was the young orphan who had come to help out in the Sutton household while Mrs. Sutton was entering the last months of her . . . seventh pregnancy, was it?

or was it her eighth? It was hard to keep count of the burgeon-ing Suttons, who, when they were all old enough to go to school, might fill an entire classroom on their own. Deirdre had an abundance of bright red hair, flashing eyes, and a great many freckles—an Irish inheritance, Margaret suspected. And although she was a dreamy child, she knew how to stand up for herself.

Mrs. Holland chuckled. "Deirdre gave some of it back to him, didn't she? I saw Harold take a tumble and didn't re-gret it a bit. One hates to say it, but he's an awful bully." She opened the biscuit tin and took out two for each of them. "It's good to see that Caroline Longford has befriended her. And Jeremy Crosfield, too."

"They are all three orphans," Margaret said. "Perhaps that's their common bond. And Jeremy's had his own taste of Harold's bullying."

Mrs. Holland poured hot water over the tea in the chipped Brighton teapot, a souvenir of one of Miss Crabbe's long-ago summer holidays. "Caroline is rather a surprise, isn't she? One would think she'd be doing better."

"Yes," Margaret said. "It's a puzzle." Caroline's school in New Zealand, where she had come from, had not given her a very good start. She should have been able to catch up easily, but something—Margaret had no idea what—was holding her back.

"Anyway," Mrs. Holland was going on, "you'd think that Lady Longford's granddaughter would have a governess, or be sent away to school, rather than attending here in the vil-lage. One wonders why."

"Oh, haven't you heard that story?" asked Margaret. "It's all on account of Miss Potter."

"No, I didn't know," said Mrs. Holland, with interest. "Tell me about it."

And as their tea brewed, Margaret told what had happened the year before, when Miss Potter had helped to persuade Lady Longford that Caroline should be allowed to attend the village school for a year. Now, though, Margaret understood that her ladyship was dissatisfied with Caroline's performance and had decided to obtain a governess for the girl. Caroline would not be coming back to school after the end of term.

Margaret sighed. That was the worst part of being a teacher. Just when one became attached to the children, one had to say goodbye.

5

Caroline and Deirdre Make a Plan

Caroline Longford was at that very moment relating the same story to Deirdre Malone as they walked up the road between banks of blooming hawthorn and verges bright with buttercups. Caroline, whose mother and father were dead, had come to Tidmarsh Manor the previous summer from a sheep station in New Zealand. Her grandmother, Lady Longford, had disowned Caroline's father when he stubbornly refused to marry the young woman she had chosen for him, ran off to New Zealand, and married for love. Her ladyship, an elderly autocrat with the unfortunate habit of expecting everyone in the world to follow her orders, had at first refused to take Caroline in. When she finally agreed, it was on the condition that Caroline be sent away to school as soon as a suitable place could be found.

But Miss Potter had intervened—quite miraculously, it seemed to Caroline—and persuaded Lady Longford to allow Caroline to stay on at the Manor and go to school in the village, at least for a year. Things weren't perfect, by any means. Grandmama was as ill-tempered and dictatorial as ever. She had recently forbidden Caroline to play with the village children, who were a "bad influence" over her, and kept her from doing well in school—in Grandmama's opinion. And Tidmarsh Manor was a cold, stiff house, crowded with heavy furniture and fragile bric-a-brac. It was the kind of place that makes laughing or playing, or any other kind of ordinary enjoyment, utterly impossible, and was fit only for reading, or embroidering, or doing lessons. Worse yet, it was the kind of place that makes you feel as if somebody is looking over your shoulder all the time. But Caroline had a pair of guinea pigs and a private journal where she could say anything she felt like saying because she wrote it all in her own secret code. Even if somebody was looking over her shoulder, the words would look like alphabet soup. The little animals and her journal were her dearest companions, always ready to listen to her when she was feeling sad or lonely.

And now she had a new friend. Deirdre was a year or so younger than she, and new to Sawrey. She was small for her age, with a great mass of red-gold hair that she wore in thick braids and blue-green eyes that could be lit by a dancing amusement or a fiery indignation. There was a certain dreaminess about her expression, and she had a vivid imagination that made the other village girls seem dull and stolid in comparison, or awful prigs. It was Deirdre's imagination that appealed to Caroline, who hated being told that something had to be done or thought because it was "practical" or "the usual thing." And her grandmother's refusal to let her be Deirdre's friend only made her more stubborn. It wasn't fair. She ought to be able to choose her own friends!

When Caroline had finished her story, Deirdre sighed. "Just be glad ye've got a grandmum," she said, "whether ye like her or not." She spoke in a soft Irish brogue, and her words seemed to lift at the end. "When me own mum died, there wa'n't nobody t' take me and no place in the world t' go 'cept St. Mary's Orphans Asylum." She shuddered. "Mrs. Sutton needed a girl t' lend a hand with her babes, an' came an' looked us all over. She picked me 'cause I look strong, an' I picked her 'cause she said I could go to school. And 'cause she di'n't look like she'd take a stick t' me very oft'n," she added matter-of-factly. "I don't mind hard work, but I despise bein' thrashed."

Caroline shivered, not liking to think of the contrast between her own private luxuries—books and pets and presents and pretty clothes—and Deirdre's work-a-day world, filled with too many tasks and the threat of thrashings.

"I shouldn't think Mrs. Sutton would thrash anybody," she ventured. The Sutton boys and girls wore merry faces, and never seemed to care if their clothes weren't clean. Mrs. Sutton was clearly overwhelmed with the task of caring for house, children, and the business end of her husband's veterinary practice. "Do you like living at Courier Cottage?"

Deirdre chuckled grimly. "Livin' is fine, it's the workin' that's hard. There's always heaps of laundry an' piles of washin' up after meals. Might've stayed at the asylum if I'd known there was six babes already, soon to be seven, an' Lizzy—she's the oldest—not yet nine." She shrugged. "But I've me own pallet in the attic an' a candle t' read by and me own scrap o' mirror, which is more'n I had at the asylum. An' tatie pot for supper is more'n the bread and treacle I had at home with me mum."

Laundry and dirty dishes and a pallet in the attic, Caroline thought guiltily, remembering the servants at Tidmarsh Manor, and the quantity of food on her grandmama's table, and her own spacious bedroom, with a bed that was wide enough for two, and a paraffin lamp, and a mirror with two wings on her dressing table.

"Now, don't ye be feelin' sorry for me," Deirdre warned, with a quick glance, as if she had read Caroline's mind. "I'm stronger 'n I look, and I'm glad t' have a place. I don't need nobody t' pity me." She turned quite remarkable blue-green eyes on Caroline and added fiercely, "Or call me a witch, neither."

"They don't mean it," Caroline said uneasily. "They're just teasing because you're new." She had experienced her own share of teasing, especially because she spoke with a New Zealand accent. And because she never quite came up with the right answer when she was called on—most of the time because she wasn't listening. But even when she listened, she didn't seem to get it right, and so the others teased her constantly.

"O' course they mean it," Deirdre retorted. She pulled her strong, thick brows together and stuck her balled fists into the pockets of her gray pinafore. "It's 'cause I have red hair an' my eyes're green an' I'm as freckled as a red pig. It's also 'cause I have an Irish name they can't get their fat tongues around. And," she added astutely, "it's 'cause everybody's talkin' about that red-headed witch at Raven Hall. Or maybe she's a ghost."

Caroline nodded, having heard about the mysterious Mrs. Kittredge.

Deirdre tossed her head. "But they're all a lot of ign'rant heathens. They c'n eat worms, 'spesh'ly Harold Beechman. I'm even with him, though." She grinned slyly. "Told him I'd spell him into a frog if he di'n't leave off."

"So that's what you said to him," Caroline exclaimed, with a horrified delight. Harold Beechman was a notorious bully who loved to pull hair and tweak noses. Everyone longed to see him get his comeuppance.

Deirdre's mischievous grin widened. "An' then I yelled out some gibberish an' waved my arms an' the cowardy custard ran away, he did." The grin again. "He di'n't look where he was runnin' an' stumbled over the water bucket an' whacked his nose proper an' smeared blood all over his shirt." The grin became a chuckle, and then a hearty laugh. "Which pleased me ever' bit as much as if he'd turned into a frog, it did. If he likes t' think I'm a witch, that's just jolly good."

Deirdre's Irish laughter was infectious, and Caroline found herself joining in without reservation. "Maybe," she said, when she could get her breath, "you could catch a frog and bring it to school and—"

"—An' tell everybody he used t' be a lad that called me a witch an' I turned him into a frog!" Deirdre finished, with a giggle. "Aye, that's grand, that is. Do y'know whereabouts I c'n find one?"

"Ask Jeremy Crosfield," Caroline replied. "He'll show you lots of frogs, down at Cunsey Beck."

"Jeremy's nice," Deirdre replied thoughtfully. "He doesn't tease."

"No, he doesn't," Caroline said. Jeremy and his aunt had moved into the cottage at Holly How farm, one of the Tidmarsh Manor farms, and they often walked to school together. He always surprised her with what he knew, for he seemed to have a personal acquaintance with almost every animal in the Land between the Lakes, and he was an accomplished artist. But for all that, Jeremy never made a show of what he'd learnt, or made her feel that he was smarter than she, the way the others did.

"He's clever, Jeremy is," Deirdre added in a respectful tone. "I'll wager he's the clev'rest lad in the village."

"Oh, yes," Caroline said, and sighed. "This is his last year at Sawrey School, you know. He passed the exams for the grammar school in Ambleside with high marks. But he can't go."

Deirdre turned a surprised glance on her. "He can't? Whyever not?"

"It costs too much. His aunt can't afford it."

"Well, I call that a shame, I do," Deirdre said definitively. "Them that wants t' go t' school should have their chance. If I could really do spells, I'd spell it so Jeremy could go." Leaning over the nettles at the foot of the stone wall, she broke off a twig of delicate white hawthorn blossoms and tucked it over her ear. "I ain't a real witch," she added over her shoulder, picking another sprig. "But I c'n see fairies. I don't tell that t' just anybody, an' it's not for spreadin' around. But it's true. Or it used to be, anyway."

Caroline eyed her. "See fairies?" She herself had never seen one, although she had read enough stories about them to know that quite a few people thought they were real. For Christmas, Miss Potter had sent her a book called *Peter Pan in Kensington Gardens,* by Mr. J. M. Barrie, who had also written a play about Peter Pan. Mr. Barrie (who obviously believed in fairies, which was unusual for a grownup) said that children sometimes declared that they had never once seen a fairy when they were looking right at one, who was at that moment pretending to be a flower, or a tree, or something else. So Caroline wasn't quite ready to state categorically that Deirdre could never have seen one.

"Stand still," Deirdre commanded, and stuck the hawthorn over Caroline's ear. "Me mum gave me the gift, she did. She was Irish from the top o' her red hair down t' the tips o' her toes, an' y' know how the Irish are about fairies an' elves an' leprechauns an' the like. She got the gift from her mum, who got it from hers, so I got a good strong dose—although, sad t'say, I ain't seen a fairy since me mum died. I'd like t' see one, just to know I've still got it." With light fingers and a half-sad smile, she rearranged Caroline's hair. "There. Hawthorn keeps away evil, it does. Ye c'n walk through storms an' the lightnin' won't strike ye. Me mum told me so."

Caroline regarded her new friend, thinking how sad it would be if Deirdre had lost not only her mother, but some special gift her mother had passed along to her. She herself hadn't got a special gift from her mother, just a pair of eyes and a nose. When she looked into the mirror and saw those familiar features, she sometimes pretended she was looking into a magic window, and what she saw wasn't her reflection, but her mother looking out at her, and smiling, and sending love and kisses.

And then it occurred to her that perhaps Deirdre was pretending, too—or both pretending and believing, at the same time. Perhaps her gift was like the mirror, a way of holding on to her mother, who was gone.

Well, if that's what it was, Caroline thought with compassion, she could help Deirdre pretend. "Your mother knew that hawthorn was magic?" she said tentatively.

Deirdre laughed with delight. "Why, o' course, silly. Ye've never heard the old saying? 'Beware the oak, it draws the stroke. Avoid the ash, it courts the flash. Creep under the thorn, it'll save ye from harm.' Hawthorn's magic, for sure. In Ireland, the fairies use the wood t' build cradles for their fairy babies, an' wear the blossoms for hats, an' sew them into skirts."

"And you've seen the fairies." Caroline tried to sound convinced, for she truly wanted to help Deirdre pretend.

Deirdre slanted her a reproachful look. "Ye're doubtin', aren't ye?" And then she suddenly straightened and said, with intensity, "Well, then, Caroline Longford, ye're in for a surprise. May Eve is comin' up next week, an' that's the very best time t' see fairies. So we'll just go out on May Eve, and we'll find us some fairies."

Deirdre's seriousness—her eyes were narrowed and her mouth was screwed up tight—was almost comic, but Caroline knew that if she laughed, she'd lose a friend forever. And there were all those books about fairies, and the authors behaving as if every single word they wrote was true. If she couldn't actually believe in them, she would pretend she did, which as far as Deirdre was concerned, was as good as believing.

"Where shall we go?" she said.

Deirdre pushed out her lips. "You know the land hereabouts better 'n me, I reckon. Fairies like oak trees an' beech trees 'cause they're ancient an' magical. Mossy hummocks, too, an' ferns an' clear running water. An' hawthorn, o' course."

"Well, there are lots of oaks and beeches in Cuckoo Brow Wood," Caroline replied, trying to sound encouraging, yet feeling cautious and unsure. Cuckoo Brow Wood was not a very comfortable place. In fact, she was forbidden to go there—although that shouldn't matter very much, since she was forbidden to go anywhere with Deirdre.

She took a deep breath. "And there's moss, big cushiony pillows of it, and quite a few clear springs, and everything looks very green and dim and magical, as if you'd stepped back in time. It's wild, though." And scary, she added to herself, as they reached the stile that climbed over the stone fence, where the path to Tidmarsh Manor began.

"The wilder the better," Deirdre said definitively. "Fairies don't like t' be around Big Folk. We'll go t' Cuckoo Brow Wood. It's best t' go at twilight, o' course."

"At twilight?" Caroline didn't like the idea of wandering through Cuckoo Brow Wood after dark, although she didn't want Deirdre to think she was a coward, like Harold. She tried to think of something. "But . . . but won't you have work to do?" was the best she could manage.

"Don't worry, I'll find a way," Deirdre said with a careless shrug. "We'll need some wild thyme an' rue an' hawthorn—thyme an' rue t' help us see fairies an' hawthorn t' keep us safe. An' I'll hunt up some yarrow. Rosemary would be good, too."

Caroline nodded. "We have rosemary in our garden. I'll bring some." She hesitated, trying to sound casual. "It might be better to find the right place beforehand, so we don't waste time on May Eve. We could go scouting first." Deirdre might decide that a twilight expedition wasn't necessary, depending on what they found. Of course, it wasn't that she was afraid of going out at night, Caroline told herself. But her grandmother would never allow it. She would have to sneak out of the house, and then sneak back in, which wasn't as easy in real life as it was in books, where children were always climbing out windows and going off at night and getting back in again without anybody knowing.

"Jolly good," Deirdre said approvingly. "Saturd'y afternoon? Mrs. Sutton lets me off from two to seven."

"Saturday afternoon, then," Caroline agreed. "If you'll come to the garden gate behind the Manor, we can start from there." She thought of something else. "Would it be all right if I asked Jeremy to go with us? He's been much deeper into Cuckoo Brow Wood than I have. He might not believe in fairies," she added, "but he believes in a great many things nobody can see. Germs and bacteria and microbes and wireless telegraphing. And the North Pole, which somebody has gone looking for but hasn't found yet."

"He don't have t' believe," Deirdre asserted. "He just has t' keep an open mind." She frowned at Caroline. "The same with you, Caroline. You're only pretending to believe, too, but there's no harm in that. Just keep your mind open, and your eyes. That's the only way you'll ever find anything in this world, anyway."

"Of course," Caroline replied, feeling cross that Deirdre had seen through her, and thinking that the girl didn't need to be so preachy, when she was only trying to help.

"Good." Deirdre sighed heavily. "Well, then, I s'pose I'd better get on. Mrs. Sutton is sure t' have a long list of chores for me, an' there's the children's tea, and baths, and bed-times." She pulled a face. "Sometimes I think the asylum would've been an easier place."

But as Caroline climbed over the stile and looked back, she saw that Deirdre was skipping as she went up the lane. And if the anticipation of Saturday's fairy hunt lightened her step, Caroline was glad.

6

The Mystery Deepens

The mystery of Mrs. Kittredge was under discussion again on Thursday afternoon, this time by Captain Miles Woodcock and Mr. Will Heelis, in the law offices of Heelis and Heelis in the market town of Hawkshead, some three miles west and north of Sawrey.

Captain Woodcock was clearly irritated.

"It's nothing but scurrilous gossip," he said. "One doesn't know whether to laugh or cry at the thought that these ignorant village people actually believe in witches and ghosts. But it's bound to cause Major Kittredge some worry." He stopped pacing and sat down in the wooden chair across from Will Heelis. "I don't know the fellow well, but he's had a bad time of it since the war. It's a pity the poor chap can't be let alone."

"I certainly agree with that," Will Heelis replied. He opened the drawer of the table that served as his desk and took out his tobacco pouch. "One would think the villagers would have better sense. But this other business—well, that's more troubling, wouldn't you say?"

Outside in Red Lion Square, a group of schoolchildren on their way home were singing lustily, a cart's wheels rattled on the cobbles, and the clanging of the blacksmith's hammer could be heard in the busy yard behind the Heelis office. Will had been admitted a solicitor in 1899, and since then had practiced law in his cousin's firm in Hawkshead. It was a busy practice, for Heelis and Heelis handled most of the property transfers in the District, as well as wills, trusts, and estates. The map table that stood along one wall was stacked with detailed surveys of the area; the shelves in the adjacent file room contained deed boxes full of conveyances, titles, and deeds; and the safe in the corner held a great many confidential documents. Will Heelis was likely to have an advance knowledge of any owner's plans for his property.

"By 'this other business,'" Miles said, crossing his legs, "I suppose you mean Mrs. Kittredge's stage career."

Will stared at him. "Stage career?"

"News to you, is it?" Miles raised his eyebrows. "I learnt of it from Henry Stubbs, the ferry man. The lady was an actress. Kittredge is said to have married her on a fortnight's acquaintance."

Will digested this with some surprise. Understandably, Christopher hadn't mentioned his wife's profession during their conversation, or said how long he had known her before they wed. Of course, the stage was quite respectable these days. People thought nothing at all of going to Kendal to see *Romeo and Juliet*, or a play by George Bernard Shaw. But going to the theatre was not at all the same thing as marrying an actress. Lakelanders were conservative folk, and old-fashioned. There was bound to be talk.

"Yes," Miles went on dryly. "An actress. It simply deepens Mrs. Kittredge's mystery, of course. The gossip mill will be kept grinding on this tasty bit for weeks."

"But that wasn't what I meant by the 'other business,' " Will said. "Whatever the lady was before Kittredge married her, she's Mrs. Kittredge now, and I wish them every happiness. It's the property matter that's worrying me." He tamped tobacco into his pipe and paused, seeing his friend's raised eyebrow. "You haven't heard, then?"

"No, I'm completely in the dark. Are you talking about the Raven Hall estate?"

Will hesitated. Discussing a client's affairs was unethical and revealing a friend's business plans amounted to disloyalty. And Christopher was both a client (he had just rewritten his will, leaving his entire estate to the new Mrs. Kittredge), and a long-time friend, he and Will having played together in the Hawkshead Bowling Club before the major went off to South Africa. Will hadn't seen Kittredge since the war, and friendships do not always survive as people and circumstances change, but he had been glad at the easy way they had bridged the gap. He admired the man's courage and his stoic acceptance of his painful and disfiguring war wounds. A tragic thing, for a fellow once considered handsome, to have half his face burned away.

But friend or no friend, the building scheme the major was considering would affect the whole area. It was very serious matter—extraordinary, really—and Will thought he ought to mention it to Miles, who had a good head on his shoulders and a deep commitment to protecting the Lake District from the threat of commercial land development. Miles served as Justice of the Peace for Claife Parish and had been a member of the Lake District Defense Society ever since he had moved here, so he had a special interest.

"Perhaps I had better tell you," Will said reluctantly, "but only on your promise of complete confidentiality. I shall tell Kittredge I've brought you into the matter, but I should like him to hear it from me first."

"He won't get a word from me," the captain said.

Will put a match to his pipe and drew. "Well, then. You know, I suppose, that the Kittredge property extends from the site of Raven Hall at the top of Claife Heights right down to the shore of Lake Windermere."

Miles nodded. "There must be . . . oh, a half-mile or so of frontage along the lake, isn't there? Very pretty land, especially in autumn when the trees are in color. In the Kittredge family since the 1840s or thereabouts. It must have been Christopher's great-grandfather who built that gloomy old Gothic mansion. Rather ruins the view, I must say, although according to some it's a good example of the style."

"His great-great-grandfather built it, according to David Bryce's design." There had been Kittredges at Raven Hall until the major's mother and father and elder brother had been killed when their carriage went over a cliff. The major had inherited the estate, but he had been in South Africa when the tragedy occurred and after that in hospital. He had come home—with his new wife—just the fortnight before.

Will blew a puff of fragrant smoke toward the low ceiling and spoke in a carefully neutral tone. "It seems that the Kittredge property may be developed."

"Developed?" Miles asked, frowning. "How would he develop it?"

"Not Major Kittredge himself," Will said cautiously. Christopher hadn't the capital for such a large project. "He is considering turning it over for development to a fellow named Augustus Richardson. Richardson, I understand, proposes to build holiday villas along the shore. Nothing definite," he added, "but there it is."

"Villas!" Miles leapt angrily to his feet. "Those appalling bungalows that are springing up all over? Entirely out of the question, Will! It can't be allowed to happen!"

"I don't see how you intend to stop it," Will said. It was one thing to organize against the railway from Windermere to Ambleside, and another to oppose improvements to the road through Sty Head Pass—all of which had been managed successfully, thwarting the commercial development of the remoter parts of the Lake District. But preserving desirable land against residential speculation was a much more difficult thing. And the Kittredge land, with its scenic location on the lakeshore and its proximity to the ferry and railway, was the most significant property on the western side of Lake Windermere.

"But the major's grandfather was one of the founding members of the Lake District Defense Society!" Miles cried distractedly. "Old James Kittredge would turn over in his grave if he heard—" He put both hands on Will's table and leaned forward, his expression accusing. "It's the money, isn't it? And that new wife of Kittredge's, I'll wager. From what I know of the major, he isn't likely to have come up with a thing like this on his own."

Will was beginning to regret that he had brought up the matter. "I can't speak to that, I'm afraid," he replied. "I've probably said more than I should already."

"It's that new wife, I'm sure of it," Miles muttered grimly. He clenched a fist. "Major Kittredge's family has always stood behind the need to preserve the landscape, rather than build more houses and roads and the like. He can't be meaning to—" He broke off. "This man Richardson. Augustus Richardson. What do you know of him, Will?"

"Nothing, other than his name."

"Another mystery," Miles said dismally. "By Jove, I—"

"But perhaps not a mystery for long," Will went on. "The major said that Richardson will attend the reception at Raven Hall on Saturday. I suppose we will all have the pleasure of being introduced to the fellow. We can form an opinion then."

"We'll have the pleasure of meeting the major's new wife, too," Miles said darkly. "But I'm already beginning to form an opinion about her."

"You and the entire village," Will said, and took another pull on his pipe.

7

Miss Potter Has an Encounter

As it happened, Miss Potter would be the first person in the village to encounter (if not to actually meet) the mysterious Mrs. Kittredge *and* the mysterious Mr. Richardson, together. This interesting event happened on Thursday afternoon, at approximately the same time that Captain Woodcock and Mr. Heelis were discussing these very persons in the Heelis office in Hawkshead.

Early that morning, Beatrix had driven the Hill Top pony cart down the hill to the ferry, for a trip across the lake. She drove to the nursery at Windermere to buy laurels, forsythia, and lilacs for her new garden, then went to the High Street to do a bit of shopping for Dimity Woodcock, who needed colored crepe paper to make streamers for the May Pole. On the way back to the ferry, she stopped for a cup of tea and a bite of lunch with Dimity's childhood nurse, Mrs. Corry, a comfortable old soul with a face as wrinkled and brown as an old oak leaf, now retired and living in a small cottage near the ferry landing. Dimity had introduced the two of them several months before, and the old lady had promised Beatrix some plants from her own garden. When it was time to take the ferry back across the lake, the pony cart was heavily loaded with pots and bags and cardboard boxes, and Mrs. Corry had entrusted Beatrix with a scarf knitted of the brightest shade of emerald green, to take to Captain Woodcock, her "dear little boy."

When Beatrix arrived at the landing for the trip back across the lake, several people were already waiting for the ferry, some having come on the coach from the railway station. Since her girlhood, Beatrix had cultivated the habit of noticing and recalling interesting or amusing things—things she saw or heard that were out of the ordinary. This was a surreptitious habit, and one to which she did not like to call attention. It had served her well as an artist, for many of the things she saw found their way into her drawings. But it also served her well as a student of human nature, for people often did and said very revealing things when they did not think they were being observed.

Beatrix noticed the woman at once. She was so extraordinarily vivid as to be almost beautiful, with an uncontained wealth of very red hair—too red, Beatrix thought, to be entirely natural—that escaped in unruly tendrils from under a wide-brimmed black hat trimmed with sweeping red feathers. Her cheeks and lips were too red to be natural as well, and she was wrapped in a black velvet fur-trimmed cape, which she flung about with a great flair. Her elbow-length gloves were black, her boots red, and she wore an astonishing quantity of exotic jewelry. The mysterious Mrs. Kittredge, Beatrix felt sure.

The man who accompanied this wondrous creature was shorter than she, barely reaching her shoulder. He was quite rotund, with a round head and large, popping eyes, rather like a toad, Beatrix thought with amusement. He wore a pale green coat and silvery straw hat with a green ribbon the same shade as his coat, and carried a walking stick with a gold top. His name, it seemed, was Augustus. The lady's name (or so he called her) was Diana. The two of them appeared to be quite intimate.

At first, Beatrix wondered if Augustus might be Major Kittredge, but then remembered that Dimity had said that the major's given name was Christopher, that until losing an arm and an eye in the Boer War, he had been very handsome. Since this toadlike gentleman possessed the requisite arms and eyes and could by no stretch be called handsome, he was obviously not the lady's husband. They were standing close together, away from the rest of the waiting ferry passengers, and were looking across the water as they carried on an animated discussion. They were deeply engrossed with the view and each other. Although they spoke in lowered voices, Beatrix, who was standing nearby, could hear them clearly.

The man had just arrived on the railway train from London, it emerged, and this was obviously his first visit to the area. Mrs. Kittredge was pointing to the place where the outline of a large stone house—Raven Hall, as Beatrix knew—could be seen behind the oaks and beech trees at the top of Claife Heights.

"And there it is, the Kittredge baronial mansion, in all its grotesque Gothic grandeur." Her throaty laugh was richly sarcastic. "From this distance, you can't quite see how appalling it is. Truly a torture chamber to live in, but as I told you earlier, it would make a splendid hotel. It commands an unrivaled view up and down the lake. The view will be even better, of course, when some of those trees are taken out."

The man, who seemed to want a better look, whipped a collapsible spy glass out of his coat pocket, extended it to full length, and examined the hillside.

"I see," he murmured appreciatively, and swung the glass along the shore for a wider view. "Indeed. Yes, indeed, this is really quite splendid, my dear Diana. Marvelously picturesque and scenic."

"I thought you would like it," Mrs. Kittredge said with satisfaction. She put her hand on his arm. "Is it not all that I described to you, and more, Augustus? Is it not worth all the trouble you have been put to, all the discomfort of your railway journey?"

"Indeed, indeed," replied the man. "An extraordinarily desirable location, Diana. I can see them now—a dozen holiday villas, each of the most modern architecture and construction, arranged above the shoreline, just there." He made an expansive gesture. "And each villa shall have its own boat dock, so that the residents can keep their own yachts. And a garage for their motor cars, of course." He pressed his lips together. "I foresee the need for a new road along the shore, so that the villas can be easily reached from the ferry landing."

"The hotel, Augustus," Mrs. Kittredge put in eagerly. "Don't forget the hotel. Tourists will simply flock to it. Why, there's even a resident ghost!"

Beatrix pulled in a startled breath. A dozen holiday villas strewn along the unspoilt Windermere shoreline? Raven Hall made into an hotel? The thought was unthinkable.

But not, it seemed, for Mr. Augustus Richardson. He smiled up at Mrs. Kittredge, a smile that seemed to have a certain edge to it. "And Major Kittredge—he has agreed to the syndicate's proposal? The investors want assurance that their project is going forward. The drawings are even now being prepared. Timing is everything in matters of this sort, you know, and every moment Major Kittredge delays is costing money. Villas do not sprout up overnight."

Don't they? Beatrix thought darkly. They seemed to her to pop out of the ground like toadstools. Why, just the previous year, an entire row of modern houses—little more than bungalows, really—had erupted along the road to St. Peter's, in Far Sawrey. Their gardens were still raw and muddy, but they were fully occupied, and there was a rumor that even more were to be built.

The lady heaved a dramatic sigh. "I cannot tell you that Major Kittredge is in total agreement. Not yet. After all, the family has owned the land for a very long time, and he has the idea that there will be Kittredges here forever. I suppose it would be better if you did not mention the hotel. The villas are enough for him to swallow just now."

Mr. Richardson frowned and tapped his walking stick on the ground. "I didn't realize that the Kittredge line was to be extended. An heir is expected, then?"

"Oh, good heavens, no!" said Mrs. Kittredge, with a flutter of eyelash and a gay little laugh. "It's just that . . ." She gave him a sideways glance. "He hopes, you see."

"And I hope," Mr. Richardson said significantly, "that you will be able to persuade him to agree to the villas. Soon, Diana. Very soon."

Mrs. Kittredge tossed her head in a careless way. "Oh, I shall, Augustus, never fear. I have a way, you know, of working on him. And now that you are here to explain the whole business to him—especially the part about how much money the Sandiford Syndicate will pour into the Kittredge purse— I am sure that the affair will move more smoothly."

"I daresay, Diana. I have every confidence in your skills of persuasion." He chuckled. "I've often said that you are a witch, you know. An enchantress."

Whatever Mrs. Kittredge might have said to this remark was unfortunately lost in the shrill whistle of the approaching steam ferry, and the two prepared to board.

As they left the spot where they had been standing, however, Beatrix noticed that something had been left behind: a white calling card, dropped, perhaps, when Mr. Richardson pulled the spyglass out of his pocket. She stooped, picked it up, and then, without the slightest twinge of guilt, tucked it into the pocket of her gray woolen skirt and went to lead her pony onto the ferry.

8

The Vicar Tells a Lie

At the same moment that Miss Potter was boarding the ferry, Vicar Samuel Sackett sat down at his desk in the vicarage at Far Sawrey, took up his pen, and returned to the essay he was writing: a scholarly work on the sufferings of Job. The piece was nearly finished. Only the conclusion remained, in which he would argue that life constantly presents us with unexpected and unwelcome challenges, and that while we may never understand the purpose of suffering, we can only do our best. It was an argument that the poor vicar was taking to heart, for he himself had been suffering greatly for the past several months.

The week before Christmas, Vicar Sackett had received a letter from a distant cousin, Harold Thexton, saying that he and his wife Gloria were traveling through the Lake District and would be delighted to drop in for a brief visit at any time that was convenient to the vicar. However, since they

planned to be in the area on the following Tuesday, it seemed
that time would be the most convenient for themselves, if it
would not too terribly inconvenience the vicar.

Now, it happened that the following Tuesday was Christmas Eve, a dreadfully inconvenient time to entertain guests
at the vicarage, what with the carol singing and the festive
decorations and the choir party and the gifts to be collected
and distributed to the village poor. Since there was no Mrs.
Sackett—the vicar had lost his dear wife to scarlet fever
shortly after their marriage—all these duties fell upon him,
in addition to the burden of several additional holiday worship services. If the vicar were honest, it was most definitely
not the best time of the year to receive guests. Nor could he
recall a branch of the family that went by the name of Thexton, although it was to be admitted that the Sackett family
tree had a great many odd branches and there might have
been a Thexton offshoot or two among the distant twigs on
his father's mother's side.

However, the vicarage had several guest rooms and the
vicar's housekeeper and cook, Mrs. Thompson, could just as
easily turn out dinner for three as for one. So Vicar Sackett
swallowed his reluctance and extended a cordial invitation
to Mr. and Mrs. Thexton to join him for a few days over the
holidays. When they arrived, he learnt that Mr. Thexton, a
burly gentleman of middle age with a drooping mustache
and an affected manner, was a great-great-nephew of the
vicar's grandmother's sister, that is, on the Lessiter side of
that family. In the course of their conversation, it emerged
that he was engaged in writing a book about the folklore of
Cumbria, and that he and Mrs. Thexton were traveling
about the area so that he might collect local folktales.

The Thextons had planned to leave shortly after Christmas,
but were prevented by a snowfall. (Mrs. Thexton was fearful

of traveling when the roads were covered with ice and snow.) By the time the snow had melted, however, the lady had contracted a nasty cold, and their departure was delayed once again. Her recuperation took rather longer than expected (she had a delicate constitution and was unfortunately susceptible to bronchial ailments), so that the vicar felt obliged to extend his hospitality until the beginning of March, at which time it emerged that Mr. Thexton had uncovered a promising vein of local folklore and thought he should like to stay and mine it—that is, if dear Cousin Samuel would not object to their company for just a little while longer. They would be very good and as quiet as a pair of little mice, promised Mr. Thexton, and would not impose upon the vicar in any way.

Vicar Sackett was by nature a mild-mannered man much preoccupied with reading, writing, and the cares of his little flock, and as a rule did not take much notice of what was going on immediately around him. However, even the vicar could not fail to notice, at the beginning of April, that the Thextons were still in residence at the vicarage, and that he was beginning to feel . . . well, just a little weary of their company. It wasn't that he didn't like them—the pair did possess a certain charming and ingratiating amiability—and he was, after all, a man of the cloth whose Christian duty it was to be tolerant of all sorts of people.

But the vicar's tolerance was severely tested. Mrs. Thexton's sensibilities being most delicate, pipe smoke made her violently ill. The vicar had to go out into the garden to smoke his pipe, or on days when the weather forbade, into the unheated porch. Mr. Thexton, however, might comfortably smoke his cigar in the parlor, for Mrs. Thexton quite enjoyed cigar smoke, which the vicar detested.

And although she was an attractive woman, Mrs. Thexton could in no sense be likened to a quiet little mouse. In fact, she talked so continually and so volubly about such a variety of inconsequential subjects that she put the vicar in mind of Alfred Lord Tennyson's famous babbling brook: "Men may come and men may go, but I go on forever." The vicar began to fear that Mrs. Thexton would indeed go on forever, and that as long as she was a resident in the vicarage, he should have to hear about the lamentable felt hat that Miss Woodcock had worn at Sunday service; the difficulty of finding cerise velvet ribbons in Hawkshead or Alceon lace in Kendal; and the relative inferiority of cod as an entrée, as compared to pheasant or sirloin of beef.

Mr. Thexton, on the other hand, had only one subject of conversation—his researches—and the disagreeable habit of reviewing his most recent findings at breakfast, whilst the vicar was reading his newspaper, or of popping into the study with them, just at the moment the vicar was about to wrestle into submission the most unyielding paragraph of his Sunday sermon. Mr. Thexton, as it turned out, had a profound interest in the supernatural, a passion which the vicar, a man of God, might under other circumstances have shared. But Mr. Thexton's fascination with the supernatural seemed to be directed toward—of all things—fairies, elves, and other such creatures, and on that score, the vicar was forced to confess ignorance. This did not, unfortunately, discourage Mr. Thexton, who seemed determined to bring to light all evidences of the past or present existence of fairies in the Lake District, so that he could put them into his book.

Other things vexed the vicar. Mrs. Thompson, who kept a careful eye on the accounts, reported that the cost of the vicarage's table had risen sharply, in inverse proportion (as the vicar himself had noticed) to the alarming decline in the stock of port in the vicarage's cellar. Worse, certain unfamiliar charges—cigars and an ebony walking stick, a cashmere shawl and pair of lady's boots—appeared on the vicarage accounts in several shops in Hawkshead. Pressed by the vicar, Mr. Thexton assured him that repayment would be made as soon as expected funds arrived. And it was, although not promptly, and several new charges brought the total to an even higher amount.

Faced with this evidence, the vicar began to suspect, with a growing horror, that the Thextons belonged to that dreaded race of *spongers*: free-loading parasites who lived at the expense of others and who, once comfortably established, could not be got rid of.

Altogether, it was enough to try the patience of Job. And while Samuel Sackett did not pretend to saintliness, he knew himself to be a man of peace—not a coward, exactly, but . . . well, a man with something of a timid nature, who deeply disliked confrontation. But clearly, it was time that something—several somethings, actually—were done.

So he closed all of the vicarage accounts in Hawkshead, with instructions that they were not to be reopened until personally authorized by himself. He locked the wine cellar and directed Mrs. Thompson to serve cod three times a week. And finally, he suggested that the Thextons might move down to the Sawrey Hotel, where there was rather more interesting society, or to the Tower Bank Arms, which carved a fine joint of roast beef every night. But Mrs. Thexton sighed and said that she found country hotels most shockingly boring, so he did not pursue the subject. He did, however, take to spending longer and longer hours in his study, where he was writing—as if from his personal experience—a scholarly article on the sufferings of Job.

And it was there, on the same bright April afternoon that Miss Potter had overheard Mrs. Kittredge and Mr. Richardson discussing the construction of holiday villas, that Mr. Thexton found him.

"I have just learnt," Mr. Thexton said with an air of suppressed glee, "that a nearby estate is one of a very few ancient houses of Cumberland which possess a relic granted to it by fairies." His thick walrus mustache bristled with excitement. "A goblet, I understand."

The vicar put down his pen. "You are speaking of the Luck of Raven Hall, I believe."

"I am indeed!" Mr. Thexton exclaimed. "And I must say, Cousin Samuel, I take it rather hard that you did not tell me about this yourself. It would have advanced my researches substantially."

"I didn't think of it," the vicar confessed. "I haven't thought of it in years, as a matter of fact—perhaps because there has been so much very bad luck there."

The story of the Luck of Raven Hall was known throughout the Land between the Lakes, and the vicar reported it as he had often heard it. The Luck was a large glass goblet enameled in gilt, red, blue, and green. It was said to have belonged to the fairies—the Oak Folk, Lakelanders called them—who lived among the ancient trees of Cuckoo Brow Wood, where the Kittredge family estate was located. Soon after Raven Hall was built, on the eve of the wedding of the eldest Kittredge son, a dairymaid went out to milk a cow. When she sat down to milk, however, she discovered to her consternation that her bucket had a hole in it.

At that moment, a trio of Oak Folk approached, dressed in oak leaves, wearing acorn caps, and carrying a beautiful goblet. They promised that if the maid should milk the cow into the goblet and give the milk to the bride to drink, they would bless the marriage, and the Kittredges' descendants for all time. But if the goblet were broken, the marriage would be doomed, and with it, the luck of Raven Hall.

Having given this warning, the Oak Folk danced off into Cuckoo Brow Wood, leaving a last fairy caution ringing in the air:

> *If that glass should break or fall*
> *Farewell the luck of Raven Hall.*

"And the goblet has been preserved intact?" Mr. Thexton asked eagerly.

"Yes, although one can't say the same thing for the Kittredge family fortunes. What with one thing and another, it's been a very rough go. The son whose marriage was blessed fell off his horse and died, and his son was struck by lightning. A few years ago, three members of the family died in an accident, and more recently, a servant girl drowned in the nearby tarn, the housekeeper went mad, and the steward made off with some of the valuables. And the major himself was horribly wounded in the war." He might have gone on to relate the details, but Mr. Thexton wasn't listening.

"What an extraordinary opportunity!" he trumpeted. "How wonderfully providential! Fairies, fairies all around us! I tell you, Cousin Samuel, if it's the very last thing I do before I leave the Lake District, I must lay my eyes upon the Luck of Raven Hall."

The vicar knew a golden opportunity when he saw one. "The last thing?" he asked hopefully. "I shall do my utmost, then, to enable you to see the Luck before you leave."

Mr. Thexton leaned forward, his eyes gleaming. "You can make that possible? When?"

"When were you thinking of leaving?" the vicar inquired.

"How soon can I see the Luck?" countered Mr. Thexton.

Now, the vicar was happily aware that an invitation to tea at Raven Hall—to celebrate the return of Christopher Kittredge and introduce his new wife to the villagers—lay in the top drawer of his desk, unanswered. He had not replied to it because it would have been rude to go without the Thextons and he found it most unpleasant to think of going with them.

But the case had altered. He was now eager to introduce Mr. Thexton to the mystery of the Raven Hall Luck and see the back of his cousin and his cousin's wife. He said: "Well, then, if you are intending to go so soon as Monday, I believe it might be possible to arrange it for this weekend. If, however, you should wish to delay—"

"This weekend!" chortled Mr. Thexton, rubbing his hands. "This very weekend! Oh, my, yes! Yes, indeed, Cousin Samuel. Yes!"

And then the vicar did something he had not done since he was a small boy, and something he hoped he would not live to regret. He lied.

"I should not like to hasten your departure," he said, childishly crossing his fingers behind his back. "Monday, is it, then?"

Mr. Thexton sighed. "Yes, Monday," he said, with the air of a man who knows he has made a hard decision but intends to stand by it.

The vicar rose with alacrity. "I will inform Mrs. Thompson that you and Mrs. Thexton will be leaving on Monday morning, and ask Mr. Cantrell to be here by nine to drive you to the ferry. And I will immediately send up to Mrs. Kittredge at Raven Hall to see if it is convenient for us to call on Saturday. She and Major Kittredge were recently married, you know. I believe they are receiving guests."

Seeming not to hear, Mr. Thexton closed his eyes. "The Luck of Raven Hall," he murmured blissfully, savoring the words as though they were sweet to the taste. "I shall see it on Saturday! And perhaps I shall even hold it in my hands!"

"Yes," said the vicar in a prayerful tone, as he went out and shut the door. "You shall see it on Saturday. And on Monday, please God, you shall be on your way."

9

Caroline and Jeremy Make a Bargain

On Thursday morning, Jeremy went early to school, so Caroline didn't get to talk to him about Saturday's plan or ask him to help Deirdre catch a frog. And when she tried to speak to him at recess and lunchtime, there were always others around. She decided to wait, since she wasn't exactly eager to be overheard discussing a fairy-hunting expedition, or finding a frog to trick Harold Beechman. She and Jeremy both took the same path home. She'd talk to him then.

So when class was dismissed, Caroline walked up the road with Deirdre until they reached the stile over the stone fence. Then she said goodbye, climbed over, and dawdled along the path, which slanted across the meadow to Wilfin Beck and then set off upstream, to Tidmarsh Manor and Holly How Cottage beyond. The stream, in full spring spate, flung itself playfully down the rocky fell, rolling and tumbling and laughing and chuckling as it skirted the shadows of Cuckoo Brow Wood and hurried toward the open meadow.

There it slowed its breakneck pace and for a time became thoughtful and quiet, as if it were pausing to wonder where in this great, wide, wonderful world its journey might be taking it. Caroline loved to walk beside the stream, for it reminded her of New Zealand, which now seemed far away and lost to her forever. The sharp edges of last autumn's homesickness had dulled and the longing was not so bitterly keen, but there was still something in her that wept for home, and the little laughing stream never failed to comfort her.

She hadn't gone very far along the footpath when she heard Jeremy calling her name. She turned and waited for him.

"I saw you walking with the new girl," Jeremy said. "I thought p'rhaps the two of you were having a private talk, so I didn't try to catch you up until she'd gone on."

"It wasn't exactly private," Caroline said, as he fell in step beside her. "We were talking about Harold Beechman. Did you notice that he's been giving her a wide berth all day? He's afraid she's going to turn him into a frog."

Jeremy chuckled. "I s'pose it's that bright red hair and that great lot of freckles. And those green eyes, of course. She does have a witchy way about her, if you'll pardon my saying so."

Caroline did not remind Jeremy that his own hair had a reddish tint, although his eyes were gray, not green, and fearless and direct. "I don't have to pardon you," she replied. "Deirdre's the one to do that. But I don't think she'd mind if she heard—not coming from you. She says you're nice. And clever." The minute she said it, she found herself wishing she hadn't, although she couldn't quite think why.

Jeremy reddened and ducked his head. "The eye of the beholder," he muttered. "How's she getting on with the Suttons?"

"I shouldn't like to have to work the way she does," Caroline said, sticking her hands in her pockets. "Laundry and dishes and babies' baths, and only a pallet in the attic to sleep on."

"You'll never have to work that way," Jeremy replied matter-of-factly. "You'll be a lady when you grow up, and ladies have servants to do all the work."

Caroline colored. She didn't like to think of it in those terms. In New Zealand, people were more alike than they were in England. It was true that her mother had hired people to help with the house and garden, but she had rolled up her sleeves and worked right alongside them, never too proud to do her own part. It was something Grandmama would never dream of doing, not in a million years. Why, she'd be completely helpless if she didn't have Emily and Mr. and Mrs. Beever to do for her.

"What if I don't want to be a lady?" Caroline asked, lifting her chin.

"It's not something you can choose," Jeremy said flatly. "Hasn't your grandmother told you that?" His grin was crooked. "Maybe Deirdre could turn all those little Suttons into frogs. Then she wouldn't have so much washing-up to do."

"Oh, yes, frogs," Caroline said, and told him about finding a frog for Deirdre to show to Harold.

"I can lend her Thucydides," he said, "if she'll promise not to lose him. He's a toad, but Harold won't know the difference."

"Thucydides?" Caroline frowned. She knew she was supposed to know who he was, but she'd forgotten. "Didn't he write something?"

"A history of the Peloponnesian War. He's the first historian who tried to figure out what really happened, rather than just retelling old war stories."

Caroline rolled her eyes, thinking that Jeremy was the only boy she knew who would name a toad for a Greek historian who had been dead for centuries. In fact, Jeremy was the only boy she knew who read the same sorts of books that adults read. Really, it was a great pity about his not being able to go to grammar school.

"Thucydides is all over warts," Jeremy said with a grin, as they reached the beck and went along beside it. "Even for a toad, he's ugly. Ugly enough to scare Harold Beechman out of his wits, if he's convinced himself that Deirdre's a red-headed witch."

"Poor Harold." Caroline ducked under a willow, laughing, then stopped herself. "We're joking about it, but Deirdre doesn't think it's funny. Nor would Mrs. Kittredge, I suppose, if she heard what the villagers are calling her."

Jeremy shrugged. "You're right—but that's not going to stop the Harolds of this world. Anyway, have you seen her? Mrs. Kittredge, I mean. I caught a glimpse of her with the major at the Sawrey Hotel, going in to dinner the other evening. A great lot of flaming red hair, a swirly black cape, and a big black hat with feathers. She must want people to see her as—"

"Unusual," Caroline interrupted firmly, finishing his sentence for him. "Lots of people don't dress the way they're expected to. And anyway, it's nobody's business what she looks like—except Major Kittredge, of course. But he mustn't care, because he married her." She paused, considering. "Speaking of witches, Jeremy, how do you feel about fairies?"

Jeremy raised one eyebrow. "Fairies? Well, there's Puck." When Caroline looked at him blankly, he added, "He's in *Puck of Pook's Hill*, by Rudyard Kipling. I read it just last year. Which of the fairies did you have in mind?" He threw out an arm. "There's quite a lot of them, you know. Giants, trolls, kelpies, brownies, goblins, imps; tree spirits and mound spirits; heath-people and hill-watchers; leprechauns, pixies, nixies, folk, and gnomes—and lots more I can't remember." He took a deep breath. "And then there's *Midsummer Night's Dream,* with Titania and Oberon and the rest. And *Peter Pan,* too, of course, but you must know about him, because didn't Miss Potter give you the book? Why are you asking?"

It was just like Jeremy, Caroline thought, to be able to recite a list of all the sorts of fairies anybody had ever described. "Because Deirdre says she can see fairies, that's why," she replied. "She got the gift from her mother and grandmother, although she says she hasn't seen any fairies since her mother died. She wants to go looking for them. She really believes in fairies," she added, trying to explain. "I thought I would like to . . . well, you know. Help her keep on believing." She glanced at him out of the corner of her eye, to see if he was going to laugh.

He didn't. Instead, he said, with complete seriousness, "Well, the old books say that fairies prefer to live among oak trees. The Druids thought the oak was sacred, and made magic wands from it. So we ought to look for someplace where there are lots of oaks."

"I thought of Cuckoo Brow Wood, of course," Caroline said in a rush. "Deirdre says that May Eve is the very best time to see fairies, but we were wondering whether it might be a good idea to scout out the best places ahead of time. Saturday afternoon, p'rhaps."

"Sounds like a good scheme to me," said Jeremy. He gave her a searching look. "Do you believe?"

"I'm . . . not sure," Caroline said. She paused uncertainly. "Do you?"

"I think it's like Father Christmas. You only really stop believing when you grow up and have to start acting the part yourself." His chuckle was edged with bitterness. "And I don't have to grow up for . . . oh, another few weeks, at least."

Caroline supposed he was talking about having to leave school, but she didn't like to mention it, for fear of making him sad. "Personally, I should like to put off growing up as long as possible," she said. She kicked at a stone. "When you grow up, you have to do what people expect you to do, whether you like it or not."

And if you didn't do what was expected of you, you made other people unhappy, as well as yourself. Her father, for instance, had refused to become an English gentleman and do the things Grandmama wanted him to do, so he had run away to New Zealand to be a sheep farmer, which hadn't made him very happy, either. Caroline had given this a great deal of thought lately, for she was beginning to realize that Grandmama expected certain things of her, as well, all in the name of growing up and becoming a lady. She had the feeling she wasn't going to like doing those things any more than her father had, but she didn't think she'd have the courage to run away, as he did. And where would she go? The sheep station had been sold and there was nobody left in New Zealand.

Jeremy chuckled. "That makes two of us, then," he said, "having to grow up and do things we don't want to do. So we shall just have to put off growing up as long as we can. Maybe we can do that by believing in fairies." Now very serious, he leaned toward her and lowered his voice. "And when we see a fairy, we can make a wish and he's bound to grant it."

"Is he?" Caroline asked dubiously. "I hadn't heard that."

Jeremy straightened and gave her a crooked grin. "That's because I just made it up."

"But it sounds as if it must be true," Caroline said, to comfort him. "I'm sure it's true, Jeremy. I'll think of a wish for me, and you think of a wish for you, and we'll find a fairy to grant both of them." Which was silliness, of course. But she wasn't going to say that out loud and spoil things.

"It's a bargain," Jeremy said. "But I don't have to think very hard."

"Neither do I," said Caroline. She had meant to wish that she would not have to be a lady—at least, not the kind her grandmother intended—but she had changed her mind.

She would wish that Jeremy could have his wish. That Jeremy could go to school.

10

Jeremy Discusses the Situation with Rascal

Jeremy and Caroline came to the place where they always said goodbye, and Jeremy watched as Caroline crossed the beck at the gravel ford and walked up the path to Tidmarsh Manor, which reminded Jeremy of a stone fortress. The sight of it always made him feel sorry for Caroline, for the forbidding old place was built of chilly gray stone, with a gray slate roof and narrow windows—not a bright and happy place for a young girl. And behind the manor, climbing the steep slopes of Claife Heights, rose the mysterious wilderness of Cuckoo Brow Wood.

Jeremy regarded the woods thoughtfully. He'd heard it said that the Fairy Folk had lived there once. They made their homes in Cuckoo Brow Wood, well beyond the open woodlands of larch and ash, up near the top of Claife Heights, hidden in secret places among the ancient oaks, where the dim forest floor was hummocked with mosses, thick and plush as green velvet. There was a path, although he'd never taken it very far. They—he and Caroline and Deirdre—could start at the gate on Saturday afternoon.

"Jeremy, Jeremy!"

A flurry of barks startled Jeremy out of his imaginings, and he turned. "Hullo, Rascal!" he exclaimed, as a small brown dog came hurtling toward him. He knelt down and opened his arms. "What have you been up to this afternoon?"

"I've spent an absolutely ripping day at Oatmeal Crag, digging out rabbits and chasing squirrels!" Rascal enthused, putting his paws on the boy's shoulders and licking him enthusiastically on the chin.

The little Jack Russell terrier, who lived at Belle Green with Mr. and Mrs. Crook, often went along with Jeremy as he tramped through the moors and up the fells, looking for animals to sketch. He had been with the boy as Jeremy drew the old badger who lived at the top of Holly How, the pair of frisky red squirrels who lived in the oak at Wise Een Tarn, and the shy pine marten they had found in Colthouse Wood. Rascal often said that Jeremy was the only boy in the village who'd rather draw and study a fox or a stoat than set traps for them.

Jeremy stroked the little dog's ears. "How would you like to look for fairies with me on Saturday, Rascal? Caroline and Deirdre are going, too. Deirdre says she's able to see them, and it doesn't hurt to pretend."

"Fairies?" Rascal barked excitedly. *"Oh, ra-ther! There once was a fairy village near Fern Vale Tarn, at the top of the woods. Oak Folk, if I remember right. The Professor would know, or Bosworth Badger."* Rascal knew, of course, that the boy—like most humans—didn't understand what he was saying. But that might change, he reasoned. It never hurt to try.

With a gloomy look on his face, Jeremy down sat on a large boulder beside the rippling stream. "I'm afraid we won't have many more tramps together, Rascal. The spring term will be finished in a few weeks, and school will be over." His heavy sigh was resigned. "And everything will change."

Rascal licked the boy's face. *"Change? I don't understand."*

Another sigh. "I'll be grown up, you see. I'll have to go to work."

"Work?" Rascal gave an astonished yip. Dogs, like a great many animals, live in the present moment and do not give much serious thought to what the future might bring. And Rascal, of course, was fully employed. He monitored strangers in the village, mediated disagreements among the other dogs, and slept with one eye open on the porch at Belle Green, keeping watch against possible trespassers. Still, he didn't think of what he did as "work," and he hadn't thought of Jeremy as needing a job, either. The idea that the boy might not be free to wander the woods and fields forever came as a thunderous shock.

Jeremy picked up a stone and tossed it into the beck, watching the ripples widen across the surface. "I'm to be an apprentice, Rascal."

Rascal stared. *"An apprentice?"*

There was an undertone of bitterness in Jeremy's voice. "I'm not a gentleman's son, you know. They go to public school, and when they've finished, they go on to university. After that, they can do anything in the world they like. But boys of my sort go to the village school, and when that's done, they're grown up. No more books or games or tramps through the woods. They go to work."

"Oh," Rascal said. Yes, of course. He knew that the village boys left Sawrey School when they were thirteen—most of them glad to be free of it, too—and went to work, usually doing the same things their fathers did, cutting wood or quarrying slate or burning charcoal or herding sheep. He

just hadn't thought of this happening to Jeremy, who liked books and learning as much as he liked the woods and fells.

A black grouse rattled out of a nearby ash coppice, tempting Rascal to a chase, but the terrier paid no attention. Of course, Jeremy was very clever, and would likely get on well in the world. But Rascal felt that there was an injustice here. He couldn't quite get his mind around it, but if gentlemen's sons were able to continue with their studies, it seemed a bit thick that Jeremy should have to go to work.

"Aunt Jane has found an apprenticeship for me," Jeremy went on in a somber tone. He picked up a stick and used it to draw designs in the dust at his feet. "Two, in fact, so I'm to have a choice. Roger Dowling has offered me an apprenticeship in his joinery. And Dr. Butters says that the apothecary in Hawkshead is looking for a boy who is good with sums. I'm sure I should be grateful. Either is better than working in a slate quarry or burning charcoal."

"Mr. Dowling would be a good master," Rascal said tentatively. The joiner's shop was a warm and cheerful place, with the sharp smell of clean wood in the air and fresh sawdust underfoot. And Mr. Dowling was a generous man, who always saved the family's soup bones for Rascal.

"I don't want to make things hard for Aunt Jane," Jeremy said, turning the stick in his fingers. "She does the best she can for both of us, so I try not to let her know how much I want to go to Kelsick."

Rascal pushed his cold nose against Jeremy's hand. *"Kelsick?"*

Jeremy sighed. "Kelsick is the grammar school at Ambleside. Miss Nash encouraged me to take the entrance examination and I passed with high marks. If I went to Kelsick, I could learn Latin and Greek and study drawing and painting.

Some of the Kelsick boys have gone on to university—to Oxford and Cambridge, even." He glanced up at a jay scolding down at them from the branch of a willow. "But there's the tuition, and books and supplies. And Ambleside is ten miles away. I'd have to have a room, and there would be the cost of meals. It's far more than Aunt Jane can manage."

"I'm sorry, Jeremy," Rascal said sadly.

Jeremy sighed again. "So either I must be apprenticed to Roger Dowling and be a joiner, or go to the apothecary in Hawkshead." He gave Rascal a crooked smile. "Which would you choose?"

"Neither," Rascal barked decisively. *"I like to drop in at the joiner's shop now and then, but I shouldn't like to spend all day hammering and sawing. I shouldn't like to count pills and pound powders, either. Both are respectable trades, I'm sure, but they're not for me."*

"I thought so," Jeremy said, reflecting that it was a comfort to discuss the situation with the little dog, who—even though he didn't understand a word you said—could always be imagined to agree with you, whatever position you took. He sighed gloomily and fell silent for a moment, trying to picture himself astride the joiner's bench all day long, a saw in his hand, wearing a canvas apron with pockets full of nails. Or dressed in a white coat, standing behind the apothecary's counter from dawn until dusk, surrounded by jars of pills and bottles of potions.

Aunt Jane was right, of course. It was all very well to dream, but he ought to be glad that he had a choice, and that whatever he chose, he would be working indoors, out of the wind and weather, at a trade that earned people's respect and enough to live on, eventually. She said the other boys would envy him, and he guessed she was right there, too.

Harold Beechman, for instance, who was going to work alongside his father in the slate quarry, which was cold in winter and hot in summer and dangerous the year round. Harold would be glad of a chance to sit on a joiner's bench and wield a smoothing plane.

But Jeremy wasn't glad. He didn't care a fig whether or not he was envied, and he didn't want to grow up and go to work. He wanted to be a schoolboy, wanted to study and learn, wanted it so urgently that he could feel the desire like a hot, sweet taste in his mouth.

"It's too bad that fairies can't really grant wishes," Jeremy muttered, thinking of what he had said to Caroline.

"Why, of course they can," Rascal replied in surprise. He knew this was true, although he had never had occasion to put it to the test.

But Jeremy only sighed, stood, and looked down at the little dog. "Tomorrow, then." He put his hands in his pockets, and turned away in the direction of the cottage he shared with his aunt.

Sadly, Rascal watched him go. Dogs, as you no doubt know from your own experience, don't need to be told what humans are thinking and feeling; they have an intuitive sense of it, sorrowing with their favorite people, and taking pleasure in the things that make them happy.

But knowing how Jeremy felt and being able to do something about it were two entirely different things. Rascal was only a terrier, and rather small and nondescript at that. He had strong forequarters and a very good nose, which were excellent attributes when it came to digging small creatures out of their holes. But he didn't flatter himself that he might ever wield any significant influence in the wide world of human affairs.

Yes, it would be wonderful indeed if Jeremy could do as he wished and continue with his education. But that would take a miracle. And even Rascal knew that miracles didn't grow on trees.

11

Ridley Advertises

In the Hill Top attic, the death of Rollo the rat, cruelly and wantonly murdered when he had sallied into the kitchen to fetch a bun, was felt to be a shocking and deeply demoralizing event, all the more because it was so sudden and unexpected. Miss Felicia Frummety had exhibited no interest in policing the place and the incumbent rats were perfectly aware of the Rule that prohibited other cats from poaching. As a result, they had become agreeably accustomed to going wherever and whenever they liked and doing whatever they liked, with the greatest confidence and sang-froid and without a whisker of fear.

The news of Rollo's death traveled at the speed of lightning through the attic, and was received in varying ways, according to the hearer's temperament. Some of the rats suddenly found that they were urgently wanted at home—an uncle had died, or a mother had lost her place—and packed their bags to leave. Others stayed, venturing downstairs or out to the barn or the Tower Bank Arms with a considerably heightened caution, warily watching their backs as they went and setting up sentinels with whistles round their necks to keep a lookout while they made free of the cheeses or biscuits or grain. A few of these even armed themselves with cudgels and cleavers, the latter sharpened by a rat from Carlisle who set up his grinding wheel just at the head of the spiral stair, requiring only that the owner of the weapon take a turn at the crank.

It soon became evident, however, that quite a number of the rats were mere unruly ruffians, of that undisciplined and excitable sort of temperament that is stimulated by the prospect of danger. They formed themselves into gangs and held rallies in the Saloon, bold as you please, where they sang war ditties and chanted fight slogans reminiscent of Mr. Churchill's political campaign and ate quantities of cold beef and drank a great deal of malt ale, vowing that they would rid Hill Top of any cat who had the temerity to threaten one of their race. When they had worked themselves up to a fever pitch of excitement, they would sally down the stairs, clanging and banging and making as much racket as possible, and charge across the kitchen and through the dairy and out to the barns, daring any cat to catch them.

Ridley Rattail, unlike the other rats, felt no sadness when he learned of the murder. He was glad to be rid of Rollo, whose offer to punch him in the nose still rankled. And the death was confirmation of the extraordinary brilliance of his idea: what was needed to rid the Hill Top attic of unwanted rats was a fierce and fearless feline. *Several* fierce felines, in fact. And Ridley thought he knew just how to find them.

On the day following Rollo's murder, Ridley shut himself up in his apartment with a quantity of paper, a quill pen made from a magpie's feather, and a bottle of very sooty ink. Within a few hours, he had fashioned several large advertising posters with the following message:

Experienced Ratters Required

Owing to an alarming increase in the number of rats of objectionable character residing in the attic, action must be taken.
Applicants may present themselves to

Miss Potter
Hill Top Farm, Near Sawrey.

(Across the lake, over the bridge, up the hill, first on the left.)
Room and board provided.
Additional compensation commensurate with skill & experience.

On the next day (which would be Thursday), Ridley stacked the posters one on top of the other, rolled them up very neatly, and secured the roll with a bit of shoelace. Then he took himself off to the Tower Bank Arms, where he waited for the brewer's dray, which always stopped just after noon. While the drayman was unloading two kegs of ale and six dozen bottles of beer, Ridley found himself a comfortable place in an empty basket. After two more stops (the spirits shop and the Sawrey Hotel, both in Far Sawrey), the dray arrived at the ferry and boarded at the three o'clock departure, the rat still on board.

Having arrived at Bowness, Ridley posted his advertisements in several places along the road where he thought they were likely to be spotted. He returned to the ferry landing in time to catch the five o'clock departure, and was delighted to find when he boarded that someone had spilt a bag of delicious buttered popcorn—exactly the sort of snack he was hoping for. And then, with the wind in his whiskers, the silver waves dancing and shimmering in an exceedingly pleasant way, and the blown spray just dampening his sleek gray fur, he settled back to enjoy the ride with the consciousness of a job well done.

He might not have been so pleased with himself, however, had he suspected the sort of cat who might be enticed by his advertisement. Ridley Rattail might just have posted his own death warrant.

12

Cats with Plain Names

It was the morning following Ridley's posting of his advertisement, which of course Miss Potter knew nothing about. She had just finished writing a short letter to Norman's sister, Millie Warne, reporting on the plague of rats, the unsettling proposal for villas along the Windermere shoreline, and the reception at Raven Hall on Saturday. She added that she hoped to see Millie soon and sent best wishes to Mrs. Warne. Norman was gone, but the Warnes were her family now, and she was bound to them with a strong bond of love and loss. She signed herself "With love yrs aff.," and folded the letter into an envelope. She was wondering whether she could catch the morning post when she heard a rap at the door.

"Oh, Miss Potter," Mrs. Jennings said, "couldst tha come to t' barn and help me give t' Galway calf her med'cine?

Mr. Jennings has gone off to market, and t' creature's turned balky—I doan't think I can manage her alone."

Willingly, Beatrix traded her felt slippers for the leather clogs she wore outdoors and followed Mrs. Jennings through the farm yard to the barn. The two of them had not hit it off when they first met, but after Mrs. Jennings had been won over by the new living quarters and the more convenient kitchen, the two women had become comfortable together. Mrs. Jennings knew a great deal about farm animals, and Beatrix was eager to learn all she had to teach.

Blossom's medicine was administered in a drenching horn, a hollow cow's horn with the tip cut off. While Mrs. Jennings held the unwilling calf, Beatrix filled the horn with the liquid and managed to get most of it down the calf's throat. Kitchen, the mother cow, watched with concern, whilst the ducks and chickens gathered around, peering curiously through the fence. There was plenty of noise, with the Berkshires grunting, the rooster crowing, the hens cackling, and Tibbie and Queenie, the Herdwick ewes, bleating in cautionary tones to their lambs in the green meadow beyond.

Beatrix loved these farmyard sounds, which seemed to her as homey and comfortable as the hiss of the kettle steaming on the back of the stove and the cricket singing on the doorstep. As a girl, she and her brother Bertram (younger by almost six years) had collected a great many animals—rabbits, hedgehogs, guinea pigs, mice, lizards, newts, frogs, rats, bats, and even a ring snake named Sally—who enlivened their third-floor nursery and could be coerced into posing for Beatrix's sketches. After Bertram went away to school, it was the animals who kept her company, allowing her to sketch them, play with them, and invent amusing stories about them. These were the stories that later, with

Norman's encouragement and guidance, had become her "little books," full of fictional animals: Peter Rabbit, Mrs. Tiggy-Winkle, Jeremy Frog, Hunca Munca and Tom Thumb, the mice.

Animals in books were all well and good, and Beatrix still loved them dearly. But at Hill Top, she was surrounded by *real* animals, animals of the farmyard and woodlands, animals with lively personalities and sometimes tragically complicated lives. There was Jemima Puddleduck, for instance, a foolish duck who lived in the barn and had the habit of laying her eggs in out-of-the-way corners, where the foxes made a meal of them. Beatrix had already decided that when she had finished her current book (a story about a silly kitten who fell afoul of a pair of scheming rats), she would put Jemima into a book. The story would also include a fox, a handsome, debonair, and clever villain with alluring manners—like the clever wolf in "Little Red Riding Hood," a tale that Norman's nieces and nephews never tired of hearing.

While Mrs. Jennings finished with Blossom, Beatrix gathered a bucket of newly laid eggs and they started back to the house. As they walked, Mrs. Jennings remarked, " 'Tis t' oddest thing, Miss Potter. Tha knowst I've been wantin' another cat, to help with t' rat problem. Well, I looked out t' window not ten minutes ago, and there was a fierce-lookin' orange tomcat with green eyes, sittin' on t' threshold and lookin' up at me, sayin' plain as day, *'I've come to lend a hand with t' rats, Missus.'* Tha shouldst see his teeth and claws, Miss Potter. Like needles and knives, they are."

Beatrix chuckled. "It sounds as if he's eminently qualified. I suppose you told this fierce fellow that the position was open."

"If you mean, did I keep t' cat, I did that," Mrs. Jennings replied firmly, not being a woman who used big words.

"Once rats gets settled, they're t' verra devil to roust out. I'm hopin' t' new tom'll do t' job." She laughed shortly. "Better'n that silly ginger puss, who fancies she's done a grand thing when she catches a beetle."

"Poor Felicia," Beatrix murmured, with some sympathy for the cat who was about to lose her place. "Does the new cat have a name?"

"His name is Fang," Mrs. Jennings said stoutly. "I doan't hold with fancy names for cats, as tha knowst. That's what's wrong with t' ginger cat. Gives herself airs 'cause she's got a fine name." She harrumphed sharply. "Miss Felicia Frummety. Plain cats with plain names is what we need."

"Fang it is, then," Beatrix said, with a little shiver. It was not a name for an amiable cat, although in the circumstance, perhaps amiability was less important than cunning. She paused. "I wonder if we shouldn't advertise."

"Advertise? For cats?" Mrs. Jennings snorted. "Tha must be joking, Miss Potter. Cats can't read."

"No, I suppose not," Beatrix murmured regretfully. "Well, I'd best hurry if I'm to catch the post. I have the feeling that Fang might need a co-worker. I'll keep my eyes open for unemployed cats."

This remark brought another snort from Mrs. Jennings.

Several other people were aiming to catch the post, as well, and had converged on the post office in Low Green Gate Cottage. Like villagers the world over, the Sawrey villagers took a great deal of interest (a great deal too much interest, some would say) in other people's private affairs. This morning, the talk was all about the mysterious Mrs. Kittredge.

"Well, I for one doan't believe she's a witch, in spite o' what Lydia Dowling says," avowed Lucy Skead, the postmistress, who was as round as a Norfolk dumpling and so short that Mr. Skead had built her a wooden box to stand on behind the counter. "There's no such thing as witches, not in these modern times, with railroads and telegraphs and electric lights. Sixpence for t' package, Mathilda."

"That's all tha knowst, me girl," said old Dolly Dorking in a scornful tone. "Auld Dolly," as she was known to the villagers, was Lucy Skead's mother, a stooped old lady who always wore a black tippet. She lived with the Skeads and spent her days sitting in a corner of the post office, knitting black stockings and exchanging remarks with the customers.

"And what's railroads an' telegraphs got to do with witches, anyway?" demanded sharp-nosed Mathilda Crook, who had brought in a package of cookies to mail to her brother's children in Liverpool. Poor motherless things didn't have a soul to bake for them, and the good Lord only knew how clean their clothes were. "Just because they doan't go round callin' folks' attention to theyselven doan't mean there's none nae more."

Auld Dolly gave a vigorous nod. "My mother, bless her soul, was born on Ash Wednesday, and knew a witch whenivver she saw one. She allus said red hair is one sure sign."

"Aye," Mathilda said, agreeing. "Another is if they go invisible when they drink t' milk from a black cow."

"Tha's both talkin' blether," harrumphed Lucy, taking Mathilda's package. "How's milk from a black cow any diff'rent than milk from a white cow, I'd like to know."

Hannah Braithwaite, wife of the village constable, pasted a stamp on a letter she was sending to her mother. "I've heard red-headed women have second sight," she said, in her sweet little voice, soft as a girl's. "An' that they'd sooner lie than smile, and're like to run off with t' fairies whenivver t' chance comes." She paused judiciously. "I woan't say anything 'gainst

Mrs. Kittredge, since I've nivver even laid eyes on t' lady. Still, I worry for our Major Kittredge, who's had more'n enough sadness, what with losin' his eye an' his right arm in t' war. He doan't need nae more."

Mathilda nodded in earnest agreement. "I worry for him, too, poor chap. He may have a deal o' courage, goin' up against t' Boers as he did, but it canna be naen too smart to wed a red-headed woman." She gave an ironic chuckle. "Mappen it's t' Raven Hall Luck, wouldst tha' say?"

"Nae t' luck," said Auld Dolly wisely. "It was t' dwelves. Remember poor Mrs. Stout, t' housekeeper, who went mad as a magpie an' threw all t' Kittredge silver into the well? T' dwelves made her do it."

"Dwelves?" asked Mathilda, raising her eyebrows. "I thought they was fairies."

"That's what everybody thinks," Auld Dolly said. She dropped her knitting into her lap. "But everybody's wrong. It's dwelves who live alongside Fern Vale Tarn, not fairies. Half elf, half dwarf. Oak Folk, some call 'em. They're t' ones who gave t' Luck. And they're t' ones who wanted t' silver, which is why they made Mrs. Stout throw it in t' well, an' made 'er mad when she wouldn't."

"Nae, Mother," Lucy remonstrated. "Dwelves, fairies, Oak Folk—'tis all nonsense, same as witches. T' steward made off with t' silver, and tha knowst what happened to him."

"Oh!" Hannah said fearfully. "What happened t' 'im?"

"Ran off to Edinburgh and fell under t' wheels of a lorry," Lucy said, with a satisfied air. She gave a gloomy shake to her head. "Bad luck all 'round. Who knows what's in store for our poor major, marryin' that actress."

"Actress!" exclaimed Mathilda and Hannah in unison.

"Tha hastna heard?" Lucy asked, pretending great surprise. "T' head housemaid at Raven Hall told her sister, and t' sister told my cousin. He saw her on t' London stage and married her in a fortnight." She gave her head a disapproving shake. "Too quick, if tha asks me."

"My brother knew an actress once," said Hannah mournfully. "A reet Jezebel, she was." She shook her head despairingly. "T' poor, poor major."

Grace Lythecoe, widow of the former vicar and one of the village's most solid citizens, had come in just in time to hear the last few comments. "Ladies, really!" she exclaimed heatedly. "It's unchristian to speak ill of people! What would Major Kittredge say if he heard you?"

"T'wasn't Mrs. Kittredge we was talkin' 'bout, necessar'ly," Mathilda Crook said defensively. "It was red-headed women in gen'ral."

"An' actresses," added Lucy.

"And we was only wishin' that our poor Major Kittredge would be happy at last," Hannah Braithwaite said in a pious tone, "which is surely a Christian thing to do. T' dear man has had a deal of trouble in his life, in spite of t' Raven Hall Luck."

"He has indeed," said Grace Lythecoe firmly. "And the Raven Hall Luck is only an old glass goblet that's had silly fairy stories told about it, which are not to be believed. Lucy, I'll have two stamps. And I should like to pay three shillings into my postal savings account, if you please."

"*Silly fairy stories?*" remarked Rascal, sitting on his haunches in the path outside the open door of the post office. "*What do you think about that, Max?*" he said to a black tail-less cat sitting next to him.

Max the Manx gave Rascal a gloomy look. "*I've not had much experience with fairies. On the matter of witches, however, I am somewhat of an expert, having served one once, in—*" He stopped and cast his eyes upward, reflecting. *"In my third lifetime, I think it was. Or perhaps my fourth. I lose track."*

"I've always envied you cats," said the little dog. *"I've got to make the best of the one life I have. Fancy having nine!"*

"I don't know why you should envy us," said Max with a heavy sigh. *"Frankly, it's just one long vale of tears after another. In this life, for instance, I am without a home to call my own. No fireside to warm my aching joints, no one to offer me milk or kippers."* Max had formerly lived with the three Crabbe sisters in Castle Cottage, at the top end of the village. After they moved to Bournemouth, he'd stayed on in the Castle Cottage barn, sleeping in the dusty hay and catching the occasional mouse. *"But then, most of my lives have been unhappy, I am sad to report. I spent one entire existence in the hold of a fishing ship. I never once saw the light of day and lived exclusively on raw eels. What's more, I—"*

"What was it like to live with that witch?" Rascal interrupted. Once Max got started on a sad story, he'd go on forever. *"A rum go, I'll wager."*

"It was a deal of toil and trouble," replied Max. *"Nothing to eat but eyes of newts, toes of frogs, and tongues of dogs. She had,"* he added meaningfully, *"red hair."*

At the mention of tongues of dogs, Rascal shuddered. *"So what do you think of Mrs. Kittredge? Is she a witch, then?"*

"I haven't met her," Max said, *"but from all I have heard, I'm sure of it."* He leaned forward and added, in a confidential tone, *"In fact, I predict that she is going to cause everyone a very great deal of trouble, especially—"*

"Hello, Rascal," said Miss Potter with a smile, coming up the post office path with a letter and several parcels in her hand. She was wearing her leather clogs and the straw hat she always wore about the village. "And Max. How nice to see you. How are you today?"

"Not very well," began Max in a dismal voice, but Rascal broke in with a welcoming yip.

"Welcome back, Miss Potter!" he cried, leaping up on his hind legs.

Miss Potter was one of Rascal's favorite humans. She was unfailingly kind and thoughtful to small dogs and very clever when it came to figuring things out. Rascal always looked forward to Miss Potter's visits to the village, and made it a point to spend as much time with her as he could when she was there.

"Max," said Miss Potter, putting her head on one side and regarding the cat thoughtfully, "it strikes me that you aren't looking very well fed. I wonder what you're getting to eat these days, now that the Misses Crabbe have gone away."

"How kind of you to inquire," said Max, his gloomy expression lightening a little. He extended a paw. *"I am not at all well fed, sad to say. I have eaten all of the mice in the Castle Farm barn and now have very little to sustain life and breath besides crickets and—"*

"Why, hello, Miss Potter!" exclaimed Hannah Braithwaite, coming out of the post office door. "How nice to have thee home again."

"Thank you, Mrs. Braithwaite," Miss Potter said. "I was just about to tell Max that if he is not otherwise engaged, I should be glad to offer him a place at Hill Top. Bread and milk regularly for supper, Max, and all the rats you can catch."

Max's green eyes grew round. *"All the rats—"* he began, in a faltering tone.

Hannah Braithwaite giggled. "Fancy thee talkin' to that old black cat with no tail. But then, I s'pose it's nat'ral, since thy stories are full of cats and frogs and t' like, and all of 'em talkin', one to another. And Max'ud be a good ratter, I'd reckon." She gave Miss Potter a slantwise look. "Hill Top could use one, I hear."

"I'm afraid you're right," said Miss Potter regretfully. "The current Hill Top cat does not have a taste for rats. Mrs. Jennings has acquired a new tomcat, but there's room for Max, should he care to come on." She smiled. "Mrs. Jennings will like him, I'm sure, since he has a very plain name."

"Should I care to come on . . . should I CARE?" Max cried, in a tone of disbelief. He began to curl himself around Miss Potter's ankles. *"Of course I should care to come on! And I am an experienced ratter, if I do say so myself. Why, in my second life, I—"*

"Just look at the beast," Mrs. Braithwaite marveled. "It's for all t' world like he understands you!"

"I shouldn't be surprised," Miss Potter replied. "I do hope that all the little Braithwaites are keeping well."

"Oh, verra well, thank you," Mrs. Braithwaite beamed. "We was glad of t' book, Miss Potter—*The Tale of Two Bad Mice,* 'twas. The children have fair read t' words off t' pages, and t' pages out of t' book."

"I'm glad," Miss Potter said warmly. "I'm working on *The Tale of Tom Kitten* just now. I'll send the children a copy when it's published. Good day."

"Just t' nicest lady," murmured Hannah Braithwaite, as Miss Potter went into the post office.

"Oh, yes," Max the Manx rejoined in a reverential tone. *"The very nicest lady!"*

13

Miss Potter Delivers

While Beatrix was posting her letter, Dimity Woodcock was arranging an armful of blooming forsythia branches in a tall vase on the hallway table at Tower Bank House. She had come to live there with her brother Miles some twelve years before, and had not for one instant regretted it. At the time, perhaps, the decision had not seemed very wise, for she was just twenty-four and had seen very little of the world. Her friends cautioned her that moving to the country would condemn her to spinsterhood, and the village of Sawrey was, as her brother put it, "quite removed from modern society." And since she had her own small fortune and did not have to concern herself overmuch about money, she could have lived anywhere she chose.

But Dimity was an old-fashioned person in many ways and did not care a fig for "modern society," especially that part of it which rushed about on underground subways and dashed off to parties and rarely slowed down long enough to take a deep breath and wonder where in the world it was. At any rate, she had flourished in the village, and intended to make her home with her brother as long as he wished to continue the arrangement. Of course, she had hoped, a few years before, that she and Major Kittredge might—

Dimity sighed and willed herself to stop thinking about the past. The major had made his choice, and she could only hope that he would enjoy every happiness. But as she stepped back to admire the flower arrangement, she could not help one last, wistful wish, that he had chosen her instead of—

Dimity made an impatient noise. She was *not* going to think such thoughts. She had a wonderful home with Miles, and she would stay as long as it was comfortable for both of them—although she did sometimes wonder if the convenience of having his sister oversee the household and manage their entertainments made Miles a little less likely to look for a wife. But her brother seemed perfectly content to go on as they were, perhaps because their society was limited and he had few opportunities to meet suitable candidates, women who were well bred, well read, educated, and interesting but who preferred life in a country village to life in the city. Perhaps if he found a suitable—

This time, it was the doorbell that interrupted her. "I'm right here, Elsa," she called to her housekeeper, Elsa Grape. "I'll answer it." She opened the door to see Miss Potter, a parcel in her hand.

"Why, hello, Beatrix," she said warmly. "How nice of you to drop in this morning. Do come in and have some tea. How are you getting on with the rats?"

"I think it's a question of how we are getting on with the cats," Beatrix said wryly, stepping into the entry hall. "So far, there are two, Fang and Max the Manx, who used to belong to the Crabbe sisters." She handed over a package. "Your crepe paper, Dimity." She glanced admiringly at the forsythia. "My, how the flowers brighten your hall."

"They do, don't they?" Dimity said happily. "Thank you for the crepe paper. You saved me a trip across the lake."

"Do you have all the help you need for the pageant?" Beatrix asked, following Dimity down the hall.

"I think so," Dimity replied. "The children make their own flower crowns. The teachers manage the games and songs, and the Ladies Guild does tea. Mr. Skead always puts up the pole in the school yard, and Mr. Llewellyn lends his old white horse for the May Queen to ride to school—this year, the Leeches' daughter Ruth will be queen."

"And what happens if it rains?"

"It doesn't dare," Dimity replied staunchly. "The sun *always* shines on May Day."

"Well, just in case it turns chilly," Beatrix said, "I have something from Mrs. Corry for your brother."

"Oh, dear," Dimity said with a sigh. "Another scarf." She brightened. "Wouldn't you like to deliver it yourself?"

"I would," Beatrix said. "Actually, I wanted to talk with the captain, if he's available."

"Yes, of course. He's in his study. We'll have our tea in there, shall we?"

And then, as Dimity opened the study door, she was suddenly struck by an idea that was so obvious, so amazingly, perfectly right that she was amazed that she had not thought of it before. Miss Potter would make Miles a wonderful wife, and a perfect sister to herself! This thought was so exciting as to send her into a state of giddy confusion from which she barely recovered in time to open the library door and say, in as normal a voice as possible, "Miles, Miss Potter has brought you something."

Miles was sitting at his writing-table, his fingers tented under his chin, scowling at nothing. But Dimity noticed that when Miss Potter came into the room, his face cleared and he leapt to his feet—surely a sign of personal interest.

"Hello, Miss Potter," he said, extending his hand cordially. "I'd heard you were back at Hill Top. Staying for a time, I hope."

"A fortnight," Miss Potter said, taking his hand.

"I'll get tea," Dimity said quickly, and left the room, feeling a warm glow of pleasure. She knew that her brother admired Miss Potter, who was certainly well read, interesting, and had a broad (if unconventional) education, having taught herself in books and museums and art galleries. She came from excellent family, and was pretty, too, in a very English way, with those bright blue eyes and beautifully pink cheeks and the clearest of complexions. Best yet, if she and Miles were married, they would no doubt live right here at Tower Bank House, and she herself could do so as well, and they would all be quite, quite happy and comfortable.

Miles Woodcock certainly did admire Miss Potter, who had provided some very helpful assistance in several difficult matters over the past two years. As Justice of the Peace for Sawrey District, he'd had to investigate the passing of old Ben Hornby, who had died in a fall from a cliff. It was thanks to Miss Potter—who struck him as a remarkably perceptive and thoughtful observer—that the case had been solved. And a few months before that, she had shrewdly unraveled a scheme of art robberies that culminated in the theft of a Constable miniature stolen from Anvil Cottage. Altogether an estimable woman, Miles thought warmly, and found that a smile had replaced his frown.

"I've brought you a knitted scarf from Mrs. Corry," Miss Potter said, her blue eyes twinkling. She handed him a paper-wrapped parcel. "I stopped at her cottage to get some plants she promised me, and she asked me to deliver it."

"Yet another scarf," Miles said ruefully, unwrapping it. "The old dear was always after me when I was a child to wear my scarf and mittens. Here I am, past forty, and she's still doing it."

"And such a . . . quickening shade of green, too," said Miss Potter with a smile. "It quite takes the eye, doesn't it? But I'm sure it gave her a great deal of pleasure to make it. When I was eight, I knitted a scarf for Mr. Gaskell, one of Papa's friends." She chuckled. "Such a kindly old gentleman. He wore the horrid thing whenever he came to visit."

"I'll be sure to wear this the next time I stop in to see Mrs. Corry," Miles said, feeling that he had been nicely rebuked and not minding a bit. "Won't you sit down? Dim will be along with our tea in just a minute."

"Actually, I have another reason for coming," Miss Potter said, taking a chair as Miles sat down across from her. She reached into her pocket and took out a calling card. "I overheard a conversation at the ferry landing yesterday afternoon, which troubled me a good deal. After thinking about it, I decided to tell you about it." And with that, she related the conversation and handed over the card, which bore a name, address, and London telephone number.

"Augustus Richardson," Miles read, in astonishment. He looked up. "I don't know how you do it, Miss Potter, I really don't. Is it magic? Are you a witch?"

"Magic?" Miss Potter's eyebrows arched. "Really, Captain Woodcock, I hardly think—"

"No, of course not," Miles said hastily. "Forgive me. It's just that you always seem to appear with the information one needs, just when one needs it." He smiled. "One can't help wondering, you see, if there's not a bit of witchcraft about it."

Miss Potter's expression softened somewhat. "I could not avoid hearing them," she said quietly. "They did not attempt to lower their voices. And when I heard the mention of villas, I'm afraid I was so incensed that I did not think to return the card Mr. Richardson dropped." She paused. "So you knew about this?"

"I knew only the man's name and had heard of the intention," Miles said, placing the card on his writing table. "The name of the syndicate—the Sandiford Syndicate, I believe you said—and the address on this card will allow me to make further inquiries."

"Yes, Sandiford. But I hope you will do more than make inquiries," Miss Potter said urgently. "I hope you will put a stop to it."

Remembering his conversation with Will Heelis, Miles sighed. "That's easier said than done, Miss Potter. Owners are generally free to do as they like with their property. You wouldn't want the villagers telling you how to manage Hill Top Farm, I'm sure."

"I understand that," Miss Potter said quietly. "But it does seem to me that land is part of the community as a whole, and that property owners should use it in a way that serves the community. Perhaps that sounds idealistic, but—"

Miss Potter was interrupted by the appearance of Dimity and the tea tray, and the conversation took a more general turn. When at last Miss Potter rose to go, Miles said, "Dimity and I are driving to Raven Hall for the Kittredge reception tomorrow. Would you care to go with us?"

"Oh, please do, Beatrix," Dimity put in, as Miss Potter seemed to hesitate. "Will Heelis is stopping here, and will be going with us, as well. We shall have such fun."

Miles remembered that Miss Potter was not overly fond of riding in his motor car. "I promise to drive slowly," he said, and smiled. "And it does have a top, so in case of rain, you and your hat are sure to stay dry."

Miss Potter looked thoughtful. Then a smile lightened her china-blue eyes, and he thought for an instant that they were her best feature—her eyes and her shy, sweet smile.

"Thank you for the invitation," she said. "I should like to see Raven Hall, which I understand was designed by David Bryce. From a distance, it looks to be a fine example of the Gothic style." She gave Miles a meaningful glance. "I should not like to think of it being turned into an hotel, with a dozen villas sprawled out along the lakeshore."

Miles sighed heavily. "Nor should I, Miss Potter. If you can think of a way to keep that from happening, I'd be most grateful."

But of course, he thought to himself, that was quite impossible. Miss Potter had certainly been of help in other matters, but even she was powerless to stop the march of what many would no doubt call progress.

14

De Parbis, grandis acerbus erit

Bosworth Badger was enjoying a cup of tea and a bit of Friday afternoon sunshine on his front porch when he heard the bracken rustle and saw a small tan-colored terrier clambering up the steep slope of Holly How. Bosworth rose from his rocking chair in alarm, recalling the Badgers' Second Rule of Thumb (*Be wary of all dogs, and especially of terriers who have been taught to tunnel, for it is safe to say that they do not have a badger's best interests at heart*) and thinking that it was time he went inside and locked The Brockery's front door.

But then he recognized Rascal and settled back down in his chair with a wave and a smile. Badger was glad to welcome the cheerful little dog, who always brought news of the village activities. And since he'd just heard some rather unsettling rumors from that direction, he was even gladder than usual.

The Brockery had been the home of the Holly How badgers for nearly two centuries and was widely judged to be the oldest badger sett in the Land between the Lakes. Beside the oaken door hung the Badger Coat of Arms, picturing twin badgers rampant on an azure field, with a shield inscribed in Latin, thus:

De Parbis, grandis acerbus erit

In English, this family motto proclaimed, *From small things, there will grow a mighty heap,* or (in the local vernacular) *Many littles make a mickle, Many mickles make a mile.* It described, Bosworth understood, the badgers' habit of excavating their burrows inch by inch, one generation after another, and piling the earth outside the door—although it could be taken, of course, to refer to a great many other things.

At the moment, the Brockery was home to five badgers: Bosworth; Parsley, the Brockery's cook; and Primrose, her daughter Hyacinth, and her son Thorn, a promising lad who, Bosworth thought, might someday take his place as the custodian of the *History.* It was also the best-known hostelry in the Land between the Lakes. Some of its residents (like the twin rabbits who helped with the housekeeping) were permanent lodgers, while others were of an itinerant bent, like the fox who occasionally popped in for a day or two, or the trio of hedgehogs displaced when their log-pile home was destroyed by a farmer, or the pair of rats who had stopped, just last night, on their way out of the District. Most paid in kind, with services or food or other useful items, like the silver thimble one of the rats had brought, and which Primrose immediately claimed for a flower vase. But Bosworth was a kindly soul, and out-of-pocket lodgers were allowed to stay on even though they could not pay their bill.

Bosworth (more properly, Bosworth Badger XVII) was not just The Brockery's proprietor. He also had the important duty of maintaining the official *History of the Badgers of the Land between the Lakes* and its companion, the *Holly How Badger Genealogy,* which were contained in some two dozen leather-bound volumes in The Brockery's library. And because earlier badger historians had recorded not only their own clan's activities but those of a great many other animals as well, the *History* was widely regarded as a reliable record of the changing flora and fauna of the Land between the Lakes. Bosworth was often consulted about questions of history, and he enjoyed thumbing through the closely written pages, looking for long-forgotten bits.

"*Hullo, Bozzy, old chap,*" barked Rascal, squatting on his haunches. "*Lovely afternoon, wouldn't you say? Looks like spring has finally arrived. Not a moment too soon, either.*"

Bosworth did not much like being called "Bozzy," but he smiled all the same. "*Hello there, my young friend. Been keeping well, down there in the village? I do hope you're full of news, and that you'll have a cup of tea and tell it all to me.*"

And without waiting for a reply, the badger picked up the brown china teapot that sat on a tray at his elbow and filled the extra cup he kept always at hand, for one never knew which of one's friends might pop in and be glad of a cup and bit of a chat.

"*Nivver say nae to a cup o' tae,*" Rascal replied, in the broad dialect of the area. He cocked his head. "*All's well here at The Brockery, is it? Seen the Professor lately?*"

Rascal was inquiring after Professor Galileo Newton Owl, D.Phil., one of Bosworth's very best friends, who lived in an enormous hollow beech at the top of Cuckoo Brow Wood.

"*I'm expecting to see him tomorrow,*" Bosworth replied, handing over the tea, and passing lemon and sugar as well. "*Did you have a special reason for asking?*"

"As a matter of fact, I did," said Rascal. *"Jeremy, Caroline, and one of Caroline's friends are planning an expedition to look for fairies. Deirdre, Caroline's friend, claims to be able to see them. I thought the Professor—since he keeps a sharp eye on all that goes on in the Wood—might know whether the Fern Vale village still exists. But p'rhaps you've an idea?"*

"Fairies?" Bosworth was mildly surprised. *"Why, nobody's asked after the Folk for donkey's years. Children hardly believe nowadays, and the grownups are too preoccupied with progress to bother about the past."*

"But you think they are still in the neighborhood?"

Bosworth gave the terrier an indulgent look. *"My dear boy, that's like asking whether there are still angels in the neighborhood! Of course there are. The difficulty lies in finding them."*

"I'm told that there once was a fairy village near Fern Vale Tarn," Rascal said. *"Do you know of it?"*

"Oh, yes, Fern Vale Village." Bosworth reflected. *"My grandfather recorded something about it. The creatures he describes, however, are not at all like those little whizzy things with delicate wings and spangles that are pictured in children's books—the sort that are commonly called 'fairies.'"* He frowned. *"I doubt that the children are prepared for the* real *Folk. They're an unreliable lot, you know. Well-meaning and often beguiling, but cheeky. Fond of trickery, and not to be trusted."*

The dog looked doubtful. *"Do you suppose they'll allow themselves to be found?"*

"There's no way of knowing," Bosworth replied. *"The children shall simply have to go and have a look. I can glance through the* History *and see if I can discover the exact location of the village. Shall I?"*

"I'd be grateful," Rascal said. He set down his cup.

"Don't go just yet," Bosworth said, putting up a paw. *"I wanted to ask about a rumor that's crept up here from the village. It concerns Hill Top Farm."*

"Miss Potter's back from London, if that's what you're asking." Rascal replied.

The badger shook his head uneasily *"This has to do with rats, I'm sorry to say. A pair stopped in last night on their way north. They'd been down at Hill Top, which they had heard was quite the place for rats on holiday. But not a very nice holiday, as they described it. They said that the place is attracting all sorts of riffraff and bad fellows. It has become . . . well, rather common. Not the sort of place for a self-respecting rat."*

Rascal made a face. *"The problem lies with the Hill Top cat—a silly, frivolous creature who let the rats take advantage. However, Miss Potter will have the matter in hand shortly, although you might want to discourage any rat traffic headed in that direction."* He paused. *"One more thing I should mention, Bozzy. This expedition—it may be Jeremy's last. The lad is leaving school and going to work."*

"To work!" exclaimed Bosworth. Jeremy, who respected animals and nature, was respected in turn by everyone at The Brockery, and always welcomed when he came around.

"Yes. He's to be an apprentice. He wants to go to the grammar school in Ambleside, but he's going to have to go to work instead." Rascal looked directly at Bosworth. *"He wants it very much,"* he added, with deliberate emphasis. *"I was wondering if the fairies, or the Folk, if you prefer, might—"* He broke off.

Bosworth returned the look, with concern. Animals usually know exactly what other animals are thinking, which is why they find it so hard to deceive. And Bosworth, who had a great deal of practice in understanding the various residents of The Brockery, understood what Rascal had not quite said.

"Oh, dear me," said Bosworth. *"Well, well. I am sorry to hear that. I shall certainly see what I can discover about the village."* He waved goodbye as the little dog trotted away down

Holly How, then poured himself another cup of tea and sat back in his chair, shaking his head in consternation.

Poor Jeremy. Of course, it was dangerous to ask the Folk to intervene, for once they were invited to become involved in human affairs, they never knew when to stop. *De Parvis, grandis acervus erit,* and one could not quite predict what sort of *grandis* they might conjure up.

15

The Power of Advertising

Beatrix awakened at an early hour on Saturday morning. The night had been a noisy one, with rats scrabbling and squeaking in the wall, the occasional yowl of a cat in one of the outbuildings (Fang and Max, no doubt, doing their job), and the frequent growl of thunder, for the weather had been stormy. She got up at an early hour, breakfasted by the fire on a bowl of oat porridge, a boiled egg, a slice of toast, and a cup of coffee, then settled down to ink a pencil drawing of the kitchen range, with its mantel-shelf of china plates, cups, and pitchers and the blue rug on the floor. The drawing would go into *The Roly-Poly Pudding,* which was to include several interior scenes in the quaint old farmhouse: the stair landing with its grandfather clock and claret-colored curtains, the old oak dresser, and the front door with its polished brass handle.

The book was about a kitten named Tom Twitchit and a pair of rats, Samuel Whiskers and his wife, Anna Maria. The kitten climbed up the chimney and into the attic and fell into the clutches of the rats, who trussed him up with string, buttered him generously, and wrapped him in dough, aiming to steam him like a dumpling. Tom was rescued and returned, sooty but safe, to his mother, Tabitha. Mr. and Mrs. Whiskers ran off to Farmer Potatoes' barn, trundling their belongings in a stolen wheelbarrow. Beatrix had already written the book's dedication, to her favorite pet rat:

In remembrance of
SAMMY,
The intelligent pink-eyed representative
of a persecuted (but irrepressible) race
An affectionate little friend
and most accomplished thief

Beatrix had just finished inking the drawing when she heard a noise outside. She put down her pen, got up, and opened the door. On the stone step sat two unfamiliar, scruffy-looking yellow cats. They looked as if they had recently been brawling—their ears were ripped, their faces scarred, their fur tattered and torn—but both were impressively muscular, with sharp claws and convincing yellow teeth.

"We've come about yer advertisement, miss," said one.

"We're rat-catchers, we are," said the other. *"We ain't much to look at, but we allus get the job done."* He flexed a claw, his eyes narrowed into slits. *"No quarter asked, none given."*

"Good heavens," Beatrix said, thinking that this pair could have made a quick meal of sweet Sammy, who had been almost too fat to run. "You gentlemen look as though you've come a long way."

"Short er long, 'tis all the same to us, miss," one said philosophically.

"As long as there's rats at the end of the journey," added the other.

"I expect you'd like some milk," Beatrix said.

"That'ud take the edge off, fer sure, miss," one cat agreed, twitching his tail.

"And then we'll get straight to work," said the other, glancing around. *"Rats is what we like, miss. Rats and the occasional bird."*

"Birds' eggs is nice, too, miss," added the first.

"I'd be glad to have you stay and give Fang and Max a hand with the rat-catching," Beatrix said, pouring a saucer of milk for each of the cats and putting them on the doorstep. "You can sleep in the barn. But you will have to promise to leave the birds alone. If I find so much as one dead bird," she added sternly, "you shall both be on your way."

The cats exchanged conferring glances, then nodded. *"We'll try our best, miss,"* they said in one voice, and addressed themselves diligently to the milk.

"Plain names," Beatrix murmured, watching them lap it up. "I can't think of anything plainer than Lion and Tiger. Will that do?"

"That'll do nicely, miss," said Lion and Tiger with one voice. And in another moment, they were streaking toward the barn, on their way to work.

Beatrix went back inside and put on the kettle for tea, thinking as she resumed her drawing that cats were very well as long as they kept their place, which was in the barn and out of the birds' nests, and as long as one had no pet rats about. She had just finished the picture and was examining it critically when there was a knock on the door. She opened it to Mrs. Jennings, who was carrying a pitcher.

"Thought tha might like a bit of Kitchen's milk, Miss Potter," she said, handing over the pitcher. "And tha cans't stop worryin' about t' rats. Another cat arrived this morning, a big, wicked-looking gray fellow about t' size of a small dog. A reet ratter, I'd swear."

"Another one?" Beatrix asked, startled. "I just took in two yellow cats—Lion and Tiger."

"Lion and Tiger." Mrs. Jennings gave an approving nod. "Good plain names for cats. Mappen they'll live up to 'em."

"Yes," Beatrix said, with a little smile. She put the eggs into a bowl and handed back the basket. "What did you name the gray?"

"Claw," said Mrs. Jennings firmly. "Big an' sharp, his claws."

Beatrix pursed her lips. "Fang, Max, Claw, Lion, and Tiger." She ticked them off on her fingers. "Five cats. I'm sure that's enough."

"Oh, no, Miss Potter," protested Mrs. Jennings. "Nobbut seven 'ud do, or eight."

Beatrix frowned at the prospect of seven or eight strange cats, but did not disagree. Cats were well as long as they kept their place. "There are plenty of rats in the barn and sheds," she said firmly. "I do not expect to see any cats in the house."

"Oh, aye, Miss Potter," said Mrs. Jennings, in an off-hand tone that Beatrix feared did not sufficiently reflect the seriousness of the business, and left. Beatrix went back to her work, feeling slightly cross. It was not that she held any personal ill-will against cats; she did not keep them simply for fear that they might try to snatch one of her little animals—the rabbits, hedgehogs, mice, and guinea pigs she kept as models for her drawings. She had not brought Josey or Mopsy or the others on this trip, but if she had, a cat would certainly threaten them.

An hour or so later, Beatrix put on her hat and went out to do some weeding in the garden. She was on her way to the rhubarb patch when she noticed an unfamiliar figure, a young girl with thick red braids, at the foot of the garden. She seemed to be searching for something amongst the herbs, some of which had not yet fully emerged from their winter's sleep. Beatrix usually discouraged the village children from coming into the garden, for they came in pairs or gangs and could do a great deal of damage if they climbed the new little fruit trees, or walked down the row of little lettuces.

But this girl was alone, and she was obviously watching where she stepped. Beatrix was curious about her.

"Hello," she called. "May I help you find something?" And since she thought she sounded like a out-of-temper shop clerk, she added, in a softer tone, "What sort of plant are you looking for?"

The girl had jumped, startled. "Yarrow," she replied, adding defensively, "Mrs. Jennings said I could." She was wearing a blue cotton dress and a gray pinafore, with a shawl flung over her head against the mist that had come down from the fells. She spoke with an engaging Irish accent.

Beatrix walked down the path, thinking that the girl's green eyes and much-freckled face, framed in red curls, reminded her of Norman's favorite niece. "If you've come for yarrow flowers," she said gently, "you're several months early." She pointed to a gray-green mound of feathery leaves. "In July, there'll be stalks with flat yellow blooms, but for now, this is all there is."

"Leaves'll do as well," the girl replied with surprising assurance. She picked several and added them to the sprigs of rue and hawthorn she held in her hand. She threw a curious glance at Beatrix. "You're Miss Potter, are you? The lady that makes the books?"

Beatrix nodded. "And you are—"

"Deirdre. I work for Mrs. Sutton. She reads your books out loud to the kids at bedtime, she does."

"Oh, yes," Beatrix said, remembering what Sarah Barwick had told her about the girl. She nodded at the small bouquet. "Is that for Mrs. Sutton?"

Deirdre shook her head. She had, Beatrix thought, more freckles than she had ever seen on a child's face. "For me. An' me friend Caroline."

"I know Caroline," Beatrix said, adding with a smile, "I like her very much."

"She likes you," Deirdre replied, cocking her head with a knowing air. "She told me."

Beatrix glanced again at the little bouquet. "Yarrow, rue, lavender, and thyme. You and Caroline are looking for fairies, then?"

Deirdre's blue-green eyes opened wide. "You *know*?"

"I've tried it myself," Beatrix confided. "I've even thought I had a glimpse of them, dancing on the smooth turf under the moon."

It was true. Perhaps it was the influence of the old Scottish woman she'd known when she was a child, who was so utterly convinced of the reality of fairies that she had made them seem real to Beatrix, too. Or perhaps it was the delight she still felt when she imagined—as she liked to do when she went for walks through the countryside—that the whole of the Land between the Lakes was enchanted, all of the crags and meadows and woods, but especially the woods; and that each of the trees in the forest had a fairy of its own, birch fairies and beech fairies, alder and fir and pine fairies, and especially oak fairies.

Or perhaps it was the same sort of impulse that compelled her to make her children's stories: the secret wish that she would never have to leave the spirit-places of childhood and join the adult ranks of skeptics and cynics who delighted in throwing cold water on dreamers. Whatever it was, Beatrix was glad to admit to believing in fairies when she was a girl and to wishing that she could still believe—and sometimes pretending that she did—now that she was fully grown up.

And perhaps it was this that caused her to bend over and pick a primrose and hold it out to the girl. "Take this, too, then, if you're looking for fairies." And then, half to herself and half to the child, she recited,

> *"There came a lady from Fairy-land,*
> *Who carried a primrose in her hand.*
> *The green grass leapt after, wherever she trod,*
> *And daisies and buttercups danced on the sod."*

"I like that," Deirdre said, adding the primrose to her bouquet. "Daisies and buttercups really do dance. I've seen them." She paused. "Is it one of your stories?"

"Not yet," Beatrix replied sadly. She had written the rhyme for *Appley Dapply,* a book of illustrated nursery rhymes she had been working on when Norman died. The book might never be finished now, for she always thought of him when she read the rhymes and felt a deep, sad loneliness that kept her from working on the drawings. She often thought that Norman himself had had a child's imagination. He loved building dolls' houses for his nephews and nieces and putting on magic shows and dressing up as Father Christmas to hand out candy and gifts. "There came a lady from Fairy-land" was a rhyme he'd especially liked. If he were here just now, he and Deirdre would have been walking hand-in-hand through the garden, exchanging playful stories about the fairies they had seen or hoped to see. And perhaps she and Norman would have had their own children, and told them fairy stories every night before they went to sleep. A sharp pang of loss struck her, and she drew in her breath.

"Well, I think it should be in a book," said Deirdre in a decided tone. "And you should draw the Fairy Lady's picture. With a primrose in her hand."

"P'rhaps I will." Beatrix smiled. "Are you planning to look for fairies on May Eve? I understand that's the best time to see them."

The girl cocked her head to one side, as if she were not sure whether to take Beatrix into her confidence. "If you were hopin' to see fairies, where would *you* go?" she asked at last.

"I'd look for a place where there are lots of ferns and moss," Beatrix replied thoughtfully. "Oh, yes, and fairy rings—rings of fairy fungi, I mean. That's where the fairies are said to dance. Although I'd be very sure not to step into the ring, because—"

"I know why!" Deirdre said brandishing her bouquet. " 'Cause the fairies might carry you off! Or change you into one of them."

"Exactly," Beatrix said, very seriously. "So be careful where you put your feet. Of course, you're more likely to see fairy rings in autumn, but May Eve is certainly a magical time. You may see all sorts of things." She paused, thinking that perhaps it wasn't wise to encourage this child to go wandering through the woods at twilight—although she had certainly done just that, and as often as she could, when she was a girl on holiday. "If you're going on May Eve, will Caroline be with you?" she asked tentatively.

Deirdre nodded. "But we're going this afternoon, first. To Cuckoo Brow Wood, to find the best places to look. Jeremy Crosfield is going with us."

"Oh, well, then, that's all right," Beatrix said, feeling relieved. "I'm sure he can show you just the right places." She had met Jeremy in difficult circumstances, when he was accused by the previous head teacher at Sawrey School of stealing the School Roof Fund. Jeremy was her favorite amongst the village boys, in part because they shared an interest in drawing woodland creatures. Jeremy had shown her a place on Cunsey Beck where there were a great many frogs, and they had often gone there together when she was making the drawings for her frog book.

Deirdre looked down at the bunch of herbs and flowers in her hand. She hesitated, frowning, started to say something, and then stopped. At last she took a deep breath and blurted out, "Do you s'pose you could go with us on May Eve? You know all about fairies. We might have better luck if you're with us." She pursed her lips and frowned darkly. "But o' course, you'll have to cross your heart an' promise not to tell a single soul."

Beatrix felt, rightfully, that she had been paid an enormous compliment. She didn't want to impose herself on the children, but if they intended to tramp through the wilderness of Cuckoo Brow Wood at twilight, it would certainly be sensible if an adult went along—just in case. In case of what, she wasn't sure, but it did seem a good idea.

"Let's agree to this, shall we, Deirdre?" she said. "When you see Caroline and Jeremy today, ask them whether they would like me to come. If all three of you say yes—without reservation, mind—I should be glad to join your party."

"I'll ask 'em," Deirdre said with satisfaction. She bobbed a quick, old-fashioned curtsey. "Thank you, Miss Potter," she said, and was gone.

Beatrix, smiling to herself, was on her way back to the farmhouse when she caught a glimpse of a very large black cat, perched on the lowest limb of the ash tree. At first she thought it was Max, but knew immediately that couldn't be right. This black cat was twice the size of Max. His black fur was shaggy and unkempt and he had a long, rumpled black tail, where Max had no tail at all.

"Good morning, miss," said the cat. He stood up to stretch his forelegs and arch his back.

Beatrix stared. This was no ordinary cat. He was so large and so black that she almost thought he must be a panther, escaped from a traveling circus.

"My goodness gracious," she said, and discovered that she was holding her breath. She let it out. "Who are you?"

"I am the Cat Who Walks by Himself," said the cat, who had once lived with a Yorkshire schoolmaster who enjoyed reading Kipling's *Just So Stories* aloud to the children. The cat (previously called by the undistinguished name of Puss) was deeply impressed by the last two sentences of Mr. Kipling's story about a cat: "When the moon gets up and night comes, he is the Cat that walks by himself, and all places are alike to him. Then he goes out to the Wet Wild Woods or up the Wet Wild Trees or on the Wet Wild Roofs, waving his wild tail and walking by his wild lone." The cat liked this so much that he memorized it and whispered it over and over to himself. And then he adopted the Cat's name, feeling that it conferred upon him a great distinction and individuality.

After the schoolmaster died, the Cat (who had forgotten that he was ever called Puss) took to the open road, traveling here and there and everywhere but never lingering for very long, for all places were alike to him. That's what Mr. Kipling's Cat had said, and that's what the Cat said, whenever he thought of it: *I am the Cat who walks by himself, and all places are alike to me.* He had happened on Ridley Rattail's advertisement as he came along the road, and thought he would just take the ferry across the lake to Hill Top Farm and make an application for Miss Potter's position. All places were alike to him, it was true, but he had never visited Sawrey, and places with rats held a special attraction.

"As an exceedingly large fellow," he went on, with ill-concealed pride, "I am able to accommodate any number of exceedingly large rats. If you are Miss Potter, I am pleased to offer you my services." He lifted up one forepaw and extended his claws, flexing them expertly. "I am accustomed to making my living with these." He bared his needle-sharp teeth. "And these." He grinned in a good-natured, ingratiating way. "You will not find a more efficient ratter than myself anywhere in the Land between the Lakes. Or anywhere in the wide, wild, wicked world beyond, for that matter." His grin widened and became rather more ominous. "I have, you see, an insatiable appetite for rats. I am not ashamed to own that I take a very great pleasure in killing as many as possible." And at the thought of rats, he began to purr, a deep, rumbling purr that rattled the twigs on the tree.

Beatrix was reminded of Alice's Cheshire cat and half expected the animal to begin disappearing, leaving his toothy grin behind. To forestall this, she spoke out loud.

"Since you are here, you might as well make yourself at home." She pointed. "The barn is that direction. I'm sure you'll find the situation to your liking. We presently have five other cats, but there are more than enough rats to go around."

"Thank you," said the cat, and leapt gracefully out of the tree, landing as lightly as a feather in the green grass beneath. But he didn't go to the barn. Instead, he followed Beatrix right up to Hill Top's front door.

She turned. "And just where do you think you're going?" she demanded, putting her hands on her hips and standing in front of the door. "I don't want a housecat. I am not a cat person. The barn is down the hill. You'll catch all the rats you want there."

"But I am not a barn cat," said the cat firmly. *"I am the Cat Who Walks by Himself, and barns do not appeal to me. Your advertisement says that your rats live in your attic. If I am to exterminate the brutes—exterminate ALL of them—I must work in the attic, too. And that's all there is to say about that."* He pushed past Beatrix and through the door, brushing her skirt with his long black tail.

"What cheek!" Beatrix exclaimed, reaching in vexation for the broom. "To the barn, puss!"

The cat turned, amused. *"There, there, Miss Potter,"* he said in a soothing tone. *"Just sit down and enjoy a nice cup of tea, and allow me to take care of those ugly rats for you."* He leapt up the stairs to the landing, where he paused and added, over his shoulder, *"I prefer a saucer of fresh cream for breakfast, if you don't mind, and perhaps a bit of cooked vegetable, egg, and cake. A cat cannot live on rats alone."* And then he leapt up the second flight, taking the stairs two at a time—obviously an athletic creature.

"I dislike unbiddable cats," Beatrix muttered, now feeling very vexed. But she could already hear the heavy tread on the floor above, and regardless of how she felt about having a cat in the house, especially a very large cat who refused to take instructions, it was indisputably true that there were rats in the house. Perhaps one large cat in the attic would do the work faster than several cats in the barn.

But just one cat in the attic, she promised herself firmly, as she went to upstairs to get ready for the afternoon reception at Raven Hall. Only one. And anyway, she reflected, as she took out her best blouse and brushed her best hat, with that gigantic beast prowling around up there, there wouldn't be room for another.

16

Evicted!

Whilst Miss Potter was in the garden discussing fairies with Deirdre, Ridley Rattail was handed an ultimatum.

His Saturday morning had begun like any other since the explosion of the rat population in the Hill Top attic. He had appeared at the crowded breakfast table only long enough to pour a cup of coffee, snatch a plate of bacon and scrambled eggs from the sideboard, and say a dark and decisive "No!" when asked to join the others in morning games. He turned his back on the company and retreated with his meal to his room, shaking his head and muttering severely, *"Too many rats. Too many rats!"* As was his habit following his breakfast, he read the newspaper from back to front, then (being a compulsively tidy fellow) swept his floor, made his bed, and straightened his bureau drawers, all the while trying to ignore the noise of rats running up and down the hallway outside his door.

Ridley was wondering whether his shoes needed a polish or whether the task could be put off for another day when suddenly his door flew open and there was Rosabelle, her broom and dustpan in her paws, her whiskers all a-twitter.

"Oh, Ridley!" she cried. *"There has been another horror! Another horror!"*

"Oh, dear," murmured Ridley, and sat down on his bed with a shoe in each hand. He did not, after all, think a polish was required today. He bent over to put them on, with difficulty, for he had grown very stout.

"Six rats were cornered in the corn bin, Ridley! It was a massacre." Rosabelle dropped her broom and used the tip of her long white tail to wipe her eyes. *"The killers were two yellow cats—mercenaries, disgraceful-looking creatures, with torn ears and scruffy fur. They killed all six, every one, and then they cut off the tails and nailed them to the barn door! Oh, horrible, horrible!"*

Ridley straightened up. *"Quite,"* he agreed, pleasurably imagining the six rat tails nailed to the barn door. The cats did not sound like village cats. They must have come in response to his advertisement. *"And which rats were these?"* he asked hopefully.

"They were Hawkshead rats, friends of Rollo. Ridley, you must do something!"

"What would you have me do, Rosabelle?" Ridley asked, managing not to smile. *"To be quite blunt about it, there are far too many rats in this attic, and most of them are rats of the worse sort. The loss of a few—or a many—is hardly to be mourned."* He rose and went to brush his whiskers, admiring his reflection in the scrap of a mirror that hung over his bureau.

"But they are our guests, Ridley!" Rosabelle protested, with a despairing wail. *"Like them or not, surely you can't stand idly by and see them massacred! Why, when word of this gets out, Hill*

Top's reputation for hospitality will be ruined! I shall never be able to hold up my head in rat society again!"

"I think, Rosabelle," Ridley said severely, *"that you had far better worry about Hill Top's reputation as a place of comfort and high moral tone. Have you visited the east end of the attic lately? Why, it is nothing but a den of corruption! A cesspool of licentiousness and depravity! Gambling, dancing, billiards, bawdy song, and beer—all out in plain sight for the youngsters to see and emulate. And all on account of your sister's husband, who was the first to invite these ruffians and rowdies into our quiet attic."*

"You leave Bluebell out of this," Rosabelle said, stamping her foot angrily. *"It's not her fault. You are the one to blame, Ridley. You should have stopped Rollo from inviting all those horrid creatures. You should be doing something now!"*

"As to that," Ridley replied loftily, *"I am doing something. I am doing something right this very minute."* He took his pocket watch from the bowl on top of the bureau, wound it, held it to his ear to make sure it was ticking, and put it into his watch pocket. *"I am advertising."*

Rosabelle stared at him, uncomprehending. *"You are . . . advertising?"*

"Exactly." Ridley looped his watch fob across his waistcoat. *"I have posted several advertisements on the east side of the lake. For cats."*

"For CATS!" Rosabelle shrilled hysterically. *"Ridley Rattail, have you lost your mind? Oh, I cannot believe it. I simply cannot believe it. What were you THINKING?"* And with that, she grabbed her ears and began running in mad circles, shrieking.

Ridley, who fancied himself a reasonable man and a philosopher, ignored her histrionics. *"I have advertised for cats to rid us of these rats,"* he said calmly. *"What's more, I imagine that the cats who killed the rats in the corn bin came to Hill Top in response to my advertisement. If that is the case, I am glad to take the credit."*

"But what's to keep the cats from killing US?" Rosabelle cried. *"You and me, Ridley. And my sister and her children? Her four little innocent children. Have you thought of that, Ridley? Have you thought of THAT?"*

"Of course I have," Ridley said in a reassuring tone. *"I have thought it all out, every step of the way. I shall simply explain that you and I are the original occupants of this attic, and that we— and our personally invited guests, Bluebell and her children—are to be let strictly alone."*

"Oh, you shall, shall you?" Rosabelle replied with a mocking scorn. *"And whatever makes you think they will listen? Ridley, you are a fool. A half-wit, a dunce, a dolt, a NINCOMPOOP."* The more names she thought of to call him, the angrier she became. *"An imbecile, a simpleton, an IGNORAMUS!"* By the time she reached this point in her tirade, she had worked herself into such a remarkable passion that she began to beat poor Ridley about the head with her broom and dustpan. *"A dimwit, a BLOCKHEAD, a BOOBY!"*

Ridley put up his arms to fend off her blows, but she managed to land one so squarely on his nose that he saw stars and was required to sit down on the floor. He was trying to find the words to tell her that she was being appallingly unkind and ungenerous, when she suddenly uttered the most unkind, most ungenerous words she could have said.

"And what's more, Ridley Rattail, you are no longer welcome here. I want you packed up and out within the hour."

Ridley stared at her, uncomprehending. *"Packed? Out? You can't be serious, Rosabelle!"*

"Oh, can't I?" Rosabelle asked in a steely voice, narrowing her eyes to ratty slits. *"I have reached the end of my patience. Ridley, you are evicted."*

Ridley's heart plummeted down to his toes. *"Evicted! But I have nowhere to go!"*

"That is really too bad," Rosabelle replied unfeelingly. *"But it makes no difference to me. You are a comfortable fellow in many respects, Ridley, but you have lately become so surly and selfish that no one can bear to be around you. I have defended you to the others over and over, but now I have reached the end of my rope. Advertising for cats is the last straw, the very last. I shall thank you to leave. Within the hour, do you hear?"*

And with that, she aimed one more thwack with her broom at Ridley and marched out, slamming the door so hard that the picture of Ridley's mother fell off the wall and smashed onto the floor with the sound of breaking glass.

For a long time, Ridley sat staring blankly into space, his brain in a fog, his thoughts in a complete muddle. And then, as he gradually began to comprehend the awfulness of his situation—no more warm, cozy bed, no comfortable apartment nor cheering meals, no companionable conversations with Rosabelle—he began to feel very sorry for himself. Rosabelle had no idea how hard he had worked to rid the attic of their unruly guests. She didn't appreciate—but how could she? for she was merely a female—how extraordinarily difficult it was to be a male rat. She didn't comprehend the burdens he had borne on her behalf, the terrible travail, the enormous effort.

And then, thinking how put-upon he was, and how little appreciated and loved—he, the most mannerly and affable and wittiest of rats—Ridley began to sniffle, and then to whimper and sob, until finally he fell prostrate on the floor and wept for a long time.

But at last he stood, wiped his eyes, and took out his watch. Within the hour, Rosabelle had said, and Ridley was nothing if not punctual. Sadly, his shoulders bowed and his head bent, he shuffled to the closet, hauled out a portmanteau, and began to empty his bureau drawers of their contents. When he had done, he picked up the picture of his mother, brushed off the broken glass, and put it on top of his shirts. He looked disconsolately around the room, with its comfortable furnishings: his loyal bed, his devoted chair, his willing footstool beside the fender, his smiling and friendly fire. The two of them—he and this dear little room—had been happy together, but that was all over now. He took out his pocket handkerchief and blew his nose. Over now, forever.

Ridley's portmanteau, fully packed, was so large and so heavy that he had to drag it down the stairs. Once in the kitchen, he saw a toy wheelbarrow filled with tiny seashells, sitting beside the geraniums on Miss Potter's kitchen windowsill—just the thing to manage his heavy load. He dumped the shells on the sill, heaved his portmanteau into the barrow, and wheeled it out the door. Then it occurred to him that he had no idea where in the world he was going. He pushed the stolen barrow under the lilac bush, sat down beside it, and tried to think.

Should he move to the Tower Bank Arms, just down the hill, where there was always a great deal of food, but where (it was rumored) the proprietor set wicked traps to catch unwary rats?

Or to Buckle Yeat Cottage, which had a delightful garden but a dark, cramped attic and a miserly pantry that was locked up every night?

Or to Farmer Potatoes' barn, which was roomy and dry and within easy walking distance of Miss Barwick's Anvil Cottage Bakery?

He had just decided on Farmer Potatoes' barn and was getting up to push the barrow in that direction, when he heard Miss Potter, speaking in an unusually sharp, scolding tone. He made himself as small as he could amongst the leaves, then peeped out to see what was going on. As he did so, a black cat walked past.

Ridley's eyes widened in astonished horror, for he had never seen such an ugly beast. The cat was the size of a dog—no, the size of a tiger!—with muscular shoulders, sinewy legs, sharp yellow fangs, and scimitar-like claws. He was informing Miss Potter, in a very firm tone, that he was not a barn cat.

"I am the Cat Who Walks by Himself," said the cat, *"and barns do not appeal to me. Your advertisement says that your rats live in your attic. If I am to exterminate the brutes—exterminate ALL of them—I must work in the attic, too. And that's all there is to say about that."* And then he pushed past Miss Potter and into the house.

Panic, like a snake, wrapped its chill, scaly self around Ridley's neck, clutching him so hard that he felt he would suffocate. His advertisement had summoned a monstrosity, a monster, a brute, a basilisk! And what was just as bad as the gorgon's size and ugliness was his obstinate, unbiddable nature, for Ridley himself had just heard, with his very own ears, the insolent Cat refuse to take orders—and from Miss Potter. Miss Potter herself!

Ridley's heart failed him as he realized the enormity of what he had so innocently and naively and hopefully done. He might, as he had assured Rosabelle, have been able to reason with the yellow cats, and persuade them to ignore himself and Rosabelle and a few others in return for easy access to the rowdies and perhaps a special tribute, such as ale from the Tower Bank Arms or sticky buns from Miss Barwick's bakery. But if such a firm and forceful person as

Miss Potter failed in her efforts to direct the Cat Who Walks by Himself, it was appallingly evident that nothing Ridley could say would have any effect whatsoever.

And then poor Ridley thought ahead to what now seemed to be the inevitable end of this terrible misadventure. This devil of a cat would establish himself in the attic and rapidly—in little more than a day or two, Ridley was sure—eliminate all of the rowdies and ruffians, even those who were brave enough to stand up against him. It would do them no good, of course, for no rat, no six rats or a dozen rats, not even a hundred rats together, could fight off such a monster. They were doomed, every single rat who lived in the Hill Top attic. And that included Rosabelle and her sister and all Rosabelle's little nieces and nephews. They would be utterly defenseless against the Cat.

Ridley closed his eyes and moaned softly, imagining Rosabelle in the clutches of that dreadful demon, her beautiful gray fur tattered and torn, her generous heart's red blood spilled all over the floor. Rosabelle, who had welcomed him in his hour of need. Dear Rosabelle, she of the unselfish spirit and sympathetic soul, whose hospitality he had so cruelly abused.

What could he do to save her? What could he do to redeem himself?

But the answer, Ridley knew to his great shame, was *nothing.* Some, like St. George, might be so brave that they would fling themselves against a fire-breathing dragon and fight to the death. Others, like Napoleon, might be so powerful and charismatic that they could summon an entire army and annihilate the fiend. And still others, like Merlin the Magician, might be so clever that they could outwit any foe.

But cleverness had already got him into this fix, and Ridley knew very well that he was neither courageous nor charismatic. Not to put too fine a point on it, he was nothing but a stout, slow-witted middle-aged rat who liked his comforts, a rat without a valiant bone in his body or an heroic whisker on his face. He was a duffer. He was an awful muff. He was a coward.

Ridley bowed his head, while the ignominy of the word— the disgrace, dishonor, disrepute, and discredit of it—washed over him like a flood of filthy water.

Coward.

17

The Professor Makes a Recommendation

At the same moment that Ridley was confronting his cowardice, Bosworth Badger was surveying his surroundings with a great deal of understandable pride.

The badger had always thought that the library was quite the nicest room in The Brockery. He loved the family portraits that hung on the walls, the comfortable leather chairs on either side of the fireplace, and the heavy oak table he used as a desk, where his pencils were laid out in a careful row, and his knife for sharpening the pencils, and his quill pens and inkpot and blotting paper, all very helpful to a badger who enjoys his work as an historian. The fire was especially cheering on damp mornings—and this Saturday morning was decidedly damp, as the badger had noticed when he put his head out the front door to sample the weather.

Bosworth, however, had no business that required him to be out and about in the wet, and indoors and underground, the weather was as it always was: perfectly perfect. He'd had a letter recently from a badger cousin who lived in the Wild Wood to the south, asserting that underground life was the very best life to be had: "No builders, no tradesmen, no remarks passed on you by fellows looking over your wall, and, above all, no *weather*." Bosworth found himself in full agreement with his cousin's remark. A drizzly morning was exactly the right sort of morning to spend underground, toasting his toes at the crackling fire and looking through the *History*, as he had promised Rascal.

Each volume of the *History* was indexed, so it wasn't difficult to find the most recent mention of Fern Vale Village, recorded by his grandfather (Bosworth Badger XV) some forty years previously. The badger lit his pipe and settled down in front of the fire to read his grandfather's entry, and to trace the story of Fern Vale Village recorded in earlier entries. He was so deeply engrossed in his reading that he scarcely heard the clang of the brass bell that hung beside The Brockery's front door—until, that is, it was rung again, and yet again.

He cocked his head. The bell had been rung with an unusual insistence, as if the animal who rang—a peremptory sort of creature—meant it to be answered without delay. The third peal had scarcely died away before it was followed by a fourth, even louder and more insistent.

Bosworth got to his feet, opened the library door, and looked up and down the hall. Seeing no one, he called out loudly, *"Flotsam, Jetsam! Will someone please answer the doorbell before that rude fellow rings it off the wall?"*

There was no reply to his call. Flotsam and Jetsam were the rabbit twins whose job it was to answer the doorbell, ask guests to sign the register, and settle them in their lodgings, although it seemed to Bosworth that the girls were always off doing the laundry or having a bit of a sit-down and a chat when they were wanted.

So when the bell clanged for what must have been the fifth time, Bosworth muttered, *"Oh, bother, I'll answer it my-self,"* and stumped off down the hallway. He flung open the door and was about to demand, *"What's all the hurry, then?"* when he saw that the peremptory person who was ringing the bell was a dear friend of his. He was clearly very wet and was scowling even more sternly than usual.

And then Bosworth remembered who had promised to drop in that morning, and felt guilty for having forgotten all about it.

"Oh, it's you," he said in a careless sort of way, as if he hadn't forgotten after all. *"Do come in and dry off, old chap. It's very drizzly outside."*

"Drizzly indeed," said his caller, *"especially at tree-top level, where the clouds all seem tooo be huddled tooogether. My apartment was quite damp this morning. And I have been standing here, ringing and ringing, and getting damper by the moment."*

Bosworth might have pointed out that if his guest lived underground, clouds at tree-top level would not trouble him, and he could visit many of his friends without getting out into the weather. But the Badgers' Sixth Rule of Thumb forbade him from criticizing other animals' living arrangements, how-ever unreasonable they might be, so he held his tongue.

His caller stepped through the door and onto Bosworth's cocoa-fiber mat, where he raised his wings and flapped them, shaking raindrops in all directions and drenching Bosworth quite thoroughly. *"I should certainly be glad of a cup of tea. Hot, if yooou please, Badger. And one of Parsley's scones would goo down nicely."*

"A cup of tea you shall have, old chap," Bosworth returned cordially, taking out his handkerchief and mopping his face. He clapped his paws and roared, *"Flotsam! Jetsam! Tea and scones in the library, please, chop-chop!"*

It was always an honor when the Professor dropped in for a visit—for it was indeed he who was dripping onto the badger's welcome mat: Professor Galileo Newton Owl, D.Phil., the oldest, largest, and most important tawny owl in the Land between the Lakes. The Professor had gained wide recognition for his studies in celestial mechanics and astronomical navigation, and could be found from midnight to dawn in the celestial observatory at the top of his beech-tree home in Cuckoo Brow Wood. But his meticulous scholarship in applied natural history was also well regarded. He carried out these investigations on the wing, as it were, from dusk to midnight, and often insisted that two or three of his tastier research subjects come home with him for dinner, for he was also something of a gourmet.

Between his evening researches and his intimate relations with the District's smaller residents, the Professor usually knew everything that was going on in the Land between the Lakes, and naturally felt a certain amount of responsibility for it. He had, however, been away for several days, attending an academic conference, and had come to catch up on the news. So when the owl was settled in front of the fire with a woolen shawl over his damp feathers and a hot cup of tea and plate of Parsley's raisin scones beside him, the badger gave him a full report, including what he had heard about the rats at Hill Top Farm and Jeremy Crosfield's pending apprenticeship. He concluded by mentioning the children's intention to look for the fairy village that afternoon.

The Professor shook his head. *"I gooo away for a few days, and when I return, what dooo I find? The village about tooo be overrun by unruly rats, and a promising lad forced tooo leave off his studies. I am most troubled by Jeremy's situation, Bosworth. I admire the boy. I wish I could help him, but I confess I cannot think how."*

Bosworth could see the gloom, like a dark cloud, settle over his friend. The Professor liked to think that everything that happened in the Land between the Lakes was his own personal affair, and hated nothing worse than feeling he could not control it.

The owl sighed again. Bosworth, who felt his friend's sense of impotence as he might feel his own, tried to think whether there was anything at all that the Professor might be able to do, any task he might be encouraged to undertake which would restore his dignity and self-esteem.

"I expect you could help with the rat problem at Hill Top," he ventured at last. *"I believe you have a taste for rats, do you not?"*

"I certainly enjoy an individual rat or twooo, properly prepared and served," admitted the Professor. *"In fact, I have a recipe for fricasseed rat that is quite delicious. But I dooo not fancy rats by the dozen, as if they were oysters."* He shuddered. *"I recommend that Miss Potter obtain the services of a cat. I shall inquire amongst a few of my friends."* He took a notebook and pencil out of his pocket and jotted down a few words, brightening at the thought of being able to do something helpful. But he lapsed into gloom again, muttering, *"It's toooo bad that there's nothing tooo be done for the boy."*

A long silence followed, during which Bosworth puffed on his pipe and the owl stared into the fire. Finally, Bosworth suggested, in a tentative sort of way, *"We might at least give the children a hand with their fairy project."*

"Fairies!" the owl hooted scornfully. *"The children are no doubt picturing those dainty, wispy-winged creatures whooo are all the rage on the stage and in children's books. It's quite clear that the creators of those silly fictional creatures have never met a real fairy."* He gave a disgusted shake of his wings. *"There's nothing dainty about our local Oak Folk. They are elves, although this particular branch of the family got itself mixed up with dwarfs a*

century or so back, no one is certain quite how, since the Fern Vale family tree is extraordinarily complicated, so that they are more properly called dwelves. A dwelf is smaller than a dwarf but larger than an elf, and his features are somewhat dwarfish. He has a tip-tilted nose, green eyes, six fingers on each hand, and a gingery beard (elves, of course, don't have beards). However, like many of our native British elves, they are shape-shifters and can take whatever appearance they like. They are good-natured, but impish, rather like the hobthrushes. And they—"

"*Indeed,*" said Bosworth, since the Professor appeared to have launched into his lecturing mode. If unchecked, he was likely to go on for the remainder of the morning, pausing only now and then for breath. *"I was just reading what my grandfather and others wrote about their antics. Pranksters, these Oak Folk are. Stealing sheep and changing babies. And there's that business about the Raven Hall Luck, which the Big Folk have got completely upside down,"*

The real story of the Luck, according to Bosworth's grandfather, was very different from the popular version that was told with such enthusiasm around the village. The truth of the matter was that the Fern Vale dwelves out-and-out lied when they said that the goblet would bring good luck to the Kittredges. They had been outraged when old Mr. Kittredge built his Raven Hall on one of their magical sites. The goblet they gave to the dairymaid on the eve of the eldest son's wedding had conferred not a blessing, but a *curse.*

"*A curse,*" Bosworth repeated emphatically. *"The Oak Folk cursed the Kittredges, and the family remains cursed to this very day."*

"*Exactly,*" said the Professor. *"I'm not at all sure, then, that the children should be encouraged tooo look for the Oak Folk. However—"* He broke off with a thoughtful expression.

"*Yes?*" inquired the badger after a few moments.

The Professor pondered. *"On the other hand,"* he said after a time, then lapsed again into silence, broken once or twice by a yawn.

"If you have an idea," Bosworth said, beginning to be irritated, *"I do wish you would tell me what it is, Owl. I have not yet met the girl Deirdre, but Jeremy and Caroline are both worthy youngsters. If they would like to meet the Oak Folk—fairies, elves, dwelves, whatever they may be—I should like to help them."*

"Yes. Well, it would certainly be a pity for them tooo walk tooo the top of Cuckoo Brow Wooood and have nothing tooo show for their effort." Yawning so widely that he nearly dislocated his beak, the owl helped himself to a second cup of tea and another of Parsley's raisin scones.

Bosworth pulled on his pipe and blew a ring of smoke toward the ceiling. *"Then, Professor, what would you suggest?"*

The owl closed his eyes. *"Give me a moment tooo reflect,"* he murmured, *"and I shall make a recommendation."*

And for the next little bit, Bosworth smoked his pipe as the Professor reflected, until at last a wheezy snore revealed that the owl had fallen asleep, tea and scone untouched. Bosworth sighed, knowing that nothing would be gained by waking the fellow, who spent his nights out and about and needed a good nap during the daytime.

So the badger poked up the fire, poured himself another cup of tea, and went back to the *History* to read the curious story of the Fern Vale dwelves, a story (he suspected) that was mostly unknown to the Big Folk. Of course, that sort of thing wasn't at all unusual, for although the human residents of the Land between the Lakes thought they knew everything about their surroundings, and although scholarly books related the history, inventoried the animals and plants, and catalogued the folktales, people were aware of only a fraction of what went on around them. One was not criticizing when one said this; one was simply stating the fact. Humans, by and large, were ignorant of the mysteries of life and land.

At last, the Professor woke up from his nap, rubbed his eyes, and ruffled his feathers. *"Well, then,"* he said, with his customary authority. *"Where were we?"*

"You were about to make a recommendation," Bosworth replied. *"Regarding the children's expedition."*

"Ah, yes," said the Professor. *"So I was."*

And so he did.

18

The Village Goes to a Party

Saturday morning had been gray and gloomy, and the rest of the day continued in the same fashion. A gray blanket of mist hung over the meadows and forest, tattered veils of fog hugged the streams and low places, and even the spring blossoms—the marsh marigolds and wood violets and pasque flowers—had folded their petals and retired for the afternoon. But the lamps burned cheerfully in the houses and cottages and there was a great deal of unaccustomed bustle as people got ready to go to the Raven Hall reception, where they might finally lay eyes upon the mysterious Mrs. Kittredge.

At Belle Green, Mathilda Crook had second thoughts about her yellow frock when her husband George told her that she looked "just like a ray o' glisky sunshine." Feeling that the dress might be too bright on such a gloomy day, she took off the yellow and put on the navy. Then, when that seemed much too dark, she added a red silk scarf, red belt, and red hat, and went to make sure that George was getting his tie on straight. But George, who usually detested parties, had managed not only his tie but also his fingernails, and had already hitched up the farm cart and was waiting for her at the front gate.

"Navy's just t' thing," he said gruffly, as his wife got in, raising her umbrella against the mizzle. "Tha dust look nice, Tilda."

"Thanks," Mathilda said, very pleased. "Wonder what she'll be wearin'."

"Who?" George said, clucking to the pony.

"Why, t' witch, o' course," Mathilda said, and settled her skirts. "Doan't ferget we're to fetch Mrs. Lythecoe and Miss Barwick."

At Rose Cottage, Grace Lythecoe fed her canary, Caruso, put a saucer of milk on the back step in case Tabitha Twitchit happened by, and stirred the pot of soup—beans and a ham bone—on the back of the kitchen range. Then she went upstairs to dress in her very best Sunday suit, a pretty pale yellow with a handsome elbow-length cape, and pinned a yellow silk rose to her lapel. Back downstairs, she put on a gabardine duster, took her umbrella, then went out on the front step to look up Market Street in the direction of Belle Green.

Ah, yes, they were coming, the Crooks in their farm cart, looking very fine. And there was Sarah Barwick, locking the door of Anvil Cottage behind her and crossing the street.

Mrs. Lythecoe smiled. She had grown so accustomed to seeing Sarah Barwick in trousers that it was almost a shock to see her in a skirt. It was lovely, she thought, that the villagers were putting on their very best finery to welcome

Mrs. Kittredge into their midst. After all the major had been through in the war and after, he certainly needed their support and friendship. One hoped that the worst was behind him now, and that he and Mrs. Kittredge could settle down and have a family and be a part of the community.

Mrs. Lythecoe put up her umbrella and called to Sarah to join her under its shelter. It was beginning to rain.

Up Market Street, at Croft End, Hannah Braithwaite was admonishing her eldest daughter to watch the baby carefully, mind that the children stayed well away from the lamps, and keep little Jack from going into the garden and getting his feet wet.

Then she went to fuss with her hair (which always frizzed so in the damp) and make sure that her husband's boots were presentable. John, the village constable, had argued that his blue dress uniform with its splendid brass buttons would be just the thing to wear to the reception, but Hannah had stood her ground. John was now dressed in his black wedding suit and a high starched collar. He blushed when Hannah told him he looked "mortal handsome," and received her affectionate kiss with a shy pleasure.

"Haven't been at Raven Hall since t' servant girl drowned there," he said. He frowned. "I'll call that back. I was summonsed there when t' steward made off with t' silver. Great lot o' janglement o'er that business, there was, some sayin' one thing, some another. But the chap didn't profit, after all. Fell 'neath a lorry and was cut to shreds by t' wheels." His frown became a scowl. "Only bad luck at Raven Hall."

"Let's nae talk ill on such a grand day," begged Hannah, fastening the buttons on her blue bombazine, which she hadn't worn since her sister's wedding.

"Nae grand at all," her literal-minded husband objected, with a glance out the window. "Ower-kessen'd, it is. Gloomy as t' inside of a barn."

"Mappen it'll be grand at Raven Hall," Hannah replied in a comforting tone, and smoothed her skirt. "There's to be a gae lot o' sandwiches an' cake. An' champagne."

"There'd better be champagne," John said grimly, running a finger inside his collar. "I'd hate to've got trussed up like a roast goose fer cider."

Across the Kendal Road, in one of the Sunnyside Cottages, Margaret Nash and her sister Annie had brushed their hair until it shone and then topped it with their Sunday-best hats, both of wide-brimmed straw, Margaret's trimmed with lace and silk roses and Annie's with a red velvet bow. They were enjoying a cup of tea in the kitchen as they waited for Mrs. Holland. Had the weather been nice, the three of them would have walked to Raven Hall. But since it had turned off damp, they were riding with Frances and Lester Barrow, in their old victoria. The four ladies could stay dry under the folding hood, whilst Lester drove.

"I'm anxious to meet her," Annie said. "Mrs. Kittredge, I mean." She leaned forward. "But I must confess to being a little nervous at the prospect of seeing him. Do you remember when he went off to war?" She sighed tragically. "So handsome, he was. And now he has only one eye and one arm."

"Of course I remember," Margaret said. She had once been madly in love with Major Kittredge (as had every unmarried woman of any age in the entire area). She had been distressed when she'd heard of his wounds and hoped very much that the new Mrs. Kittredge would make him happy. She frowned. "Where are your gloves, Annie?"

"I have to look for them," Annie said distractedly. She shook her head. "So much misfortune at Raven Hall. One would almost think the place was cursed."

"Cursed!" Margaret scoffed. "You've forgotten about the Raven Hall Luck." There was a knock at the front door, and Margaret rose to gather up the cups. "Let Mrs. Holland in, will you? And do find your gloves, Annie. You can't go without them, and we don't want to be late."

At Tower Bank House, Miles Woodcock opened the front door to find Will Heelis, holding his hat in his hand.

"Just about ready?" Will asked.

"Dimity's putting on her best," Miles said, stepping back to admit Will, who was driving to Raven Hall with them. "I never saw her make such a fuss about a tea party."

"And with good reason," his sister said in a reproachful tone, coming down the stairs. "It's a very important social occasion, and everyone will be there." She was wearing a champagne-colored silk dress with a lace yoke and high lace collar, the gored skirt falling neatly over her hips, the hem just brushing the instep of her shoes. Her wide-brimmed hat was heaped with ivory flowers and draped with tulle.

Will glanced past Miles, his face lighting. "Hello, Dimity," he said shyly. "What a pretty frock you're wearing this afternoon."

Dimity lowered her head, and Miles saw that she was blushing. "Thank you, Will," she said, pulling on her gloves. "Shall we wait in the library while Miles dresses? Miss Potter will be joining us, as well."

"I'll go and change, then," Miles said. "Shan't be a minute." But he was in no great hurry as he went up the stairs, leaving the two alone. There was plenty of time before the reception, and he was glad to give Will and Dimity a little time in private.

Although his sister was now at the age when she was in danger of being thought a spinster, Dimity still preserved an attractive and youthful appearance, with ivory skin, large brown eyes, and smooth brown hair. Miles had very much enjoyed their life together for the past twelve or so years, for his sister was not only a pleasant but a sensible companion, with vast resources of goodwill and energy. She managed the Tower Bank household with the same care and attention that she applied to her work in the parish, where she was praised far and wide as an indispensable volunteer. Dimity might occasionally seem a bit dithery, but she hid a great common sense behind that sometimes vague exterior.

Miles took off his shirt and put on a freshly laundered one, adding cuff links, collar stays, and tie. For some months, he had thought that it wasn't fair to his sister to monopolize her life as he did. Although Dim had fended off several possible suitors in the past few years, he was sure that she would prefer a loving husband and a household of her own to life with a stodgy old brother. What's more, his service as Justice of the Peace took him away at odd hours and brought a parade of strangers into the house. Even when he was at home, he was generally reading or attending to business. And whilst Dim brought a sister's sweetness and loving concern into his life and was an elegant hostess besides, he supposed he could manage without her.

Miles put on his waistcoat, buttoned it, and added his fob watch and chain. Of course, he knew that Dim had once had her heart set on Kittredge, but the major's marriage had put that entirely out of the picture, and Dimity was far too sensible to spend any time grieving about the past. It was high time that serious thought be given to her future, and

Miles had begun to do just that. His friend Will Heelis would without a doubt make Dimity a fine husband, far more suitable than Kittredge. Will was a partner in a successful law firm, so there was no question about his being able to support a wife. A bachelor, he lived with his two spinster cousins, Cousin Fanana and Cousin Emily Jane, at Sandground, in Hawkshead, where the Heelis family—a large, gregarious lot—often gathered for dinners, picnics, and family parties. Will was an avid sportsman, and he and Miles often enjoyed golf, tennis, bowling, and shooting together— an asset, as Miles was comfortably aware. Dimity certainly would not consider marrying a man her brother disliked.

Miles shrugged into his jacket and straightened its lapels, reflecting happily that there could never be any question about Will's judgment, his amiability, or the steadiness of his temper. Wherever Heelis was asked to deal with matters of property, estates, or family legal questions, there was no one more admired. He was attractive, too, which no doubt mattered to Dimity, as it would to any woman: tall and lean, he had a pleasant face with strong, regular features and his brown hair fell across his forehead in a boyish shock. The handsomest bachelor in the district, some called him, and wondered aloud why he had not married.

The answer, Miles knew, was Will's shyness in the company of ladies. Dimity should have to encourage him, something she seemed reluctant to do. Oh, she was friendly enough—the two were on first-name terms now, which was definitely a step forward. But she was not . . . well, flirtatious. That is, Miles thought regretfully, she did not look at Will with the kind of affectionate regard that would fire a fellow's romantic interest—at least, not yet. He should have to have a talk with her, and soon. She would undoubtedly be glad that her brother was taking an active interest in her future.

Miles inspected his reflection in the mirror, frowning a little. He was eager to renew his acquaintance with Major Kittredge and find out just what the man intended to do with his property. He was also increasingly curious about Mrs. Kittredge, and of course about Augustus Richardson. After Miss Potter had given him the name of the syndicate and the fellow's calling card—it had been a deuced lucky chance that she had overheard the conversation—he had sent off several letters to London bankers and brokers whom he knew, requesting information about Richardson and the Sandiford Syndicate. With luck, there might be a response by mid-week.

He smoothed his hair. He would try to find a moment, privately, to tell Heelis what Miss Potter had overheard. But he didn't want to spoil the afternoon for Dimity. She was looking quite lovely in that party dress of hers, and he intended to give Will every opportunity to appreciate her charms.

Back downstairs, Miles was glad to see that Miss Potter had joined them. She, too, was smartly dressed for the occasion, in a gray velvet-trimmed suit and blue and gray striped blouse, with a bunch of blue violets in her lapel and blue silk flowers on her gray straw hat. Miles smiled as he welcomed her, noticing that the violets were very nearly the color of her eyes, and that her hair curled quite becomingly around her face. Inviting her to go with them had been quite a clever idea, if he did say so himself. He would serve as her escort, which meant that Dimity and Will would necessarily find themselves a couple.

"Are we ready, then?" he asked warmly, extending his arm to Miss Potter. "All aboard for Raven Hall." He smiled down at her. "And I'll remember my promise not to drive too fast—not above ten miles an hour."

"I'm sure the village chickens will thank you with all their hearts," Miss Potter murmured, taking his arm and smiling up at him. "As will the flowers on our hats."

Miles felt himself unaccountably warmed by that smile.

19

Raven Hall

It was not possible to ride to Raven Hall in Captain Woodcock's Rolls-Royce without attracting a great deal of attention. Even though the captain held the speed to eight miles an hour, the motor car bounced along the narrow road with a fearful clatter that sent cats and dogs and chickens flying in panic and excited the boys, who ran alongside, waving their caps and screaming. Beatrix had expected that she and Dimity would be seated in the rear, but to her surprise, Captain Woodcock had insisted that she ride beside him, in the front passenger seat, leaving Dimity and Mr. Heelis to take their places behind. There was rather more of a breeze than she liked—she had to hold her hat on with one hand to keep it from being blown off—but she had to admit to a certain excitement, and perhaps even a thrill or two, as the motor car rattled along the road through Far Sawrey and then turned up the lane that zigged and zagged all the way to the top of

Claife Heights, where the fir trees thinned and Beatrix saw
Raven Hall, close up, for the first time.

The large house, constructed of gray stone and roofed with
a darker gray slate, was a Victorian version of a medieval castle, complete with battlements and crow-stepped gables and
turrets wearing conical candle-snuffer caps. Located at the
crest of the Heights, Raven Hall looked out over Lake Windermere to the east, with Cuckoo Brow Wood, like a rusty
green cloak, pulled up around its shoulders on north, west,
and south. Beatrix knew that the old house was supposed to
be a fine example of baronial Gothic, but she couldn't help
feeling that there was something sinister about it—not just
dark and gloomy, but . . . wrong, somehow. Perhaps it was
in the proportions, which seemed not quite right, or in
balance of gable and turret.

"No wonder the housekeeper went mad and the poor servant drowned herself," Dimity said, getting out of the car.
She stared up at the house towering over them. "I'm sure I'd
do both, if I had all those rooms to look after."

"Come, now, Dim," her brother said with a laugh. "Raven
Hall isn't nearly as grandiose as Wray Castle."

"I'd go even madder at Wray," Dimity retorted, adding
gaily, "Thank goodness I'm in no danger of being responsible for the housekeeping at either place."

Wray Castle was another baronial residence only two
miles or so up the lake, but larger and grander—and much
uglier—than Raven Hall. Beatrix joined the others in their
laughter but did not mention that her father and mother
had rented the castle for a two-month holiday when she was
sixteen. She could not think of a good word to say about the
place, which was cold and gloomy and abominably uncomfortable. The owner's wife had refused to live in the Gothic
horror under any circumstance and the architect had drunk

himself to death before the thing was finished. When the Potters rented it, Wray Castle had been empty for some time—and ought to stay that way, Beatrix thought.

"Come, Miss Potter," Captain Woodcock said, holding out his arm with a charming smile. "We'll go in together, shall we?"

A little puzzled by the captain's attentions but not wanting to offend by refusing, Beatrix took his arm and they walked through the stone portico and up the wide stone stairs to the front door, where they were shown up an ornate staircase and into an imposing baronial hall. The room, which was already quite crowded with guests, was brilliantly lighted by hundreds of wax tapers in glittering crystal chandeliers and wall sconces, illuminating a long refreshment table spread with a damask cloth and laden with an enormous quantity of cold chicken, salmon, lobster, game pie, sandwiches, and cakes of all kinds, including Sarah Barwick's beautiful Tipsy Cake. Frock-coated servants with silver trays circulated through the crowd, offering wine and champagne, and in the minstrels' gallery, high up the wall at the far end of the long room, a quartet of formally dressed musicians—two violins, a flute, and a cello—played a Bach fugue, the strains of which were almost drowned out by the voices of guests. A fire blazed in a huge stone fireplace on one wall of the room, and the opposite wall was opened out by a series of large bay windows furnished with velvet cushions, giving a magnificent view of the lake over the trees that spilled down the steep slope below.

Beatrix was not by nature an eager party-goer, and avoided large gatherings whenever possible. Required to attend a social event, she much preferred to make her entrance unnoticed and find a quiet corner from which she could watch the guests. She liked to study strange faces, to try to

decide what sort of person was hidden behind his or her party
finery and to make up amusing and sometimes mocking stories about them—to herself, of course.

This afternoon, though, she found that standing on the
sidelines was not possible, for Captain Woodcock would not
allow it. She tried to extricate her gloved hand from his elbow
as they walked through the room, only to find it gripped
tighter.

He leaned close to her with a teasing smile and whispered
in her ear, "Come now, Miss Potter. Let's relax and enjoy
ourselves, shall we?" He turned her so that they were facing
a tall oak cabinet, elaborately carved, which held only a single object, a large glass goblet colored in gilt, red, blue, and
green, with traceries of leaves and flowers etched in gold. "If
nothing else," he added, "we can admire the Luck of Raven
Hall." He gestured grandly. "There it is, in all its antique
glory. We are supposed to find it astonishingly beautiful,
I'm told."

"How . . . interesting," Beatrix mused. She had seen a
great deal of art glass in various museums and exhibits,
some of which she had admired. She did not admire this.

"Yes. Raven Hall's claim to fame and fortune. Good fortune, that is." The captain chuckled. "I can see that you're
not impressed, though."

"Fairies cannot be expected to have studied the design
and manufacture of art glass," Beatrix said dryly. "One must
surely take that into account, mustn't one?"

"You do have a discriminating eye, Miss Potter," said the
captain, laughing. "But no doubt half the people here have
come to ogle it—and Mrs. Kittredge."

The captain wore a smile but Beatrix felt a certain ten-
sion in him, the reason for which was revealed in his next
words, spoken in a lower tone. "Perhaps you can point out

Mr. Richardson, the man who intends to build villas along the lakeshore."

Ah, yes, those horrid villas, Beatrix thought. She turned to look around the room, searching for Mr. Richardson. After a moment, she caught a glimpse of him standing beside the refreshment table. He was wearing a pale blue frock coat and a ruffled shirt. Now that he was hatless, she could see that he was nearly bald and even more toadlike than she remembered. She had just pointed him out to the captain when they was interrupted by a tall, dark man, his right hand outstretched.

"There you are, Woodcock!" he exclaimed. "I was hoping you would be here. How good to see you. What's it been? Six years?"

The man must be their host, Beatrix decided, for the left sleeve of his coat was empty and pinned up, his right eye was hidden by a black patch, and the right side of his face, which had been seriously burned, was disfigured by a hideous scar. But he wore a welcoming smile, his voice was full and firm, and there was a certain upright dignity about him that inspired respect.

At the major's elbow stood the woman Beatrix had seen at the ferry landing. Her bright red tresses were piled on top of her head and her shoulders were bared by a low-cut gray silk dress that would have been more suitable for a London midnight soirée than a Saturday afternoon reception in the Lake District. Her lips and cheeks were brightly tinted and her eyes flashed. But now that Beatrix had a closer look, she saw that there was a very hard core of determination behind that decorative feminine façade. Mrs. Kittredge, she thought, was the sort of woman who would make up her mind what she wanted most, and then find a way to get it—whatever way might present itself, without any special regard to morality.

"Kittredge!" Captain Woodcock replied enthusiastically, pumping Major Kittredge's hand. "So good to see you, Major. And this must be the beautiful Mrs. Kittredge! Welcome to our village, my dear. We are glad for both of you, and wish you the very best." And with a gallant flourish that Beatrix thought rather overdone, Captain Woodcock bent to kiss the major's wife's hand.

"So nice to meet you, Captain," Mrs. Kittredge murmured, looking at him demurely from under her long, dark lashes. She turned to Beatrix. "And is this Mrs. Woodcock?"

Captain Woodcock's eyes met Beatrix's with a cheerful twinkle, and he shook his head. "Allow me to present my neighbor at Hill Top Farm, and quite a famous author, Miss Beatrix Potter."

"Miss Potter," said the major, bowing. "Oh, yes, indeed. I had heard that Hill Top has been purchased and is being restocked. We're delighted that you could join us this afternoon."

"An author!" Mrs. Kittredge exclaimed, raising her eyebrows. "And what sort of books do you write, Miss Potter? Do they sell well?"

Captain Woodcock took a step backward and even the major seemed to blink at that last remarkably ill-mannered question. Beatrix regarded her for a moment, and then, with a purely wicked intent, said, "My best-known work is *The Tale of Peter Rabbit.* It's about a very naughty rabbit who wants what he must not have."

Mrs. Kittredge drew herself up, as though she thought perhaps Beatrix was poking fun at her. "I don't believe I've heard of it," she said, adding, with barely disguised disdain, "A children's book, I suppose."

"It is only the most beloved children's book in all of England," Captain Woodcock retorted sharply, but Mrs.

Kittredge had already turned away to offer her hand and her smiles to someone else.

The major looked distressed. "You'll forgive Mrs. Kittredge, I hope, Miss Potter. I'm sure she intended no rudeness."

"Of course," Beatrix murmured, although she knew exactly what Mrs. Kittredge had intended, and felt thoroughly snubbed. It wasn't the first time. A great many people seemed to feel that children's books were somehow less significant than books for grownups, and did not hesitate to say so.

Captain Woodcock put a sympathetic hand on her arm, seemed about to say something, then caught sight of Will Heelis, standing by the window. "Excuse me, Miss Potter," he said hurriedly. "I need to speak with Mr. Heelis. I shall return."

A moment later Beatrix saw the two of them with their heads together, casting furtive glances at Mr. Richardson, so she assumed that the captain was passing along her information about the Sandiford Syndicate. And from the distasteful look on Mr. Heelis's face, she thought he might be acquainted with the man. She was glad Mr. Heelis was involved in the matter. She knew that his law firm handled most of the property sales in the area, and when it came to property, she had every confidence in him.

Relieved to be left alone, Beatrix found a corner where she could watch the gathering, which included many people she recognized. There was Dr. Butters, from Hawkshead, whom all the villagers thought must be the finest doctor in the world. And the Braithwaites and Crooks, huddled together like sheep, looking as if they were overawed by the greatness of the place. Lester Barrow, the owner of the Tower Bank Arms, was hovering like a harrier over the refreshment table, as if comparing its offerings to his own less ample bill of fare. And Miss Nash, recently appointed head teacher of Sawrey School, and her sister Annie, who taught piano lessons to the Sawrey children, were chattering as gaily as two robins with Sarah Barwick, who had forsaken her trousers for a feminine white shirtwaist with puffy sleeves and a high lace collar and a beige skirt with a dressy flounce. Sarah looked pleased with herself, and well she might, for many of the baked goods on the table had come from her kitchen, and her Tipsy Cake (made from Mrs. Beeton's famous recipe) was fast disappearing. Bertha and Henry Stubbs were there, and Elsa Grape, and Lucy and Joseph Skead, and the Jenningses and the Suttons and even Lydia Dowling, who had said she intended to send her regrets.

And there was the vicar, Samuel Sackett, looking unaccustomedly merry as he greeted Major Kittredge. Beatrix was close enough to hear him introduce his cousin, Mr. Thexton, and Mr. Thexton's wife, who had been staying with him for several months—the guests, she assumed, who could not be budged from their comfortable accommodations at the vicarage. She smiled to herself when she heard the vicar, with an unmistakable cheeriness, repeat the news that they were planning to depart on the following Monday.

"I've just learned about the Luck of Raven Hall, Major," said Mr. Thexton. He was a burly man with a pink face; small, dark eyes; and a bulbous nose over a bushy, drooping mustache. He put Beatrix in mind of a walrus, and she had to suppress a giggle at the thought.

"Oh, really," said the major, without much enthusiasm.

"Oh, yes," Mr. Thexton replied earnestly. "I am, you see, a collector of folk tales, with a very special interest in all things Fairy. I am presently engaged in writing a book about the folk tales of the Lake District. My dear cousin, the vicar"—with a bow in the vicar's direction—"who has extended the greatest hospitality to my wife and myself, has been so kind as to relate to me the remarkable story of your Luck. I should delight in examining it, truly I would, and hearing once again, and in greater detail, the astonishing tale of its fairy origins. And I should be even more pleased to hear about the good fortune it has brought to your family. I intend to include it in my volume, you see." He stroked his mustache and smiled in an ingratiating way. "I hope I am not being immodest when I say that this will amplify the quite natural public interest in your goblet, and will very likely increase its worth as an *objet d'art.*"

Major Kittredge grunted. "You may certainly have a look at the blasted thing." He waved a hand in the direction of the oaken cabinet. "It's right over there, for all to see. As to worth, I have no idea. But where good fortune is concerned, I can't say that Raven Hall has been blessed. Quite the contrary, in fact. The family has had a dismal streak of bad fortune ever since it appeared. My father always said he wished the wretched thing would be broken. Perhaps things might change."

Mrs. Kittredge was having a conversation with Lady Longford, Caroline Longford's grandmother. She turned and, over her shoulder, tossed her husband a pretty little pout. "Oh, but Christopher, my sweet, don't you think our marriage signifies a change in the Kittredge luck?"

"Of course, my dear," the major said in a repentant tone. "But we've been married for only a few months—and the damnable Luck has been in the family ever since this house was built."

"Well, well, well," Mr. Thexton said eagerly, rubbing his hands together. "I must say, this is all extremely interesting, Major Kittredge." He glanced at Mrs. Kittredge in a casual way, then bent forward, as if to give her a closer look.

"Some people seem to think so," said the major, in a tone that suggested he didn't think so himself and wished that Mr. Thexton would go away and stop bothering him.

"Oh, yes!" Mr. Thexton exclaimed, in a loud, booming voice, still looking at Mrs. Kittredge. "Oh, I am anxious—anxious indeed, sir!—to see this marvelous relic of a magical past. Perhaps your wife would be so good as to show it to me."

"Diana, our guest would like to examine the Luck," Major Kittredge said dryly. "Would you be so kind as to oblige him, my dear?"

Mrs. Kittredge did not appear pleased to have been given the assignment. Reluctantly, she excused herself to Lady Longford and, scarcely looking at the man, said, "Come with me, Mr. Sexton."

"Thexton," the vicar's cousin corrected her. "With a *th*." In a lower voice, as the pair passed directly in front of Beatrix, he remarked, "My dear Mrs. Kittredge, I can't help wondering if you and I have met before."

Mrs. Kittredge tossed her head lightly. "I do not think so, sir."

"Oh, but I am confident of it," Mr. Thexton persisted. "Just give me a moment, and I'm sure it will come back to me. I have a quite remarkable memory, you know. I have committed entire books and plays to memory. And I never forget a face, especially a beautiful face, if I may be pardoned for expressing my admiration."

Mrs. Kittredge did not answer. The pair paused in front of the oaken cupboard, where the lady reached up to take down the heavy goblet.

At Beatrix's elbow, Lady Longford spoke imperiously. "Fairies," she scoffed, snapping her black lace fan. "And Mr. Thexton a grown man. How very embarrassing for the vicar.

If I were Reverend Sackett, I would not tolerate such behavior, not for a moment."

"I must own to having believed in fairies myself, as a young person," Beatrix said mildly. "And sometimes I think I still do believe."

"Allowances can be made for you, Miss Potter," her ladyship said in an acid tone, "because you make books for children. It is to your advantage to believe in magic, or to pretend that you do. How else could you write with conviction about speaking animals and the like?" She gave a complaining sniff. "However, such beliefs do not at all become a gentleman of Mr. Thexton's obvious education and breeding. I simply cannot think why he should persist in such—"

Beatrix, however, was not listening to Lady Longford's complaint. Her attention had been attracted to the drama unfolding in front of the oaken cupboard, although afterward, when she thought about it, she had a distinctly different impression from the one she formed as she watched.

What she saw was Mrs. Kittredge, handing the goblet to Mr. Thexton. He was reaching for it but did not quite have it in his grasp when he stopped, peered intently into her face, and exclaimed, loudly and impulsively, "By thunder, I remember now! I do know you, of course I do! You are Irene—"

Mrs. Kittredge's eyes opened wide and her face turned dead white. The Luck slipped from her fingers, fell to the floor with a splintering crash, and shattered into a thousand brightly colored pieces.

20

Half of One, Half of Other

As the party-goers were arriving at the Raven Hall reception, eager to see the mysterious Mrs. Kittredge, the children—Caroline, Deirdre, and Jeremy—were making their way through Cuckoo Brow Wood in search of fairies. They were accompanied by Rascal, the village dog, who was guiding them with the aid of a map provided (yes, it's true) by Bosworth Badger.

At mid-morning on Saturday, at Belle Green, where he lived with Mr. and Mrs. Crook, Rascal received a caller: the badger boy Thorn, who handed him a roll of paper and a note from Bosworth Badger. Bosworth wrote that he had searched the *History* and found several entries recorded by his grandfather, documenting the location of a fairy village on the bank of Fern Vale Tarn. He could not, of course, be sure that the village still existed and he rather thought that it had actually been occupied by a family of dwelves, which were a different and more problematic sort of creature than the conventional Oak Folk. But he hoped that the map would be of some use to Rascal and the children, and wished them every success in their expedition.

"Dwelves?" wondered Rascal, who had never heard the word. It suggested its own meaning, of course. A dwelf must be something between a dwarf and an elf—although what the badger meant by "problematic," he couldn't guess. Still, he supposed it didn't matter what they were, at least as far as the children were concerned. A fairy was a fairy, be he elf, dwarf, dwelf, Folk, goblin, or any of the myriad nature spirits who occupied the Land between the Lakes long before humans came on the scene.

"You'll stop for a bite of something?" Rascal asked the badger boy politely.

Thorn shook his head. *"I've another errand,"* he said, and grinned. *"Good luck!"*

When Thorn had gone, Rascal unfolded the map and studied it until he had all the details by heart—not having any pockets, he couldn't take it along. On the map, Fern Vale Tarn, a smallish lake, lay cupped in a hollow near the top of Claife Heights, not far below Raven Hall. This was the darkest, oldest part of Cuckoo Brow Wood, which was itself the oldest and darkest forest in the area, a remnant of the old, dark forests that had once covered all of the Land between the Lakes. The path leading to the tarn began from just beneath Holly How. It forked several times, with branches shooting off in different directions, but Rascal thought he could make out the way to the tarn. Badger had drawn an X at the south end of the small lake, and printed *Supposed site, Fern Vale Village* beneath.

Well, thought Rascal, as he folded up the map, this was quite encouraging. The Folk or dwelves or whatever they were might not live there any longer, but at least he knew that they had lived there, once upon a time.

The drizzle was just ending when the group met at the gate at the bottom of the Tidmarsh Manor garden, after Lady Longford had gone off to the Raven Hall reception. When Rascal joined them, Deirdre was distributing a handful of herbs and flowers.

"Rue, yarrow, lavender, thyme, primrose, and rosemary," she said. "We won't be needin' these herbs today, for we're not likely t' see fairies in daylight. But it won't hurt to have them with us. We can always leave them as an off'ring, when we get to a place where we think fairies might live."

Jeremy poked a blue-green sprig of rue into his button-hole. "Where'd you find all this?"

Privately, Jeremy was thinking that believing in fairies was not going to be enough to stave off the inevitable. Just this morning, Dr. Butters had dropped in to talk with Aunt Jane about the Hawkshead apothecary, Mr. Higgens, who wanted an apprentice. The doctor believed the apothecary to be a man of good character, and Aunt Jane thought that working in a shop would be more pleasant than working in a joinery.

But within himself Jeremy could feel the resentment seething, like a boiling kettle. He didn't want to work in either place. He wanted to go to school at Kelsick. But that was impossible. And no matter how much he wanted things to be different, they weren't. So he had tried to smile—Aunt Jane was watching him with such concern—and said he would do whatever they thought best.

"It's agreed, then," Dr. Butters had said, with a sympathetic look at Jeremy. He promised to bring the indenture papers the following week, and he and Jeremy would go to the Justice of the Peace, where the indenture would be signed, witnessed, and sealed. It was final and inevitable, and Jeremy had to resign himself. He would be grown up shortly, and go to work as a man. So his last, or nearly last, expedition as a boy might as well be in search of fairies. And if by some magic a fairy happened to pop out of a tree or a bush, he thought bleakly, he knew exactly what he would wish for.

"I brought the rosemary from the Manor garden," Caroline said, in answer to Jeremy's question.

"An' I got the yarrow an' rue an' lavender from Miss Potter's garden," Deirdre added, kneeling down to weave lavender and thyme into Rascal's leather collar. "It's the queerest thing, but she felt like a friend. I asked her t' go with us on May Eve." She straightened and pushed her hair out of her eyes. "She told me a poem she's written about a fairy lady, and gave me a primrose. I know she's a grownup, but she's diff'rent from the others. I think she believes."

"Of course she does," Rascal yipped.

"I hope she said yes," Caroline remarked, tucking a yarrow leaf behind one ear and trying not to think about the difficulty of getting out of the house on May Eve.

Caroline glanced at Jeremy to see if he was feeling silly about looking for fairies, but if he was, he didn't show it. Deirdre, of course, didn't seem to feel silly at all. She obviously believed wholeheartedly. Although, Caroline reflected, if you thought you had the gift of seeing fairies, you'd have to believe in fairies, or you couldn't believe in your gift. And once you had the gift (or thought you did), you'd surely want to hang on to it as long as possible, which meant that you had to keep on seeing and believing, whether you actually did or not.

"I wouldn't agree to any of the other grownups going with us," Jeremy remarked, "but Miss Potter's a bit of all right. Did she say yes?"

"Only if you agreed," Deirdre said, and smiled. "I'll tell her, then. I'm glad." She looked at Jeremy. "Any idea where we should go? Caroline said you'd know the best places to look." She paused and added wistfully, "I ain't seen a fairy since me mother died, y'know. I'm hopin' we'll find where they live, so we can go back on May Eve an' see 'em."

"From everything I've read," Jeremy said, "they like old trees, and moss and clear water, and ferns. I think we should go to the top of Claife Heights."

"*I'll show you!*" Rascal barked authoritatively, and trotted off, glancing back over his shoulder and barking again, as if to be sure that they were coming after.

"Looks like he knows where he's going," Caroline said.

"He probably does," said Jeremy. "He runs all over these woods." He grinned. "And if we're to believe in fairies, we might as well believe in a dog who knows where to find 'em."

"Then let's follow," Deirdre said. She tossed her braids over her shoulder and set out after Rascal.

So the children followed the terrier, who headed at first for the foot of Holly How, then turned to the right up a narrow ravine, and when they reached the top, took a fork in the path that led them up another steep climb and deeper into Cuckoo Brow Wood. The little dog seemed to feel confident that he was taking the right path, even though it branched out in a great many confusing directions.

But as far as Caroline was concerned, the direction itself didn't matter, as long as it was *away*. The earlier rain had stopped and the gray mist that trailed like wisps of tulle through the trees seemed to wreathe the woods in an ancient mystery. It was easy to pretend that she was worlds away from her normal existence, from lessons and etiquette and Grandmama telling her what to do, even though they had come only a little way up the hill from Tidmarsh Manor. In fact, if she turned and looked back, she'd see the roofs of the manor house and barns not far below—except that when she tried it, she found to her surprise that she couldn't, for the pearly mist had fallen like a curtain, and everything behind them had disappeared. They might have been journeying through a completely unknown land, somewhere back at the beginning of time, with nobody else around them for hundreds of miles—and hundreds of years.

It was a thought that made the goose bumps rise on Caroline's arms. When she had suggested today's fairy-hunting adventure, it had been as a lark, really, a sort of play-acting that might take Deirdre's mind off her troubles. Now, she had her own reason for going. Her grandmother had asked her what she intended to do that afternoon, and she had answered truthfully: she and Jeremy and Deirdre—the girl who helped at the Suttons'—were going to walk into Cuckoo Brow Wood.

But Grandmama, who could sometimes be cruelly imperative, had ordered her to stay home. "It's time you began behaving like a young lady," she said with a scowl. "Young ladies don't go wandering through the woods with dirty village urchins. You are to stay in your room and read or work on your embroidery."

Caroline had a willful streak and occasionally did things she knew her grandmother wouldn't approve, but this was the first time she had ever disobeyed a direct order. She couldn't quite explain why, but going into the woods today—and on May Eve, if she could somehow manage it—had become very important. The longer she thought about it, the more it seemed that these mysterious woods were full of hidden secrets begging to be uncovered and age-old tales longing to be heard. There were no rules in the woods, and it was not a place where ladies went. And now that the rest of the world had vanished into the mists behind them, there was nothing to do but go in search of the secrets, and nowhere to go but straight ahead, following the little dog who seemed so full of confident authority, as though he were carrying a map in his head.

For a short distance, the path had slanted up through an open woods that had the look of a magical garden, so graceful were the larches and willows just going green over their heads and the yellow catkins swinging blithely on the hazels. The narrow path was bordered by delightful spring flowers, cowslips and bluebonnets and nodding harebells, anemones and wild hyacinths and wood spurge, with its red stalks and pale green flowers. In the brighter places, where the spring sun had been able to reach down and stroke the earth, there was heather and bilberry and Jack-by-the-hedge and white stitchwort, which was also called milk maids, and in the boggy places, beds of bitter cress and thick mounds of marsh violets. A little deeper into the shadow of the woods, the green banks were hung with fronds of Hart's tongue and oak fern, with Herb Robert and ivy-leaved toadflax in flower, with here and there the tidy blooms of white dead nettle. And all around them and over their heads sang the birds, as if they were very glad to have the children's company in this lovely woods on this gray, misty day: thrushes and chaffinches and robins and the cheery cuckoo, the harbinger of spring.

But as they climbed higher and deeper into the woods, they left the birds behind. The path grew narrower and darker, for the branches of the fir trees were interlocked overheard, arching together like the wooden ribs of a great cathedral, so that the sunlight, if there had been any, which there wasn't, was entirely shut out. It was chilly here, and even mistier and more mysterious, for the tree trunks were gnarled and twisted, the forest floor was thickly blanketed with brown leaves and needles, and here and there heaps of rocks and clumps of fern emerged out of the mist and then vanished into it again, as if by magic, so that one never quite knew whether one had seen them or not, or whether they were real or imagined. There were odd rustlings, too, and whisperings and scufflings, and shapes that slipped warily from behind trees or rocks or out of holes in the ground, shapes with ears and eyes that stared unblinking as the children passed. Without the sun there were no shadows, and without shadows, it was impossible to tell what time it was, or how long they had been walking, or which was east, west, north, or south. There were only two directions, uphill (the way they were taking) and downhill (the way they had been), and the path had now become so indistinct that it was impossible to tell whether they were actually walking on it or not. Caroline certainly hoped that Rascal, who was trotting some distance ahead of them, knew where he meant to go, for she certainly didn't.

Rascal, for his part, knew exactly where he was going. For one thing, he was confident in Bosworth's map, which he had got by heart, and while the path did not always branch or climb or dip exactly as he expected, it was still taking them in the general direction of Fern Vale Tarn. For another thing, his nose was a great deal keener than any of the children's noses, and for the past several hundred yards, as the three of them labored up a particularly steep bit of hill, he had been ranging quite a distance ahead, lured on by the earthy, exhilarating smell of a lake filled with frogs and tadpoles and water lily pads and decaying ferns and surrounded by fine, damp moss. He couldn't see it yet, but his nose told him it was somewhere up ahead, and if there was anything in this world that Rascal could trust, it was his nose, which always told him the truth.

And then the path reached the top of a particularly steep

place, hesitated, and then plunged down so precipitously that Rascal went right over the brink, tumbling over and over, nose over stubby tail. He barely had time to bark a startled *"Watch your step!"* to the children behind him before he landed on a thick pillow of green moss.

Rascal sat up, rubbed his nose, and checked all four legs to make sure that nothing was broken. Then he gave another warning bark—*"Watch your step, I say!"*—and looked around. He was sitting on a mossy cushion, among the roots of a very large oak tree that spread itself like a green umbrella over a green glade ringed with wood anemones and primulas, their scent intoxicatingly sweet. At the farthest edge of the glade lay a small lake, its surface as smooth and green as a sheet of green glass. It was draped in mist and rimmed with emerald ferns, and the very air itself seemed to shimmer with a green radiance. There was no breeze and everything was very quiet, as if the trees and the lake and the grass and the flowers were all transfixed in the silence of a deep and timeless enchantment. Rascal knew beyond a doubt that they had reached Fern Vale Tarn. And if Bosworth Badger's grandfather was right, this was the site of the Oak Folk village!

There was a rustle of foliage at the top of the path, and Jeremy peered over. "I think we're here," he said over his shoulder, "but do be careful. There's quite a drop on the other side." He clambered carefully down the steep incline, holding on to tree roots and branches, and arrived, breathless and awed, next to Rascal. A moment later, in a shower of pebbles and leaves, the girls had climbed down, too.

"I don't believe it," whispered Caroline, sitting beside Jeremy and looking around.

"Oh, don't say that, Caroline," Deirdre begged. "They'll hear, and think you're speakin' of them."

"She doesn't mean it that way," Jeremy pointed out. "She means—"

"I know what she means," Deirdre replied. "But *they* don't, do they? If they think we don't believe, the magic won't work. Personally, I'm going to believe just as hard as I can." She narrowed her eyes and screwed up her mouth to demonstrate how hard she was believing. "This is an enchanted place, and everything here is magic, and—"

"Listen!" Caroline said suddenly. "Is that music?"

And then they heard, as if it were drifting from far away or long ago, the sound of violins, high and sweet, floating eerily through the green air. And with the music the feeling of magic grew, until Caroline was almost afraid to speak or even to breathe, for fear of shattering its fragile beauty.

But Deirdre wasn't, of course. "Sure and it's music," she said, her eyes popping open. "It's the fairies singin'! I told you so! They're here! They're all around us. It's an enchantment!"

Jeremy chuckled. "Those aren't fairies, they're violins. It's the party at Raven Hall we're hearing." He pointed. "If I'm not mistaken, the Kittredges' manor house is just on the other side of the lake."

"Raven Hall?" Caroline asked uncertainly.

"Of course," Jeremy said. "We climbed up through the west side of Cuckoo Brow Wood. Raven Hall is at the top, and on the other side is the lake." He looked at them. "You've heard the story of the Raven Hall Luck?"

Caroline frowned. "Does it have anything to do with Mrs. Kittredge? She's the one the villagers like to call a witch."

"What kind of luck is it?" Deirdre asked. "Good luck? Bad luck?"

"Not that kind of luck at all," Jeremy said. "The Luck is what they call it. It's a big glass cup, like a goblet or something, and it doesn't have anything to do with Mrs. Kittredge. The fairies gave it to the Kittredge family a long time ago. As long as the Luck remains unbroken, the Kittredges are supposed to have good fortune."

"The fairies!" Deirdre exclaimed excitedly. "Then we must be in the right place!" And with that, she scrambled off the mossy hummock and began to poke through the ferns and flowers that bordered the little glade.

"What are you looking for, exactly?" Caroline asked, glancing around. She herself was content just to sit and take it all in, the mysterious green light, the overhanging tree with its huge, twisted roots, the grass, the lake.

"I don't know," Deirdre said. "I'll know when I see it. I—" She broke off suddenly, pointing. "Look!" she said, in a hushed, breathless tone. "On that tree. A piece of paper!"

Caroline felt a prickle of apprehension run across her shoulders and down her arms. "Is it a NO TRESPASSING notice?" she asked worriedly. That wasn't what it looked like— most NO TRESPASSING warnings were in big, bold letters, and said things like TRESPASSERS WILL BE PROSECUTED TO THE FULLEST EXTENT OF THE LAW. But what else could it be?

Jeremy scrambled to his feet and went to the tree. "It looks like a note!"

And that's exactly what it was, folded in half and pinned to the trunk of a very large, very old tree with a very small, very sharp silver knife, about the size of a bird's wing feather.

Jeremy pulled out the knife and turned it in his hands. "It's too small to be of much use," he said. "I wonder—"

"It's a fairy knife!" Deirdre cried in triumph. "Read the note, Jeremy!"

"*Yes, read it!*" Rascal yipped, as excited as the children.

Caroline watched nervously as Jeremy examined the folded paper. "It's addressed to us," he said in a strange voice. He held it up. "See? Here, on the outside. 'To Jeremy, Caroline, and Deirdre.'"

"To us!" Deirdre cried. "To us!"

"But not to me?" Rascal asked, disappointed. That was just the way, wasn't it? Dogs never got the respect they deserved.

"To . . . *us?*" Caroline whispered, feeling that it was very uncomfortable and even frightening to have come so far through the wood, not knowing where in the world you were going, and then to find a piece of paper with your name on it, pinned to a tree. "But that's impossible! How could any-one know—" She looked at Jeremy, her eyes wide. "Did *you* know we were coming here?"

"No, I didn't," Jeremy replied, shaking his head, obviously puzzled. "I don't even know where here is." He frowned at her. "Did you?"

"Of course not," Caroline retorted. "How could I? I'm not allowed out of the garden." She frowned at Deirdre. "You did it," she said accusingly. "You put the note here, to make us think of fairies."

"Nonsense," Deirdre snapped. "I did no such thing. How could I? I've never been in this place before." She turned urgently to Jeremy, her hands clasped. "Oh, don't be such a slow coach, Jeremy! What does the note say? Is it a guide to buried treasure? Or maybe it tells us how to do magic!"

Jeremy unfolded the paper. "It's a riddle."

"A riddle?" Caroline was dumbfounded. Of all the things that might have been on that paper, a riddle was the very last thing she would have guessed.

Jeremy frowned. "Well, I think it's a riddle. But maybe . . ." His voice trailed off.

"A riddle!" Deirdre exclaimed, and laughed. "Well, I call that jolly, I do! Is it about magic? Read it, Jeremy!"

Jeremy took a deep breath and began to read:

> *Half of one, half of other,*
> *Daughter of father, son of mother,*
> *Behind the beech, under the oak,*
> *Many fair and merry folk,*
> *All around but changing form,*
> *Here a blossom, there a thorn,*
> *Tall or short, thick or thin,*
> *Guess the shape we are in.*

There was a silence. Then, "Half of one, half of other?" Caroline managed at last, between numbed lips.

"*Precisely!*" Rascal yipped. "*A dwelf is half a dwarf, half an elf!*"

Deirdre's eyes were as round as teacups. "Guess the shape WHO are in?"

" 'Many fair and merry folk,' " Jeremy said. "That must be who." He paused. "There's a P.S. It says 'Come on May Eve, and maybe we'll be here, too.' "

"Maybe we'll be here?" Caroline repeated, disappointed. "That doesn't tell us anything."

"Of course it does, you silly goose!" Deirdre crowed, flapping her arms. "It tells us—"

"It tells us that somebody knew we were going to be here this afternoon," Jeremy interrupted. He looked sternly from Deirdre to Caroline. "All right. Which of you is responsible for this?"

Deirdre stamped her foot. "Neither of us is responsible," she cried, hands on hips, her chin thrust forward. "Can't you see? Why are you actin' so thick, the both of you? It's the fairies! Fairies know everything. They knew our names, and they knew we were coming, and they knew why. And what's more, they're inviting us to come back on May Eve. To come back *here*." She dropped her voice to a dramatic whisper. "This place is magic. Don't you feel it?"

And then they all fell silent, because they could all feel it, even Rascal. And if they had wanted or needed evidence of fairy magic, Jeremy held it in his hand. The riddle that shouldn't have been there, especially with their names on it, because nobody knew that they would be in this enchanted glade. The tiny silver knife that had pinned the paper to the oak tree, the violins' intoxicating melody shivering through the air, the lake and trees and ferns as silent and immobile as if no breath of air, no breeze, had ever stirred them—it was all fairy, all enchantment, and all completely unbelievable.

Caroline was the first to speak. "Well," she said breathlessly, and found that she needed to clear her throat. She tried again, steadying her voice. "I suppose this is the place we should come on May Eve, then." Although she had no idea how she was going to get out of the house.

"Of course it is," Deirdre said firmly. "We need to be here just at twilight."

Jeremy hesitated. "It won't take long," he said finally, "now that we know the way. But we can't plan on the moon to light our way home. I'll bring Aunt Jane's bicycle lantern."

And then even Caroline had to give in. "I suppose we should leave our herbs," she said, laying her bunch at the foot of the tallest oak. "As a present."

"Exactly," said Deirdre, following suit. "That way, the fairies will know we believe in them." She looked up at the tree and raised her voice. "Whatever shape you're in."

"And I suppose," Jeremy said, "that we should leave the knife, too."

"Yes," Caroline said. "Let's put it back in the tree, where we found it."

"No," Deirdre said. "Let's hide it *under* the tree, and see whether the fairies can find it. As a kind of test, I mean." So, since that seemed a reasonable sort of thing to do, they did it.

And then, as if by magic, the clouds parted, the sun came out, and flooded the little green glade with its welcome light. And on an oak tree, over their heads, a red squirrel with a perky tail began to chatter excitedly. A moment later, he was joined by two others.

The trio watched as the children and the dog climbed up the embankment and set off down the path through Cuckoo Brow Wood.

21

"She's Destroyed the Luck!"

At Raven Hall, a shocked hush fell on the guests as everyone craned their necks to see what had caused the tremendous crash. The entire gathering was silent for what seemed a full minute, every person frozen in place, every breath held, even the musicians ceasing to play—until Lady Longford spoke, in a voice that was heard round the room.

"She's dropped it!" she exclaimed shrilly. "She's destroyed the Luck!"

That broke the spell. Beatrix pulled in her breath, everyone stirred, the musicians picked up the tune where they had left off, and the room buzzed with the hubbub of hushed voices.

The major, showing great presence of mind, strode over and put his arm around his wife's shoulders. "Thank God," he said in a hearty voice that rang above the others. "Rid of that ugly goblet at last! Well done, my dear. Well done!"

Mrs. Kittredge buried her face in her husband's shoulder. "I really am very sorry," she said, in a barely audible voice. "It . . . it was heavier than I thought, and—"

"The fault was mine and mine alone, Major," said Mr. Thexton, sweeping a gallant bow. "Your wife is entirely innocent. I did not have my hands firmly on the Luck when it so tragically fell. I mourn the loss. I am heartsick, I am devastated." He bowed to the major's wife. "Mrs. Kittredge, I humbly pray that you will allow me to call upon you and express my further—"

"I'll not have another word," the major said firmly. "The Luck is of no consequence at all, in my opinion. Nothing but an ugly old bit of glass with a silly legend attached to it."

"But I insist, sir," Mr. Thexton said. He put out his hand. "My dear Mrs. Kittredge, pray do allow me to call on you privately and extend my—"

"No more apologies, please." The major nodded to a servant to clean up the shards of glass, and turned back to his wife. "Come, Diana. Let me get you a glass of champagne."

He led her away, leaving Mr. Thexton to swallow his unfinished sentence, but not before Beatrix had noticed a glance thrown at him by Mrs. Kittredge, a glance of pleading, and almost certainly of fear. Mr. Thexton, Beatrix saw, had a very odd gleam in his eye.

Lady Longford gave a peremptory laugh. "Just like his father, the major is. Every virtue of brains and breeding except the sense to marry well. Mrs. Kittredge was an actress, someone told me. He married her straight off the stage."

Beatrix thought she might have guessed. Mrs. Kittredge had quite a dramatic flair.

"An actress." Her ladyship's voice was heavy with disapproval. "When he might have had our dear little Miss Woodcock."

Oh, poor Dimity, Beatrix thought in dismay. It was difficult enough to lose the person one cared for; to lose him in full sight and knowledge of a village was immeasurably worse. And now that the major had returned home with a wife, Dimity's loss was no doubt on the tip of everyone's tongue.

Lady Longford sighed. "One does pity Miss Woodcock, Miss Potter. She must have felt the marriage to this . . . person as a shocking rejection. However, it may all turn out in the end, and to Miss Woodcock's better advantage." She gestured with her gold-handled lorgnette in the direction of Dimity, who was standing quite close to Mr. Heelis at the window, looking out over the lake. "Quite a romantic couple, wouldn't you agree?"

Dimity turned just then and looked up at Mr. Heelis, and Beatrix saw clearly her light, lithe figure, the brown hair ruffled around her face, the bright eyes, the thoughtful expression. Mr. Heelis, who was very tall, bent to say something in her ear, and Dimity nodded in a serious, considering way.

Beatrix had known Mr. Heelis since her first days at Hill Top Farm, and had thoroughly enjoyed their acquaintance, which had included a winter's walk during her December visit and a comfortable tea at the Sawrey Hotel. She had not thought of him as having a romantic interest in Dimity, but now that she did, it made a certain sense. Mr. Heelis was a friend of Captain Woodcock and a frequent visitor to Tower Bank House, and Dimity was an attractive woman. A very attractive woman.

Beatrix bit her lip, aware of a sharp feeling deep inside. What was it? Disappointment? Longing? A sense of loss?

Yes, that must be it. The loss of the only love that would have completed her life. Norman, whose loss was still a raw wound, a painful memory evoked by the sight of two people discovering their love for each other. And if she would be brutally honest with herself, there was a certain envy mixed with the pain, for Dimity was free to encourage Mr. Heelis if she liked. No one would object to the match, as Beatrix's mother and father had so angrily objected to her marrying Norman. Dimity was free to follow her heart, without any delays or postponement, other than suited her and Mr. Heelis.

Lady Longford had turned her sharp gaze on Beatrix. "Wouldn't you agree, Miss Potter?" she repeated, raising her eyebrows.

"I suppose," Beatrix said, not quite sure what she was agreeing to. Very firmly, she put the thought of Dimity and Mr. Heelis aside and changed the subject, to bring up something that had concerned her since she had heard about it from Sarah Barwick. "If you don't mind my asking, Lady Longford, I wonder whether you have taken any decision about Caroline's education."

"I don't mind your asking at all." Lady Longford raised her lorgnette and regarded Beatrix through it. "I have become rather fond of my granddaughter. I see a certain promise in her, although one that requires refinement. She has not lived up to my expectations in school this year, whether through inadequate preparation or lack of attention, I do not know. Perhaps she is simply dull-witted."

"Dull-witted!" Beatrix exclaimed in shock. "Surely not! Caroline is highly intelligent!" Beatrix knew this for a fact through her acquaintance with Caroline the previous autumn.

Lady Longford did not acknowledge the interruption. "And while the school provided a transition from Caroline's sketchy education in New Zealand," she went on, "it has had the unfortunate effect of encouraging her to associate with the village children. They are not, as I am sure you will agree,

Miss Potter, suitable companions for the child. She was a hoyden when she came to me; she has become rather more so, I fear. Why, just today, I had to forbid her to go running off into Cuckoo Brow Wood with that servant girl of the Suttons and the boy who lives at Holly How Farm." She paused and added firmly, "I have decided that Caroline needs a governess."

Forbid her to go into the woods? Beatrix wondered. Did that mean that Caroline hadn't been able to go with Deirdre and Jeremy on their expedition? That was too bad.

Beatrix frowned. Lady Longford was a strong, formidable woman with an intimidating manner that was obviously intended to strike alarm into anyone who had the temerity to disagree with her. But Beatrix's long experience with her own dictatorial mother had taught her that there were times when she simply had to say what she thought and refuse to allow herself to be bullied. And she and Lady Longford had had some dealings the previous year, when her ladyship's health—and perhaps her life—had been threatened by her unscrupulous companion. Lady Longford might not always show it, but she respected those who stood their ground.

"I do not mean to be impertinent, but I cannot agree with your ladyship about the village children," Beatrix replied. "Some of them are rather boisterous, certainly. But Caroline is a sensible girl, and there is nothing dull-witted about her. I should trust her to choose her friends wisely." She thought with a pang of her own solitary childhood, and added, in a softer tone: "And besides, the child is apt to be lonely, left entirely to herself."

"Well!" Lady Longford drew herself up sharply. "I expected you, of all people, Miss Potter, to understand Caroline's situation. However common her beginnings in New Zealand, my granddaughter is to be a lady. She requires a lady's upbringing for a lady's social responsibilities."

Beatrix stiffened, hearing in Lady Longford's harsh, strident voice the same nagging tones she heard at home. From her earliest childhood, her mother had continually reminded her that she must learn to act like a lady. Mrs. Potter herself spent the greater part of every day keeping up her own social responsibilities, driving out in her carriage to sip tea with other ladies or dressing for the many dinner parties the Potters enjoyed. Beatrix had not been allowed to play with other children and had been raised by nannies and educated by governesses until she was nineteen, because that's how young ladies were raised. And when she had wanted to marry Norman Warne, Mrs. Potter had refused to allow it, because the Warnes were not of the Potters' social class and Norman worked for a living. If that was what it meant to be a lady, Beatrix had long ago rejected the idea—not only rejected it, but positively rebelled against it. And that was the kind of life Lady Longford intended for her granddaughter!

But Beatrix had learned that it was possible to get around Lady Longford, if it were done in the right way. In the least impertinent tone she could manage, she said, "I might be able to suggest some possible candidates for governess, if your ladyship would like."

Lady Longford inclined her head. "Most kind, Miss Potter," she said, a glint of victory in her eye. "I should certainly be willing to give special consideration to anyone you might care to recommend. As long as she is of good family," she added.

Good family! Beatrix thought acidly to herself. No doubt her ladyship meant to employ a governess who would instruct Caroline in exactly the sorts of behaviors "good family" entailed. "I shall give the matter careful thought," she said. "Perhaps I'll write to my own former governess."

"Do," Lady Longford said, and swept away with a rustle of skirts. Beatrix looked after her, glad that her feelings could not be read on her face. If she had anything to do with it, Caroline would have something in her life besides instruction in how to conform to her ladyship's social expectations.

After the shattering of the Raven Hall Luck, the party never seemed to regain its sparkle, and within the hour, Captain Woodcock, accompanied by his sister and Mr. Heelis, came looking for Beatrix. The four of them said goodbyes and polite thanks and went back down the wide stone steps, through the portico, and down the path to the place where the captain's motor car was parked. The mist had blown away, the sun had come out, and the late afternoon sky was very blue.

On the path, they caught up with Sarah Barwick. She had come with the Crooks but they had gone home early, and when the captain invited her to ride back to the village with them, she was only too glad to accept. Beatrix, Dimity, and Sarah all squeezed into the back seat, with Beatrix in the middle. Mr. Heelis sat in front with the captain and the two of them discussed the business of the villas as they began the drive back to the village.

Straining to listen over the clatter of the motor car's engine, Beatrix learned that Mr. Heelis had introduced himself to Mr. Richardson, pretending to be interested in investing in the Sandiford Syndicate. Mr. Richardson, however, had informed him that the syndicate was closed to new investors and asked, with a frown, how he had come to hear of the business.

"I told him there were rumors flying everywhere," Mr. Heelis told the captain, "just to see how he would respond. He said that rumors couldn't be trusted."

"I spoke with him, too," Captain Woodcock said, "and he told me the same thing. But he also admitted that there was truth behind the rumor, although he wouldn't say whether any contracts had been signed. I spoke to Kittredge, as well," the captain added, "although I couldn't put my objections to him openly, of course—not as a guest at his reception. I daresay he took my meaning, however. We really must have a serious talk with him before this thing goes any further, Will. Appeal to his sense of family and duty. Let him know that he will face vocal opposition to any building on that shore. We can't let him go forward without knowing how deeply people are likely to feel this thing."

"Exactly my thinking," Mr. Heelis said. "Unfortunately, I must go to Carlisle on business on Monday, and won't return until Wednesday. The earliest we can see him is Thursday or Friday, unless you want to talk with him yourself."

"You're his solicitor—and his friend," the captain said. "I think a meeting must wait on you." He shook his head bleakly. "Although by the time we see him, the contracts may have been signed and the business underway. I tell you, Heelis, this is shaping up to be a nasty affair, with no easy way out. I—" Beatrix would have dearly liked to hear more, but the captain had lowered his voice at the same time that he had speeded up the engine, and she had to give up the effort.

In the meanwhile, in the back seat, the conversation was all about the mysterious Mrs. Kittredge. To their great surprise, Dimity and Sarah had learnt (as had Beatrix) that the major's new wife had been an actress before they were married. Sarah was excited by the news while Dimity seemed resigned and rather saddened, as if her faith in Major Kittredge's judgment might be weakening.

Sarah turned eagerly toward Beatrix. "Did you see how it happened that Mrs. Kittredge dropped the goblet, Bea?"

"Oh, yes," Dimity put in. "You were standing close by. What happened?"

"I'm not sure," Beatrix said. "I think I saw——" She broke off, recalling what she knew she had seen: Mrs. Kittredge with her hand extended and the goblet in it. Mr. Thexton, leaning forward, saying something, saying—what?

"I beg pardon?" Dimity said, and added, helplessly, "Really, this motor is so loud I can scarcely hear myself think. A horse is ever so much quieter."

Beatrix raised her voice. "When it happened, I thought Mrs. Kittredge had simply been startled. But now that I think back——" She stopped, not quite sure whether she ought to say it, but feeling somehow that it ought to be said. Finally, she said, "I have the impression that it might not have been as accidental as it seemed."

Dimity turned to stare at her. "Not accidental? Why, whatever can you mean, Beatrix?"

"I think she might have dropped it intentionally."

"Oh, surely not!" Sarah exclaimed, her eyes widening. "Break the Luck on *purpose*? Really, Beatrix, that can't be right!"

"I don't believe the major's wife would deliberately destroy a Kittredge family heirloom," Dimity said loyally. "Why would she do such an awful thing?"

"To prevent Mr. Thexton from finishing what he had started to say," Beatrix replied uncomfortably.

Sarah's eyebrows were raised so high that they disappeared behind her fringe of bangs. "*Really?* But what on earth could Mr. Thexton be saying that would cause her to do such a horrible thing?"

Beatrix took a deep breath. "He had been wondering aloud where he had seen her before. And then he said, 'By thunder, I remember now! I do know you, of course I do! You are Irene—' "

Dimity looked at her blankly. "You are—*Irene?* But Mrs. Kittredge's name is Diana. I took special note of it when we were introduced."

"Yes, I know," Beatrix said. "That's the name I heard Major Kittredge call her. Diana." Mr. Richardson had called her that, as well.

"So what do you think it means?" Sarah demanded, puzzled. "Could Irene be a stage name?"

"I suppose that's possible," Beatrix said, "although I'm not sure why she should be so dreadfully alarmed at someone's recollecting a mere stage name." And Mrs. Kittredge had been dreadfully alarmed. Her eyes had held a shocked look and her face had turned absolutely white. Beatrix looked from one to the other. "It's already known, isn't it, that she was an actress before she married Major Kittredge?"

"Oh, widely known, I should say," Dimity remarked, with just the barest hint of malice. "One of the guests mentioned that a cousin or someone had seen her on the stage. She only smiled and tossed her head. She seemed to take it as a compliment."

"So she wouldn't be startled by Mr. Thexton's recognition of her as an actress," Beatrix said seriously.

"I doubt it," Dimity replied.

"Well, it's certainly a mystery, if you ask me," Sarah said, opening her bag and taking out her cigarettes. "Who is Irene? And what does Mr. Thexton know about her?" With a dramatic flourish, she lit a match and applied it to the tip of her cigarette. "I don't suppose we'll ever know, will we?"

But Sarah Barwick, who was so often right, was on the wrong track this time.

22

Miss Potter Counts Her Sheep

Beatrix had been back from the Raven Hall reception just long enough to go upstairs and change into her farm clothes, then come back downstairs to put on the shoes she always wore outdoors. She smiled as she slipped her feet into the sturdy leather clogs made for her by Charlie Brown, a cobbler in Hawkshead. The old-fashioned clogs were magical, like Cinderella's glass slippers, but in reverse. They didn't take her to a glamorous ball or marriage with a prince, but to her real, true life. The minute she took off her smart leather town shoes and put on the clogs, she became a woman born to the country, rather than to the city, the kind of woman she longed to be.

But would she ever be able to trade her city self—responsible for looking after her parents and their social obligations and their big city house—for the freer, more interesting life she lived at Hill Top? The answer, sadly, was "probably not." Sarah Barwick would call her old-fashioned, but Beatrix had been raised to honor her family commit-ments, which meant that she would leave her parents only to marry. But the man to whom she had given her heart was dead, and she could not imagine loving another—certainly not the sort of gentleman her parents would find acceptable! That kind of man would never understand what Hill Top Farm meant to her. No, she was sentenced to living a double life, shuttling between the city and the country, until her mother and father were both gone. And by that time, she told herself with a rueful self-irony, she'd be too old to care where she lived.

But Beatrix was a practical person. She stayed cheerful by focusing on what she had and what she could do, rather than making herself unhappy by longing for what she would never have or couldn't do. When the manuscript of *The Tale of Peter Rabbit* was rejected by all six of the publishers to whom she sent it, she had published it herself and sold out two printings straightaway—at which point the Warne company had offered for it. She had met Norman and he had requested more books, and more, and the books had earned enough to buy Hill Top.

And that was the way she intended to deal with every-thing else in her life—her family responsibilities, her life in London, her life on the farm. There was no predicting what surprises the future might hold, or the way one failure might lead to an even greater success. One could only meet each day as it came, and let the future take care of itself.

She took her shepherd's crook out of the umbrella stand and reached for the woolen jacket that hung on a peg beside the door. It was nearly half past seven in the evening, but the sun wouldn't set for another hour and the reception's sandwiches and cakes would do for her supper. It was too wet to work in the garden, but not too wet to walk through the sheep meadow and look over her flock, which now numbered some fourteen ewes and lambs. She was anxious to see how they were getting on.

The sky overhead had cleared, the sun was dropping into a pool of lemon and lavender clouds behind the western fells, and the air was as sweet and clean as a freshly laundered sheet. Looking up, she saw two white-fleeced sheep on the flank of the hill to the east of the house. They looked like a pair of cotton puffs, grazing on the lush green grass. The others were probably on the far side of the hill.

As she went down the walk, Rascal ran around the corner of the house. *"Wait for me, Miss Potter!"* he yipped. Behind him, running to catch up, came Deirdre, her eyes shining.

"Miss Potter!" Deirdre called breathlessly. "I have something t' tell you! Something wonderful!"

"Well, tell away," Beatrix invited, and listened as Deirdre spilled her story, all about a fairy glen, and a riddle pinned to an oak tree with a silver knife, and an invitation to come back on May Eve. "My goodness," she said at last, not quite sure how much of the tale to believe—although it was quite obvious that Deirdre herself believed every word. "You *have* had a magical adventure, haven't you?"

"Oh, yes, yes, yes!" Deirdre exclaimed, her eyes dancing. "And Jeremy and Caroline say they want you to go with us on May Eve. You will go, won't you?" She sucked in her breath. "Won't you?"

"Of course I will," Beatrix said. She remembered her conversation with Lady Longford and her ladyship's assertion that she had forbidden Caroline to go out with Deirdre. "So Caroline went with you?" she asked, heartened at the thought that Caroline had defied her grandmother's unreasonable order. Defiance wasn't ladylike, of course, but that was the virtue of it.

" 'Deed she did," Deirdre replied. "I've got to go now. I'm late, and Mrs. Sutton's goin' to be put out at me."

"Well, then," Beatrix said, "I'll see you on May Eve. And just to be safe," she added, "I'll let Mrs. Sutton know that I've asked you to go for a walk in the woods that evening." The village children came and went pretty much as they chose, but Deirdre was in Rose Sutton's employ. And how did Caroline expect to get away from Tidmarsh Manor?

Deirdre gave a cheerful wave and was gone.

"Come with me, Rascal," Beatrix said. "I'm going out to check my sheep."

"Of course!" Rascal barked. He enjoyed escorting Miss Potter, and took it as one of his responsibilities when she was staying at Hill Top Farm. They usually happened on something interesting, and she always chatted with him as if he were Big Folk.

"I wish you'd been with us this afternoon," he barked happily, dancing along beside her. *"If you could only have seen their faces when Jeremy read that riddle! Of course, nobody could guess it. Why—"*

"Miss Potter! Miss Potter!" They turned to see Mr. Heelis, waving his hat and running toward them.

"I'm glad I caught you, Miss Potter," he said breathlessly. "Would you have a moment to talk? I have something important to discuss with you."

"Of course," Beatrix said with a smile, feeling very glad to see him. She gestured toward the hillside. "I'm surveying my sheep. You're welcome to come along."

She gave an involuntary and completely unconscious sigh. If Mr. Heelis was romantically interested in Dimity Woodcock, she could only be glad. Dimity would indeed be fortunate in her choice, for Mr. Heelis, who was very good-looking, had a solid, sensible head on his shoulders and was widely respected. He was shy with women, perhaps, but that would surely disturb Dimity no more than it bothered Beatrix, who was herself a shy person.

Will Heelis, who had no idea that he was being romantically linked to anyone, was just as pleased to see Miss Potter as she was to see him, and remembered their previous encounters with a great deal of pleasure. He admired her quick wit and her willingness to say exactly what she thought, an unusual quality in a woman, he had found. Even more important, she was so straightforward and comradely that she made him feel easy and comfortable. He was glad that this affair at Raven Hall, unpleasant as it might be, had given him an excuse to talk with Miss Potter again.

"Thanks for the invitation," he said, and fell into step beside her, George Crook's little terrier following along behind. "Enjoying the springtime weather?" he asked, feeling self-conscious. Small talk was never easy for him, but he didn't want to jump into the Raven Hall business right off the mark.

"I love the spring," Miss Potter replied, in her soft, light voice. "The sight of the green meadows, the fells, the lakes— it washes away unhappiness, don't you think? I'm sorry I can't just settle in and stay forever." And then she bit her lip and fell silent, as if she might have said too much, or didn't want to mar the fragile beauty of the evening by talking of something that made her unhappy.

Will could guess what she was thinking. According to those who knew her parents, the Potters were stern, exacting people who disapproved of their daughter's spending time at her farm. And her artistic life must be demanding, as well—he understood that she wrote and drew two books a year. Between her parents and her work, it was surprising that she managed to get to Sawrey as often as she did.

And although Will knew very little about Miss Potter's

personal life, it was rumored in the village that there had been a short engagement—angrily disapproved by the Potters—which ended when her fiancé had suddenly died. His loss must have come as an unimaginable shock, especially if she had accepted the proposal in the teeth of her parents' disapproval. The ring she wore on her left hand was probably an engagement ring, which meant, he supposed, that her heart still belonged to her dead lover.

He said, in a casual tone, "Well, I'm always glad for spring, when it comes. I'd a great deal rather be going about the countryside than reading papers at my desk." He chuckled reminiscently. "I grew up in Appleby, you see—the valley of the Eden River, not far from here. Lovely place. Plenty of fishing, hunting. I'm glad my property work takes me out so much."

"Property." Miss Potter turned her head and gave him a measuring glance. "I suppose you know what's likely to be available. Before it's offered for sale, I mean."

"I often do." He spoke ruefully, for he had not anticipated the development of the Raven Hall estate. "Are you thinking of acquiring more land?"

"I might be," Miss Potter replied, "as an investment. I'd be grateful if you would let me know if you should hear about something." She stopped and pointed, laughing, "Oh, look, Mr. Heelis—there's Tibbie, one of the Herdwick ewes I bought from Mr. Hornby. And she has twin lambs! Aren't they beautiful? I've already counted two," she added, "so these make five. There are fourteen in all."

Rascal saw the sheep, too. *"Hullo, Tibbie,"* he called, and trotted over to talk to her, not having seen her for quite some time. The lambs were doing what lambs always did in the springtime, he saw, gamboling through the grass and meadow flowers while their mother looked on anxiously, making little worried bleats.

"Laaambs," she cried. *"Stay away from the nettles! Mind that you don't tumble down the rocks!"* She frowned at Rascal. *"Aaand you stay away from my laaambs, Raaascal. Daisy and Marigold are still very young. They don't understaaand dogs."*

"I will," Rascal promised. *"Listen, Tibbie, I wonder if you know anything about Fern Vale Village."* Tibbie had lived at the edge of Cuckoo Brow Wood until just last year, and was always informed about the local goings-on.

"Whaaat's to know about it?" Tibbie asked crossly. *"You caaan't trust those Fern Vale dwelves aaany faaarther thaaan you caaan see them, aaand you caaan't see them very faaar, the naughty things. What's more, they may be something entirely different the next time you see them."*

"Something entirely different?" Rascal asked, bewildered. *"What does that mean?"*

But Tibbie was in no mood to answer questions. *"My advice to you is to stay away from them. They're nothing but trouble to us civilized creatures. They—"* The ewe raised her head in alarm. *"Daisy, don't eat thaaat thistle!"* she bleated. And with that, she dashed off to discipline her lambs.

Will had been watching the little dog approach the ewe. "Herdwicks," he said thoughtfully. "You like the breed?"

Miss Potter tossed her head. "I do indeed. I know they're considered old-fashioned, and that their fleece is nearly worthless, now that linoleum has replaced wool carpets. But I'm not expecting the farm to do anything more than pay its way. And Herdwicks are native to the Lake District. They belong here, as I do, and I'm very fond of them." She glanced at him and added, with something like defiance, "I'm sure that sounds sentimental."

"Perhaps." He smiled down at her, thinking that she was prettiest when her cheeks were pink, as they were now. "But it's a sentiment I share. Like the sheep, I'm heafed to the land." He watched her face to see if she understood. "Heafing" was a word that described the Herdwicks' almost uncanny ability to return to their native fellside, no matter how far away they might wander.

The sudden, bright smile seemed to transform her face. "And so am I, Mr. Heelis. Heafed, that is. So we both have something in common with the Herdwicks." She began to walk up the hill. "Tell me—what was it you wanted to discuss?"

Rascal hurried back to join them, his ears perked. It sounded as if they were about to get down to business.

"Actually, there are several things," Will said uncomfortably, clasping his hands behind his back. "I must confess to overhearing some of the conversation you had with Miss Woodcock and Miss Barwick when we were returning from Raven Hall this evening. Captain Woodcock's motor car was so loud that I couldn't hear all of it, but—"

"I'm surprised that you could hear any of it," Miss Potter retorted with a little laugh. "But I wasn't speaking confidentially," she added. "And anyway, I listened to what you were saying to the captain about those dreadful villas, so we're even."

Will nodded soberly. "Tit for tat, then. I was interested in your observation about Mrs. Kittredge dropping the goblet."

"She dropped the goblet?" Rascal yelped in surprise. *"Did it break?"*

"Major Kittredge is a long-time friend of mine," Will went on, "and a client. I have the feeling that he's cutting himself in for some serious trouble about those villas. And if there's anything in his wife's life that might cause him difficulty—" He rubbed his hand through his hair, feeling that he wasn't explaining his interest very well. "I'm not a man who takes pleasure in gossip, Miss Potter. I am concerned for my friend's welfare, or I wouldn't be asking."

Miss Potter glanced over her shoulder, noticing a ewe and her lamb under an oak tree. "That would be seven," she said, half to herself. To Will, she said, "I was standing nearby when it happened, you see. Like everyone else, I thought at the time that it was simply an unfortunate accident, and felt sorry that the Luck was broken."

"So it DID break!" Rascal cried excitedly.

"But when I had a moment to reflect," Miss Potter continued, "I felt—no, I was sure—that this was not the case." She gave Will a steady, unapologetic look. "It is my opinion that Mrs. Kittredge dropped the goblet on purpose, Mr. Heelis."

"On PURPOSE?" Rascal could hardly believe what he had heard.

Will was staring at her. "On purpose? But in heaven's name, why?"

"Just before this happened, Mr. Thexton was saying he thought he recognized Mrs. Kittredge, but didn't seem quite sure. And then he said, 'By thunder, I remember now! I do know you, of course I do! You are Irene—' And that's when she dropped the goblet."

"Irene?" Will frowned. "You're sure about that?"

"I am positive, Mr. Heelis. I was in a position to hear, and I have an excellent memory. I memorized nearly all of the plays of Shakespeare when I was a girl, so Mr. Thexton's simple remark is scarcely taxing." Miss Potter lifted her shepherd's crook and pointed to a ewe and a lamb lying together in the roots of a tall fir. "Nine."

"Maybe it's a name she once used," Rascal offered tentatively.

"Perhaps Irene was the name of a character Mrs. Kittredge once played." Will cleared his throat. "I suppose you know that she was a stage actress before she and the major married."

Miss Potter inclined her head. "Yes, I have heard. But I doubt that the mention of a mere character's name—or a stage name—would have had such an astonishing effect. The lady was terrified that Mr. Thexton would complete his sentence. In fact, she was so deeply distressed that one wonders whether she—" She hesitated, as if she were not sure that she ought to speak.

Rascal bounced up and down. *"What? Go on, Miss Potter. Go on!"*

"Whether she—what?" Will prompted, beginning to feel apprehensive.

"One can only speculate, of course." Miss Potter took a deep breath. "But one wonders whether the lady is who she says she is."

"Ah," Rascal said. *"Of course."*

Will's apprehension grew. His companion had already proven, on several previous occasions, to be quite an astonishing judge of character, and he trusted her reading of what had happened. What's more, he knew (although he wouldn't tell Miss Potter) that Christopher had fallen passionately in love with the lady who was now Mrs. Kittredge and married her on only a fortnight's acquaintance. What if there had been some sort of awkwardness or unpleasantness in her past? He did not want to be involved in Christopher's personal relationships, but if there was something badly awry, something that might somehow damage his friend, he wanted to know what it was.

"I see," he said. "So you're thinking—"

She interrupted him firmly. "I don't know what I think, Mr. Heelis." She paused. "I did not mention this to Miss Woodcock or Miss Barwick, but I am convinced that Mr. Thexton knows, or believes he knows, who this lady is. And she, for her part, understands, and fears him for it. I could read it in her face."

"Fears him?" Rascal said with interest. The whole thing was beginning to seem quite melodramatic. He could hardly wait to tell Tabitha Twitchit and Crumpet this interesting news.

Will pulled in his breath, startled. "Oh, come now, Miss Potter—"

"I am not overstating the matter, Mr. Heelis," she said decidedly. "The look that Mrs. Kittredge gave to Mr. Thexton was a look of great fear. And before Major Kittredge took his wife away, Mr. Thexton had attempted to get her to agree to receive him, privately. He said that he wanted to apologize, but I doubt whether an apology is what he has in mind."

Will thought for a moment. "Perhaps I should speak to Mr. Thexton, then—although of course, I'll leave you out of it."

Miss Potter frowned. "Out or in, it's up to you. I doubt, however, that Mr. Thexton will tell you what he knows. If he is hoping to use it to somehow gain an advantage—" She stopped. "I'm not sure what I mean, Mr. Heelis. It's just a feeling I have."

"I take your point. I'm to talk with Major Kittredge late next week. Perhaps it would be better to speak to him first. By then—"

"Yes. By then, the situation may be clearer." She paused and added, emphatically, "I hope you'll be able to dissuade the major from allowing villas to be built along the lakeshore."

"I shall do my best," Will said, "but I am afraid that the business may have gone too far to be stopped now. Mr. Richardson implied that the funds have already been raised. The matter may rest on Kittredge's agreement."

They had reached the top of the hill, a point from which they could see across Wilfin Beck and Sawrey Fold, to Far Sawrey and St. Peter's Church. Will glanced around. "There are some more sheep," he said, pointing to a corner of the meadow, where several were grazing together, heads down in the green grass. He counted. "Four, I make it."

"Thirteen," Miss Potter said, and frowned. "I haven't seen Queenie. She's the other ewe I bought from Mr. Hornby."

"There's something on the other side of that coppice," Rascal barked. *"I'll just pop around for a look."* And with that, he was off, bounding through the grass.

Miss Potter paused. "You said you wanted to discuss two things, Mr. Heelis? What's the other?"

"It has to do with Jeremy Crosfield," Will replied.

"Jeremy Crosfield?" She glanced at him, concerned. "Is something the matter?"

"Dr. Butters tells me that Jeremy is going to have to leave school at the end of this term. He's to apprentice to Mr. Higgens, the apothecary in Hawkshead."

"Apprentice?" Miss Potter's china-blue eyes grew dark. "That would be unfortunate," she said gravely. "It's hard for me to imagine Jeremy being happy as an apothecary. He has a fine artistic talent, and he's very interested in natural history. He should continue his education. I wonder—have the papers been signed?"

"Dr. Butters says that's planned for next week," Will replied. "He tells me that Jeremy has already passed the entrance examination for the grammar school at Ambleside, but there are no funds for tuition or board and room. You know, I suppose, that his aunt is a spinner and weaver. Not much money for extras, I should imagine."

"I do know." Miss Potter passed her hand over her woolen skirt. "She wove this for me, from Herdwick wool. It's so sturdy, I'll probably be wearing it forever." She gave Will a sideways glance. "Do you have something to suggest about Jeremy?"

Will nodded. "The idea came to me after I talked to Butters, and I wanted to discuss it with you before I thought further about it. I wonder if you and I might prevail upon Lady Longford to underwrite the boy's education. She can certainly afford it, and since she owns the manor farm where the boy and his aunt are living, it seems appropriate to ask her."

Surprised, Miss Potter turned to face him. "You and *I*? You're asking me to help with this, Mr. Heelis?"

Will met her gaze. "Her ladyship continues to believe that you were responsible for saving her life last year. She might be more easily persuaded if—"

"I didn't save her life," Miss Potter protested. "I knew she was ill, and thought of arsenic poisoning, especially when her maid told me about that dreadful companion of hers brewing up some sort of 'medicine.'"

"Don't be so modest," Will replied, thinking that it was like Miss Potter to refuse to take credit. "You thought of it when no one else did, not even Dr. Butters, and she was his patient. If her ladyship wants to believe she owes you her life, why not allow it?" He grinned mischievously. "In fact, why not trade on it? On Jeremy's behalf, of course."

Miss Potter gave him a dubious glance. "You don't think the vicar would be a better emissary than I?"

"Lady Longford doesn't feel that she owes the vicar anything, Miss Potter," Will said candidly. "To tell the truth, her reputation as a skinflint is well deserved. I've seen her count out pennies when pounds would have better answered. But if anyone can convince her that she ought to be generous with the boy, you are that person."

"I really don't—"

"And I'll be with you," Will interrupted. "She is my client, you know, and does on rare occasions take my advice. Between the two of us, we may actually be able to do Jeremy some good." He paused, grinning. "What do you say, Miss Potter? Are you up for it? Shall we have a go at the old girl?"

At that, Miss Potter had to smile. "I'm not as confident as you are that the old girl will do what we ask. But I shall be glad to give it my best effort."

"Hurrah!" Will cried. "Bravo, Miss Potter. Shall we say Monday afternoon?"

"Tuesday would be better for me," she replied. "Mr. Jennings and I are to look at a heifer calf on Monday. She's a bit dear, but her mother is said to be a fine milker, so I shan't begrudge the cost."

"Tuesday, then," Will said, amused at the idea that this well-known London artist, who could no doubt choose amongst all the entertainments that the City offered, chose instead to spend her time and money on cows and sheep.

There was a flurry of motion off to the left, and the dog appeared, nipping at the heels of a slow-moving sheep.

"*Oh, Miss Potter!*" Rascal barked. "*Look what I've found! Your lost sheep!*"

"*No nipping, now!*" the sheep bleated. She glanced over her shoulder. "*Come along, laaambs. Look smaaart, and don't laaag behind. Miss Potter waaaants to meet you!*"

Miss Potter turned. "Oh, see, Mr. Heelis!" she exclaimed delightedly. "Rascal has found Queenie. And she has twin lambs with her! The flock is larger than I expected, by two!"

"Sixteen Herdwicks." Will chuckled, now vastly amused. "Well done, Miss Potter. I congratulate you."

"I think," Miss Potter said crisply, "that you had better congratulate Queenie. She produced the lambs."

But Rascal saw that she was smiling.

23

The Village Goes to Sleep

Saturday evening slipped quietly into Saturday night, and the villagers, quite worn out with the day's many excitements and surprises, were preparing to go to sleep.

At Belle Green, at the top of Market Street, George Crook finished winding the alarm clock and climbed into bed, while Mathilda Crook, wearing her flannel nightgown, put her hair up under her pink-ribboned sleeping cap.

"I cudna b'lieve my eyes," she said, for the seventh or eighth time since they had come home. "Dropped t' Luck, she did, reet on t' verra floor. Broke it all to smithereens."

"Aye, Tildy," said George wearily, closing his eyes and pulling the covers up under his chin. "Tha'st said that a'ready, more'n onct, Tildy."

"And then t' major says, 'Nivver mind, m'dear,' like t' sweet gen'leman he is," Mathilda went on in a satisfied tone. "Fancy that, George. Just fancy that! Why, if I'd dropped thi Luck and broke it, tha wud'st thwacked me a gud 'un."

"Aye, Tildy," said George darkly, and pulled the covers up over his head. "Aye, that I wud."

Mathilda wasn't listening. " 'Nivver mind, m'dear,' t' major says, sweet as cud be." She got into bed beside her husband, shaking her nightcapped head in wonderment. "Even though t' lady is wearin' a gray silk dress, and has broke his Luck."

"What's a gray silk dress got to do with it?" George asked, his voice muffled by the covers.

"What's a gray silk dress got to do with it?" Mathilda laughed. "Why, silly man! T' ghost of Raven Hall wears a gray silk dress. Everybody was talkin' about it, and wonderin' if she wore it on purpose. But our major didna care, did he? He leads her off to sip champagne, just like a prince and princess in a fairytale, and all t' while, t' music playin' so sweet, and all t' candles twinklin' like stars." She gave a gusty sigh. "Canst tha think of anything more beautiful, George? Canst tha?"

"Nay, Tildy," cried long-suffering George. "Nay, nivver."

"Oh, George," Mathilda said dreamily, and lay back on the pillow, gazing up at the ceiling. "If we cud only live like that, George! If we cud only have champagne and cake at ever' meal and music whilst we eat and a big house and maids and a cook and—"

"If we cud only go to SLEEP, Tildy!" George roared, from under the covers. "If we cud only go to sleep!"

In the upstairs bedroom at Croft End, Hannah Braithwaite was tucking her eldest daughter into bed and enumerating (not for the first time) all the astonishing things that had been set out on the refreshment table at Raven Hall.

"There was cold chicken an' smoked salmon an' ham an' pickled tongue, an' t' tongue had a paper ruffle round it, an' it was glazed an' sliced ever so dainty, an' had cloves an' bits of parsley stuck all over. An' there was oyster patties an' sausage rolls an' lobster mayonnaise an' cold boiled prawns with their tails all stickin' up in a circle. An' cakes an' custards an' Sarah Barwick's tipsy cake an' raspberry cream an' all sorts of things to drink an'—"

As Hannah ran out of breath, she saw that her daughter's eyelids were drooping. "So we ate an' we ate," she said, finishing the tale, "until we was so verra full we thought we'd pop all our buttons, an' listened to music an' admired t' lake, and then we came home. An' your dad looked splendid in his suit, he did, an' all t' ladies were ever so beautiful, an' especially Mrs. Kittredge, who had t' most beautiful dress of all, an' jewels all over her."

Hannah paused, thinking about that gray dress. The ghost of Raven Hall was said to wear a gray silk dress, a fact that had not escaped the village ladies this afternoon. Hannah herself had heard them whispering about it, saying that—

The little girl's eyes had popped open. "Will I ever have a beautiful dress an' jewels an' be a lady, Mum?"

"Oh, tha'lt have ever so many pretty dresses," Hannah said, and tucked the covers under her daughter's chin. "Go to sleep, now, dear. Tomorrow's church."

In the kitchen at Anvil Cottage, Sarah Barwick had finished putting her sticky buns to rise for an early morning baking. There were always Sunday day-trippers going up and down the road past her cottage, and though there were a few old stick-in-the-muddish villagers who thought shops ought to be closed on Sunday, Sarah wasn't one of them. She was in business to make a living, not to please her neighbors, and she'd sell whenever a customer rang her bell. At the moment, she was smoking a cigarette and sipping a cup of hot milk as she finished a letter to her second cousin Lydia in

Manchester, telling her all about the reception at Raven Hall.

"But the queerest bit of all," she wrote, after listing the cakes and delicacies she had been hired to provide and describing the rest of the food and the drink and the ladies' dresses and the doomed Luck, "was Mrs. Kittredge dropping the Luck, which Miss Potter says was meant to cover up Mr. Thexton calling her Irene, when her husband thinks she's Diana. Whatever her name, Lydia Dowling still says she's a witch and not a white one, either. Myself, I suspect she's the ghost of Raven Hall, come to life. The place is supposed to be haunted by a woman in a gray silk dress. And guess what she was wearing at the party? A gray silk, cut very low, which got everyone talking, believe you me."

Sarah paused, scratching her nose with the end of her pen. It was altogether a queer thing, when she thought about it. She would never pretend to know much about the manners and breeding of gentry-folk, and she certainly laughed her fill at the way they put on airs and graces and acted like they were better than anybody else. But it was clear to her that Major Kittredge was a fine gentleman, even if he did have just one arm and one eye, and that there was something about his wife that made her not quite a lady, no matter how hard she tried to pretend.

The major didn't know that yet, of course. He was still frightfully keen on his wife, and might be, for a long time to come. But character was bound to come out, sooner or later, and what then? He had married her, and marriage was a final sort of business, which was one of the reasons Sarah had not considered it for herself. What if you married somebody and he turned out not to be the person you thought he was? What if he drank and used his fists on you, or spent all your bakery earnings at the betting parlor? You were lumbered with him forever, like him or not. So even if the major woke up and realized he didn't want to be married to Mrs. Kittredge, there wasn't anything he could do about it.

Sarah sighed, thinking of her friend, Dimity Woodcock, who was bravely trying to hide her disappointment over the major's marriage. Poor Dimity. Major Kittredge would have done much better to have married her. Sarah wished—

But it was too late for wishing. There was nothing that could be done now. Not a blessed thing.

At Tower Bank House, Miles Woodcock was lying in bed, unable to sleep. His hands clasped behind his head, he was staring at the ceiling and frowning. His conversation with Mr. Richardson had done nothing to ease his mind, and although he hadn't been able to broach the matter with Major Kittredge, he had the feeling that the scheme to build the villas was all but signed and sealed.

This was a calamitous business. The western shore of Lake Windermere was pristine and beautiful. Villas would not only mar its scenic beauty, but bring in a great many more people, along with their horses and carriages and delivery lorries and even motor cars. The ferry was already taxed beyond its capacity, and one often had to wait for an hour or more to get to the other side of the lake. And the road—well, the road didn't bear thinking about. The road would have to be widened and paved, and the parish rates would certainly have to be raised.

Miles sighed. If Kittredge himself was determined to build, there was little that could be done to dissuade the man. However, from what Miss Potter had told him of the conversation at the ferry landing, he guessed it was Mrs. Kittredge who was behind the scheme. And without any leverage, he doubted that she could be persuaded to drop her support—and of course, there was no leverage.

With a groan, Miles rolled onto his stomach. Better to think of something more pleasant. Think of Dimity and Will Heelis, who had seemed so congenial a couple that afternoon. Why, even old Lady Longford had observed that they made a delightful pair, although Miles had overheard her remark that she hoped Mr. Heelis was about to replace the major in "poor, dear Dimity's affections"—a remark that Miles had found both surprising and offensive. He hadn't been aware that anyone other than himself might know of Dimity's attachment to Kittredge, or imagined her as having been jilted by the major, in favor of a red-haired actress who was clearly no lady. And if Lady Longford knew, so did the rest of the village, which meant that it was probably being discussed at this very moment, as people settled down in their beds.

But he refused to allow a little village gossip to tarnish his pleasure in the thought of his sister comfortably married to Will Heelis and established in a home of her own, not so far away that she could not continue to manage her bachelor brother's household.

And with that happy image shimmering in his mind and a pleased smile spreading across his face, he fell asleep.

In the bedroom on the other side of the hall at Tower Bank House, Dimity Woodcock lay awake and restless. She was deeply troubled by the thought of Christopher Kittredge married to a woman who did not deserve him, who might even be capable of hurting him and making him unhappy. Poor Christopher had already suffered a great many misfortunes. It would be dreadful for him if he had married badly, for there was nothing he could do to change the situation.

And did Dimity give any thought at all to Will Heelis? Well, yes, it must be said that she did, in a rather muddled, foggy, sleepy way. She thought of the shy smile that quirked one corner of his mouth, and the light in his brown eyes and the warmth in his voice, and she could not help but feel a certain comforting gratitude to him for being the sort of friend one could count on when other friends (or a person one had considered a friend, but who had married a person so much prettier than one, and with the most amazingly un-natural red hair) let one down.

And borne upon that mazy and meandering reverie, Dimity drifted at last off to sleep.

At Hill Top Farm, Miss Potter blew out the candle—gas was available but she did not choose to have it installed—and settled into her bed. She was thinking of all the inter-esting things that had happened that day: the business with the cats that morning, the reception at Raven Hall and the queer affair of Mrs. Kittredge and Mr. Thexton, her promise to recommend a governess for Caroline, Deirdre's strange tale about a fairy riddle, Queenie's new lambs, and Mr. Heelis's concern about Jeremy's education.

She smiled to herself as she pulled the covers up close. If she were in London, she'd be troubling about the linen, the dinner menus, her mother's cough, her father's liver. And while an outsider might think this little village was a very peaceful place, it wasn't, really. It was full of conflict and con-tradictions and secrets and, yes, riddles. It was full of life.

And that was why she loved being here, she thought hap-pily, as she lay watching the stars through her bedroom win-dow, too full of contentment to welcome sleep just yet. It was why she belonged. It was why she never wanted to leave.

*   *   *

At the vicarage, Vicar Sackett was not yet asleep, either. He was still at his desk in his study, having stayed up late to put the finishing touches on his Sunday morning sermon, the topic of which was "Thankfulness." He had taken as his text Colossians 3:15: "And let the peace of God rule in your hearts, to the which also ye are called in one body; and be ye thankful." It was an appropriate sentiment, he had decided, with which to see his Thexton cousins on their way. He, for one, was certainly thankful.

Reveling in the silence, the vicar believed that the rest of the house had gone to bed and so was greatly surprised when his study door opened without a knock and Mr. Thexton appeared, in slippers and a dark blue velvet dressing gown. He was carrying a largish plate of sandwiches and cake.

"I wonder if I might interrupt you, Cousin Samuel," he said diffidently.

Remembering that this was the very last Saturday night he should have to suffer such unwelcome interruptions when he was writing his Sunday sermon, the vicar swallowed his annoyance and said with a small smile, "Yes? What can I do for you?" He glanced at the plate in some surprise. He had seen both Mr. and Mrs. Thexton helping themselves enthusiastically at the Raven Hall refreshment table and afterward, at the vicarage table, where Mrs. Thompson had left a cold supper. He had not thought it possible to be hungry after that.

Mr. Thexton followed his glance. "Mrs. Thexton gets a bit peckish at night," he explained, adding, in an offhand way, "I thought perhaps I should mention that we shall be staying on a few more days—past Monday, I mean."

The vicar felt as if he had taken a hard punch in his midsection. "A few more days!" he exclaimed.

"Perhaps a little longer," said Mr. Thexton. "Oh, and Mrs. Thexton wanted me to tell you that she has asked Mrs. Thompson to remove cod from the menu for the coming week. She is sure that you must be growing exceedingly weary of cod." His smile became ingratiating. "If I may be allowed to say so, dear Mrs. Thexton is always more concerned for the tastes and welfare of others than for her own. Cod suits her perfectly, of course, but she realizes that it must be trying for you."

The vicar attempted to gain control of himself. "A few more days?" he repeated, in a strangled voice. "But I thought we agreed—"

"Oh, yes, we did. Indeed, we did, Cousin Samuel," said Mr. Thexton quickly. "And it was my full intention to bring our visit to an end on Monday morning, with regret, of course, for we are mindful of—and most grateful for—your hospitality. But I am sure you must recognize the extent to which the situation has changed."

"Changed?" asked the vicar feebly.

"Of course." Mr. Thexton seemed surprised that his cousin did not appear to understand. "I had only a brief opportunity to view the Luck before it was so disastrously destroyed. But my glimpse was sufficient to point me to several more areas of research which require investigation. I'm sure you'll agree that this is of vital importance, and will extend your hospitality through Monday week, at which time we can discuss the matter again."

Monday week! "But the Luck is broken!" the vicar protested. "Surely you can't—"

"I have an appointment to interview Mrs. Kittredge early next week," Mr. Thexton went on in a businesslike tone.

"She had quite an affinity for the piece, you see, and was of course the last person to have it actually in her hands. I am hopeful that she will be able to give me a few more particulars about it." He glanced down at the plate in his hand. "I'd love to visit with you longer, but I really must take this up to Mrs. Thexton. She often feels quite faint if she is not able to have a little something at night. I wish you very pleasant dreams, dear Cousin Samuel."

The wretched fellow left, and the vicar buried his head in his hands. He sat in that manner for nearly a quarter of an hour, trying to think whether there was anything—anything at all—that might be done to persuade his horrid guests to leave. But he could think of nothing.

Well, not quite. He reached for his sermon and made a notation at the top of the page. Tomorrow's Scripture reading would begin with 1 Samuel, 28:38: "And Jonathan cried after the lad, Make speed, haste, stay not."

And with that, the vicar, filled with an enormous frustration, took himself off to bed.

24

Nocturnal Affairs

By midnight, all the lamps and candles in the village—even the gaslights in the Tower Bank Arms, where the men had been drinking their Saturday night half-pints and tossing their Saturday night darts—had been extinguished, and all the residents of the Land between the Lakes were fast asleep.

The humans, that is. The animal inhabitants of Sawrey—the cats and dogs, rats and field mice, garden voles and hedgehogs and shrews and bats—were mostly wide awake, for a great deal of their business was transacted after the sun went down and the Big Folk put out their lights and retired. (Horses, cows, pigs, sheep, and chickens, of course, mostly kept the same hours as humans did, since they were often wanted for something or another in the middle of the day and saw no point in staying up half the night, as well.)

On this particular Saturday night, Tabitha Twitchit, Crumpet, and Rascal were gathered in the tool shed at the bottom of the Anvil Cottage garden, where they often met to talk things over. They began by trading notes on what they had learnt from various humans about the events at Raven Hall that afternoon. Big Folk being the vague and imprecise and inventive creatures they are, each animal had heard a slightly different version of how the Luck came to be smashed.

Tabitha had heard it from Lucy Skead, who had discussed it with Elsa Grape when she dropped in at Tower Bank House to return the gloves she had borrowed from Elsa. Lucy reported that it was Mr. Thexton who had dropped the Luck, and that Major Kittredge had been so angry that he refused to accept poor Mr. Thexton's apology.

Crumpet had heard the tale from Bertha Stubbs, who was so full of the story that she had run next door to tell it to old Mrs. Abbey, whose bad chest had kept her in bed and away from the festivities. In Bertha's version, someone had bumped into Mrs. Kittredge, forcing her to drop the Luck. She had then fainted and had to be revived with champagne.

Rascal had more to tell than either of the cats, since he had heard Miss Potter tell Mr. Heelis what Mr. Thexton had said and what had happened after that, which seemed to suggest that Mr. Thexton had some sort of knowledge about the mysterious Mrs. Kittredge which she did not want him to share.

"Who is she, then?" Crumpet asked, feeling confused. *"Is she Irene, or is she Diana?"*

"Does it matter?" Tabitha replied with a shrug. *"Humans often have more than one name, anyway."*

"It seemed to Miss Potter that it mattered," Rascal replied seriously, *"and I'm inclined to take her word for it. She's jolly observant, you know. She sees things other people don't. And things that other people don't want her to see."*

The cats certainly agreed with Rascal's statement, but since they could make neither heads nor tails of the matter, they went on to a topic that all three of them definitely knew something about. Rats, and how to deal with them.

"It looks as if the recruitment project has gone very well," Tabitha said with satisfaction. *"There are now four experienced ratters assigned to the Hill Top barns and outbuildings. They are working eighteen hours each, with six off to sleep. Claw and Fang came over from Hawkshead, where they were formerly employed in Mrs. Goforth's grocery. Tiger is from the barn at the Sawrey Hotel. And Lion's previous employment was in the brewery at Ambleside, where he was responsible for keeping rats out of the grain. The four of them tell me that they should have the situation under control shortly."*

"Don't forget Max," put in Rascal, loyal to his friend. *"He's doing a rum job, too."*

Tabitha frowned. *"Max is an amateur. He kills for his dinner, and when he's not hungry, he doesn't. The others are professionals. Killing rats is their business. They kill round the clock, whether they're hungry or not."*

Rascal felt that the term "amateur" belittled Max, but he had to own that Tabitha was describing him accurately—and the others, too. They were professional killers, mercenaries.

"Who's doing the Hill Top attic?" Crumpet wondered. *"Isn't that where the rats actually live?"*

"I have good news to report there, too," Tabitha replied, with the pleased smugness of a cat who has everything under control. *"I don't know his name or where he came from, but a very large, very masterful cat is now patrolling the attic—an amazingly efficient rat-killer, according to Fang."*

"I'm not half surprised that Miss Potter's gone and let a strange cat into the house," Rascal remarked. *"I know she doesn't mind you lot, but I thought all the new cats were supposed to work in the barn."*

"According to Fang, this is a cat who does not take no for an answer. He prefers to work in the attic." Tabitha smiled, taking

personal credit for this splendid outcome. *"With him on the job, I'm sure we have nothing to worry about."*

Crumpet frowned. Tabitha was always too quick to declare everything settled, when there were often loose ends that wanted tying up. *"P'rhaps we'd better put out the word. If there are a great many rats in the attic and this phenomenal cat of yours allows some to escape into the village, we could be in for trouble."*

"Not to worry," Rascal said with a grin. *"Jack Russell terriers are jolly good at going after rats, once they're out in the open."*

"And what about after?" Crumpet went on. *"What's to keep this cat at Hill Top? If he's such a great muchness of a killer, what do we do if he decides to move into our gardens?"*

Tabitha frowned. *"But that would violate the Rule, Crumpet."*

"So?" Crumpet asked. *"Who's going to stop him? Are you?"*

Tabitha twitched her whiskers. *"I really don't think he will—"*

"That's exactly the trouble, Tabitha," Crumpet interrupted. *"You haven't thought far enough ahead. A cat who listens only to himself is a cat who is out of control. The next thing we know, he will be going about as a roaring lion, seeking for whom he may devour. First Peter, Chapter five, verse fifty-eight."*

"Crumpet," said Tabitha in an indignant tone, *"you are making far too much of this. As usual, you—"*

"As usual," Crumpet put in loftily, *"I am pointing out something you have overlooked. You may be the oldest cat in the village, but you are not necessarily the wisest. You—"*

"Dry up!" barked Rascal. *"Right this minute!"* With sulky glances, the cats subsided, and Rascal went on. *"If that's all there is to say about that, ladies, I have something to tell you."*

He told about the magical glade that he and the children had discovered and the riddle they had found pinned to an oak tree with a silver knife—although he said nothing about the plan for May Eve, since the cats would undoubtedly want to go along, which he didn't intend to allow. May Eve was *his* show, and he wasn't sharing it.

Tabitha frowned. *"I shouldn't think you'd want the children to be involved with those dwelves, Rascal. They're a trying, troublesome lot. You're lucky you got back safely."*

Rascal hated to reveal his ignorance, but he felt he had to know, especially since Tibbie had said more or less the same thing. *"Tell me about those dwelves,"* he said. *"Who are they?"*

"They're Oak Folk," Crumpet replied. *"Several generations ago—a generation is a very long time, where Folk are concerned—some dwarves and some elves became . . . well, friends. Then there were a few weddings, and the Fern Vale dwelves are the result."*

"What do they look like?" Rascal asked, now feeling anxious.

Crumpet snickered.

Tabitha frowned. *"Well, I've never seen one myself, but—"*

"Just how do you know?" Crumpet challenged, twitching her tail. *"Why, you might be talking to one at this very moment!"*

"Excuse me?" Rascal said, even more anxiously.

"They're shape-shifters," Crumpet explained. *"They take whatever form they like. Just when you think you know what they are, they're something else altogether. They can look like a leaf, like a tree, like a human, like a squirrel."* She gave Tabitha a meaningful glance. *"Like Tabitha."*

"I am definitely ME," said Tabitha frostily, *"although I'm not too sure who YOU are, Crumpet."*

"Don't fret yourself, Tabitha," Crumpet replied in a knowing tone, and licked her paw. *"If you are Tabitha, that is. When one is dealing with dwelves, one never knows."*

"Oh, really!" Tabitha exclaimed, now thoroughly irritated.

"Oh, Jimminy," Rascal muttered, remembering the riddle. *"Tall or short, thick or thin, Guess the shape we are in."*

"That's it, exactly," Crumpet replied. *"It's all guesswork with dwelves. You're never quite sure what to expect, and before you*

know it, you're upside down and inside out. That's why most com-monsensible animals avoid them. They may be very helpful—"

"Or they may make things difficult," said Tabitha, forgetting her irritation. *"They may give you perfectly reliable directions for going on a long trip somewhere—"*

"Or they may happily send you off on a wild-goose chase," said Crumpet. *"With dwelves, there's no predicting."*

"Indeed," Tabitha said, and her eyes grew round. *"Why, they've even been known to carry off kittens, and make slaves of them. And children, too!"*

"That's beastly!" Rascal exclaimed.

"It's nonsense," Crumpet said. She frowned at Tabitha. *"It's just talk, Tabitha. You know how Big Folk are. They love to sit around the fire on a winter's night and make up stories. The Folk are mischievous, but they're not deliberately malicious."*

And although you (like Crumpet) might be inclined to dismiss this last bit as a midwinter night's tale, Rascal was definitely feeling worried, for if these dwelves were as untrustworthy as Tabitha said they were, it might not be safe for the children to go back to the glade on May Eve. Still, perhaps Crumpet was right, and it was all just talk. Perhaps the dwelves were gracious and charming and entirely hospitable.

And anyway, worried or not, there was nothing he could do to stop the children from going. Their plans were made, and there was no way he could persuade them to change.

The only thing he could do was go along, and try to keep them safe.

25

Foul Murder Afoot

While the Big Folk slept and the village animals discussed village business, appalling events were happening just across the road and up the hill.

Foul murder was afoot in the Hill Top attic, in the person of the Cat Who Walks by Himself.

The Cat had not yet lived up to his promise to exterminate all of the rats in the attic, but he had every expectation of doing so quite soon. By eleven o'clock on Saturday night, he had made short (but bloody) work of the concertina player and the trio of can-can dancers, along with a half dozen of the billiard-playing crew. Next, he set up an ambush behind a stack of boxes at the top of the staircase, where, with a regrettable lack of gallantry, he lay in wait until a party of revelers emerged with a string of sausages and a large cheese they had hauled from the dairy. Without warning—the Cat was restricted by no rules of gentlemanly warfare—he sprang silently on the lot and tore them limb from limb, scattering rat tails and shreds of rat fur and bitten-off rat ears far and wide, leaving scarcely anything behind to serve for a decent funeral. Then he helped himself to the sausages, too, and a goodly portion of the cheese.

Satisfied, the Cat went down to the dark kitchen and sorted through the cupboards until he found Miss Potter's store of medicinal brandy. He took several hearty nips and, feeling very sleepy, padded up the main staircase to Miss Potter's second-floor bedroom, where he jumped up onto the foot of her featherbed. She woke up and pushed him off, but he was the Cat Who Walks by Himself and had a distinct preference for soft, warm featherbeds, as opposed to hard, cold floors. He jumped right back up, turned around several times to make a cozy little nest, and purred himself to sleep.

But while the Cat and Miss Potter slept, there was chaos in the attic. Glimpsing the fate that awaited them, many of the rats made a precipitous departure, taking with them only what they could carry and abandoning the attic like . . . well, like rats leaving a sinking ship. But once they got outdoors, they discovered (as had Ridley Rattail) that there was nowhere to run. They couldn't go to the Hill Top barns, for the outbuildings were now being guarded by a formidable federation of five cats—Fang, Claw, Max, Lion, and Tiger.

So the fugitives faced a dilemma. Should they go to Tower Bank Arms, with its deadly traps? Or Buckle Yeat Cottage, with its cramped attic and miserly kitchen? Or Farmer Potatoes' barn, which was warm and dry and just a short scamper away from Sarah Barwick's bakery?

One didn't have to be a precociously clever rat to decide in favor of Farmer Potatoes' barn. Before long, the place was full to the rafters with refugee rats, and the first fetch-and-carry units were being dispatched in the direction of the bakery, where a reconnaissance team had discovered a batch of yeast rolls rising.

But not all the rats fled the attic. There were quite a few who had been absent when the initial attacks took place and had not seen the Cat at work. When they came home and found their friends and colleagues slaughtered, they were more angry than terrified. They gathered in groups, snarling and gnashing their teeth and vowing to wreak a terrible vengeance on the Cat who had committed these foul murders.

At last, after an extended discussion which (rats being rats) occasionally and regrettably deteriorated into name-calling and fisticuffs, the pack decided it was time to take matters into their own paws. They chose a commander, a rugged, robust, rough-looking rat named Custard, who had gained his military experience when he lived for two years under the floorboards of the training barracks of the Cold-stream Guards. Commander Custard knew a thing or two about going to war. Following his orders, the rats began to gather their weapons: stout cudgels constructed from clothes-pins, lances fashioned from hatpins stolen from the pin cushion on Miss Potter's chest of drawers, cutlasses crafted from broken knife blades, and slings made of shoelaces and scraps of leather, with marbles stolen from the Jennings children for missiles.

While the male rats armed themselves, the female rats embroidered the regiment's motto, *Nulli Secundus* (Second to None), on scraps of material left from Miss Potter's red curtains, and rolled bandages from strips of white cotton stolen out of her work basket. The boy rats who were too young to fight made pipes out of hollow willow twigs and drums from Miss Potter's best napkin rings, with pieces of wash-leather bound on top and bottom with cobbler's thread, and drumsticks from matchsticks found beside the fireplace in Miss Potter's parlor. A very old rat, blind in one eye, had grown up in the mess hall of the B Company of the Scots Guards and had learnt a great many military ditties. He taught them to play "The Soldiers of the Queen, My Lads," and within an hour, they were piping and drumming with good spirit.

While the ladies sewed, the pipes piped, and the drums drummed, Commander Custard formed his troops into squads and platoons. For the rest of that night and into the early hours of Sunday morning, they drilled and ma-neuvered in the middle of the attic floor, their squad lead-ers counting cadence—*"One-two-three-hup!"*—and barking orders—*"Column left, march!" "Right flank, march!"*—as well as shouting general exhortations: *"Look smart now, boys!"* and *"Keep up the cadence."* Some of them practiced flinging them-selves flat onto their bellies and crawling through an ob-stacle course created from broken clay pots, old boots, a discarded umbrella that had belonged to Miss Potter, rolled-up carpeting, and piles of magazines, while others deployed from columns into lines and assaulted dummies hastily manufactured from woolen socks stuffed with bran. I tell you, it was a stirring sight. Any rat with an ounce of martial instinct in his soul would have been moved to tears.

Meanwhile, the sergeants and lieutenants gathered with Commander Custard around an improvised map table to develop a battle plan. The troops would be stationed at the top of the stair, with the cudgels on the right flank, the cut-lasses on the left flank, and the lancers in the middle. The slingers, well back, would launch a deadly barrage of mar-bles into the killing zone. When the Cat crept up the attic stairs, they would converge upon him all at once, take him by surprise, and—before he could unsheathe his terrible claws or bare his frightful fangs—they would kill him dead.

It was an admirable plan, and when Commander Custard announced it to the troops, the rafters rang with enthusiastic cheers. Within the hour, the army was deployed with their weapons at the ready, while their sergeants and lieutenants went up and down the ranks, exhorting the troops to do their best and fight as bravely as they could, and the troops replied with loud cheers and huzzahs and other things of that sort, as soldiers do when they are trying to hearten themselves to do something they really do not care to do.

Yes, it was a splendid plan, masterfully conceived and executed with discipline and devotion to duty. And when the Cat for whom they were waiting opened the door and stepped out onto the field of battle, the rats made a splendid, spirited, heart-stirring effort. The lancers lunged, the cutlasses slashed, and the cudgels bludgeoned. The pipers piped and the drums drummed and the spectators cheered at the top of their lungs. Throughout the attic could be heard the sounds of brutal battle and the valiant cries of *"Fell the fiend!" "Slaughter the swine!"* and *"Butcher the brute!"*

But all the lunging and slashing and cudgeling, all the piping and drumming and cheering and shouting, availed them nothing. The Cat who faced them was three times larger and five times more powerful and ten times more savage than any cat they had ever seen. He brushed off the lances, swatted the cudgels, slapped away the cutlasses. The hail of marbles bounced harmlessly off his fur and rolled away, unnoticed. He began to use his claws and fangs with cruel abandon.

Commander Custard, who had led the lancers' charge against the foe, was amongst the first to die, his brave rallying cry—*"Stand your ground, boys, stand your ground to the last!"*—ringing through the ranks.

And within a matter of minutes, the battlefield was littered with headless rat corpses, broken weapons, and trampled flags. The blood of brave warriors ran ankle-deep, while the desolate wails of bereaved widows and orphans filled the air.

Custard's Last Stand was over. The army was defeated.

26

Ridley Rattail Has a Dream

Ridley Rattail was not present at the battle, but no doubt he would have been pleased if he had watched it happen. Wasn't this what he wanted? Wasn't the utter rout of the rats exactly the outcome he had intended when he posted his advertisement? The Hill Top attic was rid of its rowdy rabble-rousers at last, and life would soon return to normal.

Ridley did not witness the bloodbath because he was hiding in a manger in Farmer Potatoes' barn, where he had taken refuge after being evicted from the attic. His eyes were squeezed shut and he was holding his paws over his ears, trying to shut out the terrifying tales of the Cat's first killings, carried by the rats who had fled Hill Top and taken sanctuary in the barn. But he couldn't keep his eyes shut and his paws over his ears forever. And when a few badly wounded survivors dragged themselves into the barn and began to describe in grisly detail the carnage of Custard's

Last Stand, Ridley's horror knew no bounds, and he felt his cowardice and timidity even more than before.

It was not that Ridley mourned the deaths of all those dozens of rats, for he was scarcely even acquainted with them, and anyway, they were the rowdies and ruffians who had caused all the difficulties in the first place. No, he was transfixed with horror because he knew what was bound to happen next.

The Cat who had killed and eaten so many rats would now retire to sleep off his exertions. But in a matter of hours—six or eight, ten at the most—he would rouse himself and return to the attic refreshed, reinvigorated, and ravenous, to finish his work. And because he had polished off all the rats who dared to confront him, he would next target the defenseless Rosabelle and her sister Bluebell and Bluebell's children, along with all the widows and orphans left in the attic. Of course, many of these would flee rather than face certain death at the hands of the killer. But Ridley knew his Rosabelle, and understood with an appalling clarity that she would never leave the place where she had lived for so long and so happily, and where she had extended her generous hospitality to so many hapless wayfarers, including Ridley himself. And look at the way he had repaid this selfless lady! Reprehensible coward that he was, despicable ingrate, *he* was to blame for what had happened. He and he alone had called this calamity down upon Rosabelle's innocent head. The fault was his, and the guilt was his. He would never be able to forgive himself.

Ridley closed his eyes, feeling dull-witted and doltish. He would be the first to admit that complex thought was his *bête noire,* and that his small brain was already so full of desperate self-reproach and awful foreboding that there was scarcely any space left for the serious consideration of what should be done.

But he had to apply himself. He had to think of some means of disposing of the Cat. He had to imagine some method of bringing the creature to justice, envisage some way to protect poor Rosabelle and preserve the peace of the Hill Top attic, conceive of some . . .

But so much focussed concentration was exhausting. Before he could tax his poor, weak brain any further, Ridley Rattail fell asleep. And as he slept, he dreamed of a long and winding passage in *Alice in Wonderland,* his favorite childhood book, which his beloved mother had read aloud to him in her sweet, comfortable voice every night before he went to bed, cuddling him up against her plump, warm body:

> Fury said to a
>   mouse, That he
>   met in the
>   house,
> "Let us
>   both go to
>   law: I will
>   prosecute
>   YOU.—Come,
>   I'll take no
>   denial; We
>   must have a
>   trial: For
>   really this
>   morning I've
>   nothing
> to do."

Said the
mouse to the
cur, "Such
a trial,
dear Sir,
With
no jury
or judge,
would be
wasting
our
breath."

"I'll be
judge, I'll
be jury,"
Said
cunning
old Fury:
"I'll
try the
whole
cause,
and
condemn
you
to
death."

But as Ridley went on dreaming (and smiling, for this
was a sweet dream, and his mother's warmth was consoling
and her voice comforting), his dream seemed to modulate
and mutate and metamorphose in the meandering manner

of dreams, until it was no longer a dream of the mouse's tail.

It had become a dream about a rat's tail, or tale, if you like.

The rat in this tale was a fat, ugly old rat named Samuel Whiskers, and he lived with his wife Anna Maria in the Hill Top attic—at least according to Miss Potter, who was putting the two of them into a book. The pages lay, unfinished, on her work table, where Ridley had read them. In the story, the mischievous Tom Kitten climbs up inside the Hill Top chimney and blunders into the attic, where Samuel Whiskers and Anna Maria fall upon him and pull off his blue coat and roll him into a bundle and tie him with string in very hard knots, intending to make him into a roly-poly kitten dumpling for their dinner.

Now, this little book was a fine book for a rat to read (at least as far as the dumpling scene, which was as far as Miss Potter had got in writing it). But it proved an even finer book for a rat in Ridley's position to dream about, for his dream took one odd turn and then another and yet another, and when Ridley woke up a little while later, his dreaming brain had solved the problem that had baffled his waking mind.

Thanks to his dream, and thanks to his reading of the tale of Samuel Whiskers, Ridley knew exactly what had to be done to dispose of the Cat who had caused so much grief and anguish in the Hill Top attic.

27

Miss Potter Takes a Walk

Beatrix woke up on Sunday morning to find the cat asleep on the foot of the bed. She remembered trying several times in the night to push him onto the floor, but it was of no use. It was becoming very clear that this cat was a problem. Rats or no rats, she would have to get rid of him.

But not today. As she threw open her window and put her head out, she was cheered and refreshed by a glorious blue sky and warm southerly breeze. The night had been a long one and she had been restless, disturbed by the recollection of what had happened at the party, as well as by a great deal of noise in the attic. Really, one would have thought a war was being waged up there!

The weather in the Land between the Lakes was as changeable as a child's temper, especially in the spring—slate-gray clouds in the morning, a smiling of sunshine in the afternoon, and a brisk north wind in the evening, rattling the shutters and chilling one to the bone. Tomorrow might be a day to spend indoors, while today was just right for that long tramp through Cuckoo Brow Wood that she had been promising herself. She was already starting to think about Jemima Puddleduck's book, which was next after she finished the roly-poly pudding book, and she wanted to sketch a fox. There was one that denned in the badger sett at the top of Holly How—if she went there and waited quietly, she might get a glimpse of him. And there was Fern Vale Tarn, at the top of Cuckoo Brow Wood, where there were oak trees and very old beeches and a great many ferns, which might be useful as backgrounds. She hadn't been up that way since the previous summer, and she was yearning for a nice long walk.

So she boiled some eggs and made up two sandwiches with slices of cold mutton and put them into a canvas pack, along with an apple and a Thermos of tea and her sketchbook and pencils. She pulled on her stout leather walking boots, took her hat and her walking stick, shouldered her pack, and started out.

It was still early and this was a Sunday morning, so there was no one about in the village except for old Spuggy Pritchard, who was carrying two buckets of milk from Castle Farm on a wooden yoke slung over his shoulders, and a trio of Mrs. Llewelyn's chickens scratching in the grass in front of High Green Gate. A thrush was singing his dawn song from a chimney top and people must be up and about in their cottages, for Beatrix could smell bacon frying and hear the voices of mothers urging their young children to wash their faces and get dressed for church. Beatrix's family was Unitarian and she didn't usually attend Sunday morning services at St. Peter's, although she and Dimity Woodcock sometimes went to Evensong together.

Filling her lungs with the fresh, clean air, so different from the sooty stuff in London, Beatrix walked up to the top of Market Street, where it became Stony Lane, then followed the little three-rutted track: two ruts for the wagon wheels, with a rut in the center where the horse walked. The verges were green with fresh grass and bright with buttercups and daisies. The lane curled over the cusp of Oatmeal Crag, dipped down into the green valley of Wilfin Beck, and joined into a contented partnership with the little brook, which leapt and swirled and chuckled beside it, until the lane took its own way again, up the fellside. Beatrix crossed at the rocky ford between Tidmarsh Manor and Holly How Farm and climbed the narrow, zig-zag path that the sheep had made to the top of Holly How, near the badger sett.

She sat down on a rock, took out her pad and pencil, and waited, the sunshine warm on her face. She never felt dull or bored when she walked out into the countryside, for there was always something to see and sketch—something quite naturally magical, she always thought, for the wild places had their own kind of natural magic. She had felt this from her childhood, during the long holidays she and her brother had spent in Scotland, where they could escape for hours and even whole days from the parental rules and regulations of the Potter household, into the magical places.

This place was magic, too. In the next few minutes, a brown mouse with large brown eyes dashed past, chittering nervously that if she was late to breakfast, someone should have to answer for the consequences. Then a shiny click-beetle blundered across Beatrix's boot, stopped to mutter an apology, and then blundered back again the same way he had come, like a half-blind old gentleman who had forgotten his spectacles. When the beetle had gone, a smug, self-satisfied lizard with a flickering tongue crawled out to sun himself on a warm, flat rock. He reminded Beatrix of Toby, the pet lizard that she and her brother Bertram had brought from Ilfracombe while they were children.

And then, to her enormous delight, a red fox poked his narrow, pointed nose out of one of the sett's side entries, sniffed the air, and ventured outside, stretching himself, forelegs out, rump and tail up, a dog's stretch. His fur was tufted and tatty from his spring molt, giving him a rakish charm and making him exactly right for the part of Jemima Puddleduck's would-be seducer. He lay down in the sun for a time, licking his paw and smoothing his ears, like a cat.

Beatrix sat very still, moving just her pencil and breathing as little as possible. If the fox was alarmed when he looked up and saw that a lady artist in a flopping straw hat and walking boots was drawing his picture in her sketchbook, he didn't show it. Finally, he got up and trotted down the hillside toward the meadow, where he was no doubt hoping to find an unwary rabbit or vole who might agree to join him for breakfast.

Amused, Beatrix put away her sketchbook and got up, too. She cocked her head, hearing the call of the cuckoo, the clear, sweet bell that tells the world that spring has come at last to the Land between the Lakes. Like the timely cuckoo in the grandfather's clock that sat at the foot of her stair, it reminded her that if she dallied all day, she would never get to Cuckoo Brow Wood.

So she took the path that circled round behind Holly How, where last summer she and Sarah Barwick had searched for the Herdwick sheep she'd bought from old Ben Hornby. The narrow meadow just beyond was as bright as a painting, blue with harebells, golden with cowslips, and accented by purple pasque flowers and red campion, and beyond rose the great, green wildness of Cuckoo Brow Wood. She would stop for a bit to sketch wildflowers in the meadow, then climb through the wood to the top of Claife Heights and walk along the ridge to the little tarn she remembered, which sported a green ruff of fern along its banks. She would come back down again by the road Captain Woodcock had taken yesterday, going to and from Raven Hall. It would be a longish walk, but she had the whole pretty day for it, and no need to hurry.

And so she loitered along the path, delighting in the spring flowers that brushed against her skirt and the very blue sky that arched over her head, sitting for a time to sketch, then going on again, completely unaware that this was the very same path along which, just the afternoon before, Rascal (following Badger's map) had led the children through the ancient woods to Fern Vale Tarn, in search of the fairy village.

Beatrix had been up to the tarn the previous summer, but the path she took on that occasion had led to the lake's north end, rather than the south, as it seemed to do now. So when she climbed the last steep hill and put her head over the crest of the bank as the children had done, she found herself looking down into a magical green glade that was entirely new to her. In fact, she was every bit as astonished and delighted as they had been at the sight of the velvety pillows of moss, the soft carpet of leaves, and the emerald lake just beyond, fringed with fern and floating water-lilies. And just as they had, she imagined the little glen transfixed in the silence of a magical enchantment.

But her imagination was framed by what she had read. She remembered Mr. Barrie's description of the fairy balls in the Fairy Basin at Kensington Gardens, and the magical woodland in Shakespeare's *A Midsummer Night's Dream:*

> *I know a bank where the wild thyme blows*
> *Where oxlips and the nodding violet grows*

Quite over-canopied with luscious woodbine,
With sweet musk-roses and with eglantine . . .

Then she thought of the old Cumbrian saying, "Fairy folk live in old oaks," and the country people's belief that the huge, gnarled roots of the oak and fir and beech trees concealed the doors to the houses where the Folk lived.

And when she remembered Arthur Rackham's drawings of fairy doorways in *Grimm's Fairy Tales,* she got down on her hands and knees to look for a door amongst the roots, which might have a gold doorbell hung beside it and open into little hallways, with miniature umbrella stands and pegs for hanging coats and hats and signs that said MIND YOUR STEP.

She wasn't surprised when she didn't find a door, for she had the feeling that fairies were extremely rare these days. If any still lived in this glen, they would have taken the trouble to hide their doors so that an inquisitive person would not be easily able to find them. But if there were fairies, they would need some fairy furniture, and so she collected some twigs and bark and leaves and small vines as pliable as twine, along with several other interesting woodsy bits. She sat down on a hummock of moss and constructed a tiny table with two fat red toadstools for stools. And then, inspired, she built a canopy of branches over it, with slabs of bark at the back and sides and ferns for a roof and a path of white pebbles leading across the mossy turf to a nearby rock, overlooking the tarn. She set two acorn caps on the table for plates and filled them with tiny red berries, and stuck a sprig of wild thyme in a bit of moss for a centerpiece. And all the while she was smiling at herself for fancying that fairies and Folk were real, and then smiling at herself for fancying they weren't.

Now, you may think it strange and perhaps even silly that a woman of Beatrix Potter's age (I won't say exactly what that is, but some might say she was old enough to know better) would get down on her hands and knees to hunt for fairy doorways in the mossy roots of old oak trees, or stop to build a little garden-house for fairies who wanted to have their supper out of doors.

But if that's what you think, you must think again. When Beatrix was a child, she played with fairies in exactly the same way she played with the animals who shared her third-floor nursery at Bolton Gardens. She believed (or wanted to believe, which came to the same thing) that real fairies lived amongst the real creatures of the real forests and fields, and that even though she might not have been lucky enough to see them on her last visit to the garden or the woods, she was bound to see them the next time, or the next, or the next. If she believed, there was always hope.

Grown up at last and required to live all day long in the real world, it now seemed to Beatrix that imaginary fairies were of a great deal more use than real ones. And I think we must agree with her on that score. It is undeniably true that the imagination is far more powerful than knowledge, and that it is much more important to believe in something than to know it! There is, after all, a limit to the things we can know (even if we are fortunate enough to be geniuses), but no limit whatsoever to the things we might imagine. And if we cannot imagine, we will never know what we have yet to learn, for imagination shows us what is possible before knowledge leads us to what is true. For Beatrix, dreaming, imagining, creating, improvising, and fancying redeemed the stern and sometimes frightening world in which she lived, and allowed her to transform it.

Well, if the fairies wouldn't open their doors and come out and let her draw them, there were certainly many other things that belonged in her sketchbook. She drew her fairy table with its red toadstool chairs. Then, thinking about Jemima Puddleduck and the fox, she drew several trees and a view of the path, which might come in handy as a background. Then she spent some time drawing lichens growing on a larch and others on a fir tree and put a few samples into her pack, so she could take them back to Bolton Gardens and look at them under her microscope. After that, she sketched the ferns and the sedge grass along the lakeshore, and a red squirrel who ran out onto an oak branch and perked his ears and flicked his bushy tail and watched her curiously with his brilliant black eyes. (Since Beatrix didn't know about the dwelves, she couldn't know that they are shape-shifters and enjoy turning themselves into squirrels and magpies and even fish or frogs, when the day is very warm and they feel like having a swim. And it is, of course, quite impossible for me or you or anybody to know whether the red squirrel on the oak was really a squirrel, or a dwelf having a bit of a squirrel-frolic. Only the dwelf could say for certain and only if he wanted to, which he probably wouldn't, since his purpose in shifting his shape in the first place was to deceive.)

It was in this way that Beatrix completely lost herself for quite a time in this magical glade, beside the small, placid tarn, imagining that she was in a primeval forest far removed in time and space from the rest of the world. In fact, it seemed so ancient and so completely, delightfully, naturally wild that when she looked up and glimpsed, at a distance through the trees, the shapes of round towers and battlemented turrets, their conical roofs silhouetted against the very blue sky, she thought at first that it had to be an enchanted castle, where a princess was waiting to be released from the spell that bound her.

And then she realized that what she was seeing was no enchanted castle, but the solid stone shape of Raven Hall. This recognition brought her back to civilization with an unpleasant thump, and looking around, she saw that the little lake (which she had thought to be far away from anywhere, away at the back of beyond) must lie instead at the bottom of Major Kittredge's garden. She glimpsed a wide, mown lawn that sloped up to Raven Hall, the green shape of a neatly trimmed yew hedge with an arch cut into it, and the outline of an elaborate folly, like a Greek temple.

Beatrix was taken quite aback and felt really rather disappointed, as you would no doubt feel if you thought yourself in the middle of a great wilderness and suddenly discovered that you were in somebody's garden, with the real world of houses and people not a stone's throw away. And the realization of where she was made her remember that she had not yet had lunch and was feeling rather empty, so she looked around for a place to eat.

After a bit of searching, she found a pleasant willow-hung bank cushioned with a hummock of green moss exactly the size and shape of an overstuffed chair, and every bit as comfortable and welcoming. She took off her hat, sat down on the mossy bank, and unwrapped her mutton sandwiches. She ate both of them, and then, because the view of Fern Vale Tarn was so serene and the mossy bank so nicely warmed by the sun, she thought she would take a few quiet moments to relax. She was dozing dreamily, her sleepy mind turning over this and that—the farm, and the fox she had seen on Holly How, and the fairies she had not seen in the fairy glen—when something bounced off her nose and into her lap. She opened her eyes and saw that it was a plump acorn, and that a red squirrel (the same one she had seen earlier, or its cousin) was perched on the limb over her head, his head cocked, his tail twitching. And then the squirrel stopped twitching his tail and sat very still, listening. Beatrix listened, too, and heard voices.

Two voices, a man's and a woman's.

She thought at first that perhaps she was asleep and the voices were part of a dream, and then she remembered that Raven Hall was not so far away, which woke her up fully. It was probably the major and his wife, and they were coming closer. Perhaps she ought to jump up and declare herself before they got any nearer, so that they would not think she was spying on them. But perhaps that wasn't a good idea, after all, since popping up like a jack-in-the-box in front of two unsuspecting people would startle them, to say the least, and might lead to a disagreeable encounter. Anyway, she was sitting on the opposite side of quite a large bank, under an overhanging willow. If she made herself as small as possible and sat very quietly, perhaps they wouldn't notice her.

By then, of course, it was too late to do anything at all, even if she had wanted to, for the man and the woman were no more than a dozen feet away, just on the other side of her bank. The woman was indeed the major's wife (to judge by her throaty voice), but the man was definitely not the major. After a moment, Beatrix recognized the unmistakable voice of Mr. Thexton, and with that came the guilty realization that the conversation was something that she ought not be hearing. It was obviously intended to be private, and Beatrix had been taught since childhood that listening to other people's private conversations is extraordinarily impolite.

But Beatrix was in no position to stop listening. She could not escape without calling attention to herself. And worse, the more she heard, the more she knew she had to listen.

(Ever afterward, when she thought of this extremely uncomfortable moment, she would remind herself of the lesson it taught her: that sometimes when you get into an adventure, there is no easy way to get out, and you simply have to carry on the way you are going and hope for the best.)

"I have told you and *told* you, Mr. Thexton," the lady was saying, her voice tight and shrill with vexation, "I have nothing whatever to give you! Every shilling belongs to my husband, who is a very hard man when it comes to money. I haven't a prayer of getting anything from him—much less the thousand pounds you're asking."

A thousand pounds? Beatrix pulled in her breath. Mr. Thexton was demanding a thousand pounds from Mrs. Kittredge? But . . . but that was extortion. It was *blackmail*!

Mr. Thexton's voice was cold and unpleasant. "You have a great deal of fine jewelry. That necklace you're wearing, for instance. If the emeralds are real, as I don't doubt they are, I should put its value at twelve or fifteen hundred pounds. I suggest that you sell it."

"I can't sell it!" Mrs. Kittredge wailed. "It's not mine. It belongs to my husband's family."

Mr. Thexton chuckled disagreeably. "But Major Kittredge is *not* your husband, my dear lady. Your husband is my friend, James Waring. And Mr. Waring is very much alive, as I am sure you know—Mrs. Irene Waring."

Beatrix, by now thoroughly shaken, could scarcely believe her ears. The lady couldn't be two people! She couldn't be Mrs. Irene Waring and Mrs. Diana Kittredge at the same time. It was impossible. It was—

But of course, it was all too possible. Beatrix, an avid newspaper reader, had happened on many accounts of people who changed their identities, some of them many times. She had also read about the crime of bigamy: being married to two people at the same time. Sometimes this happened accidentally, as when a soldier went away to war and was reported dead and his wife married someone else, only to open her door one day and discover her first husband standing on the stoop. Of course, everybody felt very sorry for the people involved in this unhappy situation, and the law usually left them alone to sort things out as best they could.

But sometimes this was deliberate, as when a married person pretended to be single and (motivated by a desire for money or property or respectability) married someone else. Then it was a crime, and charges were pressed, and the bigamist could be sent to gaol.

The lady gave a low moan. "I didn't know he was still alive, Mr. Thexton. I swear I didn't! I thought James had died when his ship caught fire."

Mr. Thexton's "Really?" was full of scornful disbelief. "But he told me that he had written to you from South America, assuring you that he had escaped unhurt, and that you had written back to him in reply. At the time of that exchange, you were quite aware that he had not been killed when his ship went down. Granted, that was eighteen months ago. But he still had your letter in his possession when I spoke with him just last month."

"My . . . my letter?" There was a tearful little gasp. "I didn't . . . I don't remember. I've been ill. I've—"

"Oh, come now, Mrs. Waring. Poor James has been looking everywhere for you. It was very unkind of you to drop out of sight as you did, changing your name and leaving no forwarding address. James has been quite beside himself, searching all over London. Anyone might think that you disappeared deliberately, to avoid being reunited with your lawfully wedded husband." Another disagreeable chuckle. "I am sure that Major Kittredge will be terribly disappointed to learn that his wife isn't who she says she is. That she isn't his wife at all, but somebody else's. What do you think he'll do? Will he press charges? Or will he simply pack you off to your husband, where you belong?"

Beatrix bit her lip. Poor Major Kittredge! What *was* he likely to do?

"Oh!" the lady cried pitiably. "Oh, Mr. Thexton! You wouldn't tell him! You *can't*!"

Mr. Thexton gave a ironic sigh. "I shouldn't like to, of course. What a wretched string of misfortune the poor chap has had. I should hate to be the one to tell him that the woman he thought was his wife is married to another man."

"Oh, then don't!" the lady pleaded desperately. "Don't tell him!"

"I shall delay until Friday, Mrs. Waring. That will give you ample time to sell some of your fine jewelry." Mr. Thexton's voice hardened. "But only until Friday. After that, I shall be forced—oh, quite regretfully, you may be sure—to discuss the matter with Major Kittredge."

Beatrix heard a man shouting in the distance, and the woman said, "He's calling for me. I must go back."

Mr. Thexton chuckled. "Oh, yes, you mustn't disappoint the major, my dear Mrs. Waring. By all means, go to him. I shouldn't think you'll want to tell him anything about our conversation, though. It will be our little secret, won't it? Just between the two of us. At least until Friday. After that—"

There was a little cry, and the rustle of silk skirts, and then the sound of running footsteps. After a moment, Mr. Thexton began to whistle, tunelessly. He must have walked away, for shortly, Beatrix could hear nothing at all.

She sat very still for quite a long time, thinking what she ought to do. There were two crimes afoot here, involving several different people. Reluctant as she might be to meddle in people's private affairs, she knew she could not simply go home and forget what she had heard. But what should she do? Confront Mr. Thexton or Mrs. Kittredge—or Mrs. Waring, or whoever she was—with what she had heard, and demand that they do the right thing? Take her story, instead, to Major Kittredge, whom she barely knew, or to the constable, or to Captain Woodcock, the Justice of the Peace? The whole affair was very complicated, and it was difficult to know what was best to do.

At last, she got cautiously onto her knees and peeked over the top of the rock, to be sure that the garden was empty. Then she gathered her pack and her walking stick, put on her hat, and set off.

She did not like to be the bearer of bad news, but Mr. Thexton could not be permitted to blackmail anyone. And Major Kittredge must be told that there was a serious question about the legality of his marriage. She shivered, feeling suddenly apprehensive. There was altogether too much duplicity and deception in this world. Appearances could not be trusted: people were not always who they pretended to be. And even though the sun continued to shine and the sky was just as blue as ever, the day seemed suddenly darker.

And back at Fern Vale Tarn the red squirrel, chittering happily, jumped off the willow branch and scampered across the mossy glade until he came to Miss Potter's fairy garden-house, where he paused and peered under the canopy. He took one of the berries off one of the acorn plates and nibbled it appreciatively, then skipped across the glen and disappeared under the root of a very large oak tree.

28

Ridley Finds a Fifteen Percent Solution

As you no doubt know by now, Ridley Rattail is by nature a timid, irresolute, and definitely unheroic individual. Throughout his life, he has placed his personal comfort and safety above all other things, above family, friendship, and the society of other rats. Not once in his life has he put someone else first, or exerted himself in any way on another's behalf, or—I am especially sad to say—offered a helping paw to a rat in need. Ridley has spent his entire existence caring nothing for anyone but Ridley and getting as much for Ridley as he possibly could, and making Ridley's life as comfortable and convenient as possible. There it is, I'm afraid: we would be hard pressed to find a more selfish and self-satisfied rat in all of the Land between the Lakes—indeed, perhaps in all of England—than Ridley Rattail.

But fate has a mysterious way of offering us opportunities to redeem ourselves, and this occasion has now come to

Ridley. A scheme for disposing of the Cat who was wreaking such havoc in the Hill Top attic had been sent to him in a dream—a gift from whatever deity guards and guides the rats of this world—and Ridley now knew what he had to do. The thought of confronting the Cat, of coming anywhere within striking distance of those horrific claws and fangs, might make him feel dizzy and faint, but he knew he could not give in to his fears, or allow himself to delay even one moment. There was no way of predicting how long the Cat was likely to sleep after last night's battle. Ridley had to act now, and act fast.

So the rat left the sanctuary of Farmer Potatoes' barn and ran as fast as he could back to Hill Top Farm. But instead of entering Miss Potter's part of the house, he ducked through a hole in the masonry under the main room of the Jenningses' addition, a hole made by the rats so they could have easy access to both the old and the new parts of the farmhouse. It was Sunday, and Ridley was well aware that Mr. and Mrs. Jennings and all of their children would be spending the morning attending worship services at St. Peter's Church in Far Sawrey. In fact, Sunday mornings had always proved an excellent time to raid the Jenningses' cupboards and pantries, and since Ridley knew his way around the place, he wasted no time in going about his business.

On this particular morning, however, Ridley was not headed for the pantry or the bread shelf or the potato bin. He went straight to the bedroom, and the shelf beside Mrs. Jennings's side of the bed, where she kept a flat brown bottle of something that Dr. Butters had prescribed to help her get a good night's rest. The medicine was potent and she did not use it often, for it made her sleep so soundly that she did not hear the children crying or her husband getting up, and she worried that she might even sleep through a fire, if nobody woke her up. The bottle had two labels on it. On one label, there was a cautioning notation:

𝔑ot to be administered to infants

And on the other was written:

𝔏audanum

Ridley could read (hadn't his dream come from his reading of Miss Potter's little book about Samuel Whiskers and Anna Maria Rat and Tom Kitten?), but his vocabulary was not very large and while he might be able to sound out a word (*laud-a-NUM*), he did not always know its meaning. He did not, for example, know that laudanum was a solution of opium poppies prepared with alcohol, usually in a fifteen percent solution, or that it was one of the most powerful narcotics available. He did not know that bottles of the stuff sat on the shelf of almost every household in the country, or that colicky infants were regularly given doses of it (in spite of the caution on the label), or that such famous people as Queen Victoria, Charles Dickens, Lewis Carroll, and Elizabeth Barrett Browning had been addicted to it, or that it was a socially acceptable way of taking opium, which most people recognized as a dangerous drug.

But Ridley *did* know that whatever was in that brown bottle sent Mrs. Jennings into such a sound sleep that a rat could run across her chin and never wake her, which made it the perfect potion for his purposes. So he stole it, by the simple expedient of chewing a length of string from the string ball Mr. Jennings kept on the mantelpiece, wrapping it three times around the neck of the bottle, taking the free end in his teeth, and pulling the bottle along behind him like a sled—a very clever trick for a rat whose brain was not the biggest.

Dragging the bottle, Ridley went through a hole in the wainscot and into Miss Potter's part of the house, and from thence made his way up the spiral staircase to the attic. He pushed open the attic door, and stood stock still. Prepared as he was by the stories he had heard from the surviving rats, he was still struck dumb by the sight that met his eyes. As far as he could see, the attic floor was littered with what remained of Custard's Last Stand: bodies of the dead and wounded, broken lances, snapped cutlasses, splintered cudgels, empty slings, torn flags, bloodied banners, and loose marbles. And everywhere there were the mourners, crying and wailing and bemoaning their losses, picking their way through the rubble to find their loved ones.

Ridley was still staring stunned and speechless at the carnage, when Rosabelle marched up to him, pushed her face up against his, and snarled, in an ugly tone: *"What do you think you're doing here, Ridley Rattail?"*

Rosabelle was joined by her sister Bluebell, whose left ear was torn and bleeding. *"Yes, why are you here, Ridley?"* she cried passionately. *"Have you come to celebrate our defeat?"*

Ridley was jolted to the bone. *"Celebrate?"* he cried. *"You can't think that of me, Bluebell! Surely you can't!"*

"Surely we can," Rosabelle said bitterly. *"Now, get out, Ridley. You don't live here anymore."*

Ridley bowed his head. *"I know I don't,"* he said in a voice of great humility. *"You were right to evict me, Rosabelle. There is nothing I can say or do that will in any way atone for posting that advertisement. I am a thoroughly wretched rat, a rat of no redeeming virtues. But I can get rid of the Cat who has caused this horror, and I mean to do it."*

By this time, they had been joined by other rats, who—when they heard Ridley's assertion—burst out in mocking, malicious laughter.

"You?" Bluebell scoffed. *"Ridley, the greatest coward who ever wore a tail, thinks he is going to get rid of a Cat who is as fierce as a ferret and strong as an ox? What utter nonsense!"*

"You?" cried Bluebell's friend Maybell. *"What can you do to save us? Why, you couldn't even save yourself, you ridiculous rat!"*

And even Rosabelle had to agree, although she said it in a kindlier tone. *"Don't be foolish, Ridley. This isn't your fight now. You're no match for that cat, any more than we are. Get out of here, and let us mourn our dead in peace."*

But Ridley knew that if he did as he was told, Rosabelle, Bluebell, Maybell, and all the others would shortly be dead. So, ignoring the sneers, jeers, taunts, and teasing that rang in his ears, he began to work at putting his plan into action. To do so required making several more trips down to the Jenningses' kitchen, first for one thing and then for another.

And finally, on the third trip, he returned with Mr. Jennings's ball of string. He was ready now to put his fifteen percent solution into operation.

The Cat Who Walks by Himself was in a very fine temper that Sunday morning. After the Battle of Hill Top Attic (as he thought of it), he had come downstairs, washed his paws and ears, and jumped up onto Miss Potter's featherbed. She tried to push him off as she had the previous night, but he resisted, for while all places were alike to him, any Cat who had a ha'p'worth of sense would prefer a featherbed to a floor.

So, curled into a contented ball of fur, well fed and delightfully warm, the Cat slept a deep, dreamless sleep for the entire night. He didn't bother to wake when Miss Potter got up, straightened the covers, dressed, and went out for the day. He finally roused himself at midmorning, yawned, stretched, scratched, and jumped up on the windowsill to see what sort of day it was.

The weather was truly glorious, with the sun spilling across the garden, the green hill rising steeply beyond, the sheep grazing contentedly, the animals in the barnyard going busily about their appointed tasks, and everything just right with the small world of Hill Top Farm. It was the sort of day on which a Cat Who Walks by Himself might prefer to go out into the fresh air, have a bit of a dig in the soft earth of a flower bed, relish a tasty green grass salad, sharpen his fine claws on a wooden post, climb a tree, catch a bird, admire his reflection in a puddle, and amuse himself by chasing the mother hens and their baby chicks in the barnyard.

The Cat sighed. Yes, he might prefer any or all these things—and he was entitled, wasn't he, after the splendid work he had done during the Great Battle of the night before? But all places were alike to the Cat Who Walks by Himself, who knew that he was duty-bound to fulfill his obligations before he enjoyed his pleasures. In this case, he had undertaken to exterminate all of the rats in the Hill Top attic, and what the Cat undertook, that was what he would do, preferences or not.

So he took one last look at the pleasant morning, leapt lightly from the windowsill onto the floor, strode up the attic stairs, and pushed the door open. He knew that it would not be easy to catch the remaining rats, who would surely not be so stupid as to array themselves before him *en masse,* as had the army. So he was prepared to begin a thorough, methodical search of all the nooks and corners and crannies and cubbies, killing every rat he found, large or small or in between. It would be tedious work—slow, hard, and dusty—and not nearly as much fun as the Great Battle, where he could wipe out ten or a dozen rats with a single swipe of his paw.

Which was why the Cat was so pleased to find, just inside the door, that someone had thought to leave him a dish of tempting rabbit stew, swimming in tasty brown gravy and enriched with delicious bits of potatoes and carrots. It was, no doubt, a tribute, offered with the hope of placating him or buying him off.

Well, it wouldn't do them any good, he thought, gobbling up the bits of rabbit. They could offer all the tribute they wanted, but when all was said and done, the only rats left in the Hill Top attic would be dead rats. He polished off the meat and vegetables and licked up the gravy. There would not be a single living rat in the attic, for when the Cat Who Walks by Himself undertakes to do a job, he does it, to the bitter end.

For the next ten or fifteen minutes, the Cat prowled around the corners of the attic, searching methodically under boxes, cartons, broken furniture, old curtains, and stacks of newspapers. At first, he worked swiftly and surely, catching here a cowering rat, there a rat napping, and every now and then a cockroach, cricket, or spider. But it was dull, monotonous work, and as the moments wore on, the Cat found himself feeling unaccountably muzzy-headed. This was very odd, since he was not usually a cat who needed a great deal of sleep, even after great exertion, and he had enjoyed such a comfortable night's sleep on Miss Potter's featherbed. He could not explain it, but definitely felt himself wanting a quick forty winks. He fought off this desire as long as he could, but finally, with a weary sigh, decided that since all places were alike to him, one place was as good as another for a bit of a lie-down.

And that was the last conscious thought the Cat would think for quite a time, for within the next instant, he had fallen fast asleep. And since that bowl of tasty rabbit stew had been generously laced with laudanum—the opiate that made Mrs. Jennings sleep so soundly—there was no doubt that he would sleep for a very long time.

Ridley's fifteen percent solution had done the trick.

29

The Vicar Hears a Story

It was nearly teatime when Beatrix returned to Hill Top Farm. She had made up her mind what she had to do, and despite the fact that she was not at all looking forward to doing it, she was hungry. She ate several slices of bread-and-butter, with a piece of cheese and an apple, and drank two cups of strong tea. Thus fortified for what was likely to be an unpleasant interview, she went upstairs and changed from her walking clothes into a skirt, jacket, shoes, and hat suitable for attending Evensong, noticing with some relief that the cat was nowhere in evidence. Then she set out on her second walk of the day, down the footpath that led across Wilfin Beck and Sawrey Fold, a large meadow shared by a flock of sheep and a dozen black-and-white cows.

St. Peter's Church, built of local stone in the same Gothic style as Raven Hall, crowned a green hill to the south of the village, surrounded by the gray granite headstones of the parish cemetery. Beatrix was not a regular church-goer, for while she had a deep inner awareness of her own relationship to the Supreme Being, she was a skeptic as far as most religious practices were concerned. She thought they caused many unhappy divisions amongst people. "Believe there is a great power silently working all things for good," she had written once in her journal, "behave yourself and never mind the rest."

Still, she occasionally attended church, and Evensong was the service she liked best, since it was mostly choral, except for Scripture reading and prayer. There was no choir at St. Peter's Evensong, so the congregation sang the responses and the canticles as Miss Annie Nash played the organ, which was quite a fine instrument. As Beatrix sat in the pew and looked up at the stained glass windows, lit by the western sun so that they glowed like splendid jewels, she listened to the *Magnificat* and the *Nunc Dimitis* and remembered St. Augustine's words: "Anyone who sings, prays twice."

There was need for prayer tonight, Beatrix thought, and reflecting on what she had to tell the vicar, did not find the service as comforting as she usually did. When it was over, she stayed behind as everyone else filed out, lingering until the vicar, in his robe and surplice, had said goodnight to all the other parishioners. She was not sure how her news would be received, for the vicar was a gentle, scholarly man, rather vague and dithery. He was inclined to placate difficult people, rather than confront them. Still, there were things that had to be done to resolve the dreadful situation, and she couldn't do them without his cooperation. So she crossed her fingers and hoped for the best.

Vicar Sackett had just closed and locked the heavy oaken church doors when he was startled to see the square, solid figure of Miss Potter step out of the shadows and around the baptismal font, wearing her usual tweed suit and small gray hat.

"Oh, good evening, Miss Potter," he exclaimed with some surprise. He had noticed her in the congregation and expected to say goodnight to her, but when she did not appear, thought she must have left by the side door. He reached for the key where it hung on a wooden peg. "I'm so sorry, dear lady. I didn't mean to lock you in. Come, and I'll open—"

"I waited to see you," Miss Potter said quietly. "It's rather important, I'm afraid. May we take a moment?"

"Of course, oh, of course," the vicar said heartily. He admired Miss Potter and wished that she were able to spend more time in the village. Of course, he also wished that she would attend services, but he wasn't the sort of vicar who would make a point of asking her. She would come as the Spirit moved her or not at all. "Why don't we walk back to the vicarage and have a cup of tea in front of the fire in my study?"

"I don't think that would be a good plan," Miss Potter said gravely. "What I have to say is for your ears alone." She hesitated, lowered her voice, and added, "I should particularly *not* like your guests to hear."

The vicar felt a moment of acute misgiving. Miss Potter could only be referring to the Thextons, and judging from her somber expression, the subject must be unpleasant. The vicar, who had got on rather comfortably in life by avoiding as much unpleasantness as possible, was suddenly uneasy.

"Well, then," he said, with a false heartiness, "I suppose we should go to the vestry. It may be chilly, but—"

"Thank you," Miss Potter said.

Hearing her tone, the vicar sighed, feeling even more uneasy. He led the way up the side aisle, and a few moments later, they were seated on wooden chairs in the small room that was used for occasional meetings.

"Now, my dear Miss Potter," the vicar said, trying to keep the apprehension out of his voice, "what is it you would like to discuss?"

"I shall begin at the beginning," Miss Potter said. Looking troubled but composed, she crossed her ankles and folded her hands in her lap. "I overheard an intimate conversation today and felt that you should know about it. It took place between Mr. Thexton and Major Kittredge's wife."

"An intimate conversation!" The vicar stared at her. Of all things Miss Potter might have said, this was the most unexpected.

"Yes." Miss Potter cleared her throat. "It was not my intention to listen, I assure you, but I was caught unawares and could not escape without revealing my presence and embarrassing both them and myself. Then, when I realized the nature of their discussion, it was much too late." She paused. "If what I heard had been only trivial, I would certainly keep it to myself. But it was incriminating, and so I fear I must trouble you with it."

"Incriminating?" the vicar asked weakly. "Oh, yes, Miss Potter, do go on."

Miss Potter nodded. "I had walked up to Fern Vale Tarn, you see, through Cuckoo Brow Wood. I did not realize that the lake was adjacent to the Raven Hall garden, and was certainly not expecting to encounter anyone there. I was seated on a bank and had just started to eat my lunch when I heard the voices of Mr. Thexton and Mrs. Kittredge, who were apparently out for a walk together. My seat was hidden from their view, and since they didn't know they were overheard, they spoke freely." She met his eyes steadfastly, and then, in precise sentences and a matter-of-fact tone, told him what they had said.

The vicar listened, at first with an almost involuntary incredulity and then with growing shock and dismay. If the woman making such preposterous statements had been anyone but Miss Beatrix Potter, he would have thought her deluded, or even an out-and-out liar. But Miss Potter was entirely trustworthy and a very astute observer, and he had to confess to having his own private reasons for believing her. Even before she had finished her story, he was convinced of the truthfulness of it.

The question now was not one of belief, but of action, and the vicar, although he was a man of good heart and deep compassion, had never found it easy to act. In fact, when he was confronted with a dilemma, he often found himself feeling quite helpless. That was how he felt now.

"Oh, dear," he said softly, shaking his head and thinking that things were so much worse than he could have imagined. "Oh dear oh dear oh dear."

"I am truly sorry," Miss Potter said sympathetically. "I know that Mr. Thexton is your relative and your guest. This must weigh heavily upon you."

Indeed. The vicar felt as if the entire weight of St. Peter's Church rested on his shoulders. But it was much worse than Miss Potter could know. "My guest, yes," he said sadly. "It seems, however, that he is not a relative."

"I must confess that I am not surprised," Miss Potter murmured. "Of course, there is no law that requires that relatives be exactly like one, but there is usually some resemblance, however faint. You and Mr. Thexton are not at all like."

"I'm afraid I must agree," the vicar said ruefully. "In fact, several weeks ago, I wrote to a cousin on the Lessiter side of the family, a genealogist who has spent a great deal of effort in reconstructing our family tree in great detail, down to the last branch and twig. I received his reply in yesterday's post, but did not read it until this afternoon. He is not able to find Mr. Thexton anywhere on our tree." He sighed, thinking of the hospitality he had naively extended for the past four months. "It appears that the man is sailing under false colors."

"I see," Miss Potter said thoughtfully. "Of course, such deception is unforgivable. One must regret it, but in a way, it makes things easier."

"Yes, I suppose it does." The vicar peered hopefully at her over his glasses. "There is no doubt about what you heard? No chance that you . . ." He sighed. "No, of course not."

"No," Miss Potter said. "Mr. Thexton's demand was clearly blackmail, and Mrs. Kittredge understood it as such. Her responses made it unmistakably clear that his charges struck home. We have two crimes here, both of them very serious."

"Oh, dear," the vicar muttered, beginning to fear that he was in for a disagreeable confrontation with Mr. Thexton. But perhaps Miss Potter had thought of other options. "Can you suggest a way to approach him?" he asked, in a diffident tone.

Miss Potter coughed. "It is a matter for the authorities, wouldn't you say?"

The vicar bit his lip. Mr. Thexton might not be a relative, but he had, after all, been a guest at the vicarage. "I don't suppose," he suggested tentatively, "that there is a way of dealing privately with this—without bringing in the law, that is?"

"I fear not," Miss Potter said firmly. "If Mr. Thexton were threatened with exposure, he might well simply withdraw his blackmail threat and leave the area. But the lady's previous marriage cannot be so simply handled. In my opinion, it is better to deal with the two crimes together. What

Mr. Thexton proposes is very nearly as reprehensible as Mrs. Kittredge's actions."

"Yes," the vicar said. The room had begun to seem uncomfortably warm, and he took out his handkerchief and mopped his forehead. "Yes, of course," he said despairingly. "I suppose I must go and see Constable Braithwaite this evening."

"If you don't mind," Miss Potter said, "I should like to make a different proposal."

"Oh, by all means," said the vicar eagerly, looking at her with new hope. Miss Potter seemed to have such a clear, unmuddled understanding of situations, even the most complex.

"I propose that you and I go to see Captain Woodcock, early tomorrow morning. I would suggest going tonight, but the captain and his sister are visiting friends in Hawkshead and do not plan to be back until very late. In any event, nothing will be gained by acting sooner. Mr. Thexton has given Mrs. Kittredge until Friday to sell the jewelry and hand over the money. It might even be good if she were allowed an opportunity to move in that direction, which would be as clear an indication of guilt as we are likely to get, barring a confession—although I am sure that the prior marriage can be easily verified."

The vicar shuddered, but he had to agree. "Yes," he said. "Yes, indeed. Let us meet at Tower Bank house in the morning. Shall we say nine?"

"Yes, nine," Miss Potter said. She stood, smiling slightly. "I don't think it will be necessary to speak of this to Mr. Thexton, should you see him when you return to the vicarage this evening. It would be better to consult with the captain first."

The vicar felt a sense of relief. "Yes, you're right, of course. I really shouldn't like to see Mr. Thexton at all, under the circumstances." He gave a rueful laugh. "I must confess that I am not very good at dissembling. He would no doubt be able to tell from my expression that something is seriously amiss. And he might even get the story out of me."

"I hope you will put a lock on your tongue, then," Miss Potter remarked with a little frown, though her light tone took most of the sting out of her words.

"I shall endeavor to do my best," the vicar said humbly, thinking that he would go up to his bedroom by the back stair. And if he were inclined to say anything at all to Mr. Thexton, the thought of Miss Potter's frown would certainly dissuade him.

30

The Cat Who Went for a Ride

On Sunday night, just about the time Miss Potter was returning from Evensong, Ridley Rattail was preparing to explain the rest of his astonishing plan to the two dozen surviving rats, who could still not quite believe what they were seeing.

It had been just about noon when Mrs. Jennings's laudanum did its work and the Cat fell sound asleep onto the attic floor. Ridley Rattail had been waiting, the ball of string at the ready. But he could not do the work alone, so he turned to Rosabelle, who was standing beside him, speechless, staring at the Cat, who seemed even larger, stretched out flat on the floor.

"Rosabelle," Ridley said humbly, *"I need your help. We are going to roll up the Cat and tie him with string."*

Rosabelle's eyes were as big as ha'penny pieces. *"Tie up the cat?"* she gulped. *"But he's as big as a house!"*

"Tie him," Ridley repeated patiently. *"With very hard knots."*

"But . . . but what shall we do if he wakes up?" she cried, her eyes fixed on the dreadful claws. *"He'll murder us!"*

"He's not going to wake," Ridley reassured her. *"Not for a very long time. And he can't murder anybody if he's completely tied up. Now, start by tying your end of the string around his right paw, then pass it over to me."*

And so, with much twisting and turning and tying and tightening, the two rats used all of Mr. Jennings's string to truss up the Cat. When they were finished, the animal was so completely immobilized that he could not have twitched a whisker. Even when he wakened from his drugged state, he wouldn't be able to move.

Rosabelle cast an admiring look at the Cat, who was now reduced to a tightly wrapped bundle, and then back at Ridley. *"I never would have thought you'd manage it, Ridley, not in a million years. You've captured the Cat!"*

"Yes, Ridley," Bluebell said, *"I have to confess that I didn't believe it could be done."* She gazed in admiration at the sleeping cat. *"Such a novel approach. Where in the world did you get the idea?"*

"From Miss Potter's story," replied Ridley. *"The rats tie up the kitten with string, you see. And then they roll him up in a blanket of dough, with the idea of making him into a roly-poly pudding."*

"A pudding?" Rosabelle said, regarding the huge cat doubtfully. *"But we don't have a pot that's large enough to steam him. And I don't think I should care for steamed cat. I am not opposed to experimental cookery, but it doesn't strike me as a tasty dish."*

"We're not going to steam him, dear Rosabelle. I have another plan. We have to wait until after dark to carry it out, however." He looked around. *"And I'll need some help."*

Two of the rats—the ones who had jeered the loudest when Ridley announced that he intended to capture the Cat—stepped forward without hesitation. One of them, a Cockney rat named Brutus, snatched off his hat respectfully. *"We'll 'elp, Mr. Rattail, sir. You just tell us wot t' do, and we'll do it."*

"Us'ns too," chorused several others. *"You're a right rum chap, Mr. Rattail. You give the orders, and we'll carry 'em out."* And then, without any prompting, they all broke into a round of applause and cheers and a chorus of "For He's a Jolly Good Fellow."

Enormously touched by their admiration and respectful address, Ridley almost wept. And when Rosabelle suggested that, since the danger was now past, they should all sit down together and share a meal of thanksgiving, he got up the courage to say, with a huge hope rising in his heart, *"Does that mean I'm not evicted, Rosabelle?"*

"That's what it means, Ridley," Rosabelle said, and gave him a generous hug. *"You've saved us from certain destruction, and we're enormously grateful. Now let's all have some lunch."*

So that night, when Miss Potter had blown out her candle and gone to sleep, Ridley gathered the rats together. Following his instructions, they lined up along the sleeping Cat's length and began rolling the creature across the floor to the top of the spiral stair, just as though he were a rolling pin. And then, on the count of three, they gave the Cat a very hard shove. He rolled and bounced and thumped all the way down to the bottom, still fast asleep. The rats rolled him across the floor, out the door, and down the starlit hill to the pub, where they gathered in the back garden.

"Now what, Mr. Rattail?" Brutus asked, dusting his paws. *"Wot's t' be done with the 'orrible creature?"*

Ridley pointed to a wooden ale keg standing, empty, beside the back door. *"We'll turn that keg on its side,"* he directed, *"take off the lid, and roll the Cat into it."*

Two dozen pairs of paws made light work, and the task went smoothly. In five minutes, the keg was upright again, with the lid on. But it was no longer empty. It contained a Cat.

Which is why, when the brewer's draymen arrived with their horses and dray early on a very wet Monday morning to deliver two full kegs of ale to the pub and take away two empty ones, the bewildered Cat (by this time beginning to wake up, his mouth parched and his head throbbing), found himself wound completely round with string, bouncing up and down in the bottom of an empty keg which smelt so much like ale that it nearly intoxicated him. Somewhere along the way, the lid of the keg popped off. Now, you might think this was unfortunate, and so, no doubt, did the Cat, since by this time the gray skies had opened and a cold rain was pouring down and there was a good chance that the Cat might drown before he got wherever in the world he was going. As things turned out, however, the loss of the lid was a bit of good fortune, for when the draymen reached the brewery and began to unload their dray, one of them glanced into the Cat's keg.

"Well, I'll be blowed," he said to his partner, taking his hat off and scratching his head. "It's a wet cat, trussed up like a roly-poly puddin'. Guess some boys done it for a prank, eh? What kids'll get up to these days is a wonder." He took out a knife and cut the string, freeing the Cat. "Be on your way, you," he said, tossing him out of the wagon. "We got all t' cats we need round here."

A moment later, the Cat Who Walks by Himself could be seen running away from the brewery as fast as he could, out into the woods and up a tree and from thence onto a roof, exactly like the cat in Mr. Kipling's tale: *"Then he goes out to the Wet Wild Woods or up the Wet Wild Trees or on the Wet Wild Roofs, waving his wild tail and walking by his wild lone."*

And if you had asked him whether he would like to return to Hill Top Farm and have another go at the rats in Miss Potter's attic, he would have given you a very nasty piece of his mind, in language that I should not have wanted to include in this book.

But if he were to be perfectly honest, he would reflect that all places are no longer quite alike to him.

31

Dimity Woodcock Cooks Breakfast

Captain Woodcock's breakfast was a little later than usual on Monday morning. Elsa Grape's sister-in-law, who lived in Windermere, had just given birth to a new baby, her seventh. Elsa (the Woodcock's cook and housekeeper) had gone across Lake Windermere on the Saturday evening ferry to help out, but the Monday morning ferry was prevented by the very same rainstorm that drenched the Cat. The wind whipped the waves and the lightning flashed and Henry Stubbs, the ferryman, wisely decided to beach the ferry until the storm passed.

So Dimity Woodcock (who would be the first to admit that she was not a very good cook) found herself in the kitchen at Tower Bank House, frying bacon and eggs and making toast. Things were going fairly well until she put the toast too close to the fire and it burnt to a cinder. Since there was no more bread in the house, she sent Jennie, the kitchen maid, running down the garden through the rain to Sarah Barwick's kitchen door and back again with a plate of Sarah's finest, freshest, tastiest sticky buns.

"Just look at that!" Miles exclaimed with satisfaction, when Dimity appeared in the dining room at last, flushed and with her hair all awry but bearing a handsome tray of bacon, eggs, kippers, and fragrant sticky buns. "Dimity, you're a wonder! The cook's out of commission, but the eggs are just as I like them. And fresh sticky buns as well. Thank you very much, my dear." He picked up a bun and took a bite. "Delicious!"

"Thank you," Dimity said modestly, failing to mention that Miss Barwick should, by rights, receive praise for the buns. "I'll just get the orange juice and coffee and—" She was interrupted by the doorbell. "Oh, dear," she lamented. "Not company so early!"

"It's already gone nine," her brother observed, putting down his napkin and rising. "You get the coffee, Dim. I'll get the door. Whoever-it-is will have to wait until we have finished our breakfast."

But when Dimity got back to the breakfast room with a pitcher, she found that whoever-it-is was Vicar Sackett and Beatrix Potter, and that Miles had seated them at the breakfast table. They were protesting that they had already eaten at home, but Miles was urging them to sample his sister's buns.

"Elsa is stranded on the other side of the lake, but Dimity came to our rescue," he said proudly. "She baked the buns fresh this morning, before breakfast. They're delicious. Please have one."

"Oh, yes, do," Dimity heard herself saying, as she put down the coffeepot and went to the sideboard for more cups. "And hot coffee, too. That rain is coming down in buckets, and there's thunder and lightning. You must be wet through."

"It is very damp," the vicar admitted, and helped himself to a bun. One bite, and he was beaming. "My dear Miss Woodcock! These are every bit as good as Sarah Barwick's, and that is saying a very great deal."

Flushing, Dimity could think of no convenient way to say that they *were* Sarah's buns. Instead, she asked hastily, "You've really eaten, have you? Wouldn't you care for some kippers and—"

"We've breakfasted, thank you," Beatrix said quickly. "But coffee would be very good." Her expression was somber. "We've come about a rather unfortunate matter, I'm afraid."

"If this is Justice of the Peace business," Dimity said, "you'll want privacy." She turned toward the door.

"Nonsense, Dim," Miles said firmly. "You just sit right down and eat. After all that baking this morning, you must be hungry." To their guests, he said, "If you don't mind, Dimity and I will just go on with our breakfast while you tell us what's brought you out on this rainy morning."

Beatrix and the vicar did not object, so Dimity poured two cups of coffee for their guests, and one for herself. Then she helped herself to bacon and eggs, sat down at her usual place nearest the hallway door, and began to eat.

The vicar cleared his throat. "I think Miss Potter should be the one to tell you what has transpired," he said uneasily. "She was a witness."

Dimity was indeed hungry. But when Beatrix started to talk, she forgot all about the food on her plate. And when Beatrix finished her story, she cried out in horror, "Oh, how shocking! Poor Christopher! Poor, sweet Christopher!" and burst into a storm of tears.

At the opposite end of the breakfast table, Captain Woodcock was also horrified by what he had just heard, and troubled by his sister's unusual show of emotion. Surely she couldn't harbor any affection toward Kittredge. But this wasn't the time to go into that. He applied himself to the matter at hand, beginning with the obvious question.

"You're sure, Miss Potter? You realize that you might have to testify to this in court."

"In court?" Dimity asked, aghast. "Oh, Miles, surely Christopher won't have to parade his private troubles before the whole—"

"Hush, Dimity," her brother said sternly.

"I should not like to testify," Miss Potter replied, "but if I must, of course I shall. I have an excellent memory. The conversation was just as I have related it to you."

Miles felt apologetic. He was aware that Miss Potter had a first-rate memory—Dimity had told him that she had memorized almost all of the plays of Shakespeare as a girl. He also knew that she had an amazingly acute observational ability, and could see and understand things that others did not. He did not doubt that she had heard exactly what she said she had heard. But it certainly did raise a host of problems, and left him wondering where to start.

"Well, then," he said, feeling very much at sea. "I suppose we must—" He was interrupted by the doorbell.

"I'll go," Dimity said in a strangled voice. A moment later, Will Heelis was standing in the breakfast room door.

"Mr. Heelis!" Miss Potter exclaimed, smiling. "I'm glad you were able to come, in spite of the rain."

"How could I not?" Will asked with a shake of his head. "Poor Kittredge. This is a frightful business."

"Yes, indeed," Dimity said distractedly. "Poor Christopher. It will kill him. Sit down, Will, and let me pour you some coffee. Have you eaten?"

"I doubt it will kill him," Will replied, pulling out a chair. "But it's going to be deuced unpleasant. Coffee, please."

Miles looked from Miss Potter to the vicar. "Would someone please tell me how Heelis got into this? Not that I mind, of course," he added. "It's just that—"

"Mr. Jennings had to take the butter and eggs to Hawkshead very early this morning," Miss Potter explained. "I took the liberty of sending a note to Mr. Heelis, with a brief explanation of the situation. I knew him to be a good friend of Major Kittredge, and hoped he might agree to speak with the major about this delicate situation. After Mr. Thexton has been interrogated," she added, to Miles. "One has to begin there, of course."

"Oh, of course," Miles said. He stared at her. "You've sorted it all out, have you, Miss Potter?"

"Well, it does seem rather logical, wouldn't you say?" Will said, taking the cup Dimity handed him and helping himself to sugar and cream.

"Yes, it does," put in the vicar. "Miss Potter has thought it out completely. If Captain Woodcock were to question Mr. Thexton, he could ascertain the truth of the charge against Mrs. Kittredge." He paused uncomfortably. "I suppose I should call her Mrs. Waring—that is, assuming that Mr. Thexton's charge is true."

"Which must be determined," Miss Potter said, "before anything else."

"Yes, I see," Miles said. "Yes, you're right. That should be the first step."

"Once Mr. Thexton has been persuaded to reveal the whereabouts of Mr. James Waring," the vicar continued, "Captain Woodcock could telegraph the gentleman and ask him directly whether he is Irene Waring's husband—and request that he provide a photograph of his wife."

"And then," Miss Potter said, "if the photo proves that she is also Diana Kittredge, perhaps Mr. Heelis might have a conversation with the major and lay the entire matter before him." She paused sympathetically. "It is all so difficult, and delicate. It does seem that Major Kittredge should know as soon as possible—and from a friend."

"I very much agree," Will said gravely. "While I'm not eager to be the bearer of this appalling news, I think Kittredge would rather hear it from me than from anyone else. He is a client, as well—and there are some legal knots to be untied here."

Dimity looked up quickly. "Untied?"

"Of course, we do not yet know the facts in the matter, Dimity," Will said in a quiet, steady voice. "But if Mr. Thexton's allegation is true, Major Kittredge's marriage cannot be valid."

Miles turned his head just in time to catch the look of rosy gladness that passed over his sister's face. Surely she wasn't— He was stopped from pursuing this thought by the vicar, who spoke with the air of a man steeling himself to something unpleasant.

"I am willing to accompany you, Captain Woodcock," he said, "to speak with Mr. Thexton. He is, after all, a guest in my home."

"And a relative," Miles said regretfully. "This must be difficult for you, vicar."

"I am glad to say that he is *not* a relative," the vicar replied, with unaccustomed firmness. "The Lessiter side of the Sackett family tree has been carefully examined, and Mr. Thexton's branch cannot be found."

"Oh, well, then," Will said, in a joking tone, "if he's not one of yours, Vicar, we'll just toss him in gaol and throw away the key. And while he's there, we'll get to the bottom of this Waring business, once and for all. If Kittredge isn't well and truly married, we should know it shortly."

Dimity picked up the platter of buns. "Please, Will," she said, in an extraordinarily cheerful voice, "wouldn't you like a sticky bun? Everyone says they're delicious."

Miles stared at his sister, an uneasy thought taking an uncomfortable shape in his mind.

32

The Village Gets Ready for
a Celebration

The next two days were busy ones in Sawrey, with all the ordinary activities that go on when April turns into May and the landscape is fresh with delightful scents and sounds and colors and the whole world feels new and optimistic and full of importance. Monday was Washing Day, so when the skies finally cleared on Monday afternoon, the women hurried into their gardens to hang their freshly washed laundry, ensuring plenty of work for Tuesday, which was Ironing Day. Since cows and sheep often give birth in April, the men had new calves and lambs to tend to, along with the usual spring chores that keep every farmer occupied. The village smith was shoeing horses (all the village horses seemed to have lost their shoes at once), and Roger Dowling, the joiner, was building a new wooden counter for the village shop, which was operated by his wife Lydia, in their cottage.

The schoolchildren were excitedly rehearsing their program for Wednesday's May Day celebration. Tuesday brought showers, but everyone was confident that Wednesday would be fair, for no one in the village could remember a time when it had rained on May Day morning.

The May Day celebration was a village affair, the preparations taking several days and involving any number of people. On Monday afternoon, Dimity Woodcock (who had charge of the May Day tea) sent Lester Barrow's youngest boy around the village, reminding members of the Ladies Guild to bake enough cakes and biscuits and tarts so that each schoolchild could have at least two sweet treats, as well as a cup of lemonade. On Tuesday, fearing that they might be short on biscuits, she sent Jennie with a note to Sarah Barwick, asking her to do some extra baking for the event. Sarah, who had laid in an extra supply of flour and sugar in case she was asked, was glad to oblige.

On Monday night, the Village Volunteer Band (Lester Barrow on trombone, Mr. Taylor and Clyde Burning on clarinet, Lawrence Baldwin on coronet, and Sam Stern on the concertina) met for practice in the pub—thirsty work, to judge from the several half-pints required to wet their whistles. While the band practiced, the band members' wives brushed their red wool coats and red hats and made sure their Sunday boots were polished. Meanwhile, several fathers were setting up the wooden platform in the schoolyard, where the May Queen would be crowned, Captain Woodcock would make his usual speech, and the usual prizes would be awarded for perfect attendance, scholarship, and deportment. When that was done, they retired to the pub to listen to the band practice and wet their whistles, too, for building wooden platforms is also thirsty work, as you will know, if you've ever done it.

On Tuesday morning, at High Green Gate, Mr. Llewellyn washed and curried David, his large white horse, who had the honor of carrying the May Queen to the grand event. David would be led by Mr. Llewellyn and wear the new blue horse blanket that Mrs. Llewellyn had already made for the occasion, as well as the flower garlands that Abigail Llewellyn was making. Whilst Mr. Llewellyn was washing David, Mrs. Llewellyn washed Mr. Llewellyn's best Sunday shirt. And whilst Mrs. Llewellyn was pegging the shirt on the clothesline, Mrs. Grace Lythecoe, who lived over the way in Rose Cottage, was writing the May Queen's annual proclamation, calling on all creation to join together in peace and love (which is, after all, the point of any spring celebration).

On Tuesday afternoon, the schoolchildren went out into the lanes to gather flowers and then back to school to construct hawthorn garlands and daisy chains and ropes of primroses and apple blossom. Meanwhile, Head Teacher Margaret Nash undertook the important task of making the May Queen's crown under the critical eyes of the May Queen and her Court. The May Queen herself (this year, she was Ruth Leech) was already so nervous that she had to go outside and throw up, but the other girls were happily discussing their dresses and ribbons, and the boys' mothers were making sure that their sons' best white shirts had all their buttons and their Sunday neckties were not berry-stained.

Joseph Skead, the sexton at St. Peter's and the man who helped to maintain the school, was charged with the task of attaching Dimity's colorful crepe paper ribbons to the top of the May Pole and planting the pole in the middle of the school yard, in preparation for the Ribbon Dance. Traditionally, the boys went one way round the May Pole and the girls went the other, holding their ribbons taut. Each girl was supposed to carry her ribbon under the ribbon of the first boy she met, then carry it over the ribbon of the next boy, while the boys did the opposite. If this rather complicated pattern was done right, the dance created a colorful basket-weave of ribbons all down the pole, and everybody congratulated everybody else. If it was done wrong, and somebody went backward instead of forward, or over instead of under, there was a huge tangle of ribbons and dancers, and everyone ended up in a helpless heap of giggles.

But forward or backward, perfectly woven or irretrievably tangled, the children always had a great deal of fun, and the mothers and fathers who cheered them on enjoyed the spectacle immensely. After all, when they were children, most of them had danced that very same Ribbon Dance around that very same May Pole in that very same school yard on this very same day, and perhaps that memory was as fresh and sweet as the happy scene before them, a reminder of a gay and innocent time, before the grownup cares of work and family began to weigh on their shoulders.

So as far as the village was concerned, May Day was one of the very highest points of the year, the day when winter's chilly gloom faded into the past and all of the Land between the Lakes could look forward with cheerful smiles and light hearts to a season of sunshine, clear skies, warm breezes, and bright flowers.

May Day morning could not arrive soon enough.

33

Major Kittredge Learns the Truth

But behind all this happy flurry of preparations, another, darker game was afoot. Immediately after breakfast on Monday morning, Captain Woodcock and the vicar drove through the rain to the vicarage and confronted Mr. Thexton with what they knew—without, of course, mentioning the source of their information.

At first, and with a great deal of outraged sputter and vehement indignation, Mr. Thexton denied the whole thing. But when he saw Captain Woodcock's threatening expression (which seemed to suggest dungeons and thumbscrews) and heard the detailed report of the conversation in the Raven Hall garden, he became rather more cooperative. In fact, he may even have thought that since he and Mrs. Kittredge (or rather, Mrs. Waring) had been entirely alone on the occasion of their talk, she must have decided to make a clean breast of things. It must be she who now accused him of attempted extortion—an idea that Captain Woodcock did not attempt to discourage. So, convinced that he had been betrayed by the woman he was attempting to blackmail, Mr. Thexton decided that he had no other choice. With the hope of making it easier on himself when he stood in front of the magistrate, and to discredit his accuser, he agreed to tell as much as he knew about the Waring marriage.

Which turned out to be just enough. Mr. James Waring, who had indeed survived the blast that had wrecked his ship, resided at a London address which Mr. Thexton was able to provide. Captain Woodcock immediately dispatched a telegram of inquiry—without revealing the circumstances, except to say that a woman meeting his wife's description was living in the Lake District.

The answer arrived within a few short hours. Mr. Waring confirmed that he had married a red-haired actress named Irene some five years previously, and that they remained legally married. She had left her lodgings, leaving no forwarding address, and he had been searching for her frantically. He was posting a photograph of his wife with the hope that it would confirm that she was the lady who had been discovered living in the Lake District. He would be arriving at the Windermere Station on Wednesday and would bring with him a copy of the marriage certificate, in case further proof were required. He was prepared, he said, to take her back immediately and without question.

The photograph—a wedding photo—arrived by the Tuesday morning post, and when Miles Woodcock and Will Heelis opened the envelope and studied it, there was no doubt in either of their minds. Mr. Thexton had been correct in his identification. Mrs. Irene Waring and Mrs. Diana Kittredge were, regrettably, the very same person. (Mr. Thexton himself was conveyed to the Hawkshead gaol, to await to magistrate's hearing. Mrs. Thexton, saying not a word, packed her bags and left the vicarage, leaving Vicar Sackett feeling that his prayers had indeed been answered.)

So, just after luncheon on Tuesday, armed with the tell-tale photograph, Will took himself off to Raven Hall for a quiet talk with his old friend Christopher Kittredge. They met in Major Kittredge's study, and when Will was sure that they were alone and that the door was securely shut, he told the major the full story, from beginning to end.

The major was at first incredulous and disbelieving, as I daresay you would be, if someone told you, completely out of the blue, that the person you thought you had married was already married to someone else. But when he had read James Waring's telegram for the third time and looked at the photograph for the second and third and fourth, the major had to agree that the woman he had thought was his wife was legally married to another man. He paced back and forth in front of the fire, his incredulity turning into a sense of tearful injury.

"She has stabbed me in the back," he muttered brokenly, taking out his handkerchief and wiping his eyes. "I thought she loved me. How could she wrong me so unmercifully? How could she betray me?"

Will had no answers to these rhetorical questions and felt that he wasn't very good at this sort of thing. He stuck his hands in his pockets and said nothing.

Finally, after a few moments of this sort of tearful blame, the major's injury turned to anger, first at the lady's unfeeling deception and betrayal, and then at himself, for jumping into marriage with a woman about whom he knew next to nothing—in which, of course, he was entirely right, for he had taken the decision without the proper thought.

"If I hadn't acted so hastily," he said in a tone of bitter self-accusation, "if I had waited, had insisted on learning more about her, I wouldn't be in this situation. I gave in to my passion, and to her flatteries. I failed to look any further than her beautiful face and her attractive figure. I never asked myself who she was or where she came from, or why she wanted to attach herself to me. It is my fault. All my fault."

Will, now feeling completely out of his depth, tried to say something that might make his friend feel better, something to the effect that a man in love rarely asks such questions, and that Kittredge ought not blame himself for being merely human.

But the major, anguish written all over his face, overrode him. "No, don't try to excuse me, Will," he said brokenly. "I should have known better. No woman in her right mind could love a man like me, face hideously scarred, missing an eye, missing an arm. Diana—Irene, rather—had to have wanted something else from me, my money, my property, my name. How could I have failed to see through her?" His tone was bitter with self-reproach. "How could I have been such a conceited, dull-witted *dolt*?"

At last Will found his voice. "Please don't reproach yourself, Christopher. You have been ill-used, yes. But you're not unique. It's happened to other men before you. The responsibility for her falsehoods is entirely with her, not with you. The question you must answer now is whether you want to press charges against the lady for fraud. You would be perfectly within your rights to—"

"No, no," Kittredge said, giving his head a violent shake. "I don't want to make this ugly business even uglier by dragging it into the public view. I'm at fault, too, for not insisting that we wait and get to know each other better. I must share some of the blame." He eyed Will worriedly. "I'm not obliged to go to law on this, am I?"

"Technically, yes," Will said. "Bigamy is a serious crime. But I've been consulting with Captain Woodcock, and both of us are of the opinion that—unless you want to have the lady prosecuted for fraud—it may be best to simply send her back to London with her husband. That might be punishment enough."

"Yes, I suppose," Kittredge said gloomily. He fell silent, and I don't suppose that we want to inquire what was going through his mind.

Finally, Will spoke. "What'll it be, Christopher? Do you want to decide now, or take a day or two to think things over?"

Kittredge straightened his shoulders and tightened his mouth, a man who has decided that it is time to face the music. "It'll do no good to put it off. I'll tell her to pack her things, give her enough money to tide her over, and send her off with Waring." He gave Will an oblique glance. "Once she's gone, what then? It's as if we were never married?"

"Yes," Will said, "although I would feel better if she would sign this affidavit." He reached into his pocket and took it out. "It simply states what we know and requires her to acknowledge the facts with her signature. Of course, we have Waring's telegram, and the letter that accompanied the photo. I will see to it that he signs a similar affidavit, but it would be better to have hers, too."

Kittredge nodded glumly. "Very well. I suppose I will let her keep the gifts I've given her, except for the family jewelry, of course." His eyes widened. "The jewelry, by Jove!" He went quickly to the wall, took down a large painting, and twirled the lock. After a moment, he let out an audible breath. "It's all here. For a moment, I wondered if she had somehow managed to make off with it. It's worth tens of thousands of pounds, you know."

Will nodded. "I suppose you'll want to revoke the last will and testament you executed recently." He hesitated. "And then there's that business about the villas." The villas. They had hung like a dark cloud at the back of his mind for days. "Will you go on with that?"

"I shouldn't think so. It was Diana's idea." The major stopped, his mouth painfully twisted. "That is to say, Irene, Mrs. Waring. She was the one who suggested the scheme and brought Richardson and his syndicate into the business. I must confess I didn't like the fellow very much, and put off signing the agreement he brought from London—luckily, as it turns out." He put his hands into his pockets and went to the window that looked out over the lake. "Father was never keen on developing this land, you know," he added in a lower voice. "He always thought it should be left as it is, especially as there has been so much commercial development on the east side of the lake. I was beginning to feel badly about violating his wishes. You've given me a reason to back out of the arrangement, Will."

So there would be no holiday villas on the shore of Lake Windermere, at least not now—and with luck, not ever. Will felt a very great relief. "Well," he said, "I'm sure many will be glad that there will be no building on that shore." He got up to go. "I'm to meet Waring's train at the station tomorrow morning. If Mrs. Waring would be ready at nine, I can take her with me, and see that both of them take the next train back to London. If there's no doubt in your mind that this is the right way to handle the situation," he added.

"There's no doubt," the major said shortly. "Yes, do stop by. I'll see that she's ready, with her bags." He turned around. "One more thing, Will. You said that the scheme— Thexton's blackmail, that is—was discovered when someone overheard his conversation with my . . . with Mrs. Waring.

I should like to know who overheard it, if I might, and in what circumstance." He cleared his throat. "I'm concerned that this person might . . . well, that he might not be inclined to keep this in confidence. It's a private matter, and deeply embarrassing. I don't want the entire county talking about it until I myself am ready to make some sort of public statement."

Will smiled briefly. "As to the circumstance, it took place at the foot of your garden, where Mr. Thexton and Mrs. Waring had gone for privacy. Miss Potter—the lady who purchased Hill Top Farm two years ago—happened to be sketching there. She's the one who overheard the conversation."

"Miss Potter?" The major frowned for a moment, and then his expression cleared. "Ah, yes. Miss Potter. The lady who makes the children's books. She was at the reception on Saturday, as I recall."

Will nodded and went on. "She had walked up through Cuckoo Brow Wood and was not aware that Fern Vale Tarn lay adjacent to your garden. She overheard the conversation inadvertently. I gather that she felt she could not escape without embarrassing them—and by the time she understood what they were talking about, it was impossible to declare herself." He hesitated. "Don't worry that she will spread the tale around, Christopher. You can trust her not to speak of it."

The major's nod was gloomy. "Saturday." He sighed. "The afternoon the Luck was broken. It seems such a short time ago."

"In fact," Will replied, "it was the breaking of the Luck that alerted Miss Potter. That evening, she told me she thought Mrs. Waring might have dropped it in order to forestall Mr. Thexton, who was on the point of announcing her real name."

"If I am ever able to recover from this, I am sure I will be grateful to Miss Potter. I loved Diana, or rather the woman I thought she was. But somewhere down deep inside, I think perhaps I never really trusted her." The major shook his head. "I wonder if I shall ever be able to trust again."

"I believe you shall," Will said quietly. "You have many friends here, Christopher. Friends who can be trusted to be exactly as they seem." He thought of Dimity Woodcock, and the happy relief on her face when he had told her that the major, in effect, had never been married. Kittredge had a friend in Dimity. "The next months are bound to be difficult. I hope you will count on all of us to help."

"I shall," said Major Kittredge. "Thank you, Will. And thank Miss Potter for me. Tell her that I am grateful to learn the truth—however much it hurts."

"Of course," Will said warmly. "I'll be seeing her within the hour."

"Oh?" The major raised an inquisitive eyebrow. His lips quirked. "Do I detect—"

"No," Will replied, in a firm voice, "you don't. The lady is still grieving over the death of her fiancé. All other thoughts are very far from her mind."

Kittredge nodded. "Well, then," he said. "Be sure and give her my thanks. It is better to know the truth than to be deceived."

34

Lady Longford Receives Callers

Beatrix had not forgotten that she had promised Mr. Heelis to go with him on Tuesday afternoon to call on Lady Longford and try to persuade her to help Jeremy Crosfield. She was not especially looking forward to the meeting—Lady Longford was a prickly sort of person, and not at all likable—but she felt strongly that something should be done to help the boy. And anyway, there was the problem of getting Caroline out of Tidmarsh Manor for their May Eve fairy hunt. Besides, she was eager to learn from Mr. Heelis whether the photograph proved that Mrs. Waring and Mrs. Kittredge were the same person, and what had transpired during his talk with Major Kittredge.

Mr. Heelis arrived shortly before two o'clock, driving a bay horse and a smart red-wheeled gig. Beatrix put on her straw hat, climbed in, and as they drove up Stony Lane in the direction of Tidmarsh Manor, Mr. Heelis told her about the photograph and what the major had decided.

"Kittredge asked me to convey his thanks to you for discovering the truth," he said. "He was deeply saddened—and angry, too, of course—but I think there may be some relief there, as well. He has decided to drop the building project." He turned and his smile lightened his eyes. "You may rest easy, Miss Potter. There will be no villas on the shore of Lake Windermere."

"I'm happy for that," she said heartily. "And perhaps, in the long run—" She stopped. "I don't mean to sound harsh. It is just that, when everything is said and done, the major may be glad to escape that marriage." She was thinking of Dimity, too, and wondering how things would turn out for her. And for Mr. Heelis, too. She hoped he would not be too bitterly disappointed if Miss Woodcock and Major Kittredge renewed their friendship.

"I fully agree, Miss Potter," Mr. Heelis said firmly. "It is my opinion that Irene Waring—for that's her real name— would have brought Major Kittredge nothing but grief. Sad to say, but he is well rid of her." And then they were driving up to Tidmarsh Manor, and there was no more time to discuss the matter.

Tidmarsh Manor was a square, forbidding-looking place, overshadowed by ancient yews. Its windows turned blank, empty eyes onto the world and its chimneys rarely showed a trace of smoke, because Lady Longford believed that fires were a waste of money, except on the coldest of days. In Beatrix's estimation, it was not an hospitable place for a child, and she hoped that Caroline was able to find her own comfort, somehow or other. She ought to have friends in the village. She might be the lady of the manor someday, but the manor was a part of the village (at least traditionally), and the stronger the connection between them, the better for all concerned.

Emily, the maid, showed them into the library, where Lady Longford was writing letters, with Dudley, her ancient spaniel, sprawled on the floor at her feet. Every time Beatrix had seen the dog (who was named for the late Lord Longford), he was cross and out of sorts. He was also growing very fat, for Lady Longford fed him ginger biscuits, which were obviously doing him no good. (Actually, he didn't like ginger biscuits very much, but like Lord Longford, he found it hard to say no to her ladyship.)

Dudley raised his head and gave a menacing growl. Her ladyship looked up from her letter and put down her pen, also looking cross, as if she was not pleased at being asked to interrupt her letter writing to receive callers.

"Well, Heelis," she said shortly. She nodded at Beatrix, with slightly more politeness. "Miss Potter, too. What brings you here this afternoon?" In a dry tone, and with a lift of her eyebrow, she added, "Together."

Beatrix understood. If Mr. Heelis had come on solicitor's business, he would have come alone. The fact that he was accompanied suggested to Lady Longford that the call was of a personal nature, and no doubt made her ladyship suspicious.

"Tea, mum?" asked Emily.

"Yes, of course we'll have tea, you silly girl. But there's no need for cake. Bread-and-butter will do." Lady Longford waved Emily away. She frowned at Mr. Heelis. "Well, Heelis? I'm waiting."

Beatrix sat down on the sofa, although she had not been invited to do so, and Mr. Heelis, with a small, quiet sigh, sat down beside her. It would have been nice to have passed some pleasantries about the weather or about village matters, but that was not Lady Longford's way. She was blunt and brusque and always went straight to the point. She expected others to be the same.

"We've come," Mr. Heelis said without preamble, "to ask for your help."

Lady Longford lifted her lorgnette and regarded him with a dour expression. "If you intend to badger me about my granddaughter, you can go straight away again. I've told Miss Potter that I intend to hire a governess for the girl, who has altogether too much freedom. She's to continue her education here at Tidmarsh Manor, and cease associating with the village children, who are hardly suitable companions for her. And you needn't try to change my mind, Heelis. It's time that Caroline was educated for the role she is to play in life." She lifted her chin, her eyes flashing. "She is to be a lady."

"No, we're not here about Caroline," Mr. Heelis said, although he gave Beatrix a questioning look. Mr. Heelis had befriended Caroline when she first arrived at Tidmarsh Manor, and Beatrix knew that he cared for the girl and was concerned for her welfare. She wondered if he knew that Caroline was not doing well in school.

"I wrote this morning," Beatrix said quickly, "to Mrs. Moore, my former governess, to ask for her recommendation." Beatrix had been nearly seventeen and hoped to be done with governesses when her mother had hired Annie Carter. But the two had quickly become fast friends, and when Miss Carter married and became Mrs. Moore, Beatrix had visited her often. It was to Annie Moore's little boy Noel that Beatrix had written the picture letter that later became *The Tale of Peter Rabbit.*

"I'm sure that Mrs. Moore is acquainted with several young women who may be suitable," she added. "I expect to hear from her shortly." Choosing a governess for Caroline was not going to be easy, since Beatrix was hoping to find a young woman who would nurture the girl's creativity and

independence of thought, while Lady Longford would undoubtedly prefer a stern older woman who would insist that
Caroline learn to follow her grandmother's rules.

But for the moment, at least, Lady Longford seemed satisfied. "Thank you, Miss Potter. Well, then, Heelis? If you've
not come about Caroline, what brings you here?"

"We've come," Mr. Heelis said carefully, "about Jeremy
Crosfield. He is the boy who lives with his aunt at Holly How
Farm—your manor farm," he added, with a slight emphasis.

"I know perfectly well that Holly How is my manor
farm," Lady Longford snapped. "What about the boy? Is he
in trouble?" She shook her head disgustedly. "These boys, always into some sort of mischief. He hasn't been tormenting
the animals, has he? If there's anything I won't tolerate, it's
teasing and tormenting the animals. I—"

"No," Beatrix said, interrupting. If Lady Longford were allowed to go on, she'd work herself into a spite. "Jeremy is *not*
in trouble," she said firmly. "He has done quite well in school
this year, according to Miss Nash. He is a fine young scholar."

"And he passed the entrance examination for Kelsick, the
grammar school at Ambleside," Mr. Heelis put in. "With an
impressively high score."

"Commendable," said her ladyship grudgingly. "A surprising achievement, if I may say so, for one of the village
children. I should not have expected any of them to be
scholars." She paused. "Well, then, if the boy isn't in trouble
and he's done sufficiently well in school to earn a place at
Kelsick, what is the problem?"

"The problem," Mr. Heelis replied, "is that Jeremy's aunt
cannot afford to send him to school. Dr. Butters has found
him an apprenticeship, with the apothecary in Hawkshead."

At that moment, Emily appeared with the tea tray. She
put it down, stood by while Lady Longford poured, and

passed the bread-and-butter. Others of her ladyship's social status would have served cakes and sweets, but frugality was the rule at Tidmarsh Manor.

"That'll do, Emily," her ladyship said. Emily left the room, and Lady Longford, her tea cup in one hand, went back to the subject. "With regard to Jeremy Crosfield, I can only speculate that you have told me about his situation because he and his aunt are tenants of my manor farm, and you suppose me to have an interest in the child. Well, then, you may tell Dr. Butters that I am glad to know of his interest in securing Jeremy a good place as an apothecary's apprentice. The boy could do much worse."

"But he could do much, much better!" Beatrix cried impulsively, leaning forward. "I have known Jeremy since I first bought Hill Top Farm. He has a fine talent for botany and natural history and a keen mind. His interests are academic— and artistic, as well. He can benefit greatly from more education, and from an opportunity to pursue his art. He can grow up to be someone of whom we will all be very proud."

Suddenly, she was aware of Mr. Heelis, who was looking at her with some surprise, and of Lady Longford's raised eyebrows.

"Indeed," said her ladyship dryly, and put down her cup.

"Yes, indeed," Beatrix muttered, thinking that she had gone too far—and then went even further. "It would be a shocking waste to train Jeremy as an apothecary, when he is capable of so much more. When he deserves an education."

Mr. Heelis cleared his throat hurriedly. "As we said—and as your ladyship is no doubt aware—Jeremy's aunt is an excellent spinner and weaver, and produces truly admirable cloth. But she barely earns enough money to keep herself and Jeremy, and there is nothing left over. It is quite out of the question for her to provide for his continued schooling."

There was a moment's silence. "So you've come to me," Lady Longford said, frowning darkly, "to ask for money. Well, it won't do you any good."

Beatrix felt her insides clench. What a disagreeable old lady! She had to steady her voice before she could speak. "We're asking you to be generous toward a young man who can benefit greatly from your help," she said in measured tones.

Lady Longford made a harrumphing sound. "It comes down to money in the end, though. It always does. People asking for a pound here and another pound there, all in the name of charity." Hearing her tone, Dudley lifted his head and growled. "It is very vexing," she went on, with a self-pitying sigh. "One does well to manage for oneself and one's household, without being expected to support every improvident Tom, Dick, and Harry who believes himself to be in need of shoes or a winter coat. I don't know why people always turn to me."

And then, just when their effort seemed hopeless, Beatrix was suddenly inspired. She put on a look of blank surprise.

"But Lady Longford, to whom else should we turn? Jeremy and his aunt *are* your tenants, and Lord Longford, as everyone knows, was widely respected for his generosity toward those who occupied his lands and cottages. Mr. Heelis and I were sure that you would want to do something for the boy in honor of your husband's memory—but perhaps we've been presumptuous."

And then, not looking at Mr. Heelis, Beatrix added, "Of course, we did discuss the possibility of asking for a special collection at the Sunday church service." She hoped that Mr. Heelis would not give her away, for they had discussed no such thing. He did not disappoint her.

"Yes," he said gravely, taking her cue, "we did think of asking Vicar Sackett to take up an offering. But we feared that your ladyship might be offended if we asked others before you had an opportunity to help."

Her ladyship grimaced. "Fat lot of good it would do you, anyway. Most villagers haven't two pence to rub together, especially after the men come home from the pub on Saturday night." She gave a dry cough. "Have you thought of asking Major Kittredge? Judging from the style of Saturday's reception at Raven Hall, the man has a deep purse."

"Yes, we've discussed that possibility," Mr. Heelis said, although they had not spoken of that, either. "Major Kittredge could certainly afford it, but he is not acquainted with the boy. And the Crosfields are not his tenants."

Beatrix put on a look of concern. "That was it, you see, Lady Longford. We feared that others would think it . . . well, odd. That is, if the master of Raven Hall should offer to fund Jeremy's education when the boy and his aunt are tenants of Tidmarsh Manor."

"I suppose you're right," her ladyship said slowly. "But I shouldn't like to set a precedent by simply giving money to the boy. There would have to be something—"

"Of course," Beatrix said in warm agreement. "Your ladyship is exactly right. He should *earn* such a great honor, and it should be public. What if it were announced—say, at tomorrow's May Day celebration—that Jeremy Crosfield was the winner of the Longford Scholarship, awarded in memory of the late Lord Longford?"

Lady Longford frowned. "But that might oblige me to continue paying—"

"If it were a scholarship to Kelsick," Mr. Heelis put in hurriedly, "it would be awarded only to a child who passes the entrance examination, which I understand is very difficult.

In fact, Jeremy is the only child to have done so in the history of the village school. So, practically speaking, I should say that his is an exceptional case."

"Still, it would be a considerable expense," her ladyship said doubtfully. "I suppose there will be board and room costs, as well as the tuition. And the boy would have to have clothes and—"

"Yes, of course," Beatrix said, feeling entirely out of patience. She put down her teacup and stood. "Mr. Heelis, we have imposed on Lady Longford's hospitality long enough."

"Yes," said Mr. Heelis, also rising. "It would undoubtedly be better to approach Major Kittredge with the plan for the scholarship. He—"

"Oh, sit down," Lady Longford snapped crossly. "You make my neck stiff, stalking about like a pair of cranes." When they had seated themselves again, she said, "I see I'll get no peace from either of you until I've agreed to pay for this boy's education. How much is it going to cost me?"

"I've taken the liberty of working up an estimate." Mr. Heelis reached into his pocket and took out a folded sheet of paper. "It comes to a fairly minimal annual expenditure of around twenty pounds, give or take a few shillings."

"Twenty pounds!" Lady Longford exclaimed, aghast.

"Of course," Beatrix said, "if that seems too much, Major Kittredge might—"

"Oh, bother Major Kittredge!" Lady Longford cried angrily, and snatched the paper from Mr. Heelis. She scanned it, then said, in a curt tone, "I shall give you a cheque for the first year, Heelis, so that there is no confusion. And I mean to be present when the scholarship is announced."

"Yes, please come!" Beatrix said energetically, thinking how the ceremony would be arranged. "There will be a place of honor for you on the platform. Captain Woodcock will introduce you as the donor when he makes the presentation of the Longford Scholarship. The vicar will say a few words of thank-you, and Miss Nash will—"

"Do leave off, Miss Potter," commanded her ladyship wearily, waving her hand. "You make me tired just listening to you. Heelis, my cheques are in the desk drawer. Miss Potter, pour me another cup of tea."

Beatrix poured the tea, and as she handed the cup to Lady Longford, remarked, in a diffident tone, "I wonder if your ladyship would allow me to borrow Caroline this afternoon and evening. I have a project with which I should very much like to have her assistance—if you can spare her, that is. She could spend the night at Hill Top and go on to school in the morning."

"I have no objection, I suppose," Lady Longford said, scarcely paying attention. "No, Heelis. It is the drawer on the left."

"Thank you," Beatrix said. "I shall go to the school and let Caroline know. Would you like another slice of bread-and-butter with your tea?"

A short while later, Mr. Heelis, with Lady Longford's cheque in the breast pocket of his coat, was handing Beatrix into his gig. "You are a wonder, Miss Potter," he said.

"I'm not at all sure what you mean by that," Beatrix said crisply. "I simply saw an opportunity and—"

"You simply read her ladyship like a book, that's what you did," Mr. Heelis said, climbing up beside her and picking up the reins. "And you lied like a trooper, with nae a blink of t'eye, as the local folk say. If you should decide to interest yourself in the practice of law—"

"I have quite enough to do already, Mr. Heelis," Beatrix replied tartly. "As far as lying goes, I cannot condone those who would be maliciously deceitful, such as Mrs. Irene

Waring. But I certainly believe that lying in the service of a greater truth is forgivable, although perhaps not entirely admirable."

"Agreed," Mr. Heelis replied, and they drove off. "The scholarship—a ripping good idea, by the way—will be the making of the boy. And it's good for Lady Longford's soul to part with some of her money. God knows she has enough of it. She could do a great deal of good for the village, if she would, which she probably won't." He chuckled. "The next time I need to persuade someone to agree to something unpleasant, Miss Potter, I'll be sure to bring you along."

Beatrix looked at the watch pinned to her lapel and changed the subject. "I see it is nearly time for the children to be dismissed. Perhaps we could drive to the school and let Caroline know that her grandmother has given her permission to spend the night at Hill Top Farm."

"Of course," Mr. Heelis said, and added curiously, "If you don't mind my asking, what are you planning?"

Beatrix chuckled. "I fear that I have written about too many excessively impertinent bunnies, Mr. Heelis. My sympathies lie with the rebellious."

"Ah," Mr. Heelis said. "And so you are aiding and abetting Miss Caroline's rebellion?"

"Something of the sort," Beatrix replied. "I resisted being trained up to be a lady, which is apt to wring out all one's original and creative spirit. I am sorry to say that this seems to be Lady Longford's aim for Caroline. However, tonight's little escapade is almost entirely innocent. It is May Eve. We are going to look for fairies."

There was a moment's silence, long enough for Beatrix to wonder if Mr. Heelis thought she should not be involved in anything that thwarted Lady Longford's intentions for her granddaughter. But when she turned to look at him, she saw that the corners of his mouth were quirking.

"Fairies, eh? I remember watching for fairies myself as a boy. There was a place along the Eden, where they were said to live—a very pretty place, with overhanging willows and spring flowers. We used to go there, on May Eve. If you'd like, I should be glad to accompany you." He glanced down at her, his eyes smiling. "In case of goblins, of course. Or trolls. May Eve brings out all sorts, and some of them are dangerous."

"Why, thank you, Mr. Heelis," Beatrix said, genuinely pleased. "I think, however, that the children view this rather as a special occasion, and—"

"And I would be intruding." He sighed and shook his head. "Ah, well. The price of growing up, I suppose. One does it at one's peril."

Afterward, Beatrix was to vividly remember his offer, and wish that she had not been so quick to reject it.

35

The Mysteries of May Eve

In the ancient days of the Celts, when all lived by the Wheel of the Year, May Eve (then called Beltane, for Bel, the Celtic god of fire) was one of the eight seasonal celebrations. Halfway between the spring equinox and the summer solstice, it marked the magical passage from the long months of chilly darkness to the season of light and warmth, when the fields and forests became exuberantly green and the sky became deliciously blue. This joyful event was celebrated with a night of games and feasting and merry-making, with bonfires and dancing and happy song. In the Old Tradition, it was a night when the veil between the Earthworld and the Otherworld became thin and very nearly transparent. The Fairy Folk were known to come out on that night to dance, and there would always be a few lucky humans who would see them. Or unlucky, for it has been claimed that some were carried off by fairies on this night, not to be seen again, or saw such sights that they were changed forever, and returned to their mortal existence as mad as hatters.

Of course, as the nineteenth century turned into the twentieth, much of this fairy lore was forgotten or laughed at, for the world had become far too sophisticated—and skeptical and ironic—to tolerate such nonsense. In the cities, nothing much survived of the traditional May celebration; in fact, the first day of May had become a day to celebrate workers and serious work, rather than indulge in games and frivolous play. In the villages, only the May Pole and the Ribbon Dance were left to mark this day from any other, and the games and festivities were now seen as childish celebrations fit for schoolchildren, rather than a happy ritual for all to join. And fairies were relegated to books and the stage, where readers and play-goers (chiefly children) could indulge their fantasies in safety, without fear of being carried away.

But there remained a few parts of the British Isles where fairies were not forgotten or shunned. In the rural areas of Scotland, Wales, and Ireland, many swore that the Folk still populated the hills and dales, more secluded than before, perhaps, but still very much alive. And in the Land between the Lakes, while some might not publicly own up to such beliefs, only a few would swear on a Bible that there were no fairies, or that all the elves and trolls and tree-spirits had left the woods many years before. And even fewer would venture out at twilight on May Eve to put the possibility of fairies to the test.

This might have been why Beatrix, Deirdre, and Caroline did not see a single soul as they walked up Market Street, through the village. Or it might simply have been that this was the hour when most families were getting ready for supper, the sons hurrying in from their garden chores, the fathers washing their hands and splashing water onto their faces, the daughters lighting the lamps in the cottage kitchens, the mothers dishing up the tatie pot and pease porridge. Whatever the reason, the lane was empty and Beatrix and the girls saw no one until they reached the ford over Wilfin Beck, where Rascal and Jeremy (who had brought his aunt's bicycle lantern to light their way home after dark) had been waiting for some time and wondering what was taking them so long.

Caroline had been delighted when Miss Potter appeared with Mr. Heelis to give her a lift from school, and astonished to learn that her grandmother had granted permission for her to spend the night at Hill Top Farm—something that had never happened before and seemed like quite a magical thing, all by itself. Deirdre, too, was overjoyed when Mrs. Sutton (at Miss Potter's request) allowed her not only to take the evening away from her usual duties, but to stay the night at Hill Top. Miss Potter had explained that she wanted to do some drawing and would like to use the girls as models, a request that Mrs. Sutton—who really tried very hard to be a good mother and felt guilty at all the hard work Deirdre was asked to do—was perfectly willing to grant. And since Miss Potter did not like to think herself a complete liar, she did exactly what she told Mrs. Sutton she would do: she drew the girls as they gathered rue, lavender, thyme, rosemary, primroses, and hawthorn in the garden.

In after years, when Caroline had grown up to be a lady (although not at all the sort of lady her grandmother envisioned), she had a thousand magical nights upon which to reflect. Of course, I can't tell you what these were, because they hadn't happened at the time of our story. But it is safe to say that Caroline would always remember this May Eve as the most enchanted—and one of the most exciting—of all the nights of her long life.

To the west, the sun had transformed the sky into a remarkable tissue of gold and purple, colors that lingered behind long after the sun had gone to rest. To the east, a blue haze hung over Claife Heights, and a full, round moon floated up like a silver balloon. The evening breeze, sweet and cool, brushed her face with easy fingers. Somewhere a thrush was singing, and nearer at hand, a cuckoo reminded them that the wheel of the year had turned, bringing back the long, slow twilights of summer, when the pale sky would not darken enough to see the stars until nearly eleven.

And with all this, Caroline (who was following behind Deirdre on the woodland path) kept remembering what had happened on Saturday. She was no closer to understanding than she had been then, and no matter how much and how often she and Deirdre had talked about it (and that had been almost constantly whenever they were together), they were both still completely mystified. Not even Jeremy, who always had an opinion about things—especially things that couldn't be seen, like the North Pole and the wireless— could offer an explanation. But now it was May Eve at last, and they were returning to the magical glen, and Miss Potter was with them, and perhaps the mystery would be solved. Having Miss Potter along made that seem more likely, somehow. She was the sort of person who could make impossibilities happen, like obtaining Grandmama's permission to stay all night at Hill Top Farm, or solving the mystery of the riddle pinned to the oak tree.

Deirdre, walking in front of Caroline and behind Jeremy, was also very glad that Miss Potter had agreed to come along. Not that she was afraid of the dark. Eleven was far

too old for that, and anyway, there was enough light to see
where they were going, at least until they reached the darkest woods and the path took them under the tall trees near
the top of Claife Heights. No, it was something else. If there
were fairies in the glen (and after what had happened on
Saturday, how could it be doubted?), Deirdre suspected that
they were more likely to show themselves to Miss Potter
than to anyone else in the world—if only because they
would be afraid not to. Miss Potter was that kind of person,
somehow. She took it entirely for granted that the fairies
would be there and that was simply that, no questions asked
or answered.

And Jeremy, who had taken the lead as they went up the
path, was also still in the dark, figuratively speaking, about
Saturday. No matter how much thought he had given the
matter (and he had given it quite a lot), he had never quite
got things entirely sorted in his mind. He had not the least
idea of what they might encounter tonight, either, whether
magic or fairies or something else altogether. In fact, he had
to own to being glad that Miss Potter had come along, for
she was the least likely of all of them to be taken in by whatever chicanery was afoot. He had not forgotten how she had
defended him against Miss Crabbe's accusation of theft, and
he knew her to be clear-eyed, strong-minded, and unafraid.
She would see through any sort of underhanded nonsense in
a flash, whilst all three of them were still blinded by their
belief (or half a belief, he thought ruefully) in magic.

And Miss Potter? Well, having believed in fairies when
she was a child and continuing to believe in the creative
power of the imagination, she was not at all bothered by the
possibility that she and the children might see something
they didn't understand. So she was quite content to let Jeremy and Rascal take the lead while she herself brought up

the rear of their little caravan, enjoying the magical sights and sounds of twilight, even though she didn't know where they were going. Indeed (and it is important to remember this), neither Deirdre nor Caroline had told her (or would have been able to tell her, even if they wanted to!) the exact location of the magical glen. All they had said was that it was a green place on the shore of a lake at the top of Cuckoo Brow Wood, a little distance from Raven Hall. So Beatrix had only a general idea of where they were going, which was through Cuckoo Brow Wood to the tarn at the top of Claife Heights.

It was with some surprise, then, that she began to recognize the path they were taking as the very same path that she had followed on Sunday morning. And when they reached the top of the mossy bank and slid down the other side into the green and magical silence of the glade on the shore of Fern Vale Tarn, she knew that her fairy glade and the children's fairy glade—the place where they had discovered the riddle pinned to a tree with a silver knife—were one and the same.

Which was rather nice, of course, except that it meant that the children were about to discover the fanciful garden-house she had built, with its fern-roofed canopy and table and toadstools and acorn cups full of berries, and were bound to think it had been built by enterprising Folk planning to picnic out in the open.

And that, of course, is exactly what happened, before Beatrix could open her mouth to explain. Deirdre was the first to see it, and flew to it with shouts of delight. "A fairy house!" she cried, falling onto her knees. "Look, oh, look! They've left it for us to find! It's proof they've been here!" She looked up, her eyes shining. "Why, this is as good as seein' a fairy! It means I've still got me mum's gift!"

"Miss Potter?" Caroline whispered, reaching for Beatrix's hand. "Do you suppose it's *real?*" She looked up into Beatrix's face, the question huge in her eyes.

And Beatrix, who had been about to say that she had visited this very same glen and had made the little garden-house herself, just for a lark, found herself saying instead, "It certainly looks real to me, Caroline." She let go of the girl's hand and gave her a little push. "Take a look and see what you think."

Jeremy, with Rascal at his knee, was looking on with surprise and incredulity written across his face. "Do you think," he said very seriously, "that the fairies are here? If they are, maybe I could make a wish, even though I can't see them." He glanced around. "Of course, it's hard to tell what shape they're in. Perhaps I'm looking right at them."

"Do wish, Jeremy," Rascal barked encouragingly. *"It certainly can't hurt."*

Beatrix said quietly, "I'm sure it's possible. Wishing never harmed anyone, as far as I've been able to learn, and it requires such a little expenditure of effort. All one has to do is *do* it."

So Jeremy closed his eyes, clenched his hands, and whispered something so low that Beatrix could not hear it, although she was sure she knew what it was. And then he opened his eyes again and said distinctly, "The knife."

"The knife?" Beatrix asked.

"The silver knife we found on the tree, pinning the riddle. We hid it." He went toward the twisted tangle of roots at the foot of a large oak. "It should be right here." He poked around for a moment, then said excitedly, "But it isn't where we put it! It's gone!"

Deirdre, still on her knees in front of Beatrix's garden-house, looked up at Jeremy. "Of course it's gone," she said matter-of-factly. "The fairies took it back."

"But where *are* they?" Caroline asked, looking around. "Why won't they show themselves?"

"*Because they're dwelves,*" Rascal explained, "*and not to be trusted.*" He glanced nervously over his shoulder. "*It's probably better that we don't see them, if it's all the same to you. We have no idea what form they're going to take or—*"

"Hush, Rascal!" Jeremy commanded. He cocked his head. "I hear voices."

"Right over there," Caroline said, pointing. "At the end of the lake!"

"It's them!" Deirdre gasped, jumping to her feet, her eyes nearly starting out of her head. "It's the fairies!"

But it wasn't. Beatrix recognized the voices as human voices, and knew that they came from the path at the foot of the Raven Hall garden. One voice was easily recognizable: the throaty, petulant voice of Mrs. Kittredge, now known to be Irene Waring. The other voice was . . . Beatrix frowned. She had heard that voice before. It belonged to Mr. Augustus Richardson, the toadlike gentleman who planned to build the villas on the shore of Lake Windermere!

He was saying, "I've brought the horses, my dear, as you requested—although I should have thought a carriage would have been more comfortable for you."

"Someone might have heard the wheels on the gravel," Irene Waring replied in a guarded tone. "And I am dressed to ride astride." She gave a low chuckle. "As you can see, I am wearing trousers. Where have you put the horses?"

"They are hidden under the fir trees, in the place where the carriages were parked during the reception on Saturday. Do you have your things?"

"My bag is packed. It's hidden in the pantry."

"And the gems? You managed to get them out of the safe?"

Beatrix pulled in her breath. The gems? The Kittredge family jewels?

"Of course I have them," Irene Waring snapped. "Do you take me for a fool? I'm not leaving this appalling place without something to show for all the time and effort I've put into this business. And I'm not going back to James Waring, either. That's all over and done with. The jewels will allow me a comfortable living in France."

"Your half of the jewels, you mean," Mr. Richardson remarked in a dry tone. "They are part of our bargain, as you recall. Now that the villas are out of the picture, I require something for my time and effort, as well."

"Yes, of course. Wait for me here. I'll get my things and join you—it will take me seven or eight minutes. And then we'll go to the horses."

Seven or eight minutes! That didn't give them much time. Beatrix grasped Jeremy's arm. "I need your help," she said urgently. "Can you run fast?"

"Of course," Jeremy said. "As the wind. Well, almost," he amended.

Beatrix gave him instructions, then turned to the girls. "I would like you to stay here," she said, "and keep a sharp eye out. There's no predicting what you might see, but above all, you must keep yourselves hidden."

"Yes, Miss Potter," the girls chorused.

"Thank you," Beatrix said. She looked down at Rascal. "You stay here and guard the girls," she said. "We'll be back as soon as we can."

The exact sequence of affairs over the next few minutes is rather confused, so perhaps I will tell it one bit at a time, rather than trying to put it into its original jumble. It was Jeremy, of course, who ran as fast as he could (not quite as fast as the wind, but almost) round to the front door of

Raven Hall, where he rang the bell and, when the butler appeared, insisted on seeing the major immediately, at the urgent request of Miss Beatrix Potter—all of which took (although I wasn't watching my watch) approximately five minutes, perhaps six. After that, it was two minutes more before the major could be summoned from his smoking room, where he was enjoying a cigar. Jeremy's story took another two minutes (because he had to tell it twice, to be believed), and another two minutes for the major to summon a suitable party for pursuit. And then they all had to run out a side entrance (Jeremy, the major, the butler, the valet, and the boot boy) and through the woods to the place where the carriages had been parked, some four minutes away. This entire business took—oh, let us say, some sixteen minutes, more or less. Which means that Mrs. Waring and Mr. Richardson, had they been undeterred, would have already reached their horses, mounted, and ridden off with the Kittredge family jewels.

But Miss Potter had another plan. As Jeremy ran for the front door of Raven Hall, she ran for the carriage park, taking care to be silent, so that Mr. Augustus Richardson, who was pacing up and down in the garden, smoking a cigarette, would not hear her. Beatrix was hardly as fleet-footed as Jeremy (one does not have much occasion to run in London), but she managed to reach the trees where the horses were hidden in just under seven minutes. She was quite out of breath, to be sure, and she had a painful stitch in her side, but these slight disabilities did not keep her from accomplishing what had to be done in the space of five minutes.

The horses were curious, of course, and swung their heads round to see who this person was and what she was doing. But Beatrix rubbed their necks and spoke a few quiet words into their pricked ears and they listened and nodded and agreed. After all, horses (while they are often used by people with evil intentions) are honest creatures who do not like the idea of being involved in larceny, and were actually quite pleased to see what Miss Potter was doing. When she had done what she came to do, she slipped back into the shadows, sat down on a stump to catch her breath, and waited to see what would happen next.

While Jeremy was fetching the major and Miss Potter was managing the horses and Mr. Richardson was smoking a cigarette and pacing back and forth in the garden, Irene Waring was getting her bag (filled mostly with the jewels, as well as the few pieces of silver that had not gone off to Edinburgh with the thieving steward). As she had predicted, it had taken seven minutes to get her bag out of the pantry and join Mr. Richardson, and they set off.

Always the gentleman, he offered to carry the heavy bag, but she refused. "What?" she said, laughing unpleasantly. "Give you a chance to run off with the loot? Not on your life, sir!"

"Not my intention!" Mr. Richardson protested, but Irene Waring was clutching the bag very tightly and he did not pursue the matter.

The lady and gentleman were nearly as fleet as Miss Potter (who was really quite unused to running) so they reached the horses in only ten minutes. All that was left was to climb into their saddles and ride off down the lane. No wonder Irene Waring was looking forward so confidently to establishing herself in France on her half of the stolen jewels, or that Mr. Richardson was anticipating using his share to purchase some land that was just coming up for sale at the southern end of Lake Windermere, where the syndicate might build its villas, after all.

But things did not turn out as Irene Waring intended. For when she put her foot into the stirrup to lift herself onto the horse, the saddle—without any warning at all!—slid all the way round under the belly of the horse. She was suddenly and unceremoniously flung onto the gravel of the carriage park, flat on her back. Her red hair had come loose and the breath was knocked out of her.

And in that moment, quick as a wink, Mr. Richardson seized the advantage. He snatched up the fallen bag of jewels and silver and strode to his horse. "There appears to be some sort of difficulty about your saddle, my dear," he said with an ironic chuckle. He untied his horse and gathered the reins. "How very regrettable."

Irene Waring suddenly found her voice, and spit out some very nasty names which I will not repeat here. "You cad!" she cried furiously (or words to that effect). "You rascal! You cur!" She scrambled to her feet. "You sabotaged my saddle! You meant to make off with the jewels all along!"

"I did nothing of the sort," Mr. Richardson protested, as he slung the bag onto his horse's back. "But you are clearly unhorsed, and there is no time to spare. Forgive me, dear Irene, but I must be off." And with that, he leapt gracefully into the saddle.

But this did not turn out as Mr. Richardson intended, either, for he was not even settled in the saddle when it slid away underneath him. With a sharp cry, he tumbled onto the ground on the other side of his horse, landing with a decisive thump.

Which gave Irene Waring the opportunity to seize the bag of jewels and use it to beat Mr. Richardson about the head and shoulders, which must have been quite painful, for the bag was heavy. He got to his feet and hunched over, trying to ward off her blows, remonstrating with her loudly. But there was no stopping her. In fact, she might have beat the poor fellow senseless if she had not been interrupted by a sudden firm command from the shadows under the trees.

"Hold there, you scoundrels!" It was Major Kittredge. "Stop, thieves! You're not getting away with this!"

Irene Waring screamed, dropped the bag, and turned to run. Mr. Richardson reached into his pocket for the gun he had hidden there, but just as he was drawing it out, he was tackled by the butler and boot boy and roughly wrestled to the ground. Major Kittredge's valet grasped Irene Waring's arms and pinned them behind her.

"He did it!" she shrieked piteously. "He stole them, Christopher! I was only trying to get them back so I could return them to you."

"Stuff and nonsense," Mr. Richardson growled. "She burgled them out of your safe, Kittredge. I confiscated them on your behalf."

"Quite," said the major dryly. "Come on, you two. We'll see what Captain Woodcock has to say about this."

Miss Potter, with Jeremy beside her, could not help smiling as she watched this scene unfold, for it had been she who had loosened the saddle girths, dumping the two thieves on the ground and keeping them from escaping with their loot. But she did not like to call attention to herself or to Jeremy, and she felt the need to return to the girls, who had been left all alone in the growing dark. While the major dispatched the boot boy to summon the Justice of the Peace and the constable, Miss Potter and Jeremy melted into the shadows and made their way back to the fairy glen.

A few minutes later, they had rejoined the girls and told them what had happened. Jeremy reported on his whirlwind race to summon the major, and Miss Potter told them about loosening the saddle girths. Of course, this also meant telling them who Irene Waring and Mr. Richardson were, and what they had been trying to do.

"So she *was* a witch, after all!" burst out Deirdre. "She had to've been, to do something as awful as all that! Marry the major when she was already married, and try to steal the family jewels!"

"And try to convince the major to build holiday villas along the lakeshore," Jeremy put in.

"That *does* make her a witch," Caroline said decidedly. "A very evil witch."

"You weren't afraid, I hope," said Miss Potter. Night had fallen now, but the stars were out and the moon brightened the fairy glen and shimmered across the surface of the tarn, as if someone had spilled silver paint across the water. "What did you see while we were gone? Any fairies?"

"*Of course!*" Rascal barked excitedly. "*A great many! Fairies, fairies, everywhere!*"

"How are we to know?" asked Caroline, clearly frustrated. "If they are first one thing, then another, how do we know whether we're seeing them or not? But I made a wish anyway," she added, with a glance at Jeremy. "Just to be on the safe side."

"That's right," Deirdre said, and recited the last lines of the riddle. " 'All about but changing form, Here a blossom, there a thorn, Tall or short, thick or thin, Guess the shape we are in.' " She brightened. "But I saw *something,* and I'm sure it was fairies, and I made a wish!"

And then they reported what they had seen.

Deirdre's vision had been the most fanciful: a pair of delicate creatures with golden wings and golden crowns, slanting down a moonbeam. Caroline had seen a remarkably large tawny owl, which had drifted down out of the night sky and landed in the top of the tallest oak, gazing down at them and inquiring *Whoo-whooo?* in a stern owl's voice. Both of them had seen a large badger that came out from under the ferns, regarded them thoughtfully for a time, and then vanished. And all the while, a trio of red squirrels perched on a branch above the glade, making soft chittering noises, while several other small, furry creatures—voles, perhaps, or moles, or something like—crept out of the roots of the oak trees, sniffed at the children's hands, and disappeared again.

"So you see," Caroline concluded in a matter-of-fact tone, "we might have seen fairies, or we might not. It all depends."

"But we did!" Deirdre insisted. "I did, anyway!"

"I don't know about Deirdre's winged creatures," Rascal put in, *"but the owl and the badger weren't fairies. It was the Professor and Bozzy, and I caught a word with each of them before they left."* He grinned. *"They were the ones who posted the riddle, you see. They knew we were coming, since it was Bozzy's map we were following. It was Bozzy's knife, too, so that much is solved."* He paused and frowned. *"But those noisy squirrels— If you ask me, they're dwelves. Oak Folk, in squirrel shape."*

Even though Miss Potter and the children can't understand Rascal, we can, and we shall have to be satisfied, I think, with his interpretation of events, for it is just about as close to an explanation as we are likely to come. If he is right, and if the squirrels really were Oak Folk, perhaps they were celebrating the fact that there would be no villas built along the shore of Lake Windermere, and that Raven Hall had seen the backs of Irene Waring and Augustus Richardson. They were very bad characters, after all, and it was a good thing that Miss Potter and Jeremy were on hand to keep them from getting away with the Kittredge family jewels.

But perhaps Rascal is wrong, and the squirrels were only squirrels, for there have always been a great many red squirrels in Cuckoo Brow Wood, and they are rather unruly creatures, and like to leap from branch to branch and make a great deal of noise.

When it comes to magic, and the mysteries of May Eve, none of us can know for certain, can we?

36

The Last Word

Still, there are probably some who would say that the children must have seen real fairies on May Eve, for all three got their wishes.

This surprising outcome occurred at the May Day celebration in the Sawrey School yard, after the vicar had given his invocation, thanking the Almighty for His gracious goodness, and the Village Volunteer Band had struck up "God Save the King." Everyone joined lustily in the first verse:

> *God save our gracious King*
> *Long live our noble King,*
> *God save the King.*
> *Send him victorious,*

Happy and glorious,
Long to reign over us:
God save the King.

When they began the second verse, the vicar found his heart lifted up in joyful thanksgiving for all that had happened during the past few days and cast a grateful glance at Miss Potter, who surely had done more than anyone else to bring it all about, vanquishing not only the duplicitous Irene Waring and the nefarious Mr. Richardson, but the unendurable and knavish Thextons, as well:

O Lord, our God, arise,
Scatter our enemies,
And make them fall:
Confound their politics,
Frustrate their knavish tricks,
On thee our hopes we fix:
God save us all.

And then came the moment everyone was waiting for. Ruth Leech was crowned Queen of the May and gave the May Queen's proclamation, calling on all creation to join together in peace and love, after which the schoolchildren danced the May Pole dance without a single mistake for the first time since anyone could remember. Their success was a great surprise to all, making the dancers exceedingly happy, their parents exceedingly proud, the teachers most exceedingly relieved.

But you will not be surprised by what happened next, surely, for (if you were paying attention in Chapter Thirty-four) you already know what Mr. Heelis and Miss Potter said to Lady Longford, and what her ladyship agreed to do, and that she had already written out her cheque and handed it to Mr. Heelis.

So I am sure you were expecting to see Lady Longford seated in a place of honor on the wooden platform in the school yard, and to hear Captain Miles Woodcock announce that her ladyship had graciously endowed the Longford Scholarship in memory of her dear, departed husband, whose philanthropy was known to everyone throughout the Land between the Lakes. And you will not be at all surprised but only pleased by Captain Woodcock's announcement that the first award was being made to Jeremy Crosfield, so that he could attend Kelsick Grammar School in Ambleside.

But Jeremy, Caroline, and Deirdre were expecting none of this, and their gasps of astonished delight could be heard in the jaw-dropping silence between Captain Woodcock's announcement and the round of ringing applause congratu-lating young Jeremy for his achievement and Lady Longford for her astonishing generosity.

"It's the fairies!" Deirdre whispered to Caroline. "We saw them, and we wished, and they granted our wishes!" She cast her eyes in the direction of Cuckoo Brow Wood, which rose up the hill beyond the school. "Thank you, fairies!"

Caroline had to agree, because she knew very well that her grandmother pinched every penny until it squeaked twice, and only the fairies could make her let loose of the pounds and shillings it was going to take to pay Jeremy's tu-ition and board bill.

And when Bosworth Badger and Galileo Newton Owl heard the happy news that afternoon, they, too, were aston-ished, for while they had done their part in bringing the children and the fairies together (which was why they had posted the riddle on the oak tree), they had no idea that Jeremy had received a scholarship and was therefore no longer destined to spend his life mixing powders and potions in the apothecary's shop. They received this word from Rascal, who found them together in the library at The Brockery, enjoying their tea and toasting their toes in front of a comfortable fire.

"*Oh, I say!*" the badger exclaimed, when Rascal had told the whole story. "*Bully for Jeremy!*"

"*And just whooo,*" the Professor inquired, "*is responsible for this? Such generosity on Lady Looongfooord's part has little precedent, sooo far as I am aware.*"

"*Dudley—Lady Longford's spaniel—tells me it was Miss Potter's idea,*" Rascal replied. Dudley was not always forthcoming, but the fat old spaniel had been so impressed by the adroit way Miss Potter had managed his mistress that he just had to tell Rascal all about it. "*And Miss Potter,*" Rascal added, "*was the guiding genius behind the major's capture of the two thieves. If it hadn't been for her, they would have got clean away.*"

"*And what will happen tooo the miscreants?*" asked the Professor, blinking sleepily. Parsley's raisin scones were deeply satisfying and the fire was making his feathers delightfully warm. His afternoon nap seemed imminent.

But Rascal couldn't answer that question, for the simple reason that it had no answer just yet. Irene Waring and Augustus Richardson were being held at the Hawkshead gaol and would be arraigned at a magistrate's hearing on Thursday. They would no doubt be bound over for the assizes, where a jury would weigh the charges against them and assess their punishment.

"*And what,*" the badger said, getting up to put another stick on the fire, "*has become of the Hill Top rats?*"

Rascal shook his head. *"That is a most incredible story,"* he said. *"It appears that one of the attic's regular residents—a fellow named Ridley Rattail—employed a cat to get rid of the riff-raff, then bundled him off in a beer-barrel."* He told the tale as he had heard it from Max the Manx, who was enjoying his new employment in the Hill Top barn.

"Astonishing," said the badger.

"Very gooood," said the Professor as he nodded off to sleep.

And that, I think, will be the end of our story, for the Professor always likes to have the last word.

Historical Note

Beatrix Potter in 1907*

1907 was a busy year for Beatrix Potter, between paying the proper attention to her parents and the necessary attention to her growing establishment at Hill Top Farm. It was the farm that captured her imagination, and she gave it as much time as she could.

By the spring of 1907 (when this book takes place), Beatrix owned sixteen Herdwick sheep, six dairy cows, and six pigs, including Aunt Susan, who (as she wrote to Harold Warne's daughter Louie) was "very fat and black with a very turned up nose and the fattest cheeks I ever saw [and] likes being tickled under the chin." Aunt Susan was so tame that she nibbled Miss Potter's galoshes. But while Beatrix could treat her animals as friends, she could also be realistic about them. In August of that year, she wrote to Millie Warne

*For more on Beatrix Potter's life, see the Historical Notes in *The Tale of Hill Top Farm* and *The Tale of Holly How*.

(Norman's sister), that she had gone out early that morning to photograph the lambs before they were taken to market. "Oh shocking!" she remarked dryly. "It does not do to be sentimental on a farm. I am going to have some lambskin hearthrugs."

The rats, of course, were a continuing problem. The previous fall, she had written to Millie about her struggles with them:

> *The rats have come back in great force, two big ones were trapped in the shed here, besides turning out a nest of eight baby rats in the cucumber frame opposite the door. They are getting at the corn at the farm. Mrs. Cannon calmly announced that she should get four or five cats! imagine my feelings; but I daresay they will live in the outbuildings.*

The outbreak seems to have been brought under control by the summer of 1907, in part because of the building program, which included a new barn and milking parlor, zinc strips on the bottoms of the doors, and cement skirtings around the house—as well as the cat campaign managed by the farmer's wife.

But Hill Top Farm and its animals were not Miss Potter's only concerns, for she was actively engaged with her creative work. *The Story of a Fierce Bad Rabbit* and *The Story of Miss Moppet* had been published in panorama format in November 1906. For Christmas 1906, she gave Winifred Warne an illustrated story called *The Roly-Poly Pudding,* which she continued to work on throughout the year and into 1908, using the interiors of Hill Top as her settings. (In 1928, the book was renamed *The Tale of Samuel Whiskers,* to conform with the other titles.) In late August 1907, while on holiday in Keswick with her parents, she celebrated the publication of *The Tale of*

Tom Kitten. The first printing of 20,000 copies sold out in two months and a second printing of 3,000 copies was ordered in December, for Christmas sales. Warne was soliciting French and German publishers, but Beatrix (always a perfectionist when it came to published materials) was not pleased with the translations. In September, she wrote from Wales, where she and her parents were staying at Gwaynynog:

> *That French is choke full of mistakes both in spelling & grammar, I daresay it is the English type-writer's slip-shod reading of the MSS; but we shall have to have the proof sheets read very carefully.*

In addition to these creative efforts, she had begun work on her next book, *The Tale of Jemima Puddleduck.* On all fronts, and by any standard of measurement, 1907 was clearly one of Miss Potter's most productive years.

On the matter of fairies, Beatrix Potter held a firm opinion. In a journal entry (November 17, 1896), she wrote:

> *I remember I used to half believe and wholly play with fairies when I was a child What heaven can be more real than to retain the spirit-world of childhood, tempered and balanced by knowledge and common-sense, to fear no longer the terror that flieth by night, yet to feel truly and understand a little, a very little, of the story of life.*

In 1911, she wrote a story for two little girls in New Zealand about an oak fairy who tragically loses her home when her ancient oak—"enormous, tall and bold" is cut down and the wood used to build a bridge. "The Fairy in the Oak" ends happily, however, when the oak fairy takes up residence in the oak timbers of the bridge, "and may live

there through hundreds of years; for well-seasoned oak lasts
for ever—well seasoned by trials and tears."

When Beatrix and Willie Heelis were married, Willie's
little niece, Nancy Nicholson, was delighted to discover
that her belief in fairies—she called them Oakmen—was
shared by Mrs. Heelis:

> *I remember my amazement on my first visit to Sawrey, when this
> new aunt left the grown-ups and came to me to imagine win-
> dows and doors in the trees with people peeping out.*

In 1916, Beatrix wrote a six-page story for Nancy's Christmas present, featuring the Oakmen, whom she drew as
dwarflike creatures with white beards, brown leggings, red
coats, and red pointed hats. Later, she wrote to Fruing Warne
that she would have liked to make a book of the fairy-tale
letters she had written to Nancy, adding, "I see the little
men peeping round the mossy stumps and stones whenever
I go up to the wood."

That project did not come to fruition. However, Beatrix
did write a much longer tale, *The Fairy Caravan* (published
in the United States in 1929) about a traveling animal circus that was invisible to humans, rewriting "The Fairy in
the Oak" as the last chapter. The year before she died, she
wrote that the inspiration for *The Fairy Caravan* came from
a magical sight she had seen on the fellside:

> *In a soft muddy spot on the old drove road I had found a mul-
> titude of unshod footprints, much too small for horses' foot-
> marks, much too round for deer or sheep. I wondered were they
> foot marks of a troupe of fairy riders, riding down old King
> Gait into Hird Wood and Hallilands—away into Fairyland
> and the blue distance of the hills.*

I think it is not at all fanciful to say that Miss Potter believed in fairies to the very end of her own quite magical life.

Susan Wittig Albert

Resources

There are many excellent resources for a study of Beatrix Potter's life and work and the Lake District of England at the turn of the century. Here are a few of those that I have found most useful in the research for this book and the series as a whole. Additional resource material is listed in the previous books and on my website, www.mysterypartners.com.

Beeton, Isabella. *Beeton's Book of Household Management, 1861,* facsimile edition. Farrar, Straus and Giroux, New York, 1969.

Denyer, Susan. *At Home with Beatrix Potter.* Harry N. Abrams, Inc., New York, 2000.

Hervy, Canon G.A.K., and J.A.G. Barnes. *Natural History of the Lake District.* Frederick Warne, London, 1970.

Jay, Eileen, Mary Noble, and Anne Stevenson Hobbs. *A Victorian Naturalist: Beatrix Potter's Drawings from the Armitt Collection.* Frederick Warne, London, 1992.

Lane, Margaret. *The Tale of Beatrix Potter,* revised edition. Frederick Warne, London, 1968.

Linder, Enid and Leslie. *The Art of Beatrix Potter,* revised edition. Frederick Warne, London, 1972.

Linder, Leslie. *A History of the Writings of Beatrix Potter.* Frederick Warne, London, 1971.

Potter, Beatrix. *Beatrix Potter's Letters,* selected and edited by Judy Taylor. Frederick Warne, London, 1989.

―――――. *The Journal of Beatrix Potter, 1881–1897,* new edition, transcribed by Leslie Linder. Frederick Warne, London, 1966.

Rollinson, William. *The Cumbrian Dictionary of Dialect, Tradition and Folklore.* Smith Settle Ltd, West Yorkshire, UK, 1997.

Rollinson, William. *Life and Tradition in the Lake District.* Dalesman Books, Clapham, Lancashire, UK, 1981.

Taylor, Judy. *Beatrix Potter: Artist, Storyteller and Countrywoman,* revised edition. Frederick Warne, London, 1996.

Taylor, Judy, Joyce Whalley, et al. *Beatrix Potter, 1866–1943: The Artist and Her World.* Frederick Warne with the National Trust, published by the Penguin Group, London and New York, 1987.

Recipes from the Land between the Lakes

Mrs. Jennings's Bubble and Squeak

Ridley Rattail has a preference for this traditional dish, which he finds occasionally in Mrs. Jennings's pantry (but only occasionally, for the Jenningses leave nothing left over). The Oxford English Dictionary tells us that "bubble and squeak" is named for the sounds that are produced as the dish is cooked. Or as one satirical diner put it:

> *What Mortals Bubble call and Squeak*
> *When midst the Frying-pan in accents savage*
> *The Beef so surly quarrels with the Cabbage.*
> *—John Wolcot, 1738–1819*

2 tablespoons butter
1 onion, finely chopped
1 pound potatoes, cooked and mashed

1/2 pound cabbage, cooked and finely chopped
2 teaspoons parsley, minced

Heat the butter in a large frying pan. Add the onion and cook until soft and transparent. Add the potatoes, cabbage, and parsley. Mix well. Cook over medium heat, turning occasionally, for 15 minutes or until golden brown. Serve with bacon and eggs for breakfast or as part of a supper dish.

Sarah Barwick's Sticky Buns

These are the buns that have made Sarah Barwick famous throughout the Land between the Lakes.

1 tablespoon dry yeast
1/4 cup warm water
1 cup milk, scalded
1/4 cup sugar
1/4 cup butter
1 teaspoon salt
3 1/2 cup flour
1 egg
1/2 cup butter, melted
1/2 cup brown sugar
2 teaspoons cinnamon
1/2 cup currants

TOPPING
1 cup brown sugar

1/2 cup butter

2 tablespoons light corn syrup

To make buns: Soften the yeast in warm water. Combine the milk, sugar, butter, and salt; cool. Add 1 1/2 cups flour and beat well; beat in the egg and yeast/water mixture. Gradually add the remaining flour to form soft dough, beating well between additions. Place in a greased bowl, turn to grease surface; cover and let rise in a warm place until double, 1 1/2 to 2 hours. Turn out on a lightly floured board and divide in half. Form half into a ball and let rest while rolling the other half into 8×12-inch rectangle. Brush with 1/4 cup melted butter; sprinkle with 1/4 cup brown sugar, 1 teaspoon cinnamon, and 1/4 cup currants. Roll lengthwise and seal edge; cut roll in 1-inch slices. Repeat with the second ball of dough.

To make topping: In a saucepan, mix the brown sugar, butter, and corn syrup; heat slowly, stirring often. Divide into two 8×8×2-inch pans. Place rolls, cut side down, over mixture. Cover; let rise in a warm place until double, 35–40 minutes. Bake at 375 degrees for 20 minutes. Cool 2–3 minutes; invert on a plate; remove the pan. Yield: 2 dozen sticky buns.

Mrs. Beeton's Tipsy Cake

This famous cake is based on a trifle, which has a long history of appearances on the English table. Mrs. Beeton's version, reprinted here, was the "definitive" one, Mrs. Beeton being the leading Victorian authority on all things domestic.

#1487

Ingredients: 1 moulded sponge- or Savoy-cake, sufficient sweet wine or sherry to soak it, 6 tablespoonfuls of brandy, 2 oz. of sweet almonds, 1 pint of rich custard.

MODE: Procure a cake that is three or four days old—either sponge, Savoy, or rice answering for the purpose of a tipsy cake. Cut the bottom of the cake level, to make it stand firm in the dish; make a small hole in the centre, and pour in and over the cake sufficient sweet wine or sherry, mixed with the above proportion of brandy, to soak it nicely. When the cake is well soaked, blanch and cut the almonds into strips, stick them all over the cake, and pour round it a good custard. The cakes are sometimes crumbled and soaked, and a whipped cream heaped over them, the same as for trifles.

TIME. About 2 hours to soak the cake. Average cost, 4s. 6d.

Pease Porridge

Pease porridge hot, Pease porridge cold,
Pease porridge in the pot, nine days old.
Some like it hot, some like it cold,
Some like it in the pot, nine days old.
                    —Traditional nursery rhyme

When food was cooked in an open fireplace instead of on a kitchen range, a large pot always hung over the fire, filled with a thick soup of peas and other vegetables. In the morning, before the fire was lit, any porridge left from the previous meal was eaten cold, for breakfast. During the day, more peas and vegetables were added and the porridge was eaten hot. It would be no surprise to learn that some of the ingredients were actually nine days old. Pease porridge is traditionally served with sausage or boiled bacon or spread on thick slices of bread-and-butter.

> 1 pound split peas
> water
> salt and pepper
> 1 medium onion, quartered
> bay leaf, 2 sprigs parsley, 2 sprigs thyme
> 2 tablespoons butter
> 2 eggs

Cover the soaked peas with water in a large pan. Add the salt, pepper, and onions. Bring to a boil, then reduce heat, cover, and simmer for 2 1/2 hours, adding more water if necessary. In the last 15 minutes, add herbs. Remove and discard the herbs and onion. Serve this thick soup with slices of hot bread.

Mrs. Beeton (recipe #1323) turns pease porridge into pease pudding with the addition of 2 tablespoons butter and 2 eggs. Excess water is drained, the peas are put through a colander with a wooden spoon, the eggs and butter are beaten in, and the pudding is steamed for an hour in a greased heatproof pudding basin. It is then inverted onto a platter and served hot, sliced.

Cumbrian Bacon and Onion Roly-Poly Pudding

"Anna Maria," said the old man rat (whose name was Samuel Whiskers)—"Anna Maria, make me a kitten dumpling roly-poly pudding for my dinner."
—Beatrix Potter, *The Tale of Samuel Whiskers,*
or The Roly-Poly Pudding

You certainly wouldn't want to make a kitten roly-poly, but a Cumbrian bacon and onion roly-poly would do very well.

FILLING
1/2 pound bacon, diced finely
1 medium onion, chopped finely
1 small clove of garlic, very finely crushed
1 teaspoon dried thyme
1 teaspoon dried sage
freshly ground pepper

DOUGH
2 cups flour
4 teaspoons baking powder
1 teaspoon salt
2 tablespoons lard
1 cup water

For steaming: Prepare a large oven-proof lidded pan, such as a turkey roaster or fish kettle. Set a rack or trivet in the pan, of a height that will hold the pudding above the boiling water. You'll also need baking parchment and aluminum foil.

To make the filling: Mix the diced bacon, onion, garlic, herbs, and pepper. Set aside.

To make the dough: Sift the flour, baking powder, and salt together. Rub in the lard and gradually add just enough water to make a soft, slightly sticky dough. On a floured board, roll out an 8×10-inch rectangle 1/4-inch thick. (You may need to make two smaller roly-polies if your pan won't accommodate this length.) Distribute the filling over the surface, leaving a quarter-inch border across the top and both ends. With a pastry brush and water, wet this border. Roll up tightly along the longest side, starting with the edge nearest you. Smooth the long edge where it joins the body of the roll and pinch the ends lightly to seal in the filling. Loosely roll in several layers of baking parchment, leaving room for the dough to expand, and then in two layers of foil, leaving an expansion pleat. Fold up the ends of the foil and secure, to prevent water penetrating during steaming.

To steam: Preheat oven to 325 degrees. Fill the steaming pan to an inch below the rack or trivet with boiling water from a teakettle. Place the wrapped roly-poly on the rack and cover the pan with a tight-fitting lid. Bring the water back to a boil and boil hard for 10 minutes. Check to see if you need to add more boiling water, then reduce the heat and simmer for 20 minutes. Set the pan, water and all, in the oven, and oven-steam for 2 1/2 hours. Transfer the pudding to a warm plate, open the foil and parchment, and slice. Traditionally served with potatoes and a green vegetable. Serves 4–6.

Glossary

About the Cumbrian dialect, writer Hall Caine remarks (in the preface to his 1895 novel, *A Cumbrian Romance*): "I have chosen to give a broad outline of Cumbrian dialect, such as bears no more exact relation to the actual speech than a sketch bears to a finished picture. It is right as far as it goes."

For the *Cottage Tales*, I have borrowed Caine's approach to dialect representation, and attempted only a very broad sketch—right as far as it goes, although it doesn't go very far. Some of the words included in this glossary are not dialect forms, but are sufficiently uncommon that a definition may be helpful. My main source for dialect is William Rollinson's *The Cumbrian Dictionary of Dialect, Tradition, and Folklore*. For other definitions, I have consulted the *Oxford English Dictionary* (second edition, Oxford University Press, London, 1989).

Beck A small stream (Old Norse *bekkr*).

Brow The projecting edge of a cliff, standing out over a precipice.

Dray A cart with low sides built to haul heavy loads, driven by a drayman.

Dwelf A fairy resident of the Land between the Lakes, half elf, half dwarf. Known to be a shape-shifter.

Fell A mountain or a high hill (Icelandic, Danish, Swedish *fjell*).

Folly A small pleasure-house in a garden.

Gae lot A great many.

Glisky Bright, sparkling.

Go An unexpected turn of events. *A rum go.*

Ha'p'orth Halfpennyworth. The amount that can be bought for a halfpenny, very little.

Hast tha Have you? *Hast tha a bit o'bread?*

Heafed Herdwick sheep instinctively recognize their native pastures, or heafs; that is, they are heafed to their home meadows.

Hobthrush A hobgoblin or spirit that can do useful work but is just as likely to make mischief.

How Hill.

Joiner Carpenter.

Lumbered To be burdened or encumbered with something.

Mappen Perhaps, likely. *Mappen t'weather'll be good.*

Nae, nay No (said emphatically).

Nobbut Nothing but.

Ower-kessen'd Overcast, cloudy.

Pater familias Latin for "father of the family," and used by the Romans to designate the eldest or ranking male in the household.

Reet, reetly Right, proper; rightly, properly.

Rum Good, fine, excellent, great.

Sett The system of underground burrows and chambers where a badger colony lives.

Tatie pot A favorite Lake District dish made of mutton, potatoes, carrots, onions, and black pudding (a traditional sausage made of pig's blood, beef suet, oatmeal, and onions). For a recipe, see *The Tale of Hill Top Farm.*

Thick Excessively disagreeable, too much to tolerate.

Verge The grassy roadside.

Verra Very.

Wax Anger, irritation, pique.

Wudstha Would you?